AN OCEAN FULL OF ANGELS

Other books by Peter Kreeft from St. Augustine's Press

Socratic Logic
Summa Philosophica
The Philosophy of Jesus
Jesus-Shock
The Sea Within: Waves and the Meaning of All Things
I Surf, Therefore I Am
If Einstein Had Been a Surfer

Other books from St. Augustine's Press and Dumb Ox Books

JPlato, *The Symposium of Plato: The Shelley Translation*, P. S. Shelley, trans.
Aristotle, *Aristotle – On Poetics*, S. Benardete & M. Davis, trans.
Aristotle, *Physics, Or Natural Hearing*, G. Coughlin, trans.
St. Augustine, *On Order [De Ordine]*, S. Borruso, trans.
St. Augustine, *The St. Augustine LifeGuide*, S. Borruso, ed.
Thomas Aquinas, *Commentary on Aristotle's Nicomachean Ethics*
Thomas Aquinas, *Commentary on Aristotle's Posterior Analytics*, R. Berquist, trans.
Thomas Aquinas, *Commentary on Aristotle's De Anima*
Thomas Aquinas, *Commentary on the Epistle to the Hebrews*, C. Baer, trans.
Thomas Aquinas, *Commentary on St. Paul's Epistles to Timothy, Titus, and Philemon*, C. Baer, trans.
Thomas Aquinas, *Disputed Questions on Virtue*, R. McInerny, trans.
Thomas Aquinas, *Treatise on Law*, A.J. Freddoso, trans.
Thomas Aquinas, *Treatise on Human Nature*, A.J. Freddoso, trans.
Henry of Ghent, *Henry of Ghent's* Summa of Ordinary Questions: Article One: On the Possibility of Human Knowledge, R.J. Teske, S.J., trans.
John of St. Thomas, *Introduction to the Summa Theologiae of Thomas Aquinas*, R. McInerny, trans.
Servais Pinckaers, O.P., *Morality: The Catholic View*, M. Sherwin, O.P., trans.
ames V. Schall, *The Regensburg Lecture*
James V. Schall, *The Modern Age*
Josef Pieper, *In Tune with the World: A Theory of Festivity*
Josef Pieper, *The Platonic Myths*
C.S. Lewis and Don Giovanni Calabria, *The Latin Letters of C.S. Lewis*
Edward Feser, *The Last Superstition: A Refutation of the New Atheism*
Leszek Kolakowski, *My Correct views on Everything*

Peter Kreeft

AN OCEAN FULL OF ANGELS
The Autobiography of 'Isa Ben Adam

ON THE CONNECTIONS BETWEEN
JESUS CHRIST
MUHAMMAD
DEAD VIKINGS
SASSY BLACK FEMINISTS
DUTCH CALVINIST SEMINARIANS
LARGE MOTHER SUBSTITUTES
ARMLESS NATURE MYSTICS
CARIBBEAN RUBBER DANCERS
THREE POPES IN ONE YEAR
CORTEZ
ROMEO AND JULIET
THE WANDERING JEW
THE SEA SERPENT
OUR LADY OF GUADALUPE
THE DEMON HURRICANO
ISLAM IN THE ART OF BODY SURFING
THE UNIVERSAL FATE WAVE THEORY
THE PALESTINIAN INTIFADA
THE FATAL BEAUTY OF THE SEA
DREAMS OF JUNGIAN ARCHETYPES
THE DOOMS OF THE BOSTON RED SOX
ABORTION WARS
THE GREAT BLIZZARD OF '78
THE WISDOM OF THE 'HANDICAPPED'
THE ECUMENICAL JIHAD
THE PSYCHOLOGY OF SUICIDE
THE DISGUISES OF ANGELS
AND THE END OF THE WORLD

ST. AUGUSTINE'S PRESS
South Bend, Indiana

1 2 3 4 5 6   16 15 14 13 12 11

Library of Congress Cataloging in Publication Data
Kreeft, Peter.
An ocean full of angels: the autobiography of 'Isa Ben Adam /
by Peter Kreeft.
p. cm.
"On the connections between Jesus Christ, Muhammad, dead Vikings,
sassy Black feminists, Dutch Calvinist seminarians, large mother
substitutes, armless nature mystics, Caribbean rubber dancers, three
popes in one year, Cortez, Romeo and Juliet, the wandering Jew, the
sea serpent, Our Lady of Guadalupe, the demon Hurricano, Islam in
the art of body surfing, the universal fate wave theory, the Palestinian
intifada, the fatal beauty of the sea, dreams of Jungian archetypes,
"the dooms of the Boston Red Sox, abortion wars, the great blizzard
of '78, the wisdom of the "handicapped", the ecumenical jihad, the
psychology of suicide, the disguises of angels, and the end of the
world."
ISBN 978-1-58731-590-9 (hardbound: alk. paper) 1. Metaphysics –
Fiction. 2. Identity (Psychology) – Fiction. 3. Philosophical anthropology – Fiction. 4. Theological anthropology – Fiction. I. Title.
PS3561.R3817O34 2010
813'.54 – dc22   2010027392

∞ The paper used in this publication meets the minimum requirements of the
American National Standard for Information Sciences – Permanence of Paper
for Printed Materials, ANSI Z39.48-1984.

ST. AUGUSTINE'S PRESS
www.staugustine.net

Printed in Canada

CONTENTS

To My Readers   1
(1) The Beginning of the Autobiography of 'Isa Ben Adam   2
(2) Nahant   16
(3) Papa   36
(4) Mama   43
(5) Night   47
(6) Mother   51
(7) The House of Bread   64
(8) The Housebugs   72
(9) Throwing Poems at Each Other   102
(10) The Dreams   109
(11) Saint Michael's Bloody Sword   115
(12) The Great Blizzard of '78   120
(13) Hurricano   128
(14) The Book of Love   156
(15) The Sea Serpent   185
(16) Mara's Hymn to the Sea   193
(17) The Summer of Love   200
(18) The World Splits in Two   221
(19) The Healing Power of Surf   231
(20) Islam in the Art of Body Surfing   241
(21) Data for the Universal Fate Wave Theory   252
(22) The War in the Womb   255
(23) The Ecumenical Jihad   272
(24) The Angel's Fall   278
(25) Armageddon at Fenway Park   302
(26) Into the Abyss   330
(27) Recovery   336

(28) Vikings on Nahant   349
(29) Tying Up Destiny's Threads   358
(30) The Last Dreams   369
      Editor's Postscript   373
      After-word   375

To My Readers

I am not a great storyteller, but I have a great story to tell. It is the story of 'Isa Ben Adam, the most remarkable man I have ever met.

I have taught over 25,000 students over almost fifty years, and 'Isa was the single best writer I have ever known. 'Isa wrote as sharks swim: continually and voraciously. This book consists of just some of his writings, mainly his interrupted autobiography. I was given three large cartons of his writings by Maria Kirk, his foster-mother, after his disappearance, all of them written by hand, most of them in pocket-sized notebooks.

It was the events of September 11th , 2001, that persuaded me to publish his story now, more than 30 years later. For I believe that 'Isa himself is a piece of significant data about Islam and its meaning for the future of our global civilization.

'Isa is "another kind of Muslim," in fact the commonest kind. He is neither a terrorist nor a secularist. He passionately believes in both justice and mercy, honor and compassion, toughness and tenderness, law and liberty.

This is not my story but his. I am an absent-minded philosophy professor. I have written over fifty books, but never one even remotely like this one. It is far too big for me. It is messy and diverse. If you're bothered by that, I guess you're also bothered by the Bible—or the universe.

Please do not judge this book as a novel. It is not a bad novel because it is not a novel at all. What is it? I call it an ocean full of angels. The "ocean" is the story, the events, the narrative of 'Isa's unfinished autobiography. The "angels," or islands in this ocean, are the other writings that reveal 'Isa's mind. To do justice to 'Isa, I had to do an injustice to the purity of literary form. The literary purist about "narrative integrity" is invited to simply skip over all 'Isa's interruptions of his narrative. You will either like them very, very little or very, very much.

(By the way, in this story there are also real angels, both good and evil, and a real ocean.)

Although this is 'Isa's story, I have occasionally inserted my own editorial comments into it, in this smaller typeface. The critics say writers shouldn't do that. I say writers shouldn't write for critics, but for readers. So I will often interrupt 'Isa's narrative to speak to you directly, dear reader, because I've often wished other authors would do that. And I do it because if it's good enough for Dostoyevsky, it's good enough for me.

(1) The Beginning of the Autobiography of 'Isa Ben Adam

Why I Write

I am 'Isa Ben Adam, and I am a mystery.

Every man is a mystery, a lived identity crisis. None of us quite knows who we are, once we stop fooling ourselves. We are continually sculpting our own identity. We are not the only sculptors; we do it in cooperation (or conflict) with nature, other people, and the Will of Allah, which some call Fate or Destiny.

Each human life is a different response to the question "Who are you?", the question asked of us by our Creator. In the end, in the Last Judgment, I will know the secret of my identity—if I have surrendered my identity to the Author of all identities. Therefore Islam, which means "surrender" to Allah, is the path to "know thyself." For us Muslims, Muhammad (peace be upon him!) is the answer to Socrates; the Prophet is the answer to the Philosopher.

O my reader, I tell my story to "you" in the singular, not to "you" in the plural. For only one person at a time reads a book. A hundred people at once hear a speaker, and each hearer thinks he bears only 1 percent of the responsibility for listening. But we two are alone together now, you and I, reader and writer, with no one else between us. We are separated only by time, by space, and (soon) by death.

We human beings have been telling our stories to each other ever since we first spoke words. It is our task in life to make stories and then to tell them. Sometimes we make them in our imagination, and sometimes we make them in our life. The ones we make in life are the best stories. Here is mine.

My story begins in Heaven. (If you do not understand that, ask any Muslim and he will explain it to you.)

My Confession

I am a failed Messiah.

I never wanted to be a Messiah. But when I read the following letter, I was trapped. I was an animal in a cage. The cage was my past.

I am trapped because the past is unchangeable, and my failure has already happened. It is past, and there is no escape from the past, as there is no escape from the dead. For the past *is* the dead.

This is what the letter said:

Dear 'Isa, when you read this letter, you will have already fulfilled its prophecy. This will confirm you in your appointed task. When you were young, the knowledge of it would have been a burden on your shoulders, so we have laid it, by oath, on Mahmoud Ibn Rashid, your second cousin, to give you this letter on your 21st birthday, whether we your parents are then living or dead.

The prophecy said that you were to do a new deed never done before. You were to do this deed before you became a man, and now that you are a man, it will have already been accomplished.

Your task was "to hasten the rising of the sun for all the world." This was not the sun of hydrogen but the sun of righteousness and truth. The prophecy said that as you were an instrument in helping to join your two parents together more closely (though they remain two, not one), you were an instrument in helping to join our two faiths more closely together, the Muslim and the Christian (though they remain two, not one).

When you were an infant, we brought you for the first time to the mosque and a very old man, a holy Sufi, took you from our arms and uttered a prophecy over you. We were told that he had been looking into the eyes of infants for seventy years, asking: "Is this the Hastener?" And always, he answered, "No, this is not the Hastener." And when he looked into your eyes, he said: "THIS IS THE HASTENER, THIS IS THE BOY WHO WILL HASTEN, OR ELSE DELAY, THE RISING OF THE SUN FOR ALL THE WORLD."

Today you are no longer a boy, and we believe you have done the deed that Allah has decreed. You have hastened the rising of the sun for all the world.

Praise be to Allah, Lord of all worlds, and thanks be to His prophets Adam and Noah and Abraham and Ishmael and Moses and Jesus and Muhammad, and to Jesus's mother Maryam, the perfect Muslim. Peace be upon them.

But I have not hastened the rising of the sun. I have delayed it.

As an atonement for my sin of being the Delayer instead of the Hastener, I undertake the writing of this book, the story of my life. When you read in your daily newspapers of the shedding of blood between Muslims and Christians, between Muslims and Jews, and between Muslims and Muslims, you may know that it was my failure that was in part responsible for this blood. This book is my confession.

Song of Myself

Every man is a river. His ancestors are his tributaries.

My ancestors have been global wanderers for three generations, and my friends tell me I have "a sailor's look," gazing into the far distance even when I look directly at them. They find this disconcerting.

My mother, Maria Lopez, was born in Mexico. She was part Indian and part Spanish. The Indian lineage goes back to two streams. One of these, she says, is Mohawk. It sounds impossible that a Mexican can have blood from a tribe that lived three thousand miles away, in New York and New England, and she cannot explain how it happened, but she speaks of it as a fact, because it has been passed down to her through many generations.

The other part of Mama's Indian lineage she traces back to Juan Diego, the peasant who reportedly saw Maryam, whom Christians call the Virgin Mary (blessed be her name!) on December 9, 1531, when she named herself the Lady of Guadalupe, made roses grow in the winter snow on the Mexican mountains, and miraculously imprinted an image of herself onto Juan Diego's cloak. That cloak sits now in Mexico City, miraculously preserved from age-ing. Of the thousands of pilgrimage sites where Catholics believe miracles have happened, this one is the single most popular destination in the world. The Virgin's image has not faded from Juan Diego's cloak for 400 years; the chemistry of the colors is of no known earthly origin; and the cloak is a *tilma,* made of rough burlap that normally decays in a few decades. The image on the tilma is one of a Mexican Indian lady, not a European, and many of my Mama's friends remarked on how uncannily she resembled the face on the cloak: the large, heavily lidded eyes, the thin brows, the full cheeks, the straight mouth, the calm and serious look.

I am proud of this Catholic stream of my ancestry even though I follow my father's Muslim faith rather than my mother's Catholicism; and Jesus and Mary (blessed be their names!) loom large in my faith, as they do for most Muslims. I read and know and love the Holy Qur'an first, but I also read and know and love the Bible. When I was born, my parents chose my name to rat-ify and unite both sides of my heritage; for "'Isa" is a common Muslim name ("hee-sah") as well as a common Hispanic one ("hay-soos"). I revere my namesake as the second greatest prophet who ever lived, and I revere Mary as the greatest woman, for she was not only his miraculous virgin-mother but also the perfect example of *islam* with her complete surrender to the Will of Allah and the word of His angel Gabriel.

My mother's mother's name was Fatima, and this is another bridge between two faiths and cultures, for this was the name of the daughter of the Prophet Muhammad (blessed be his name!), as well as one of the titles the Virgin Mary announced for herself ("Our Lady of Fatima") when she appeared to three children in 1917 at Fatima, Portugal. This is a Muslim title, and Mary deliberately chose it, for this town had been renamed after the daughter of the Prophet by a Muslim ruler who married a Portuguese Catholic.

Incidentally, the most widely witnessed miracle in the history of the world was Mary's appearance to over 2 million Muslims in Zeitun, Egypt, just outside Cairo, over a period of a few weeks, from the dome of the Orthodox cathedral. She spoke in signs, chief among them the sign of peace.

At Fatima, Mary predicted the course of two world wars and the rise and fall of Communism in Russia, and caused the "miracle of the sun" spinning wildly through the sky, witnessed by 70,000 people, including atheists and journalists. Guadalupe and Fatima are part of my heritage both physically and spiritually.

The little Spanish town of Guadalupe was the birthplace of my father's mother, and Papa claimed to trace part of his family blood line back to Cortez. The claim has never been documented, but I believe it.

My father's mother had moved, with her family, from Guadalupe in Spain to the Spanish protectorate of Cienta, in Morocco, and then, a few years later, to Palestine, where she met and married my father's father, a Palestinian Muslim, Ahmed Ben Adam. Their marriage was stormy, and their son (my father) planned to escape the storms by migrating to the New World once he reached adulthood. When the United States Immigration Service refused him permission, he entered Mexico instead, where he plied his trade as a fisherman. There he met and married my mother and kept alive his dream of moving to the United States. After two years on the waiting list, the door of opportunity finally opened when Khalid, a family friend from Palestine who had immigrated to Boston and taken up the trade of fisherman, lost his partner and invited Papa and Mama to come live and fish with him off Nahant, a tiny peninsula a few miles north of Boston. The three shared a little bayside fishing shack there for two more years. Then Khalid retired, prematurely aged by the New England winters, and gave Papa his boat.

The river of my identity, fed by these tributaries, runs thick with richly mixed blood. This river has carved a channel through my soul, where it now flows to its destiny in the ocean. It is an ocean full of angels.

My Philosophy of Life

The meaning of life is always absolutely simple. It is simply *Islam*, Surrender, Submission, unqualified Yes to the Perfect Will of Allah.

I am *not* "open minded" about that, and I am very grateful that I am not. I think a constantly open mind is like a constantly open mouth: something for flies to enter. My friend Jim was once urging me to "keep an open mind," and I said to him, "It is good to keep the door open when your friend is outside. But if you keep it open when he is inside too, that insults him, for it invites him to leave. My mind's friend is truth, and I will not insult my friend." He had no answer.

My Love of Nature

From early childhood I have been a natural naturalist. I have always been happier when collecting stones or shells from the beach than when playing with complicated mechanical toys. I have always found God-made things more interesting than man-made things. Naturally: they are designed by a far greater artist. Papa used to say, when waxing poetical, "Old Cape Cod was made by God, but Route 28 was made by the State." (Ask anyone who lives or vacations on Cape Cod about Route 28.)

I used to spend many happy hours at the beach when I was small, arranging and ranking stones and shells: first by color, then by size, then by shape, then by beauty. Although I did not know it, I was training to be a philosopher. I was playing games of abstracting, ordering, categorizing, and judging: philosophical games.

I love to rank things in hierarchies. I simply cannot comprehend the American preference for flat equality over hierarchy—not because I want to look down the hierarchy and sneer, but because I want to look up the hierarchy and admire. I love the lower things too, but differently from the higher things. I like to caress the poor little broken shells as if they are broken birds, or broken people.

When I was twelve, I made a painstakingly detailed map of Bailey's Hill, my favorite place on Nahant, with pet names for each feature and a complete road map of all its little paths. The most tangled place was "Br'er Rabbit's Briar Patch." If I ever have to elude a pack of pursuers like a rabbit running from hounds, I thought, this will be my refuge and "home field advantage."

Two Doors in My Soul

Let me tell you about the two doors in my soul.

This is not supposed to be the right way to write a story: to spend time telling you who I am rather than confining myself to what I have done. I know that. But Augustine did it in the *Confessions*. And I think that's pretty good company. I think if you first understand who I am, you will better understand what I have done.

As I was saying before I was so rudely interrupted by myself, my soul has two doors in it. One is like a door in the sky to Paradise, and the other is like a door in the ground to Hell. Through these doors good and evil angels come, like the angels on Jacob's ladder. I think I have a vertical soul. It feels like a spear thrown down from the sky and stuck into the ground.

They say the eyes are the windows of the soul. Mine are black—not just brown but black. Perhaps these are the two doors of my soul.

Editor's Note: 'Isa never describes his appearance beyond this suggestive analogy. And since I knew him well, I thought it would be useful to supply this missing part of his autobiography. For as Wittgenstein said, the best picture of the human soul is the human body.

'Isa's appearance would have been striking even in Palestine or Mexico. In America it turned women's heads. His intense black eyes, wavy black hair, large and slightly hawk-like nose, and protruding jaw and cheekbones all gave him the look of a conquistador.

He was six feet tall and wiry, all muscle and no fat. His skin was the color of burnished brass in dim light. His face was rectangular, like the face on the Shroud of Turin. His nose looked like it had been broken in a fight, for it was slightly bent, like a broken stick. This gave him a pugnacious look but at the same time an honest one. He seemed to be saying to the world, "No hiding places here. Here I am. I'm not afraid of you. Come out into the light of the desert sun."

His jet-black hair seemed to absorb light, like fog. It never glistened. Some people's hair looks wet even when dry; 'Isa's looked dry even when wet.

His eyes, under thick, short brows, were wide, rectangular windows. He tended to stare at a person, unaware of how uncomfortable this made others feel. He had the owl-like habit of turning his neck and head rather than his eyes when he looked to the side. He always preferred to stare straight ahead, like an angel.

Yet there was also a softness about his face, as if air-brushed. Without that aura you might have suspected him of being a violent man. It's difficult to say where the aura of softness came from. It didn't come from his hard features, so it must have come from his spirit, from the form his soul imposed on his body's matter.

He was not unsociable, but he confessed to me that he loved solitude and "felt lonely in crowds." When I asked him to explain that paradox, he said that when he was in a crowd, he missed part of himself, the part that lived only in solitude.

He was not only more facile with words than any other undergraduate student I have ever taught, but also deeply moved by words, more moved by words than most people are by music. (I wonder: Are Muslims so deeply moved by words because they are so moved by the Qur'an, or vice versa?)

Am I a Troublemaker?

Many people have called me that. I have often gotten into trouble because I am impatient in the presence of injustice. Here are two examples.

Once, in high school, I failed a quiz on "world religions" because I answered all four of the following "true or false" questions about Islam "false" instead of "true," as the textbook claimed they were:

1. Islam began in the 7th century A.D.
2. It arose in Saudi Arabia.
3. It was founded by Muhammad.
4. It spread by preaching and military conquest.

When I pointed out to the teacher that she and the textbook were wrong, she said something like, "How dare you be so arrogant as to set yourself up above the textbook?" I replied, "Are you a Muslim, Miss Ehrlich?" She was not. "Well, I am, and I don't think it's arrogant to say that a Muslim knows more about his own religion than a non-Muslim does." I then pointed out that all four statements were false, because

1. Islam has always existed. It began in eternity.
2. It arose in Heaven.
3. It was founded by Allah.
4. And it spread by divine revelation, divine providence.

I pointed out to Miss Ehrlich that any educated Muslim in the world would have given the same answers. I tried to explain how a Muslim feels when he's told that Muhammad founded Islam: the same way it must feel to a Christian to be told that that Saint Paul founded Christianity, or the way it must feel to a religious Jew to be told that that Moses invented Judaism. It really assumes that the religion's claims are false without being honest enough to say so. I concluded, "So you're punishing me with an F for saying that my religion is true, and you'd reward me with an A only if I said my religion was false. That's not freedom of religion. And it's not fair. It's not even honest."

She was livid. But I held my ground. Did I also get my grade reversed? I don't even remember.

On another occasion, in senior year in high school, I got thrown in jail for stealing my own car.

One hot day, the glue on the inspection sticker dried up (I have no air conditioning in my little blue Nash Metropolitan convertible), and the sticker came loose and flew out. (The top was down.) It was on a busy highway, and I thought it wasn't safe to back up and try to find it. But before I reached home, a police cruiser noticed the sticker missing from my windshield, pulled me over, and gave me a fine for driving without an inspection sticker. The officer did not take kindly to my reasonable question: "Tell me, officer, what should I have done? What mistake are you fining me for? For not backing up on a busy highway? Or for trusting the State of Massachusetts's glue, that came loose?"

The ticket cost me five times its face amount because my insurance company added a stiff yearly surcharge to my policy's premium. Their policy is to do that for only one offense besides accidents and moving violations: missing inspection stickers. Needless to say, arguments with the insurance company about the justice of this policy were fruitless.

The worst was yet to come. When the policeman ran a routine phone check on my registration, after he pulled me over, the police records came up with "uninsured vehicle" even though I had faithfully paid my monthly car insurance bills. The officer then removed my license plate from my car and refused to let me drive even to a phone to call my own insurance company for a tow. The police-approved towing company had to tow my car to a town ten miles from home, and they charged me daily storage fees until I cleared the mess up. My local insurance agent was not home when I called him, and when after 20 minutes of phoning I finally got through to the company's national headquarters, six states away, they told me that Massachusetts was the one state they could not handle from their central office. It had its own regional office. I'll bet I know why: because it's the car theft and insurance fraud capital of the world.

When I finally got through, I found that my insurance registration had "gotten lost in the computer somewhere." The insurance company blamed the Registry of Motor Vehicles and the Registry blamed the insurance company. Each call to the Registry, of course, took 20 minutes more. When I finally *walked* three miles to the Registry office (quicker than phoning!), after waiting on line for an hour and *then* being told that the Registry officer at the door had directed me to the wrong line, then waiting for another hour on the second line, my Islamic "submission" was, unsurprisingly, wearing thin. (A local newspaper columnist compared a trip to the Registry unfavorably with root canal work, and awarded the Registry "the Kafka's Castle Award.") I finally found out that there was "no way" the process of clearing up the mistake could be speeded up, and "no way of telling" how soon they could find and correct the mistake. As I left, I fondly fondled the thought of bombing the building.

Meanwhile, I had promises to keep and obligations to fulfill with my car, and I could not afford to rent one or pay any more storage fees. So I borrowed my friend's expired license plate, rode my bike the ten miles to the storage place, attached the license plate to my car, and stole my own car in the middle of the night.

But Murphy's Law was not yet satisfied. On my way home a policeman noticed the outdated license plate, pulled me over, and reconfiscated the car. Once it was discovered that the car came from the storage garage, I was charged with car theft and locked up in jail overnight. They told me afterwards that I would have been released if I had not argued so much with the policemen that I was also charged with "verbally abusing an officer."

Finally, my friends at the Muslim Center bailed me out, after a day and night in jail. When my case came to court, I refused a court-appointed lawyer, argued my own case, lost, and was sentenced to ten days or $2,000. Since I couldn't afford the dollars, I served the days, next to druggies, a pimp, and a *real* car thief. It was, not to put too fine a point on it, an educational experience. I did not lose my faith in Allah, but I certainly lost my faith in man; and I did not lose my faith in American democracy, but I certainly lost my faith in American bureaucracy.

Boston College

I got high grades in high school and won a scholarship to Boston College, a prestigious old Jesuit university in Newton, Boston's western suburb. I was able to use the scholarship because I had worked all through high school to save some money for college. I had to live at home in Lynn and commute to BC because I could not afford the luxury of room and board on campus, as most of BC's students can. My choice of BC came partly from my respect for Catholics and for the Jesuits as their most famous teachers, and partly from the fact that BC is also ecumenical and welcoming to other faiths.

I worked on campus, in the kitchen, fifteen hours a week, scrubbing and hauling pots and trays. Carrying ten-gallon aluminum pots filled with sudsy water has done wonders for my muscles. One day, when my friend Tim saw me sweating and straining with my big, water-heavy pots and uttered a word of pity, I corrected him. "The way I see it, Tim, I got a great deal from BC, because I'm *being paid* to do the very same thing—exercise—that you *pay for* in your expensive health club." (And I'm paid more than the legal minimum wage: Jesuits are big on social justice.)

I never fit into any of BC's cliques. Certainly not into its drinking crowd, for which the school is famous on the national student grapevine. The Irish, who founded the school, bequeathed to it their two primary institutions, Church and Pub. My faith forbids me alcohol, and I feel no temptation to disobey this law, for I have no respect for drunks. The word "alcohol" is an Arabic word, and a fitting one: it is a spit word.

As to sex, BC's other obsession, I am as temptable and as tempted as anyone, but I think my large and unfashionable contempt for the fashionable sins of the flesh that I see around me have done more to protect me from them than my small piety has done.

Most BC girls don't seem to share my respect for basic sexual morality, and the few who do seem dull. Autumn, for instance, has a beautiful body but an ugly soul, and Mary Ann has a beautiful soul but an ugly body. I wonder: If I am not able to love the girl with the beautiful soul in the ugly body, does that mean *I* have an ugly soul?

Autumn East is a provocative coed with an improbable name who set her sights on me for some reason. She is a rock climber, and probably thought of sexual conquest as a form of rock climbing, and of me as a resistant rock to conquer.

Autumn had four problems. Problem One was that she had a stunning 42-24-38 body. Problem Two was that she knew it. Problem Three was that others knew she knew it. Problem Four was that she didn't know they knew she knew it.

Once, I was in her coed dorm (boys on even floors, girls on odd floors), and Autumn caught me alone in a dead end hallway, minced up to me with a confident "Gotcha" look, smiled provocatively (she thought), wiggled her bountiful breasts under my startled face, and drawled, "How'd you like to see these hooters, Heesa?" She lifted up her sweater.

Because I was startled, or perhaps because I had to protect myself, I reverted to crudity: "I don't give a hoot about your hooters."

She laughed, thinking I was playing, so I had to be even more blunt: "You think you're sexy? You're just an ugly, stupid slut. And if I did want sex, I wouldn't want *you*. If I was looking for a whore, I wouldn't be looking for a whore who *looked* like a whore."

Her dream of conquest shattered by the rude alarm of my ringing insult, she slapped my face furiously, then slapped her sweater back down around her holy hooters. Then, to her horror, she turned to see three other students who had come up during the exchange, looking on wide-eyed. The story, of course, circulated quickly around the student grapevine, and divided those who heard it into two camps. Some felt sympathy for my bluntness but not for hers. Others felt sympathy for hers but not for mine. (They seem to believe that words demand modesty but bodies do not.)

My Mistress, Philosophy

When I took my first Philosophy course, as a freshman, I found my mind's true love. My young Muslim friends are surprised that I can love something so ethereal and abstract, and my old Muslim friends are suspicious that philosophy will undermine my faith with skepticism or rationalism or both. But to me philosophy is neither ethereal nor faith-threatening. I don't love its technicalities, but I love its existential questions: life, death, good, evil, fidelity, infidelity, hope, despair, righteousness, wickedness, man, woman, angels, and of course God.

Like most young American Muslims, I was plunged into many heated arguments about cultural accommodation, at the social club attached to the mosque. Many Muslims insisted on identifying religious purity with cultural purity; others (like me) insisted on distinguishing them. How much of American culture could a Muslim accept without compromising his religion? Compromise is what religious "liberalism" seems to mean to Christians. If that is the definition, I know of *no* religiously "liberal" Muslims. No Muslim I know has ever argued that the religion should change to conform to the culture. All Muslims are religiously "conservative." But not all are *culturally* "conservative." Some are: they want to preserve enclaves of "un-American" Muslim culture (music, dress, entertainment, art) like islands of purity in a sea of decadence. I agreed with them that the culture was decadent, but disagreed with their strategy of withdrawal rather than engagement. I think we have to be discriminating. I see nothing wrong with American cars, sports, and informal, modest clothes. But I see plenty wrong with most American rock music (brain bashing), American drug and alcohol culture (brain scrambling), and American sexual mores (your brains relocating between your legs). American Christians seem embarrassed at platitudes like #420 of the Sayings of Muhammad: "The most valuable thing in the world is a virtuous woman." Yet their own Bible says exactly the same thing (Proverbs 31).

Mama never understood my love of philosophy. "What can you do with it?" was her practical question. My answer, which seemed just as practical to me, was "What can it do with me? That's the question." Isn't what I am more important than what I do? When I told her that, Mama smiled, called me "my wise one," hugged me, and told me, "Follow your heart."

I am also following the Will of Allah as revealed through His Prophet. *The Sayings of Muhammad* tell us that "the pursuit of knowledge is a divine commandment." (280).

Are There Banks in Paradise?

Zvi is a very intelligent Jewish student at BC. (We call him Skip.) I love to argue with him about everything, especially Palestine. He is very practical and businesslike. He asked me why I chose philosophy as a career. I gave the world's most practical answer: "Death."

"What do you mean?"

"Do you think anybody will be doing economics or law or politics in Paradise?"

"I don't know if anybody will be doing anything in Paradise. What do we know about Paradise anyway?"

"Do you believe it exists?"

"Let's say I do."

"Well, then, do you think there will be banks in Paradise?"

"No. In Paradise everything is free. The streets are made of gold. So are the toilet bowls. So what?"

"But won't philosophers philosophize in Paradise? Could you imagine Socrates being happy there without philosophizing?"

"No, I can't. So there will be philosophers in Paradise. So what?"

"So I've got job security and you don't."

"Good joke, Jack. (Jack is my nickname.) But seriously, why did you go into philosophy?"

"I *am* serious, Skip. What's more serious than death?"

"So you want to take it with you."

"Yes. If I made a million dollars I couldn't take a penny of it with me. If I founded a new nation I couldn't take one of its citizens with me, or one of its towns, or one of its laws. But I can take whatever wisdom I learn on earth with me to Paradise, and I will. Philosophy is the love of wisdom, so it's death-proof. Wisdom is soul money that's stored in a fireproof vault."

"That sounds very noble, but you can't tell me that if you had to choose between finding just one more wise thought or a billion dollars, you'd turn down the money."

"Suppose I told you I would?"

"I would not believe you."

"Then you don't really know me, Skip."

"OK, Jack, I believe you. I always suspected you were a little crazy."

"That's not crazy, that's sane. Dollars burn, wisdom doesn't. A billion dollars are no more fireproof than one."

"You got a point there, Jack. Maybe you're crazy like a fox."

*   *   *   *   *

My favorite Christian author is C.S. Lewis, whom I first discovered when I saw a single sentence quoted from him printed on a poster that hit me in the heart like an arrow: "I was not born to be free; I was born to adore and to obey." I knew instantly that this was a true Muslim.

It was because of my admiration for Lewis that I adopted Lewis's nickname "Jack" (even though, traditionally, Muslims are not supposed to use nicknames). "Jack" is not a Muslim name, but it sounds right and good and clean and honest. Lewis had been saddled with the name "Clive Staples," and one day at the age of eight he announced, "Call me Jack," and the name stuck. "Jack" seems to have built bridges for me where "'Isa" has often built walls. For in using any form of the name "Jesus," pious Christians fear sounding impious and impious Christians fear sounding pious. "Jack" also short-circuits all the bad jokes about "Jesus," which sound more blasphemous to me than they do to most Christians. Why do they revere the name of Jesus *less* than Muslims do even though they say they revere the man who bore it *more*? Perhaps they just don't revere *names*.

I find that sense of reverence mainly among the "conservative" Christians, but I find respect for my faith mainly among "liberal" ones, and I rarely find both these things together. Yet neither point of respect is negotiable for me.

My Car Philosophy

I love my little beat-up, bright-blue, twelve-year-old Nash Metropolitan. A good friend who is "into" auto repair keeps it in shape for me for free, and I let him use it when he needs it. "From each according to his ability, to each according to his need."

Here is my Car Philosophy; it reflects some of my life philosophy:

1. Beauty is more important than utility. So choose a car you love even if it gives you a little bit of trouble.

2. Since beauty is more important than utility, choose a slower route over a faster one if it is more beautiful.

3. "Small is beautiful." Therefore a small car is more beautiful than a big one, and a bike is more beautiful than a car, and walking is the most beautiful of all.

4. "Small is beautiful" also means "natural is beautiful." Cars are not an improvement on horses; they are a substitute for horses. Gliders are more beautiful than airplanes, and sailboats are more beautiful than motorboats.

5. Don't have air conditioning in your car. Learn to love all weather. When it's hot, enter into the heat, just because it's there. Listen to the heat. Listen to everything. There's something almost ecstatic about opening all the windows (or letting the top down if you're blessed enough to have a convertible) and letting the wind run as it will through your hair and around your skin.

6. Don't have a car radio. Instead of the artificial music on the radio, listen to the music of nature, and of men at work and play.. There are hundreds of sounds you *hear* every day but you don't *notice* because the radio is on. Listen to Allah's humble, happy birds.

Listen to everything except "background music." Music is holy. "Background music" is like "background sex": an obscenity. It's like using the Mona Lisa to patch a broken window. It is part of the conspiracy to abolish silence from the world. The Voice of God can be heard only in silence. Omnipresent "background music" makes your soul sleepy. Music is soul food, and you are what you eat.

7. Another reason for no radio is to experience reality directly instead of indirectly. The radio is a middle man. Don't be dependent on the middle man. Use cash instead of credit cards, unless you *want* to lose track of how much you spend and lose and owe. Better yet, don't even use cash: barter; swap; touch real things. Things are better than cash, cash is better than checks, and checks are better than credit cards. You always wind up redeeming credit cards with checks and for checks with cash.

By the way, Muslims do not lend money at interest. The Qur'an says that is unnatural. I think the whole capitalist economic system is based on a philosophical lie: that money can get pregnant (interest, usury).

8. "Small is beautiful" also means that "simple is beautiful." I had an old bike that I loved because it was the simplest bike I ever saw. It was totally stripped, light and thin and it had only a foot brake, no hand brakes, and no gear shift. For steep uphills, I just pushed it, and for downhills, I just glided,

and for the flat it was perfect. It was my favorite bike in the world. Papa bought it for 25 cents back in the Forties, and rode it himself, so it was a kind of icon of Papa to me. I had no bike lock, but I engraved on it "STOLEN FROM 'ISA BEN ADAM" with my phone number. No one ever stole it.

(Editor's Note:) I interrupt 'Isa's autobiography here with an article he wrote on the town he lived in, Nahant, Massachusetts. It is written in a separate notebook rather than as part of the narrative of his autobiography, but I have included it here because it is the setting for the rest of his narrative, and his story is so deeply entwined with Nahant that the setting of his story is almost the protagonist.

(2) Nahant

Perched on the edge of Boston's urban blight like a seagull at the edge of a dump site lies an unpretentious little paradise called Nahant.

If Massachusetts were the whole world, Nahant would be its England:

> This other Eden, demi-paradise,
> This fortress built by Nature for herself
> Against infection and the hand of war,
> This happy breed of men, this little world,
> This precious stone set in the silver sea . . .
> This blessed plot, this earth, this realm, this England.

Nahant today is one of the best kept secrets of New England. But the secret was proclaimed from the rooftops throughout the nineteenth century by Henry Wadsworth Longfellow, John Greenleaf Whittier, Oliver Wendell Holmes, John Singer Sargent, Webster, and many other luminaries. Aggasiz did much of his scientific research here. Prescott wrote *The Conquest of Mexico* here, in his house overlooking Swallows Cave. Henry Cabot Lodge said he was happier here than any place on earth—and he had been in nearly all of them as U.S ambassador. There is a tiny park in his honor out on the uninhabited peninsula of East Point, with a bronze inscription quoting him: "The most prized memories of my life are of Nahant."

The park is at the very top of the windy, hundred-foot-high hill that reaches out into the Atlantic like the mailed fist of a medieval knight challenging the sea to combat. It is battered on three sides by waves having paroxysms. During major storms, you can feel the spray from the waves here, a hundred feet up. Robert Grant describes this place as "a splendid array of cliffs, more impressive in their ruggedness and bold beauty than any other on the North Shore. There are, indeed, none on the [Atlantic] coast, excepting perhaps at Bar Harbor [Maine] which surpass them in grandeur." ("The North Shore of Massachusetts," *Scribner's Magazine,* 1894.) The only other place I've seen like it is Rockport's Halibut Point. (Some go there to get the Point and some go just for the halibut.)

William Cullen Bryant called Nahant "the most striking landscape on the Eastern shore" and judged that "there is no coast on the Atlantic seaboard which presents a wider choice for the lover of marine pleasures, for the artist searching to reproduce on canvas the visible romance of nature." He mentions its "several exquisite diminutive beaches lying below jagged eminences" and notes that "the rocks are torn into such varieties of form that all the beauty of wave motion and the whole gamut of ocean eloquence are here offered to eye and ear." (*Picturesque America*, 1894.) Many sensitive nineteenth-century writers eulogized her beauty, and although the barbarism of the twentieth century allowed her to sink into obscurity, anyone with a pre-twentieth-century eye can take advantage of this forgotten gem.

Nahant is the smallest town in Massachusetts (1.06 square miles, population 3,828), and one of the oldest (1630). It is also the safest, one of the only two towns out of 117 in the state with absolutely no crime. For it is an island connected to the mainland only by a causeway, which protects it: the police can simply close the causeway and close in the criminal.

Nahant is actually two wooded rocks sticking out of the sea: 640 acres of Nahant and 80 of Little Nahant, plus three uninhabited acres of Egg Rock. Its Indian name means "the Twins." Little Nahant and Nahant (no Nahanter ever utters the oxymoron "Big Nahant") are linked to each other by a short causeway, and to the mainland by a long one, curved in a gentle, two-mile arc. On a map Nahant looks like two fish, one large and lean (Nahant) and the other small and fat (Little Nahant), snagged at the end of a thin fishing line (the causeway) and snapping at a bug (Egg Rock).

Before the causeways were built, Nahant was separated from the mainland by every high tide. It still is, during nor'easters, when the causeways are under water. The winter storms were so fierce here in 1840 that Nahant was cut off from the mainland for six months. The Great Blizzard of 1978 isolated it for a week.

Three hundred years ago, it took a whole day's walk through charming country roads to go the twelve miles from Boston to Nahant. Two hundred years ago, it took four hours to get from Boston to Nahant by horse, about as long as it takes today to get from Boston to New York by train. One hundred years ago, it took an hour's ride in a steamship. Today, you just drive for twenty minutes through ten miles of northern New Jersey—that is, Revere, Lynn, and other offenses. (Woody Allen says that on a good day even an atheist can believe in a Great Benevolent Mind permeating the universe "except of course certain parts of northern New Jersey.") Then, suddenly, at the Lynn-Swampscott rotary, you emerge into another world, like a bird hatching from its egg into the open air, or like a prisoner released from Plato's Cave into the light.

Keats must have felt this way on first discovering Chapman's Homer, and Pizarro peering at the Pacific "from a peak in Darien," and Xenophon's soldiers after the "march across country," the *Anabasis,* uttering that one unforgettable line in the book, "The sea, the sea!" (*Ta thallata, ta thallata!*) Nahant is a time machine: by moving north through space you move back through time, out of the modern world of size-seizure, time-tyranny, and a terminal case of the Uglies, into a time of innocence, simple beauties, and quiet pleasures.

Ahead of you stretches the two-mile-long causeway, arching gracefully left. As you drive along it, you have the open sea on your left, behind low, grassy dunes with bushes that look a little bit like Bonsai. On your right is the shallow, wind-whipped bay of Lynn Harbor. During very low tides, half the harbor bottom is exposed, revealing the mucky lairs of lawyerlike life forms. At high tide, the land (causeway, dunes, and beach together) can be as little as fifty yards wide between baywater and seawater. Many winters, the causeway is closed for a day by trespassing storm waves. Nahanters face this event with the same excitement kids face a "no school" snowstorm.

Nahant Beach stretches along the north side of the causeway in a moon-like arc of clean, tan sand that is hard and wriggly-wrinkled near the water but soft higher up, near the little dunes. Seen by night light, it shines like a pearl necklace. Across the bay to the south looms the Boston skyline, a mere 12 miles away. The causeway leads first to Little Nahant. From a half mile away, Little Nahant looks like a giant Russian Easter egg decorated with 328 tiny houses. They cling to its steep sides, snuggling close together against the winds. They are not mansions or summer houses for the rich, but modest cottages, year-round sturdy Cape Cods, saltboxes, mini-Victorians, or renovated barns—not pretentiously-plush, artsy-fartsy, or cutesy-poo, just solid New England sanity.

Nahant proper, past Little Nahant and across the next causeway, rises a little higher out of the sea, but it looks lower because it is a whole mile long. Nahant contains no traffic lights, neon signs, fast food, or chain stores, and only one of each of the following necessities: gas station (hard to find), police station, mini-post office, general store, sandwich shop, beachside clam shack, public restaurant, private restaurant, country club (tiny), doctor, dentist, library, town hall, golf course, elementary school, realtor, butcher, fish store, pharmacy, Little League baseball diamond, Coast Guard station, harbor, and perhaps sea serpent. (This creature was seen and certified by thousands of otherwise very reliable witnesses a century ago off Nahant, but has been understandably shy of media attention throughout most of the twentieth century.)

Nahant is surrounded by—well, non-Nahant. On the mainland side of the causeway, immediately west, lies Lynn, twenty times bigger than Nahant. More than a century ago Longfellow wrote a famous admiring poem about "The Bells of Lynn," but the most famous poem for present-day Bostonians about Lynn is: "Lynn, Lynn, city of sin/ You never come out the way you went in." Lynn's most famous product nowadays is corrupt politicians. Lynn Beach is an extension of Nahant Beach, curving north around the shoreline; but whereas both the water and the sand of Nahant Beach are almost always clean, both the water and the sand of Lynn Beach are almost always full of brown seaweed and various dead smelly things. The Fates draw their lines sharply.

To the south, between Nahant and Boston along the coastline, is Revere Beach. In the nineteenth century it was America's first seaside amusement park. The rides are all gone now, some burned down, some torn down, some blown down by hurricanes. The best way to describe Revere Beach in 1978 is by the following news item from the Boston College student newspaper, *The Heights*: A creative BC student won first prize at a Halloween costume party by dressing as Revere Beach. His costume consisted of an old brownish bed sheet to which he had glued sand, mud, rocks, broken and unbroken bottles, beer cans, paper cups, pieces of plastic, syringes, sanitary napkins, unsanitary napkins, and (of course) condoms.

However, Revere Beach also boasts Kelly's Clam Shack, which serves the best fried clams in the solar system. There always seem to be at least a dozen people on line waiting for takeout orders at any hour of the day or night, and it's open from 6 A.M. to 3 A.M. (No, that's not a typo.)

To the north of Nahant begins the prestigious and prohibitively pricey North Shore, increasing in economic inaccessibility from Swampscott to Marblehead to Beverly to Manchester-by-the-sea to Magnolia.

Just as Nahant is on the border between the urban ugliness to its south and the posh perfection to its north, it is also at the exact border between sandy beaches to its south and rocky beaches to its north. North of Nahant pretty much everything is rock right up to Labrador, with only a few rare stretches of sandy beach in between (Plum Island, Massachusetts, Hampton Beach, New Hampshire, and Old Orchard Beach, Maine). South of Nahant we have the opposite: pretty much flat sand with only a few stretches of rocky cliffs like Newport. Nahant is the southernmost outpost of the empire of rock and the northernmost outpost of the empire of sand.

It is also at the border between swimmably-warm and unswimmably-cold water. No seawater north of Nahant ever gets near 70 degrees except by miracle. So Nahant is almost the only place on the Atlantic, except Newport, to combine rocky coastline with swimmable water.

To the east of Nahant lies her glory and crown: Big Mama Sea, who keeps caressing Baby Nahant's tiny body. A hundred house owners on Nahant can say: "My back yard is the Atlantic Ocean." Wouldn't you swap your back yard for an ocean?

Nahant has the best of both worlds: the sea-surroundedness of an island and the commuter-convenience of the causeway. Unlike her richer, bigger, and more famous sisters Nantucket and Martha's Vineyard, she doesn't require ferry reservations six months in advance. Her Little League baseball field proclaims her unpretentious innocence. It has no seats, stands, or fences, just a little blackboard scoreboard. The outfield "fences" are weeds. If you love the game of baseball itself more than any of its accoutrements, you will love it here, because it is simple, pure, and unprostituted.

On Nahant you always see little kids playing ball, riding bikes, selling lemonade in summer, or sledding in winter. In fact 18.86% of her population (720) is under five. The adults are often seen walking their dogs, their babies, or their own bodies. There are almost as many walkers as drivers. They walk with leisure, like free men and women, not with hurries and scurries, like slaves in mansions or rats in city sewers. A lot of them are pregnant. For this is the perfect place for kids. I believe that one of the most potent unacknowledged forces in the world for keeping kids innocent, keeping adults kids, and thus keeping both happy, is smelling salt air every day. When I walk thorough Nahant I often hear a sound I hear nowhere else today: whistling!

I defy anyone to find another place as unspoiled and innocent as Nahant that is only ten miles from the center of a metropolis as sophisticated and fast-paced as Boston. Boston has more colleges per square mile than any other city in America. To a Bostonian, Boston is America's brain. New York is its nose: big, smelly, and in your face. Washington is its mouth: gossipy, propagandistic, and filibustering. The Midwest, the heartland, is of course its heart. Chicago, "city of the big shoulders," is its shoulder. Texas is its potbelly, Los Angeles is its anus, and Florida is . . . well, you get the idea. That is the insufferably provincial Bostonian's anatomical map of America.

I would love to take you on a tour of Nahant some day and show off all her tasteful little natural bounties that the Victorians gave pet names to on their maps: Spouting Horn, Cauldron Cliff, Roaring Cavern, John's Peril (an open-mouthed cliff fissure), Great Furnace, Little Furnace, Black Mine, Forty Steps Beach, Crystal Beach, Swallows Cave, Irene's Grotto, Maolis Garden (Solomon's "Siloam" backwards), Dashing Rock, Basking Rock, Sunken Rock, Castle Rock (complete with natural turrets, battlements, and buttresses), Pulpit Rock (shaped like a giant pulpit broken at a 45 degree angle, with a giant rock-Bible on top), and Egg Rock, which looks like a gigantic, half-submerged egg that fell out of the nest of a giant bird.

So many names for rocks! And all in one little square mile! What does it mean? It means love. Naming is an act of love. You don't name what you don't care about. It is remarkable how much more real a rock becomes when you name it.

Tolkien's dwarves would have loved this place. The rocks are alive. They acquire personalities here. There are great black square rocks that look like toy blocks tossed tempestuously to and fro by giant babies with temper tantrums. There are smooth yellow rocks poking out of the ground that look like the bald spots on a gentle giant's sleeping head. There are cliffs of vertical layers of grey granite that look like enfolded layers of the giant's beard. There are brown, sun-tanned arms and legs of rock that stretch out and down to the sea like lazy bathers. And there are gaggles of giggling rock children running into the sea like a frozen stop-action photograph.

Swallows Cave was the refuge for Narragansett Indians during King Philip's War. When the war ended, it became the refuge of hundreds of swallows. Ten feet high, seventy feet long, and open on both ends to the water, it is flooded at high tide and dry at low. There is a place on the slope next to its entrance where you can look *up* to see green grass and look *down* and see the blue sky through angled openings halfway down the cliff. It makes you feel non-horizontal, as on a pitching ship.

Fifty feet away, Irene's Grotto is an arched throne room in the cliffside that can be reached on foot only at very low tides, by scrambling on all fours over slippery, seaweed-covered rocks.

At Maolis Garden there is a cold natural spring that has flowed from the rock ledge since the world was young. (It still *is* young here.)

At a certain turn in Marginal Road, which hugs the northern shore of the island, all you see is a sea of rocks. The road is twenty feet above sea level and hugs the shoreline so closely that you feel the spray on your face if you drive with the window open at high tide or on a windy day. You think you are in Labrador or Patagonia, not ten miles from downtown Boston. An 1887 guidebook noted: "it is the very closeness of the Nahant cliffs to the hived life of cities which freshens and magnifies the impression produced by the ocean. Within the sound of bells in city steeples, its surf thunders on sand or rock. . . . The sharp contrast between the city and the shore is here felt with keenest pleasure." (*Romance and Reality of the Puritan Coast*) A hundred years later this same "keen pleasure" is undiminished.

Out at East Point, Nahant's largest archipelago, you may think you are in the Aleutian Islands. Looking east, you see thousands of sea birds and no visible sign of human life. Around the base of the hundred-foot-high cliffs the sea churns and foams incessantly. Underwater ledges and offshore rocks the size of houses break the stately swells that sweep in from the open sea, transforming them instantly into bouquets of white foam flowers flung up into the air. The surf is always active here, even when it is calm everywhere else. It curls around little caves and splashes up into rock chimneys, mutters to itself like an old hermit, and picks endless fights with itself like a schoolyard of brats. Waves rush into rock cauldrons to be trapped there and rage round like caged white tigers. The sea's mouth is never shut.

Morning fog is pure magic on Nahant. It does not so much conceal as reveal. You see more, not less: other worlds, worlds within worlds. Then the Sun King arises in glory from the sea, processes slowly and majestically into his kingdom, and dispels the fog. When you see your first sunrise here, you will find it hard to believe you have not died and gone to heaven. (This actually happened to me once, when I slept overnight on the beach and suddenly awoke to a five-S symphony of sea, sand, sky, sunrise, and seagull flying straight out of the sun. It took a minute of body checks to convince me I was still on earth.)

The variety of topography seems impossible for such a tiny place. There are beaches big and small, rocky and sandy, open and hidden. There are stone ladders, grottoes, caves, islets, inlets, outlets, bays, mounds, cliffs, breaks, and slides. There is salt marsh, tide pools, and kelp beds. Inland there are dunes, fields, marsh, hills, a stretch of pine, and even a tiny, block-square birch and poplar forest that says "Vermont."

Earth, air, fire and water all seem *larger* here. All earth seems exposed on the open beach, all air in the open sky, all fire in the summer sun, and all water in the sea.

Your senses are sharpened here. You notice a greater variety of flora and fauna than you ever did before. You notice little changes in the smell of the wind, the color of the sky, and the sounds of the sea, that you never noticed before. You find yourself breathing deeper because there's air worth breathing here, even at low tide, when the suggestion of dead fish perfumes the air just enough to satisfy the subconscious sea-lover who lives in the back of your nose. (The sea *should* smell fishy: a thing should smell like itself.)

Your heart beats faster when you come here because you are becoming the child you forgot you were. A trip to Nahant is a trip back to the time when both you and the world were young and innocent; back even farther, to the moment of creation, when everything was fresh from the Creator's hand. This place feels like it was just thrown through a curtain and onto the stage of Being, one second before you looked at it.

The books say there is no manufacturing on Nahant, but there is: Nahant manufactures vast quantities of fresh air every day. That is her primary product. Where does it come from? From God. It's His Spirit's breath. You can almost smell the Mind of God in the air.

Wherever you are on Nahant, you are never more than two blocks from the sea. In fact, the sea is closer than that: it's inside you, in your lungs and in your heart. You are on board a large, securely anchored ship.

Tiny Nahant is a complete world that can teach you everything you need to know, everything the whole planet can teach. The rocks teach you fidelity. The waves teach you the relentless, unceasing heartbeat of love. The winds teach you the power of the invisible. The high cliffs teach you to hope. The caves teach you that all things have a dark and buried side. The grass teaches you humility. The sun teaches you glory. The sand teaches you time. The trees teach you to think tall. The ants and bees teach you industry. The flowers teach you the morality of superfluity, the wild adventure of hospitality, and the beauty of prodigality. The seasons teach you that change and stability are two sides of the same reality. The night teaches you mystery and the day teaches you mindfulness. The tiny town teaches you modesty. And the surrounding sea teaches you that you are rocked at every moment in the arms of a giant angel.

But you learn all these things here only because you first learn the precious Lesson One that my Mama used to call "hushing": the wisdom of slowing down, getting all quiet inside, and entering the holy silence, where you can listen. I believe this is the single most potent of all learning arts. Most follies, of both thought and deed, cannot endure that place, that holy silence. Addictions, aggressions, and aggravations fall out of your soul, like birds with broken wings, when the air is fresh with silence. But what does it mean and how does Nahant teach it to you?

It means nothing mystical or esoteric. Just listen. Don't listen *for* anything, just listen. You *must* learn to listen, for listening is life's second greatest art. Only loving is greater. But listening well is the best aid to loving well.

Nahant teaches this art because it is an island. Islands make it easier to listen.

Most of us can't afford to live on an island. We are landlocked by many obligations. But we can slip away to this island easily, because it has a causeway.

Landlocked towns usually lack clear edges and therefore identity. Especially near cities, each suburb blurs into the next like lumps in tapioca. This is not just an aesthetic tragedy but a human one, for when things lose their identity, people begin to do the same. The unnatural becomes natural and vice versa. Life starts to feel like a load of gooey wet cement because there are no borders.

No *real* borders, I mean. For instance, the border between Lynn and Revere is only an invisible, imaginary line, a political abstraction. But the border between an island like Nahant and the rest of the world is one of the most real things there is: the sea. Paradoxically, the plasticity of the sea is the very thing that gives rigidity to the lands. The sea does to islands what light does to colors: because light transcends all colors, it brings out the different colors in each thing it touches; and because the sea transcends all lands, it defines all lands. The sky does the same to the earth, giving it the edge called the horizon. God does the same to the whole creation: since He has no finite form or limit, He can preserve all finite forms and limits instead of displacing them as a finite rival (like Zeus) would do.

Little islands like Nahant remind us that we all live on big islands: we call them continents. The difference is only one of degree, like the difference between dying tomorrow and dying fifty years from now. We all live on "this island earth," surrounded by the mystery of the heavens. Living at the edge of the sea is like living at the edge of the heavens, on a mountaintop. It is a local reminder of a universal truth. All of us, in all places and at all times, are surrounded by the sea, as we are surrounded by angels. A few of us are lucky enough to live where we can see it habitually, as a few saints habitually see angels.

Islands are surviving chunks of individuality in a mass-minded world, enclaves of excellence in an orgy of egalitarianism. They are excellent not because they are alienated from the world but because they are not alienated from themselves. They have identities because they are small and have natural limits. They can't grow indefinitely, like suburbs, or cancers. When you live on an island you belong to it, as a dog belongs to its owner (or vice versa). That's because it's a real thing, like both dog owner and dog, not an abstraction, like a political entity. You can't belong to an abstraction.

There are four different ways people feel about islands, depending on how they feel about the sea.

For some, the island is their castle and the sea is a moat. They love it because it is an escape. It shuts out the rest of the world, other people, cities, bigness, responsibilities, ugliness—whatever they came to the island to escape.

For others, the island is their prison cell and the sea is its walls. They are bored on an island and can't wait to get back to the very world the first group wanted to escape. The sea is a moat for them too, but they are the prisoners in its castle.

For a third group, the sea is not a moat at all but a highway. They define travel not by cars and roads but by boats and seas. The sea is the road that begins at their dock and joins all other wet roads on earth. It can take them to Nome, Alaska, or Hobart, Tasmania, or Istanbul, Turkey.

A fourth group sees the sea as neither a moat around the land nor a highway from one land to another, but as her own salty self. It sees the sea not as a means to any end, either protecting the island (the first group) or imprisoning the island (the second) or connecting islands (the third). Rather, the island is for the sea, not vice versa. The island is the place you can go to be rocked in the Great Wet Mother's undulating lap, and lullabied. One Nahant resident put it this way to me: "When you live here, the sea is part of your family." Her changing moods, her smells, her storms, her beauty, all become a part of your life. It's like having a very large grandmother camping out in your back yard. She's not just part of the scenery, she's a part of your family.

*   *   *   *   *

The Nahant of Nahant is Bailey's Hill. It is to Nahant what Nahant is to the world. It is the hub of the universe, the navel of the cosmos, the holy of holies, the still point of the turning world.

Bailey's Hill is one of three hills surrounding Trimountain Road. Until 1922 there was a hotel here, the Trimountain Hotel, nestled between two of the three "mountains," which are really just tiny hills. Only one of the three hills is inhabited today; the other two are virginal, with nothing on them but God-stuff. The inhabited one is one block high and one block wide. Off the steep road that climbs up its side, a dozen funky little houses crowd together like a family of proud dwarfs. The second hill is a city-block-sized forest. Out of its seaward side juts a World War II concrete bunker with a wide, curved gun emplacement. It served the same purpose as the medieval castle, but it looks less like a castle than like the top of a giant periscope sent up by troglodytes to observe the surface dwellers.

The third hill is Bailey's: a round, rocky outcropping of about four acres covered with long grasses, tall bushes, and short trees. It too was used by the Army; in fact, it is hollow, and once sheltered thousands of troops under-ground. But almost all the marks of its defacement are gone now. It is a per-fectly hilly hill, hill-shaped and hill-sized—in fact, *human*-hill-sized, just big enough to get lost in and just small enough to imagine you own it. It contains four tiny meadows, each the size of a swimming pool. It is criss-crossed with dozens of little paths, barely wide enough for one person, that turn every few feet, concealing the new worlds around each new corner. They are inviting, like red carpets rolled out by the Hill itself for you, who stride in as its king and conqueror. They look like they have always been there. Henry Beetle Hough says, "If you see a path, it is probably an old one, for we live in a soci-ety that no longer goes afoot."

Except kids. The Hill is just the right size for pre-teen kids to play on, and you sometimes see them there (but never more than a few at a time, never in gangs) playing cops and robbers or pirates, with toy guns, or with bikes or kites or fishing rods, or sleds in winter—or just poking around. Nahant is a pokey place, a place for kids and play and dogs. The Hill is dog heaven. Yet, step where I will, my feet have never been the recipients of their creative anal products. Perhaps the angels sweep them up each night with invisible pooper scoopers. There are also dozens of rabbit holes here, but you seldom see the rabbits except at night, probably because the dogs keep them underground. If the Almighty should solicit my advice for designing an afterlife for animals, I would suggest that a heaven for dogs and a hell for rabbits can be combined very economically.

An extended family of seagoing ducks lives here year round. They ride the swells like surfers waiting in the lineup for the perfect wave. I've actually seen one riding the whitewater when it was about three inches high, glued to his own perfect surfboard of belly feathers. When the ducks come on land, they stick out their necks proudly like Viking ships, thrust out their beaks defiantly, and look almost lordly—until they start waddling. One pair that roams the Hill regularly seems to expect me, and follows me around for a few minutes when I come, at a respectful distance. Of course, they will not let me touch them, much less pet them. They are proper New England ducks, they are not "easy."

On the Hill I have more than once met self-styled mystics, nature worshippers, occultists, and wiccans. They come because they say this place is a
"power point" or an "energy center" where unseen forces come together and
can be felt "like electricity." Two words they often use are "powers" and "presence." One called it a "battlefield," another a "dynamo." I think these people
are flakes and nuts, but they all say the same thing about this place, and that
gives me pause. At the top of the Hill there is an altar-sized rock, charred and
blackened by fire. This also gives me pause.

You often see lobstermen throwing out traps near offshore rocks. You can
sometimes see the lobsters crawling around the rocks at the waterline at the
foot of the Hill. Once, a rare giant *blue* lobster was caught here.

Most hills look taller from the bottom than from the top, but Bailey's Hill
is the opposite: when you reach the top, it seems much higher than it seemed
from the bottom. Here you seem to stand on the top of the world. You have a
360-degree view of everything, from skyscrapers to wilderness, mansions to
fishing shacks, Boston Lighthouse to the crowded little local harbor. You feel
like a god here, while the winds of Heaven sweep like swells through your hair.
You think of rising to the sun, like Icarus, since your spirit has already done it.
When you turn to face the east, you become Poseidon, commanding endless
oceans. When you face south toward Boston, you become Athena, custodian
of the city that calls itself "the Athens of America." When you face north and
west and see approaching storm clouds, you become Zeus, readying your thunder to intimidate your enemies.

The summit is bald and flat, and just big enough for a football field for
hamsters. In the spring it becomes a miniature Alpine meadow dotted with
multicolored wildflowers. On the hottest summer days there is always a breeze
here.

The animal inhabitants are exhibitionists. Bees buzz importantly around
the abundant goldenrod. Dragonflies and butterflies shamelessly show off their
extravagant bodies. Ants conscientiously carry little leaves across little paths.
Robins rejoice, chickadees chirp, crows complain, and all these sounds are
periodically interrupted by an assertive brass section of tiny tubas in the person of wild ducks intermittently announcing their protests against the establishment. And the stage scenery for these animal actors is purple heather, pink
wild roses, and yellow buttercups.

One of the commonest bushes here look like deer antlers after they lose
their leaves and grow a soft, strong fuzz over their tips. I don't know their
name, and don't want to. I want to be Adam and name things myself. Not
knowing their scientific name makes them more exotic. When the Englishman
G.K. Chesterton came to Times Square, he said he wished he was illiterate for
one night so that he could feel a child's wonder at the colors instead of the
adult's boredom at the words. I have my own pet names for many plants and

animals. Why should I let scientists in sterile classrooms thousands of miles away name my pets?

At the landward foot of the Hill there is a grassy park with a white gazebo where there are summer band concerts, as if it were Middle America in mid-century. Climb this gentle west slope and you think it's a tame, English hill; then, at the top, you suddenly discover the craggy west coast of Ireland. There are sudden vertical canyons into which storm waves rush *up* as a sudden rainstorm rushes *down* a drainpipe, creating for a second an upside-down waterfall. Garage-sized slabs of smooth black stone lie strewn at the foot of the cliffs. If there is a sea serpent off Nahant, as the old records claim, this is where it would come ashore, on this slab stairway, which looks evil and old enough to have seen dragons.

The steep sides of the Hill are punctuated with little bays, and the rock geometry of each one causes a different wave action: swirling spirals, frontal attacks, vertical waterfalls and runoffs, ten-second tides, aquatic explosions, gradual sand erosion, and in one place waves running around in circles and catching their own tails. It is a complete world of water, and I can watch it without boredom for hours, even though most TV bores me after two minutes. When, approaching the hill, I see that there will be great waves there today, I get so excited that I sneeze.

My favorite spot on the Hill I have christened "The Water Treasury." It is a pancreas-shaped, elephant-sized grotto into which each incoming wave makes a deposit of gazillions of gallons of seawater, then withdraws its deposit five seconds later, and for those five seconds the grotto is full of mad whitewater sloshing sideways, collecting interest and gathering momentum for the return journey. When there's a storm here, I call it "The Cauldron." It is to Bailey's Hill what the Hill is to Nahant, Nahant to Boston, and Boston to the world: it is the hub of the hub of the hub of the hub of the universe.

When it is calm everywhere else even around the Hill, the angel still troubles the water here. When the sea is asleep, it still dreams here, muttering under its breath. When invisible swells hit the Hill, they become visible here, even when they are not big enough to rise into waves. Sometimes they slither seductively by like Southern belles in crinoline. Sometimes they gurgle and burble like babies. But never do they rest. They keep coming with the single-mindedness of spawning salmon. Clearly, there is *life* in them.

As each wave enters from the sea, it is split in two by the rock in the middle of the Cauldron. Each separated half of the wave then curls its tendrils round the rock, and meets its separated half on the landward side, like two armies rushing at each other from opposite ends of a battlefield.

Just above the Water Treasury there is a large, flat, south-facing rock where I love to lie like a lizard and sop up the first precious rays of the spring or the last precious rays of the fall. It is my reserved front row seat in the

world's best amphitheater, where I listen to the water music, the longest playing show on earth. Sometimes my favorite singer comes up to me and plants a
salty kiss on my lips. Her name is Spray. Though our love is innocent, it is
supremely sensual. When I sit in this theater seat and hear the swirling surf,
feel the sensuous sun, smell the brine-bearing wind, taste the spray, and see the
jutting, jagged, ragged, and romantic rocks mirrored by the screamingly blue
skies, I feel my heart beating wildly, threatening to burst out like an animal
from a cage. It's aesthetic overload, sensory supererogation, too beautiful to
endure and too beautiful to endure leaving.

Out at the farthest tip of the easternmost outcropping of the Hill is a truck-
sized rock I call The Drum. You get to it by sliding down a slope of splendid
desolation, a hundred feet of broken blocks of granite. The Drum is half hollow on the bottom, a space worn by relentlessly repeated sloshings and slurp-
ings and crashings and cracklings and roilings and rumblings of centuries of
waves and swells.

The variety of music played by this instrument is unbelievable. Sometimes
the waves slide in sideways and spiral out S-sounds: *slishes, smishes, spits,* and
simple *sisses.* Sometimes they spank, with Whomps, Thunks, Klaps, or
Klonks. (Whomps sound like dragon tails swatting dwarves like flies. Thunks
sound like elephants stepping on octopi. Klaps sound like wooden clappers.
Klonks sound like Chinese gongs that have had all their echoes stolen.) On
quieter days, the water *flubs, glops,* or *klishes* around the weedy surfaces
exposed by the low tide. On wilder days it *kabooms* or *kerplunks.* It even slaps
loose rocks against fixed rocks with *kbonks* and *kpokks.* It also boils, roils,
whips, spits, smacks, lurches, kisses, flames, sputters, mutters, and gibbers.
Sometimes it sounds like the digestive processes of a giant with a cement
mixer for a stomach.

Its vocabulary, once you learn it, is surprisingly rich, though it consists
entirely of verbs. It comes at you like a wet, happy, irrepressible one-year-old
full of babble.

The themes of its music vary with the rhythm. You can turn your spirit into
a surfboard and surf on its sound waves. When the swell is slight, the rock is a
giant mouth slurping its food. Increase the swell a little and you elicit burps.
Add a little wind and you hear Mother burping Baby: pit-a-pat-a-pit-a-pat-a.
Sometimes the rhythm is as regular as a polka, sometimes as irregular as a Zen
garden. Sometimes the sea sings to the Drum, sometimes she spanks it.
Sometimes it Yesses the sea, and sometimes it No's her. But it always knows
her.

I call it the Seeing Stone as well as the Drum, because the sense of sight
is washed here as well as the sense of hearing. One sees deep into the deep,
where there is always peace under the sea's surface agitation. You don't see it

with your eyes but with your soul. You feel it. It acts on you. It kisses all your boo-boos and sucks all the pains out of your soul like a syringe draining pus out of a wound.

If you stand on the south side of the Hill, halfway between the Drum and the Cauldron, you see the shoreward swells moving *past* you, left to right. As they pass you can see every inch of their curl rising and falling. If you now turn right, you see these same swells moving *away* from you onto the beach. You feel like Poseidon, Lord of the Waves, sending them forth. Now turn left and you see them coming *toward* you. Different sounds correspond to these different sights: the swells that go away from you to the beach on your right break on the small, round stones of the beach with a hissing or kissing sound, while the oncoming swells to your left strike the outcroppings of rock with deeper, heavier crashes. So you feel you are conducting two parts of an orchestra, playing in counterpoint. Crash!—hiss—hiss—crash!—hiss—hiss—crash!—hiss. . . . And the rhythm changes every day. Tomorrow the orchestra will play Crash!—hiss—crash!—hiss—crash!

The swells are elegant and perfectly formed, and seem to know it. They stride shoreward graciously with heads held high, necks arched like aristocratic Victorian ladies concerned with nothing but their own perfection. Then, suddenly, they lose all their grace in an instant, falling, coming apart on the rocks or sands of their destruction—or is it their consummation?

The most scenic spots on the cliffsides of the Hill, seen from afar, seem dangerously vertical or even inaccessible. But once you are there, you find that there are always horizontal places for you to stand or sit comfortably. From these places you can look up and see little rivulets of rainwater draining down the long rock stairways, step by step, like inchworms, each drop obediently following its predecessor and merging its identity into a tiny river. The river sparkles and smiles in the sun and sings silent songs of ecstasy as it approaches its God, the sea. You can't find these places at first; you have to pay your dues to the Hill by exploring for a while before it allows you into its sanctums. The ledges look especially dangerous when the swells are big enough to send spume thirty feet up, entirely covering them from view for a few seconds. There are sizeable pools of seawater and seaweed even fifty or sixty feet up: warning signs from the sea angel: "See what I can do!"

Nahant has always been shaped by waves: not only the waves of the sea, which have sculpted her rock, but also three other kinds of waves. First, glacial waves shaped the land. Then, waves of settlers humanized it. Finally, waves of love keep breaking over Nahant and preserving it. Everything in nature comes in waves.

Nahant's history naturally divides into five eras: the Native American, the Viking, the Colonial, the Victorian, and the modern.

(1)

The Native Americans (wisely?) left no written records.

(2)

The Vikings probably penetrated into Nahant in 1000 a.d. One of them, Thorvald Erikson, may even be buried here, according to local rumors.

(Editor's Note: When 'Isa wrote this sentence he had no idea how his life would soon be changed by this fact.)

(3)

The Colonial period began in 1630, when a Puritan farmer, Thomas Dexter, bought Nahant from an Indian named either Sagamore or Poquantum for a bottle of whiskey and a suit. The seal of Nahant shows the suit but not the whiskey. Brian Doyle, an ex-Nahanter, wrote a play about the incident that is worthy of Samuel Beckett. The entire play consists of four lines:

>   **(Dexter:)**   **Hello.**
>   **(Poquantum:)**   **Hello.**
>   **(Dexter:)**   **Here's your suit.**
>   **(Poquantum:)**   **Here's Nahant.**

The Colonials pastured their cattle on Nahant by building fences across Long Beach (today's causeway), which was under water at high tide. This gave them a pen for their cattle and protection from the wolves that lived in the forests inland.

Like all the islands near Boston Harbor, Nahant was originally thickly wooded. But the practical Colonials cleared it, leaving it naked as a shaved lion. In the nineteenth century, the less pragmatic and more romantic Victorians, like Shem covering Noah's nakedness, lovingly replanted thousands of trees, mainly willows and poplars, which thrive in the salty wind.

The Colonials were hardworking, serious people with little leisure or head for natural beauty. Vacations were unheard of, travel a hardship, and the sea a threat to life. Only after the Revolution did wealth and leisure allow Americans to search out beauty spots. Nahant was the first place Bostonians found. By 1738 the first inn (Samuel Breed's) was built there. Vacationers came to look at the sea, not swim in it, for until the nineteenth century swimming in the open ocean was thought to be insanely reckless.

(4)

By the nineteenth century every house on Nahant was a boarding house. (Today there is not a single one.) In the eighteenth century almost no one moved from their house; by the nineteenth century almost everyone did who could afford to.

Nahant was Boston's Newport: the fashionable destination for the rich and famous. Only its tiny size saved it from a fate like Atlantic City's. When the local history books note that Nahant had a "glorious past," they mean it was crowded with large hotels and amusement parks with rides, midways, and gambling. Blondin the famous tightrope walker was suspended on a wire strung between East Point and Castle Rock. The world's first lawn tennis match was played on the lawn of a mansion next to East Point. A railroad was built across the causeway to bring in the crowds. It's gone now, and so are they.

For Allah in His mercy sent Nahant a mysterious series of fires that burned every single one of its hotels to the ground between 1861 and 1938. The first and most definitive fire from Heaven fell on Colonel Hutchins's Nahant Hotel. Five months after the beginning of the Civil War, in September of 1861, there was (as Joseph Garland put it, with salty irony, in *Boston's North Shore*) "one bad moment after the fire when life seemed to stir among the ashes, but the distractions of the deepening war took care of that." Through death beauty was preserved. It is nature's way. Even Egg Rock was not spared nature's judgment, when a storm destroyed its one building, a lighthouse.

Egg Rock is the smallest of the three islands that make up Nahant. It hosted a lighthouse, keeper, and family. Here are four snippets of its nineteenth-century history:

(1) In 1815 a young Italian lover sailed out to Egg Rock the evening before his scheduled departure for Italy, to pick forget-me-nots for his beloved. A sudden storm drowned him on his return trip and the girl died of a broken heart. (People actually used to do that.)

(2) One of the most famous dogs in American history lived on Egg Rock with his lighthouse keeper family, the Taylors. He was an enormous Saint Bernard/Newfoundland who once swam all night into the ocean after a loon, rescued several children from drowning, and is immortalized in "Saved," one of the most famous pictures of the century.

(3) Entry in lighthouse keeper's wife's log, 1873: "Severe rainstorm. Keeper went ashore to get some groceries and got caught in the storm; was detained away 4 days on account of rough seas. The wife kept the light all trimmed and burning bright and clear. Keeper was drunk ashore all the time."

(4) In 1873 an enormous codfish was caught on Egg Rock. When cut open, it disgorged an 18–carat gold ring with the initials H.L.)

Imagine all the hotels in Miami Beach burning down and not being rebuilt. Then imagine ordinary middle-class people building ordinary middle-class year-round houses there. Does that sound like a fairy tale? It happened on Nahant.

There was, however, one rude interruption of Nahant's return to sanity in the twentieth century: the world's jihad against a bothersome little mustachioed madman in Germany. During World War II, the Army built four massive concrete bunkers on the island, with guns that shot 100–pound shells 17 miles. Nahant was thought to be the first defense against Nazis invading Boston. (What would they want here? Beans? Cod? Harvard's library?) So it was fortified like no other place in America. Artillery bunkers on Nahant: that's about as fitting as a battleship on Walden Pond.

It can't be accidental that this ugly war picked such a pretty town and the most beautiful places on it (East Point and Bailey's Hill) to deface. And it's no accident that grass now grows over the concrete. The grass always wins.

The bunker is still there on Trimountain Hill, barely daring to poke its head out of the earth, looking embarrassed. Kids used to get inside it to play (how could they resist?), so it was sealed up. The Army also built three tall, thin concrete observation towers, four stories high, on Bass Point Hill just inland from Bailey's Hill. They are also still there; current owners have made them part of their houses. One calls it his giant refrigerator.

Town affairs in Nahant are run by direct democracy: the old-fashioned New England Town Meeting. A large percentage of its inhabitants always turn out. The Board of Aldermen's most serious task is to make it notoriously difficult to get any kind of building permit that changes the face of the place. Such stodginess is reasonable, for if you're happy with anything, why change it? "If it ain't broke, don't fix it." Conservatism is the natural philosophy of happy people, progressivism of unhappy people.

A few years ago the *Boston Globe* ran short articles on each town in the Boston area. The one on Nahant started out this way:

"The more things change elsewhere, the more things pretty much stay the same in Nahant, say longtime residents of this tiny seaside community. While other towns wrestle with issues such as explosive development and stretched-thin local services, Nahant has the luxury, mostly because of its small size (1.1 square miles), of dealing with more mundane matters. At the recently concluded town meeting, for example, there were "the usual controversies—dogs and perambulations," noted Daniel DeStefano, director of the Nahant Public Library, referring to debates about dogs on the beaches. "They are banned from all but one beach, and volunteers walk the town once a year to make sure that rights-of-way are being observed."

Nahant houses human treasures too, past and present: relics of hotels, mansions, and ships, and living specimens as strange as any ocean creature:

happy-grumpy retirees impersonating sea captains, Tony Conigliaro's house and family, a convicted Mafia chief's common-law wife (famous for wandering around town erratically, tanked and searching for parties), and the twelfth richest house of the twelfth richest man in America.

A few others have discovered this Eden, but happily no one paid much attention. Dan Levin wrote, in the *Boston Globe*, "Little Nahant is my choice for the best summer place in the history of the world." Shut up, I mutter, reading this. Do you want to let everybody in on our secret? But the mutter came only from the lower part of my soul. The upper part said simply: "Sing!"

Lucien Pierce summarized Nahant this way in the *Globe* in 1953: "Architecturally it is a period piece; socially, it registers the shift from 19th to 20th century in the small, comfortable, single-family houses in good taste; scenically, it is a sea voyage on dry land. . . . And over all this the sea winds blow, fogs roll, the sun gleams, the moon silvers, stars glitter, and storms roar . . . the world is still beautiful and Nahant is one of its masterpieces."

I will now prove that Nahant is the best place in the universe. The proof is mathematically certain and infallible.

Let us symbolize desirable features by circles designating the geographical areas where you can find them. Then, like Venn diagrams or the old Ballantine beer signs, the interlocking circles will leave only one complete and perfect center, narrowing to the single bull's eye of Nahant.

First, America, despite all her problems, is still the best country in the world to live in, the place everyone else wants to live in, the land of opportunity, the place where you can make your life pretty much whatever you want. That excludes the rest of the world.

Second, we need four seasons. Without winter, there is no appreciation of summer. That excludes the South.

Third, we need the sea. That's obvious. That's our blood. That excludes the heartland.

Fourth, we need rocks, not just sand. The mystical meeting of sea and rock preaches constant cosmic sermons. That, plus point two, cuts out la-la-land, southern California.

Fifth, we want water warm enough to swim in for at least the two months of summer vacation. That means nothing north of Boston. The West coast is beautiful all the way up to Alaska, but the water is too cold. Living by the beautiful cold sea without being able to swim in her must be like being married to a beautiful woman and knowing you could never touch her.

Sixth, we want waves. Even little ones most days will do.

Seventh, we want to be near a sophisticated city with museums, symphonies, shopping, and sports fanatics.

What's left is Nahant.

Brian Doyle wrote, in *House Beautiful* (1993):

"When my wife Mary and I moved from Massachusetts to Oregon . . . my professional self, the reasonable man with a pen in his pocket, carefully drew up a list of pros and cons. He drew it up on a sheet of yellow legal paper, with a line down the middle and items numbered on either side. There were twelve reasons to go and ten reasons to stay. Five of the reasons to stay were all the same odd word: Nahant.

"I still have that sheet of yellow paper. It is pinned to my office wall and I often stare at it in the long glow of a late Oregon afternoon. From my window I can see the vast green muscle of the Northwest forest . . . but in my heart I see Nahant.

"I found much to love in Nahant: the rich salt air, thick as wool; the muted silver clang of the buoy bell at midnight when all else was still . . . where the lawn ran into the sea and ducks slept on the porch. . . . You can smell history here. It smells like tidal flats."

I think the smell of brine and fish is the part of the island's charm that penetrates the deepest. For of all the five senses, smell involves you most totally in the world. You literally take its atoms into your body. It's the most animal, and least rational, of all the senses; the most language-transcending and mystically intuitive sense.

When I lived in Lynn, whenever a few rare free hours opened up, I fled to Nahant like a homing pigeon. I found myself singing on the way. I became a little kid again, school was out and summer vacation was just beginning. Everything gets brighter and clearer here. I notice the sound of dirt underfoot, the different smells of different grasses, the patterns of sun and shade under the trees—things I don't notice anywhere else.

Time itself seems to change here, as in Rivendell, in *The Lord of the Rings*: it doesn't seem to pass, it just is. It can no longer be meaningfully measured by clocks, only by waves, nature's pendulums. There is no need to hurry here, because everything is just right, as it should be, and right on time. Here, things determine time rather than time determining things. (Isn't that Einstein vs. Newton?) Here you can really turn back the clock if you want to. (And why not? Who's the master, anyway?) All the mornings of the world are saved here like pennies in a piggy bank. When I lie on a patch of grass atop Bailey's Hill in the summer sun, all surrounded by waves and wind, I learn the liberating truism that time is our servant, not our master, and our friend, not our enemy. The Hill teaches me this wisdom. It must have great wisdom inside it somewhere to teach me this, because you can't give what you don't have.

Say "Nahant" to me in a game of "free association" and the word that first springs back is "peace." When you cross the causeway you leave the maelstrom, you get off the unmerry-go-round. I have asked dozens of Nahanters how they feel about Nahant, and the commonest theme is some kind of contentment. Some samples:

* "It makes me love to come home."
* "Wherever I am, no matter how far I travel, I know I belong here."
* "Even when I can't get home to Nahant, I'm just happy it's there."
* "Once you come over that causeway, you're in a totally different world."
* "I remember the view of the sea outside my living room window wherever I am, even in a motel room. It's imprinted on my mind."

These people seem strange because they are not strange. They are happy, and because they are happy, they are friendly.

I remember the first time I discovered East Point and went to the top of it to see the sea shining in the sun's gold fire a hundred feet below. I just stopped in my tracks, stunned by the unexpected gift, then spontaneously wept for gratitude, simply because such beauty existed. I've done that only twice before in my life. The first time was as a teenager when I first heard Beethoven's Ninth. I was so swept away on its tides that I felt terrified that I could never get back to shore: I thought I had lost my body and become the music. The other time was first hearing Bach's "Bist Du Bei Mir." My German wasn't good enough to understand all the words, but I sensed from the music that this was about love and death, and that it said more than all the words in all the books, and that I will be happy if I can hear this music as I die.

In most places I find it hard to pray. Here, I find it hard not to.

Nahant is what you throw into the scale to counter Lynn and Los Angeles and Levittown. When I hear of some new piece of social decadence or terrorism or environmental disaster on our tortured planet and fear our civilization is swirling down its own sink hole, I think, "Well, at least there's still Nahant."

(3) Papa

The main story of my life begins when my Papa's and Mama's end. Alas, that will be very soon.

One of my most vivid early memories is from three days before Papa died. I was four years old. It was a perfect Sunday afternoon in 1961 at Nahant Beach. The heavens looked like a seagull: the blue-grey of the sky and the clean white of the cirrus clouds were his feathers, and the yellow sun was his unblinking eye. The beach was an uncrowded two-mile crescent of clean, packed sand. It was the middle of August, the one month of temperate water and warm air into which New Englanders have to cram their only perfect beachgoing. A massive offshore storm the night before and a quick clearing that morning had produced the rare and perfect combination of freshly-washed air, bright sun, and storm-driven waves big enough to body-surf. Children were playing with them as lion cubs play with their mother, and the sea was playing with the children as a lioness plays with her cubs.

I had never tried to play in sizeable waves before, and I was both afraid and enthralled. (A four-foot wave is as awesome to a three-foot boy as an eight-foot wave is to a six-foot man.) It would have been perfect weather for boogie boarding, but boogie boards hadn't been invented yet, and New Englanders hadn't yet caught on to the radical idea that surfing could be done outside Hawaii. Even Californians were just beginning to pick up the idea.

Papa had already taught me much wisdom about waves: how they are made by the wind, and how the tides are made by the moon (I found that hard to believe, but Papa was infallible), and how you can tell whether the waves come from an offshore storm only fifty miles away or from across the sea thousands of miles away, by the shape of the wave and how it breaks. [Author's Note: This is not true. 'Isa was often in error but seldom in doubt.] Storm waves break suddenly, violently, and vertically, and throw you onto the bottom; while the far-away waves, the kind that are more common at Nahant, are deep and gradual swells that break forward and thrust you horizontally toward the beach atop the breaking white water. These waves were perfect for riding, like tame horses.

Papa explained the difference this way: "The storm waves are like my words when I am angry. They are sudden, and they can hurt. The far-off waves are like my words when I take time to think. They are like words that come from deep and far away, and they are slow and well thought-out. They are the good waves for you."

That day, I had been chased by a wicked wave. I raced up the gentle slope of the beach, panting, a few feet ahead of the roaring white foam, onto my parents' beach blanket, which was an extension of Mama's lap. The wave by now had dived into the sand and muttered back into the sea; but a second wave, stronger than the first, hissed up the slope, flooding beach blankets with two inches of foamy sea water. My eyes darted like lightning from the wave to my parents' faces to assess how much I ought to fear this calamity. I was reassured to see only annoyance and then laughter as they rescued from the swirling water our faded red blanket, a pile of clothes and towels, and the yellow plastic portable radio with rounded corners that looked like a fat little diner.

Mama noticed that I was still shaking, so she glanced very deliberately at Papa, who nodded and took me by his big, hard hand. "Come here, 'Isa, and take a walk with me. I want to tell you about the angel in the wave."

I nodded acceptance. We both knew that my fear was the kind that needed Papa's words more than Mama's lap. We all knew our roles.

I had been thrown from a horse and had to get back onto it, to overcome my fear. Papa knew I would have to suffer many wipeouts in my life, and that most of those waves would not be made of water. But Papa wisely did not tell me how I ought to feel but asked me about how I did feel:

"Are you afraid of the ocean today, 'Isa?" (He was teaching me to ride my feelings as I would ride a wave or a horse.)

"Yes, Papa. I am little bit afraid."

"Are you afraid the ocean will hurt you?"

"Yes. It tried to get me."

"Do you think the wave was chasing you?"

"Yes. It was."

"Why do you think the wave would chase you?"

"I don't know. Maybe it was angry."

"Do you think the ocean can really be angry?"

"I think it was. But why, Papa? Why was the ocean angry?"

Papa did not tell me that the ocean cannot be angry because it is not alive. Papa had not gone to college, so he did not know the great modern myth that the universe was dead. As a fisherman he knew better. He knew how alive the ocean was. How could the mother of millions of life forms not be supremely alive herself?

"'Isa, I want to tell you about the ocean. I know the ocean very well. The ocean is my friend. You can trust what I say about my friend. Will you trust me, 'Isa?"

I nodded.

"Then listen. The ocean is *not* angry with you."

"But why did it chase me? Why does it run so fast? It scared me."

"'Isa, let me tell you a story about the ocean. Now this is only a story. Do you understand?"

"Yes, Papa." I *didn't* understand, but I wanted to hear the story.

"I will tell you why the sea moves, and why the sea makes waves. It is because there is an angel in the sea. That is why the sea is so alive." He waited until his words had time to sink in, like waves into sand. Only then did he add, "But it's a good angel, not a bad angel."

I tried to digest this information. "Papa?"

"Yes, 'Isa?"

"How did the angel get into the sea?"

"I think the angel leaped into the sea, 'Isa, just as we do—and for the same reason we do: because he loved the sea, as we do."

"But Papa—"

"Yes, 'Isa?"

"How does the angel in the sea make the waves?"

"I think it is like breathing. The waves are like his breaths. They come in and they go out, like our breaths. Our breath comes in waves too, but they are waves of air, not waves of water. It comes in, and it goes out. It never stops, even when we sleep."

"Papa?" (I remember my habit of asking Papa permission to ask before asking, and how comfortable that felt.)

"Yes, 'Isa?"

"Are the big waves the big breaths, and are the little waves the little breaths?"

"Yes."

"Why does the angel sometimes make big breaths and sometimes make little breaths?"

"He is like us that way. When you play hard, you make big breaths, don't you?"

"Yes."

"And when you sleep, you make little breaths."

"I do?" I had never seen myself sleeping. I resolved to try to watch next time. It did not occur to me that this was logically impossible.

"Yes. And sometimes the angel is playing, and sometimes he is sleeping."

"When there are no waves on the ocean, is that when the angel is dead?"

"No, 'Isa. The angel is never dead, and neither is the ocean. There are always some waves, just as there are always breaths in us even when we sleep. The ocean breathes as long as it lives, just like us. The life is in the breath."

Though I was only four, that last sentence stuck in my mind with liturgical force: "The life is in the breath." Then a sudden brainstorm came up and clouded my thoughts:

"Papa, what is the angel doing when there is a big storm on the ocean like that one, you know, that time when we saw the really big waves?"

"Maybe the angel is dreaming. When you dream, you breathe faster. A big storm is like a big dream."

Another liturgical formula: "A big storm is like a big dream." It felt comforting and terrifying at the same time. Then another question hit me in the head:

"Papa?"

"Yes, 'Isa?"

"Can't we wake the angel up when he has a bad dream?"

"No, 'Isa. We can't wake the angel up. Nobody can do that except Allah."

"Why can't we wake the angel up?"

"Because he is an angel. He is very, very big and we are very, very little."

Papa's explanation was obviously right.

"Papa?"

"Yes, 'Isa?"

"Why do the waves come up on the beach? Today one came all the way up on the blanket. And once, remember, when it was all cold and dark, the waves came up on the road, and they closed the road, and the road was all water. Do you remember?" My eyes and my heart were both wide open.

"I remember. Maybe the angel sometimes walks in his sleep, and gets out of his ocean bed."

I had to think this out for a long time. "Papa?"

"Yes, 'Isa?"

"Will the angel get up out of his bed at the end of the world?" I had just recently learned about the End of the World and the Day of Judgment, and was fascinated with the thought.

"Yes, I think at the end of the world the angel will wake up, and he will throw off the sea like a coat."

"Oh! And what will happen to the sea?"

"There will be no more sea. In Paradise, there will be no more sea."

This sounded like another formula, but a less rightful one. "But that will be bad for you, Papa, because they you can't be a fisherman anymore, and I can't play in the waves anymore."

"No, 'Isa, that will not be bad, because it will be Paradise, Allah's Paradise. Everything will be good. Everything will be perfect.""Well, then, there must be a sea in Paradise just like this one."

"I do not think it will be this one. I think Allah will make a better one."

"But how can there be a better one? I like this one best."

"That is a very good question, 'Isa. Yes, it is hard to imagine any sea better than this one. But Allah can do that. He can imagine something better. After all, He imagined this sea, didn't He? And then He created it."

I almost followed Papa's logic, but not quite.

"Papa, did Allah make *everything*?"

"Yes, 'Isa. Everything."

"Then He made the waves too. It was Him, not an angel."

"Very good, 'Isa. You are right. Allah makes everything. But sometimes He uses the men or angels that He made—He uses them to make other things. He made us, and we makes houses and boats. He made angels too, and an angel could make waves if Allah willed it."

"Did Allah will it? Is that how the waves come, really?"

"I know Allah willed the waves, because He wills everything that is good. But I don't know whether He really uses an angel or not. Maybe He does. Or maybe that's just a beautiful story."

"Papa?"

"Yes, 'Isa?"

"When I grow up can I make beautiful stories like you do?"

"You can make beautiful stories right now if you like, 'Isa. And you can make more beautiful ones when you grow up. You can be a poet."

"But Papa, I want to know: Is there really an angel in the wave? Is that true, or is it just a beautiful story?"

"'Isa, I think maybe you will be a scientist instead of a poet."

"What is a scientist, Papa?"

"A scientist is someone who studies all the things we see, like oceans and fish and trees and stars and winds and waves."

"Papa, can you see the wind?"

"No."

"Then how can scientists study it?—if we can't see it?"

"That's a very good question, 'Isa. I think maybe you will be a philosopher."

"What's a philosopher, Papa?"

"Someone who asks questions about everything."

"I want to be a philosopher. I want to know how scientists study the wind if we can't see it."

"Scientists study how the wind makes the waves, and we can see the waves."

"But . . . [I was searching for both words and thought] . . . does the wind make the waves or does the angel make the waves?"

"Maybe the angel uses the winds to make the waves!"

"Maybe Allah uses the angel to make the winds to make the waves?"

"'Isa, I think you will be a theologian."

I did not know what a theologian was, and I did not want to be more confused, so I did not ask. A long silence passed. It was full, not empty. Neither of us ever felt awkward about silence.

"'Isa, do you understand what I said?"

"No, not all of it. But I know it is true."

"How do you know it is true?"

"Because you said so, Papa."

"I love you, 'Isa."

"I love you, Papa." His hug sent me back into the waves, quite fearless now. Papa followed me, and we both exulted in enduring the playful battering of the angel's wings. Papa crouched down to my level to feel the full force of the waves. Soon a big wave picked me off my feet, churned me like butter, and set me down upside down. Papa shared the ride, and the somersault, so that I could see it was supposed to be fun, not fear. We both came up spitting and coughing but laughing, full of salt and sand and spit and spirit.

I was very lucky: Papa had the soul of a poet *and* a scientist *and* a philosopher *and* a theologian. What he *did* was fish, but what he *was* was more than a fisherman. He was a rock. Like the rocky coastline of Nahant, he would always be there for me. Even a hurricane could not move the rocks, as it moved the sands. Papa's guardian angel would always take care of him, and Mama, and me too, and soon there would be many more little Ben Adams to laugh in the waves with us.

Three days later Papa drowned in his angel.

A sudden storm and a rogue wave dashed his little wooden fishing boat against the rocks at the foot of Bailey's Hill, off the southeast point of Nahant. Papa was a good swimmer, but not with part of his head on a rock.

In a single day I lost both my father and my home. For without Papa's job Mama could no longer afford to live in our little fisherman's shack on Nahant. We had to move two miles inland to a too-small apartment in a too-big, ugly tenement in Lynn. I remember its peeling yellow paint, its perpetually broken plumbing, and its smell of garbage. Lynn is big on the outside but small on the inside; Nahant is small on the outside but big on the inside.

The day after Papa died, I told Mama I wanted to see where it had happened, and she generously interrupted her own grief, and all the busy preparations for the funeral, to help me to deal with mine, to say good-bye. We walked to Bailey's Hill, to the south side, and on the rocks we found a few pieces of Papa's boat. (I picked up an inch-long splinter, and kept it like a relic for many years in my bedroom. Mama just shook her head and refused to touch it.) As we surveyed the scene of destruction, I remember seeing a very curious white bird with black around its eyes. It perched on the top of the rock the boat had crashed on, cocked its head to the right, and looked at us very deliberately, then flew away. Why should a four-year-old remember such a detail?

While growing up in Lynn, I visited Nahant whenever I could, as an ongoing pilgrimage to both Papa and the sea, and to memories of earlier, happier times. It took only a bus token to sneak under the angel's flaming sword and briefly visit Eden. As I got older I spent more and more time sitting and musing on the rocks of Bailey's Hill. I sensed that my destiny lay waiting for me there, like those far-off waves thousands of miles away, the waves that nothing could stop from finally reaching me and breaking on my beach.

I never hated the sea, or its angel, for Papa's death. I was never very good at hating things, even though I was a willful and passionate child. But though my love for the sea was not polluted with hate, it was spiced with fear; and this gave it an urgency and an energy not known to casual summer vacationers.

Why did I still love the sea? Joseph Conrad knew. He wrote that "the most amazing wonder of the deep is its unfathomable cruelty," and yet he confessed an unquenchable passion for it, a love that "like any great passion gods send to mortals, went on unceasing and invincible, surviving the test of disillusion, defying the disenchantment that lurks in every day of a strenuous life, went on full of love's delight and love's anguish."

Why do I still love the sea? Because Papa loved her, and because she still teaches me the things she taught him. Things like what Papa once taught me on Forty Steps Beach.

This beach is a tiny gem of sand, big enough for only a dozen beach blankets, enclosed by thirty-five-foot-high craggy cliffs. Papa picked up a handful of sand, and dropped it into my palm as he spoke. "'Isa, look at this. All this"—Papa nodded to the sand as it dribbled into my hand—"was once *that.*" He jerked his head dramatically back up at the great rock cliff behind us. My head snapped up in imitation of his, and my mind was struck with wonder.

Papa then said, "'Isa, see the rocks up there, far up the beach? See how big they are? Now see the rocks down here, near the sea? See how small they are? The rocks get smaller and smaller as they get nearer to the sea, and finally, they turn into sand. They will have many sand children. They will disappear into their children. That is what we all must do, 'Isa."

But if Papa has disappeared into me, why do I keep hearing his voice whenever I bow over the rock where he drowned? And why does it keep repeating the words: "And the angel fell into the sea"? When Papa told me the story of the angel, three days before he died, I know he said, "The angel *leaped* into the sea," not "*fell* into the sea." Why does the voice from the sea change one word? And what does it mean? How can an angel fall, anyway?

Ever since Papa died, sixteen years ago, I have had a recurring nightmare of a great, grey, inexorable wave, hundreds of feet high, bearing everything in the world on its foamy crest, closing in on me like a gigantic hand. Usually it is slate grey, but sometimes it is black. I do not know whether to yield to it and become one with it, or to turn from it and flee. When I turn to flee, my body freezes, stiff as a pillar. When I turn to enter it, I know it is death. My only hope is to ride it, like a horse. But how? It is far too terrible to swim in. As I have gotten older, the dream has become less terrifying, but it still recurs.

They say the ear is trained by the sea. They say that those who linger long by the seaside come to hear the voices of the drowned. So they say.

(4) Mama

Mama died on September 14, 1977, sixteen years and one month after Papa.

For three years she knew she had cancer, but she hid it from me as long as she could, trying to protect my fragile happiness. As I was entering my second year of college in 1975, her doctor "gave" her one year to live—as if he were Allah, decreeing life and death! Mama quietly resolved to refute the doctor's prediction so that she could see me graduate. This resolution kept her strong for two years. But by the spring of 1977, she could no longer hide her symptoms and told me the whole truth. I was almost as shocked at how well Mama had hidden it as I was by the cancer itself. I remember every word of our conversation that day.

"Mama, why did you hide the truth from me?"

"What would you have done for me if I had told you?"

"I would have taken care of you. I would have given you anything in the world. I would have spent more time with you."

"Would you have given up college to take care of me?"

"Of course I would."

"I know that, 'Isa. See? That is why I hid it from you."

"But Mama, that makes me very unhappy."

"'Isa, the only thing in this world that makes me happy now is to see you working for your heart's desire. And that is what you have been doing at college. And that must not stop because of me. That is what I desire. Do you want to do something for me? That is what you can do for me. *For me, '*Isa. Do you understand?"

I could never win arguments with Mama. I win arguments only with everyone else.

Mama's last summer was a summer of surprising patches of happiness between the tears, like sudden sun showers between storms. It was full of simple but deep conversations about love and death and the meaning of life, and about Heaven and about God, the God who loved Christians and Muslims alike, though they use different words. (I think I have come to understand why Christians use the word "love" so much when talking about God and why Muslims do not. It is *not* because we worship different Gods but because the God we both worship is neither cuddly nor cold. Christians rightly deny that He is cold and Muslims rightly deny that He is cuddly.)

We spent many hours on Nahant Beach that summer. When Mama was taken to the hospital, on the last day of August, she knew it was the end. She silently said her farewells to the sea, the sand, the gulls, the rocks, and the waves, which she knew she would never see again. I think she saw them truly for the first time when she knew it was the last time.

Two nights before she died, when she thought I was asleep on my mat on the hospital floor next to her bed, I heard her praying very softly. It was something like this: "I thank You for all the good things You have put in my world. I will miss them, and I would dearly love to find them in Your Heaven too, because they have taught me about how beautiful You must be if You made such beautiful things. But even if I will not find them in Your Heaven, I still thank you for them on Your earth. Thank you for all the good years *You* gave me here. I don't ask for any more years. I just want to know You will take care of my 'Isa when I am gone. He will have no Papa and no Mama, and no brothers or sisters. Heavenly Father, You must be his Papa. Jesus, you must be his brother. Mary, you must be his Mama. Angel of God, you must guard him very close every day. That is all I ask."

I pretended to be asleep, but I could not help sobbing audibly. It was now Mama's turn to listen to my prayer, which had no words.

When I was tiny, Mama used to sing me her favorite lullaby over and over again when it was beginning to get dark and we were waiting for Papa to come home from fishing and I was beginning to be afraid. She sang it in a soft, low voice that put my fear to sleep like magic:

> Sweet and low, sweet and low,
> Wind of the western sea;
> Low, low, breathe and blow,
> Wind of the western sea.
> Over the rolling waters go,
> Come from the dying moon and blow,
> Blow him again to me
> While my little one, while my pretty one sleeps.
>
> Sleep and rest, sleep and rest,
> Father will come to thee soon;
> Rest, rest, on mother's breast,
> Father will come to thee soon.
> Father will come to his babe in the nest,
> Silver sails all out of the west,
> Under the silver moon:
> Sleep, my little one; sleep, my pretty one, sleep.

This was now the song I sang to her. For the first time in my life, I felt like a mother with a baby on my lap. Mama was now as dependent on me as I had been dependent on her when I was a baby. She was resting in my lap, and she would soon be going to sleep.

When the day came for her to die, she knew it. Her Indian blood had eyes in it. Perhaps the red corpuscles were eyes for life and the white ones were eyes for death. She insisted that I move her bed next to the window so that she could die in the sun. When the sunlight touched her face, she smiled faintly but deeply, and said, even more faintly and even more deeply, "I love you, son." She never called me "son," always "'Isa," so I don't know whether she meant me or the sun. Maybe both. Or maybe she meant her other 'Isa, whom she called the "Son of God."

I answered her: "I know you love me, Mama. And I love you. Forever." She smiled at me—the most precious smile I have ever seen. Then, suddenly, she opened her eyes wide, raised her head from the pillow and almost sat up in bed. (She had not had that strength for days!) She stared straight at the sun without blinking, and said, with a clear voice, "Oh, Look! Look!"

"What do you see, Mama?"

She did not answer me, but opened her eyes even wider, and her smile too. I was infinitely curious. Was she seeing Papa? An Angel? A Prophet? But she did not answer, or even hear me, I think. Her spirit was already there, and her head fell back onto her pillow. She died with the most seraphic smile I ever saw. My hand was holding her hand, and my heart was holding her heart.

I was at once assaulted by the beauty and grace of her passage out of this world, and by my own infinite loneliness now, a loneliness wider than the whole world. I felt like an abandoned baby left on the beach. Mama had crossed the sea of light and I was left alone in the dark. She had gone up in a chariot of fire and I was left in the water. My attempts at prayers fell like birds without wings. I had been preparing for this moment for months, yet nothing could possibly have prepared me for this moment. It was too *big*. There came into my mind the strains of the mournful old ballad:

> Sometimes I feel like a motherless child.
> Sometimes I feel like a motherless child.
> Sometimes I feel like a motherless child
> A long way from home,
> A long way from home.

I heard the vast silence that waits, brooding, behind all sounds, ready to flow in like a wave, that great wave of silence that waits and waits—until the end. My nightmare wave. The wave came in today.

I knew I was supposed to feel older and more adult and responsible now, but instead I felt like a tiny child, helpless before the dark. I wanted to run to Papa's arms for comfort as I had run to Papa that day when the wave terrified me on the beach, when he had comforted me with the story of the angel in the sea. When Mama would get mad at me, I would run to Papa; and when Papa would get mad at me, I would run to Mama; and when Papa died, I ran to Mama for comfort. To whom could I run now?

By sheer effort of will, in the teeth of those waves of loneliness, I said my Shahadah and accepted this too as Allah's inscrutable will. It gave me no peace, but I accepted that too. I enacted my islam.

I did not sleep in my bed that night. I slept in my sleeping bag on Bailey's Hill, where Papa died, and sobbed myself to sleep. I was a newborn, a puppy taken from its litter. I was what we all are and what we all hide. The first thing I saw when I woke was the curious white bird I remembered seeing at that same place when Papa died. Evidently this was its home, and I envied it, for I no longer had a home. It cocked its head to the right and looked at me—with pity, I fancied, just as I remembered its ancestor doing 16 years ago.

(5) Night

Most Muslims have large, extended families. I had no close relatives in America. Without a family it felt almost as if I had no body.

It was arranged that I would move in with my only American relatives, second cousins, who also lived in Lynn. I called them "Uncle" and "Aunt," to pretend a closeness and affection that was not really there and to try to create it, as if the words would create what they said. "Uncle," though supposedly a Muslim, drank heavily, and beat his wife and small children regularly. I will not dignify him by writing his name. All my attempts at peacemaking were met with the roar of a great bear—"Uncle" both looked and sounded like a bear—and with threats: "Out on the street you go, you little snake, if you dare try to tell me how to run my own family!" "Uncle" was six feet four and weighed around three hundred pounds. There was no way I could save this family from his drunken rages, either by persuasion or by force.

I knew the situation was going to be intolerable, but I had no alternative. I had no money, and no other relatives in America. I was too foolishly proud to impose myself on another family, even though many families from the mosque would have willingly extended to me the hospitality that Islam commands. My four-year scholarship and work-study grant were still in place, so I resumed my classes at Boston College out of sheer duty in September, feeling like a robot.

One day in mid-September the inevitable happened. I came home from BC to find "Aunt" badly bruised. I spoke my heart to "Uncle" and called him an infidel. This provoked a vicious attack. "Uncle" broke two of my ribs and knocked a tooth loose, but I bloodied his nose, at the price of a badly bruised right hand. (The price was worth it!) The last thing I remember of "Uncle" is his size 14 boots kicking me down the second-story stairway and kicking shut the door behind me, yelling curses through the door at me—and at my Mama and Papa.

I had already packed my few essential possessions (half of them were books and papers) and stowed them in the trunk of my car to prepare for this eventuality. All the clothes I needed fit into Papa's valise. Its age could be measured by the difference between the light tan color of the soft old leather and the black of the handle, which had been held by three generations of hands.

I "burned rubber" outside "Uncle's" driveway, vowing never to return. I headed for Nahant, hoping the place I loved best would help me to sort out whatever pieces remained of my life. I felt a burning need for Papa's wisdom, so I headed for the spot where he died, Bailey's Hill. I hardly noticed the pain in my ribs, my mouth, and my hand, because the pain in my heart was so much worse.

As I drove across the causeway, I passed the spot on the beach where Mama and I had spent much of our last summer. The sobs were shaking my ribs, the steering wheel, and the whole tiny car. I had felt as lonely and scared as this only twice before: when Papa died and when Mama died. I had felt anger and outrage like this before a few times, at other injustices besides "Uncle's." But I had never felt both such loneliness and anger at once before. One felt cold, the other hot. Without moderating each other, the two opposite waves of emotion crashed together in the sea of my soul.

The sea without was also rising. The finger of the wind was flicking the foam off the tops of the waves. I knew I had to go to Bailey's Hill. I don't know who Bailey was, but I fantasized someone like George Bailey in the movie *It's a Wonderful Life*. The Hill somehow feels like a Bailey, and tonight I wanted to feel like a Bailey.

As I had done many times before, I parked at the foot of the Hill, in front of that strangely shaped house whose back looks like the prow of a ship. As I got out of the car, I could feel the air pressure drop. The wind turned up its volume a few notches, as if someone had pushed the volume button three or four times. Dark clouds scudded across the sky like rats across an attic floor. They were tearing themselves into tatters, committing collective suicide as they ran from the terrifying wind. I knew what kind of storm was coming: a killer storm like the one that took Papa.

It was a warm September night in spite of the wind, but I felt cold, and so I wore my hooded windbreaker and took my sleeping bag with me up the Hill. I knew I was going to get wet, but I had to sleep on the Hill tonight. It was my one remaining home.

As I climbed, I felt as if I was being *drawn* up, or *swept* up the Hill by the coiling forces that swirled around it. The night followed me like a spy. The wind began to hiss through the grass, and the rain began to hiss on the rocks, and the sea began to hiss onto itself. I half expected to see a sea serpent behind the hissing.

The wind seemed to be blowing *up* the Hill from the sea into the sky. It filled the sails of the trees. If they had not been anchored by their roots, they would have scudded swiftly out to sea and capsized. The surf rose and groped at the sky hanging forever beyond its reach. The wind made a howling sound like the cry of an invisible wolf. Grizzled old men in town were probably muttering, "That's no normal wind," and superstitious old women were probably whispering, "If I believed in witches, I'd lock my doors and windows tonight."

All light faded. Nothing can be quite as black as the sea at night. It was not an accidental attribute added at dusk to the substance called the sea, like a coat of paint; it was substantial blackness itself, the Platonic Essence of Blackness. But it was not safe and still like a concept, but alive and moving like an animal. It was *coming*. It was the back of a very large panther. It was trying to heave itself up to scratch its back on these rocks.

An image suddenly appeared in my mind: Papa's boat. It appeared very small and fragile, seen from afar. My inner camera zoomed into a close-up of the gunwale, to a single board, red and faded and peeling, with its name printed on it in white: "CAN DO." I heard Papa's words echoing down my memory's hallways: "We are like boats, 'Isa, we men. We must be made of good wood. We will take many shocks during our lives, but good wood can take the thrust of a knife and still endure. Be strong, 'Isa. Be like good wood. Even when you feel like a knife has been thrust into you, you must endure."

I knew Allah had raised these words from my memory. As I reached the top of the Hill I shouted my Shahadah: *La ilaha ill' Allah! Allah akbar!* This had always been my answer to every question, my refuge in every storm. And it did not fail me now. I was borne forward and upward by this wave of faith, like a soul-surfer. Yet I also felt another, contrary wave, a dark one, that wanted to sweep me backwards and downwards and hold me underwater.

With a tropical suddenness, the incontinent clouds released waterfalls of rain. I quickly climbed into my sleeping bag, having found a soft stretch of grass on the south side of the Hill, three quarters of the way up the sloping cliff above the Cauldron, where I was at least partially protected from the northeasterly wind and rain by the contours of the Hill itself. I snuggled inside the bag, though I was already half drenched, pulled the flap over my head, and met— Nothingness.

Around me the storm was raising wild, white-capped waves on the sea and then blowing the white foam off the tops, destroying its own work. On another day I would have welcomed this spectacle with wonder. But today I was a worm, not a man.

The storm gathered even more force. It became a Dracula wrapping his cape around me. The winds became demons. Their voices were the screams of the damned. I could not distinguish the real from the imagined. Worse, I did not care.

For the first time in my life I understood the force of the word Nothing. I felt Nothing. I did Nothing. I did not complain and I was not comforted. I did not pray and I did not weep. I did not sleep and I did not think. I did Nothing. I was Nothing.

I have no idea how long I lay there, unable to move and unable to sleep. But around midnight, at the height of the storm, I was surprised to find my mind suddenly springing to life. A thought, palpable as a hand, had entered my heart, as if a giant octopus had reached an arm up out of the sea and inserted it into my chest cavity. The thought did not shape itself into a word. If it had been honest enough to do that, I would have rejected it. The word was Death.

The blackness of the raging sea was a *thing,* and it was beckoning me. Only its deep darkness could understand my deep darkness. Deep called unto deep at the roar of its waterspouts. If I became one with it, Nothingness would meet and mate with itself. I did not have to will it. I did not have to do anything. It would happen of itself. I would be free of my will, free of myself. It would just happen. It was inevitable. It was not my choice.

I did not think of Mama, or Papa, or Allah, or Muhammad, or Jesus, or Mary, or any name, or any word. The wordless thing blew itself up like a balloon. It contained only emptiness inside. It displaced everything else, everything finite, everything that had a name. All names were destined to drown in this sea. So were all the pains named in this world. I too must drown because I was a name, and I was a pain.

Slowly, mechanically, I picked myself up. I stripped off my sleeping bag. Ignoring the sheets of water falling on me from the sky, I began to walk toward the edge of the fifty-foot-high rocky cliff. I felt no hurry and no hesitation. I felt no hope and no fear. There was Nothing within and Nothing without. The sea below seemed to beckon. I had no more will. I was following another will, a will without pity and without pain. I had no fear of death. I had already died. I was impervious.

Ten feet from the edge, I suddenly heard a powerful voice behind me piercing the storm, calling out a name. It was a rich, heavy, mature, female voice, and it said: "JESUS!" Confused, I stopped, turned, and saw the utterly unexpected. It was an enormous middle-aged lady, both very tall and very fat, bounding down from the summit of the hill toward me with an agility that seemed impossible for such bulk and such age.

A tendril of thought pulled at me from the sea, putting into my mind the idea that it was not too late. I saw that this was true: I was only ten feet from the edge, while she was forty. But the name she had called out seemed to work like an incantation: from its sound I felt another tendril come out, to match the one from the sea. The two tendrils met, and wrestled. I was left alone. Free from both, I turned away from the edge.

I did not know what the enormous female Thing bounding down the hill was, but it was a Something rather than a Nothing. A whole lot of Something, apparently. I chose Something over Nothing, that was all. But it was enough.

I moved one step back, then collapsed in a wet heap. The last thing I remember, before I lost consciousness, was the feel of a pair of authoritative arms lifting me up. Then I blacked out.

(6) Mother

I woke up many hours later with my head still full of the thought of Nothingness. But when I looked around me, I found not Nothingness but Pandemonium. For a moment I thought that I had gone mad.

I was lying on an oversized, overstuffed sofa covered with a multitude of birds in garishly bright colors. It took me a few seconds to realize that they were not alive, but part of the sofa's slipcover. The sofa stood on massive lion claw legs in a corner of a big, open living room about thirty feet square, with wooden walls, floors, and rafters, like a hunting lodge. On one wall was a 6x12 foot picture window with a spectacular view of the sea, which lay only a few feet outside. It was calm now, and sparkling in the after-storm morning sun. My sleeping bag was under my head, dry now, like my clothes.

It was the inhabitants of the room that made me think I was Alice in Wonderland. The first person I noticed was the lady who had rescued me. She was plump as a planet and looked even fatter indoors than out, especially since she was wearing bright Hawaiian colors, mainly yellows and greens. Perched on her shoulder was a large parrot that matched her dress. She was smiling, humming, and puttering before an industrial-size oven (was everything over-sized here?) in a kitchen alcove off the living room. The living room was evidently also the dining room, since it had a long oak table with benches along it, under a big wooden chandelier. (I had never seen a *wooden* chandelier before.)

I found it difficult to guess her age or her race. She could have been as young as 35, prematurely aged by wrinkles of fat, or as old as 65, preternaturally vivacious. Her softly hooked nose and close-set eyes looked Semitic; their deep, dark pupils looked Hispanic; their almond shape looked Italian, her skin color looked Polynesian, her rounded faced looked Oriental, her large-boned shoulders and cheekbones looked Native American, her birdlike mouth looked English, and her full lips looked French. She had a smile-shaped face, as if her soul had a habit of happiness which had shaped and set the clay of her flesh.

The next person I noticed was sitting very still like a cat on a little window seat in a corner nook ten feet from the big picture window, looking out. She was smiling seraphically at the sea, or the sun, or Everything. She had a delicate, feminine face, pale, white skin, a large head, which was totally bald— and no arms.

I next noticed two people sitting on big wooden chairs on opposite sides of the oak table in the center of the room: a man and a woman, both in their early twenties, playing chess. The man looked like Ichabod Crane. He was very tall and his frame was so angular and awkward that his clothes did not fit, but hung. He had red hair, a very large, straight nose, and freckles. The woman was a classy-looking Black lady. Her face was soft and round and moved like waves. It seemed about to break out into laughter at any moment. She had curlers in her hair and wore a dingy, olive-colored terry-cloth robe, but it could not hide her striking, curvaceous, pleasingly plump figure. She sat sprawling over her chair like a squid, while the man sat straight as a spear. They seemed to be arguing over the chess game. I heard the gawky man ask, in a stiff accent,

"Why is it that you play the strange and inferior opening gambits once again?"

"You jes' play your move, hon, an' you'll see how inferior this ol' gal is."

"No, Libby, I did not say that *you* were inferior. It is your opening gambit that is inferior."

"I know whatcha said. I'm teasin' you, hon."

"It is hard for me to know when you are teasing. And please do not call me 'hon.' It is embarrassing to me."

"OK, hon. Your move."

I next noticed a man who looked older than time. He was creaking down the stairway next to the kitchen, from the second floor. He had a cynical frown permanently etched into his face, beneath a long, thin, hooked nose, narrow eyes, and unkempt white hair. He moved like a sigh, settling into a stuffed chair. I thought he looked like an old man who looked like an old woman who looked like an old man.

I was about to get up and introduce myself when suddenly a door from another room burst open and a wave of classic rock & roll music swept into the room. Riding the wave were two dancing Black men whose bodies seemed to be made of rubber. One was tall and very thin; the other was very short and almost perfectly round. They looked like string licorice and a bowling ball.

I had never seen anyone move like that before. It was living rubber, and I could not help laughing with delight. But no one noticed me; these two were center stage. They danced into the living room and circled the table to the happily frantic strains of Jerry Lee Lewis's "Great Balls of Fire." Everyone stopped what they were doing. Those who had arms said something to them in sign language, something apparently upbeat. (I did not know sign language then.) The tall one signed something back. Whatever it meant, they seemed to incorporate it into their dance. The music changed to "Mister Lee," and their dance became a shotgun marriage between a jitterbug and a Charleston. Back they bounced through the same door they had entered, kicking it shut behind them. The music suddenly became inaudible; the room they had come from was apparently soundproofed. I was staring at them all the time with my mouth open, but I don't think they even saw me.

Behind the dancers had come, through the same door, a fat, droopy tricolored basset hound, dusting the floor with his ears. At each high note he howled happily. (Or unhappily—who can say?) His howls seemed part of the music, and as beautiful as loons on a lake. But the hound didn't make it back into the music room fast enough to keep up with the dancers, and after the door shut in his face he turned and heaved himself down like a moving sigh next to the chair where the very old man sat. The man reached down and stroked the dog's head. The two looked like twins.

The last person I noticed, after this action stopped, was a remarkably unremarkable man, middle aged and nondescript, helping the fat lady in the kitchen. Since he was the only normal human being in the house, he looked the most abnormal and out of place.

Surrounding this tableaux was the most wonderfully homey smell in the world: fresh baked bread.

By this time, the man in the kitchen had noticed that I was awake. I heard him say to the fat lady in a quiet but clear whisper, "Mother, our young friend is awake."

Faces turned to me with smiles and hellos, as "Mother" replied to her informant, "Thank you, Mister Mumm. If I ever need another pair of eyes, it's you I'll call, OK?" Then she turned to me and said, "So how's the weather? Were you measuring the rainfall last night, or what? Here, have some tea. You drink tea? We got all kinds, decaf too. And fresh bread. I just baked it. How about eggs? Or maybe you feel like some nice homemade clam chowder?"

I blinked and said something like "Where am I, and who are you, and who are they, and why am I here, and . . . ?" For a moment I was too surprised to be gracious. Then I remembered: "Thank you for saving my life last night." I sat up and gingerly felt my broken ribs. "Mother" set down a cup of tea and a plate of bread and butter on a sturdy little side table next to the couch. I waved away her offer of everything else and gulped down the bread and tea. It was absolutely the best bread I had ever tasted.

Mother was apparently still waiting for an answer to her question. I felt embarrassed and confused, and said something like "I've never done that before, you know. I don't know what came over me."

"That was not you last night," Mother said firmly. "That was something else. This is you, here, now, in my house."

"But what is this house? And what are you? I mean, who are you?"

The two at the table chuckled over my Freudian slip. My face reddened. But Mother chuckled the loudest. "What we are is what you see. What you see is what you get." The parrot on her shoulder repeated the formula: "WHAT YOU SEE IS WHAT YOU GET. WHAT YOU SEE IS WHAT YOU GET." (The parrot never said anything only once.) She waited with a wry smile for the parrot to finish, then extended her big hand to me and said, "I'm sorry, I should be introducing myself. My name is Maria Kirk, but everybody calls me Mother."

"Maria was my mother's name too," I said, shaking her hand. "She died . . . three weeks ago." Then, quickly, to cover up embarrassing condolences, "How did you know my name last night?"

Instead of answering, Mother asked, "What *is* your name?"

"It's 'Isa. 'Isa Ben Adam. You called it out on the Hill. You called me 'Jesus.' In Arabic, that's "Isa." Do you know me? Were you calling to me?" For some reason it felt very important for me to know this. Her answer seemed evasive:

"Well, you know, I don't make a habit of calling out to the thin air." I was not satisfied, but I didn't know how to press her further without being impolite to the person who had saved my life. "So shall we call you 'Isa, or what?"

"'Isa is fine. But my friends call me by my nickname . . ."

"Well, then, that's what we'll do too," Mother interrupted, quickly and firmly. "Because we are your friends." There was a chorus of mumbled but enthusiastic yeses, followed by a low growl by the basset hound. "So what *is* your nickname?"

"Jack,'" I said, and immediately jumped, for the parrot lifted up its voice and intoned: "YAK YAK YAK YAK YAK" five times, with the timbre of an old fire horn. Everyone broke out laughing.

"That's *his* name," explained Mother. "Yak." Yak immediately launched into his fivefold amen. "Every time he hears his name he does that. He thinks you called him, I guess. Well, if we can't train him to tell a man from a goat, I guess we'll have to train you to get used to an echo every time one of us calls you. Unless you want to pick another nickname."

"I'm sort of attached to it," I said, "so I guess I'll have to learn to get attached to its echo." I was smiling and relaxing now, and Mother made bold to ask, "Please don't think I'm prying, but—well, we have no secrets in this house. So tell me, please, why in the world were you out there alone on the Hill in the middle of the night in a storm? Don't you have a home you can go to?"

"No, I have no home. My father died years ago, my mother died three weeks ago, and I just ran away from the only relatives I have in America because my uncle is an animal and a drunk who beats his wife and kids. And me."

"How awful for you!" said the Black girl immediately. There was genuine feeling in her voice. Mother added, "You must feel horribly lonely! Do you have a job, or go to school, or what?"

"I'm a senior at BC. I work on campus. But I can't afford to live there."

"Well then, you must live with us until you have some place to go." Her voice was firm and matter-of-fact. It was not an invitation; it was an announcement. "It's no accident you found us, you know."

"But *you* found *me*. How . . ."

"Whatever. It was meant to be, and you were meant to be here." There was something so naturally authoritative about her manner that the matter didn't matter. It was so. Ipse dixit.

"Where *is* 'here'?"

"This house, you mean? They call it the House of Bread."

"Why?"

"What, your nose doesn't work right? Can't you smell the answer? You just ate it."

"Mother is always baking fresh bread," explained Mister Mumm. "And we eat it by the ton."

"It was delicious," I said. "What else do you do besides bake the world's best bread?"

"I take in orphans from the storms. All kinds of people who need a place to stay, some short-term, some long."

"Where do they come from?"

"From some storm or other, just as you did." At this there were a chorus of mumbled assents. Even the dog gave a confirming echo.

"Who were those two dancers?"

Instead of answering she suddenly turned to her stove, where a Mother-shaped pot was beginning to boil over. "Laz," she called over her shoulder to the old man in the stuffed chair, "why don't you fill Jack in on who we all are, while I punish this pot for boiling over on me, OK?"

The old man harrumphed in my direction, in a gravelly voice, "I'm Lazarus. They're Diddly and Squat. Professional dancers. Go on gigs. New concept: Rent A Dancer. Or two. Nobody like 'em. Nobody in the world. They're the best. An' I know. I seen 'em all. Believe me. Squat's blind, Diddly's deaf. Both orphans. They do for each other. Everything." Lazarus was now out of breath; he evidently preferred the shortest possible sentences, with the most breathing spaces between them.

"How does Diddly hear the music if he's deaf?" I asked.

"Hears it fine. In his bones. Not just the rhythm. The sound too. Hears it from the earth. Not like us. We hear it from the air. He hears the music's heart beating."

"And we all know sign language here, so we can talk with him," volunteered the Black girl at the table. "It's real easy to learn."

Mother assured me, "You'll learn that here, and a lot more too. One thing you'll learn from them is that they will teach you more than you can teach them."

"What do they teach you?" I asked, stupidly.

"Who we are."

I nodded. "Do they just dance all day?"

Mother nodded back. "You'd never guess what jobs they used to have."

I guessed. "One's a criminal lawyer and the other's a spy, right?"

Everyone was suddenly silent and looked at me. "Good guess," said Mother. "Actually, Squat *was* a lawyer and Diddly was with the FBI."

"Was he a spy?"

"I don't know, exactly. He did something with computers for them."

"Did they leave their jobs because they got blind and deaf?"

"No. They were born blind and deaf. They left their jobs because they hated them, and they loved dancing. So they did something most people aren't wise enough to do. They followed their hearts instead of their wallets."

"Do they make enough money to live on, just dancing?"

"No, they supplement it with a little consulting. So they work part time and play full time instead of vice versa."

I said I thought that sounded pretty shrewd. "Do they dance their way through your house like that all the time, or was that a show they put on for me, to wake me up?"

"All the time," answered the Black girl. "They practice in the rec room." (She indicated the door they had come through.) "It's soundproofed. But Mother has arranged for them to interrupt us unpredictably at least five times every day. She calls it 'the Discipline of the Interruption.'"

"That's another one of those good lessons we learn from them," explained Mother. "Being interrupted teaches you to be flexible, and not fixated on *your* thing. It teaches surrender."

"That sounds like Islam!" I exclaimed. (And five times a day, too, I thought. I wondered if the parallels were deliberate or coincidental.)

"You said that like a Muslim," Mother remarked.

"I *am* a Muslim," I said, proudly.

I was looking directly at her when I said that, and I know I saw her eyes open in surprise. It was not an ordinary reaction. My first thought, I must confess, was that she was Jewish, and hated Muslims. But she replied, with unmistakable sincerity, "Well, in this house we are all Muslims even if we aren't. Because we're all trying to learn the lesson your religion teaches you, the lesson in that one word, 'islam': surrender, and the peace, the *shalom*, that comes from it. That's the heart of your religion, isn't it?"

"Yes," I said, "but it's not *my* religion. We believe there is only one true religion in the world, and that the 'people of the Book,' Jews and Christians, have the same religion we do because they submit to the same God, the only one."

"But your God is Allah," objected the gawky red-haired man.

"We call Him that *because* He's the only one. That's what the word means: not just 'God' but '*the* God.'" I replied.

The gawky man frowned, thoughtfully, but not threateningly. Mother said, "You might say Diddly and Squat help us to be good Muslims, good surrenderers—surrenderers to the things God brings into our life, and not just the things we bring in. That's why we have the Discipline of the Interruption."

"It's training for death," added Lazarus.

I took that as a test, like a Zen *koan*, and answered, "The greatest interruption of all, by the Great Interruptor."

"Exactly," replied Mother, pleased that I had passed my test and understood her bizarre custom. But before any more profundities could emerge, a scrawny black cat suddenly leaped down from the rafters and pounced on a fluffy white one which had been sunning itself near another window. The white cat took off after the black one, and both raced up the stairs.

"Is that another Interruption?" I asked, laughing.

"They do that all day long," explained the Black girl. "Say, I haven't introduced myself yet, Jack. I'm Libby."

"Hi, Libby," I said, as Yak echoed my name again.

I turned to the gawky man for another introduction, but just as he was opening his mouth Libby said, "Hey, Jack, I'll bet you can't guess the black cat's name."

"Uh . . . I dunno."

"Good guess, but it's not 'I Dunno.' Try again."

"I give up."

"Nope, it's not 'I Give Up' either."

I was wise enough to shut up. Libby said, "It's the answer to this riddle: What do you call ten thousand Black paratroopers?"

I was totally unprepared for this. "I give up. What?"

"Night."

Everyone exploded with laughter. I laughed too, but with a little uncertainty. "Isn't that a kind of racist joke?" I asked Libby.

"Of course not! Not when I tell it. Hey, Black is beautiful. And so is Night."

"And so is White, and so is Day," added Mother. "*Vive la différence!*"

"You people sound like philosophers," I said. "I'm a philosophy major, and most of the stuff I have to read makes a lot less sense than you do."

"Aha!" said the gawky, red-haired man, as if spearing a fish. His voice was as awkward as his frame. "You are a philosopher. Excellent. I am a theologian—a theology student. My name is Evan Jellema." (We shook hands.) "I am a student at Gordon-Conwell Theological Seminary, and I too am an orphan, like you. My parents were killed in a car accident last year, and I am able to continue in school only because Mother very generously received me into this house." He spoke with a thick Dutch accent, and formally, in complete sentences, as if practicing from a textbook. But he had such a friendly and sincere manner that I liked him immediately.

By this time Mother had finished whatever she had been doing in the kitchen, and she stepped into the living room brandishing a great wooden spoon like a baton. "Jack, you've met all of us now except Eva." Here she pointed with the spoon to the quiet, armless girl by the window.

"Hi, Jack," said Eva, in the most beautiful voice I have ever heard. It sounded like a warm and sparkling little river.

"Hi," I said, wondering what to say next. Eva smiled away my confusion. "It's OK, everyone feels a little uncomfortable at first when they see me. But there's nothing we can't talk openly about. You see, I'm a thalidomide baby, with a few other medical complications thrown in, and like you, I owe Mother my life. Because she literally stole me from the hospital when the doctors were about to kill me, right after I was born. I'm an abortion that didn't work." (She smiled even more sweetly when she said this.) "And I hear she plucked you from death too. You see, that's her business in life, that's what she does for fun . . ." Her speech flowed like water. Nearly every sentence started with a connective.

Mother laughed gently. "We are all a strange lot, eh, Jack? And you're not so ordinary yourself, I think—am I right, or not? Nobody in this house is ordinary. Maybe nobody in the world is ordinary, deep down."

Almost as if to contradict this, the nondescript man next to Mother in the kitchen tapped her gently on her parrot-less shoulder. "Oh, I'm sorry, Mister Mumm, I forgot about you." She turned to me and said simply, "And this is Mister Mumm."

Mutual polite smiles. No electricity, no heat, no cold either. No reaction. Strange as it sounds, I have always found it hard to remember what Mister Mumm looks like, even after living in the same house with him. I can't contrast him with other men. He's not darker or lighter, taller or shorter, fatter or thinner, older or younger. Perhaps he is exactly in the middle of everything, a pure average. He is not even fascinatingly dull, like Chang, a seraphically bland Chinese fellow at BC who looks like a fat, quiet, supernaturally contented angel. There is simply nothing to say about Mister Mumm. He was the most silent of the tenants of the house. Yet he always seems to be thinking. I can't imagine him asleep.

I later discovered that Mister Mumm often had to leave on long errands, and he would always walk instead of taking a car, a cab, or a bus. I assumed he walked to the bus stop, but once I saw him walking past the bus stop. I asked him, "Are you going far?" "Yes," he replied, and said nothing more. "May Allah's angels go with you," I said. He turned and smiled at me, and walked away. The smile remained in my memory longer than the smiler, like the Cheshire cat.

After she introduced Mister Mumm, Mother completed the introduction by pointing to the animals. "Let's not forget our little brothers and sisters. The cats are Night and Day. The dog is Dudley. Laz calls him Howler. And you already met Yak." She paused for the requisite five yaks.

"So this is your house, and these are your boarders?" I asked.

"My *friends*," she corrected me. "None of them can pay to live here—not with money, they can't. So they pay in the ways they can."

"We all pitch in," Libby explained. "Like a good family."

"From each according to his abilities, to each according to his needs," quoted Evan.

"That's Karl Marx, right?" I asked him.

"*That* is the part of Marxism that we accept," Evan replied.

"Like any good family," explained Mother.

"So you are a kind of orderly anarchy? Or is it a benevolent matriarchy?" I asked. I was feeling bold enough now to tease a little.

"I think it is both," Evan said. "And I think it will be very good to have a philosopher among us, to help us to define things."

Lazarus sighed and rose slowly from his chair. "Excuse me. Have to catch the bus. To the airport. Jack, welcome to this house. They're all nuts here, you see. But the rest of the world is worse. So please stay."

Mother explained, "Laz comes and goes a lot. So does Mister Mumm."

"Ach, it never ends," complained Lazarus.

"Yes it does," Mother corrected. Lazarus smiled wryly. I wondered what *that* was all about. Libby asked, "Where are you off to this time, Laz?"

"L.A. again. La-la-land. Craziest place on earth."

Libby turned to me and explained, "Laz is some kind of detective. Ever since he came here, he's been chasing down some kind of missing person, and he hasn't found him yet. But he can't tell you anything more than that." Then, as Lazarus disappeared out the front door, Libby commented: "There's something very queer about it, if you ask me." I was surprised that in this house anyone would find anyone else queer.

Mother called out the window, "Be careful, Laz. You're not as young as you used to be!"

Lazarus growled back something about "old" that I couldn't hear.

"So this is what you do—you take in . . . unusual people?" I asked.

Low giggles. "That's us, Jack, The Unusual People." That from Eva. I blushed. "No, don't be embarrassed," she said, with a low, gentle laugh. "You see, we can't afford to be thick-skinned in this house. That's one of the many things we've learned from living here with Mother." She turned with a loving smile to Mother, who shrugged.

"What you see is what you get," Mother said, and Yak croaked his echo from her shoulder: "WHAT YOU SEE IS WHAT YOU GET. WHAT YOU SEE IS WHAT YOU GET."

I was totally taken off guard and charmed by this place and these people, even the animals. The smell of fresh baked bread made all the strangeness seem normal. "Thank you a thousand times," I said to Mother. "I owe my life to you. Someday I must give you something in return, but I have nothing to give now."

"Oh, yes you do," replied Mother. "You can give us yourself, by staying here with us. And you'll pitch in and help just as much as the rest of us. No lazybones here. Now, I just happen to have one extra room that I can empty for your bedroom, if you don't mind sleeping in a tiny room in the attic."

"Oh, no, not at all. That's wonderful of you. Thank you." I didn't know what else to say. How could my fortunes have turned around so completely in just twelve hours, I wondered. Then I remembered that the tide did just that every day.

"Do you have any of your things to bring with you?" Mother asked.

"Not much. They're all in my car."

When she heard me say "car," Mother's eyes lit up. "Well, now, *there's* something you can do for us. You can share your car with us once in a while. We had only two cars for eight people until you came."

"Oh, that's fine. I'm used to sharing it. I only need it to go to BC three days a week for classes, and Friday to the mosque."

"Good," said Mother. "Where is it now?"

"I left it on the street, just below Bailey's Hill." I turned to look out the window that faced inland, and almost dropped my pants in surprise. "There it is now! Right out front. Is this . . . is this the house at the foot of the Hill? The one that looks like a ship?"

Like a rabbi, Mother answered my question with a question: "Is that your car there?" She pointed to the blue Metropolitan.

"Yes." I felt in my pocket, and the keys were still there.

"Then this is your house, yes: 191 Bass Point Road."

I was astounded at the "coincidence." "But I must have parked in front of your house a hundred times! I always wondered what strange people lived in such a strange house. But I never dared to just knock on your door and find out."

"Well, you found a funny way of doing just that, I think. It's not the easiest way to find us, but here you are."

"I used to live in Nahant, you know."

Everyone looked up, surprised. "How lucky you were!" said Eva. "Welcome back," said Libby. "Yes, yes indeed," said Evan.

My curiosity was bursting. "Do you mind if I just go out and look around and sniff some fresh air?"

"Of course not. You don't have to ask permission. Do you think you'll need a doctor for those broken ribs?"

"No, I've had broken ribs before. It's not so bad. I just had to wear an Ace bandage for a few weeks."

"I've got one here you can use. But if you're going out to sniff the air, take this other sniffer with you, OK? He needs a walk." Mother produced a leash, apparently from thin air, put it on Dudley, and handed it to me. I have always loved dogs, but we could never own one because of Mama's allergies. I especially love a droopy dog like Dudley; I can't look at him without smiling. He cheers me up every day because he looks sadder than I ever do. And when I'm sad, he's like a mirror mimicking me and making me laugh at myself for how funny I look.

Dudley slobbered happily on my hand, wagging not only his tail but his whole massive butt. Mother clapped her hands and said, "Dudley! Want to go OUT?" At the magic word, incanted in a rising pitch, Dudley went into ecstasy. He took me out the front door and we immediately headed for dog heaven, Bailey's Hill.

The morning was bliss-colored, sun-yellow. The air was washed and recharged with electricity—like my life. The sun was a gold coin sitting on a sapphire throne of sky and ruling over a sea of silver, which was turning to yellow fire as the rising sun ignited it. The sun was King Midas, turning the sea into liquid gold at his touch.

My eyes watered at the excess of light. I lowered them, and noticed at my feet one imperfection in this perfect world: a single crumpled beer can. It was an intolerable blasphemy. This is my home now; how dare this intruder desecrate it?

Dudley led me up the Hill. When we came to the grassy meadow on top, I knelt down on my portable prayer rug, faced east, and prayed, while Dudley waited obediently. After the required prayers, I thanked Allah for delivering me from death and from something worse, and asked forgiveness. When I confessed that I did not know I had that evil in me, Allah put into my mind the memory of a story I had once heard from the imam about what a man had in him.

In the story, a man asked Allah to grant him all the desires of his heart. Allah replied, "You know not what you ask. Nevertheless, I shall grant you the first two desires of your heart, and if then you wish for the rest, you shall have them all." The man thanked Allah profusely, and rose from his knees. The first thing his eyes rested on was his neighbor's house, which was much larger and richer than his, and which he had always envied. As soon as he looked at it, the house collapsed. He ran into the street to see this miracle and collided with his neighbor's troublesome little boy, falling to the ground and hurting his arm. He glared up at the boy, who immediately dropped dead at his feet. At that, the man looked up and prayed, "No more, O Lord, no more!"

I resolved never to underestimate the potential for darkness that lay hidden in my own heart, and once again thanked Allah, the Compassionate, the Merciful, for being what He was.

But the question I could not get out of my head was this: What had brought Mother out onto the perilous cliffs of the Hill in the middle of the night and the middle of the storm? And what had made her call my name? For some reason the question of the name seemed important. At first I accounted for her shout of "Jesus!" by the fact that Christians, as I have discovered to my surprise, often use the name of the man they believe to be God as a casual expletive, or even a curse word—something no Muslim would ever even think of doing. But the more I got to know Mother, the less possible this seemed. Two possibilities remained, then: that she somehow knew me and was calling my name, in English; or that she was calling on her Jesus for help, and was answered. If the first, how could she have known my name without supernatural aid? If the second, why would Allah send deliverance in response to a Christian's idolatrous prayer to the man they mistook for God? And why would Mother not give me a simple answer to my simple question of how she knew my name?

The other puzzle that buzzed in my mind like a bee was that tentacle-like force from the sea that nearly claimed my life. Wasn't the angel of the sea a good angel? And wasn't Papa there too? Had Papa been betrayed by the sea he loved so much? Or by the angel he mistook for a good one? Could it have been the same force that tried to kill both father and son? Or were two forces at work there, one good and one evil? What was going on behind the surface that we see? There must be an immensity of forces that lie beyond the visible scrim of the world. Is the sea a battlefield between good and evil, like the soul?

My meditations were interrupted by little barks erupting from Dudley's throat. He pulled at his leash so strongly that I wished I had roller skates on. He turned off the main path onto a tiny one, then started sniffing in earnest and headed like a slow bullet straight for the spot I had slept in last night. He nosed around it for a while, then unearthed a little leather pouch on a string from underneath some newly fallen wet leaves. I recognized it immediately: it was the locket my grandmother in Palestine had sent me. In it was a tiny laminated holy card, in gold foil, with holy words from the Qur'an, surrounded by medieval illuminations. I had worn this treasure around my neck, and it must have slipped off last night, or else come off when Mother grabbed me. I looked at Dudley with new respect and gratitude.

As Dudley and I ambled down the Hill, a seagull walking in front of us turned around, faced us, and took three ridiculous steps in our direction with its oversized webbed feet, looking like a diver walking on land with swim fins. It looked straight at me, opened its beak, and screamed five times. (The same number as Yak: is it a secret code, I wondered?) Then it took off, as graceful in flight as it was clumsy on land. If angels have a sense of humor, I think they would disguise themselves as seagulls.

In the next few weeks, I began to feel as much at home as if I had been born there. The first night in my new bedroom, Day slept with me, and I felt as comforted as a cuddling cat. I opened my little window to the sea and fell asleep to the September ocean breeze coming in through my tiny open window, warm and wet and wild, and to the sound of the wavelets worrying the round rocks beneath the house like a cat worrying a mouse, hissing and frothing in, then chittering and chattering out. That was the percussion section of Nahant's string quartet that included wild ducks on the Hill, a bassoon-like loon on the inland pool two blocks away (the one surrounded by willows), and a single owl's soft, muted, fuzzy-sounding "Hoo?"

For the first time since before Papa died, I was completely content.

Until the dreams came.

(7) The House of Bread

On the living room wall there is a real estate ad from the newspaper, laminated and framed. It is the ad Mother answered when she bought this house:

191 Bass Point Road, Nahant: sprawling, elegant 12-room Victorian "painted lady." Front yard is tiny but back yard is enormous and drop-dead gorgeous: the Atlantic Ocean

Mother's House, like Mother herself, is a refuge for anyone at any time. Someone is always home. That is the most basic rule of the House. People know that, and come here for all kinds of help. Mother says, "The most important thing we can do for people is just to be there for them, to be with them. That's what 'home' *means*: to be-with somebody, not to be alone."

The House of Bread is an extension of Mother herself. Like her, it is old, sprawling, commodious, a little mysterious, strong, and loud. There are loud colors on the outside trim, and on Mother's dresses, and on the sofa, and on Yak's feathers. It is loud also literally: you aren't afraid to talk or sing aloud here, or to say anything you honestly feel. It is "comfortable" to soul as well as body, because it is dowdy and unfashionable, like an attic or basement room with old furniture in it. Again, like Mother herself. If she were a sofa, you would spontaneously put your feet up on her.

Most of the surfaces are stained, unpainted wood, so it has something of the look of a man's house, a hunting lodge. But it is full of soft "woman's touches" in unexpected places, with live flowers everywhere, even in winter: in pots hanging from the rafters, in window boxes, on the mantel, on the dining table. Where they come from in the middle of winter remains one of the House's mysteries. The household budget doesn't have a penny for flowers. Either somebody in the House knows a florist and gets first dibs on throwaways, or some saint or angel produces fresh flowers by miracle. When I presented this dilemma to Mother, she solved it by pronouncing, "No miracles here!" It sounded more like an imperative than a declarative sentence, as if she was holding back some unruly angel child who might otherwise at any moment drown the house in a wave of miraculous blossoms. It made me think of the Christian story of Jesus stilling the storm waves with the words "Peace! Be still!" as if he was taming a dog: "Down, boy!"

Inside the House space changes into place and clock time changes to human time. There are clocks here, but they seem less real than in other houses. If I may be excused for injecting a pet philosophical idea of mine into my story, I believe clocks are the most life-changing machines ever invented. Ever since the Industrial Revolution, there has been a continuous flood tide of clock time throughout the rest of the world, but not here. Time exists here, but it doesn't seem to *pass*.

One of the secrets of the House's happiness is a simple miracle in easy reach for anyone: no TV. There is one TV set, but it is stored away and brought out only for special events. So the great conversation killer is killed, or caged, and thus there is a lot of real conversation, simple and free and flowing like the sea, sometimes quiet, sometimes boisterous. The conversation is also aided and abetted during high tides by the background chatter of the pebbles in the back yard being constantly juggled by the hands of the little waves. If the TV were on, no one would notice this comforting sound.

You can hear it only because of the silence that is the background to this background sound. It is a silence that lurks like a living creature in this noisy house—a silence that is not the mere absence of sound but the mother of sound, the womb of words.

Mother once said, "I don't understand why anyone would rather listen to some silly show on TV when there are angel wings rustling just outside the window." Another time, she said, "Why a man wants to kill another man, that I understand. But I don't understand why he wants to kill the world, the sea, the air. Why he wants to kill noise—that I understand. And I will help him commit that murder, I will. But why he would want to kill the music, that I don't understand at all." When I asked her what music, she said, "The water music. The sound of moving water. Doesn't it feel like salve on all the wounds of your soul? Why would the wound hate the salve?" I pressed the point: "But they *do* hate it. Why *do* they do that?" And she answered, "Because they're fools. You Muslims call it *ghaflah,*I think, which means 'forgetting,' isn't that right?"

I was surprised she knew so much about Islam. "Yes," I said. "But it's not just ordinary forgetting. It's a kind of 'fundamental forgetting.'"

"Exactly," Mother said. "That's part of what we Christians call Original Sin. You can call it Original Selfishness, or Original Insanity."

Mother never even tries to speak the new politically correct language. She will not bend her soul or her self or her speech out of shape for any ideology. When I complimented her for that once, she said, "That's because I'm fat. I can't bend easily—except to God, 'cause He's even heavier than I am."

The "No TV" rule is not a *rule*, but just something we do. In this and in general Mother's authority is all the more powerful for being quiet. She does not have to *say* it, only to *be* who she is. It's like the authority of the summer sun.

Better, it's the authority of mother-love. No one in this house has the slightest doubt that Mother would instantly give her life for them. Indeed, that is her life's vocation. I found out that she had literally risked her life for others besides me. Libby, for instance. Drugs and abusive men with guns were involved. I don't know, or need to know, the details. What I know, and need to know, is that her house is a Noah's ark, with strange animals aboard, all rescued from flood waters.

Architecture aids this fancy, for the rear of the house is shaped like an ark, or a large ship, prow pointing out into the ocean. The first floor porch is a large triangular deck. It looks like a diver pointing his hands together at the water before leaving the diving board. The whole house addresses the sea through this prow, which breaks the waves of storms. A ladder leads down to the stony beach, which is there only at low tide, for at high tide the sea reaches underneath the seaward half of the house (the landward half has a cellar under it), so that on a stormy day at high tide it is easy to feel that you are actually on a ship far out at sea.

The house is built on four concrete piers, sunk deep into the bedrock under the stony beach. Each pier sticks up fifteen feet, and the house rests securely on them, safe from the storms that lash the coast each winter. The piers are triangular too, turned edgewise to the sea like four impossibly tall and narrow ships. Even on the rare occasions when storm waves reach up to such an impossible height as to crash on the house itself, they find no surface to hit broadside. It is probably the most dangerous building site in Nahant, yet the house is one of the most seaworthy. The two dozen neighboring houses on Bass Point Road, along the shore, have all suffered structural damage from big storms at some time in their history, but the House of Bread has withstood even the famous 1938 hurricane that took 700 lives up and down the northeastern seaboard, with waves whipped by 130-mile-per-hour winds.

Whenever high tide sloshes under the house between the concrete piers, I can listen to my favorite music, "the stone symphony." Its instruments include a percussion section of rock on concrete, a wind ensemble blowing under the house over the face of the water, and a string section of pebbles that make that "melancholy, long, withdrawing roar" that Matthew Arnold heard on Dover Beach. Centuries of sculpting by the sea have shaped and sized the stones for this music as painstakingly as Stradivarius ever shaped a violin.

The front door is flat with the street, but then the stony beach slopes sharply down from the House. The short cellar is fitted into the rock under the landward half of the house. (Actually, it is only under a quarter of the house, but it extends out landward under the front yard.) But nothing of value is kept there. It is usually damp, frequently flooded, and has two sump pumps and eight drains in its concrete floor.

The small front yard is full of bright yellow dandelions from spring to fall.

I once asked Mother whether she wanted me to weed the lawn, and she answered, "Thank you for asking, Jack, but I don't think we have any weeds."

"Yes you do. Your lawn is full of dandelions."

"Dandelions aren't *weeds*," she retorted. "They're *dandelions*." It was a reminder of the Law of Identity. The lesson in logic made me feel like a retarded child. She explained, "Taking the dandelions out of the grass would be like taking the stars out of the sky, don't you see? Or the raisins out of my raisin bread."

The side yard on the north side more than compensates for the smallness of the front yard on the west, for it is nothing less than all of Bailey's Hill. Thus, this house has both the best back yard in the world (the sea) and the best side yard in the world (the Hill). The 150 feet of stony beach between the House and the Hill is strewn with little tide pools teeming with life, including edible mussels and inedible clams, occasional starfish or jellyfish, and even an occasional visiting lobster. Tide pools like these can be found all around Nahant. Papa and I used to scavenge them at low tide for "sand dollars" (keyhole urchins), "mermaid's purses" (the black egg cases of skates) and "minister's collars" (the egg cases of moon snails). They give out a right, proper, salty smell containing equal mixtures of life and death.

The House is the last one on private land before the Hill, right at the point where Bass Point Road, the shore road, takes a sudden ninety degree turn to climb up a steep little hill to become Trimountain Road. It is the largest house in the neighborhood. From the front it looks like a typical grand-dame three-story Victorian. A four-story cylinder sticks out of it on the south side, atop which is perched a round, pointy-roofed observation tower. The main section of the House has a widow's walk on its third story. A rickety, rambling wrap-around porch, with rocking chairs and a porch swing, begins at the front door and curves around the whole north side (the Hill side). The porch is an architectural relic from a more leisurely and humane era that valued sitting and talking, sitting and watching, or sitting and swinging.

Both outside and inside, the House is dowdy but proud, funky but formal, dilapidated but elegant. It is kept clean enough to be healthy and dirty enough to be happy. It is never fully fixed up; there is always some rotting gutter or peeling paint or broken windowpane. But just enough of these things get fixed somehow to save it from being an eyesore or an embarrassment.

Mother's finances always seem to be at the brink, never over it into either bankruptcy or solvency. Somehow, enough money always appears just in time when needed, and disappears when not. Money seems to move like the tides here.

I had no money available at all when I first came here, because of a snafu in processing my student loan. Mama's good credit reference had been lost, and to reinstate it, the department stores she had used as references demanded that she pay off the whole of her credit account, which I could not do without the loan. And since the loan depended on credit references from the store, it was a Catch-22.

But in this house money, like time, is simply displaced as master. "It will work out," Mother assured me. And it did.

The House is peppered with spicy signs. For instance, the three toilets, shared by nine people, all have "No Parking" signs on them. A little sign on the sink says, "No Cats." (Day loves to sleep in the sink.) There is even humor in the architecture itself. It is full of unexpected turns and steps and corners and cupboards and crannies. Mother says that even its crannies had crannies. (She calls them "great-crannies.") There are old doors that lead to small store-rooms, and even a hidden staircase behind the fireplace. (It leads nowhere.) Each door has a look about it that seems to say "Adventure," like Alice's rabbit hole. The house seems much larger on the inside than on the outside, like a person.

Over the big dining room table, suspended from the ceiling between the two heavy wooden chandeliers, is a flat circle of wood, about two feet in diameter and about two inches thick, curiously carved and stained ebony. I don't know its original purpose, but Mother uses it as a display case. She has dozens of unusual objects of art, but keeps them all in a closet, and takes out just one new one every month to replace the old one on this circular shelf. When I asked her the thinking behind this strategy, she explained her philosophy of art:

"People ask what makes a work of art great. I say the closer it is to being something like a person, the greater it is. I don't mean *looks* like a person, I mean *inexhaustible* like a person. It doesn't bore you. You get something different out of it every time you come back. And so I keep only things like that, things that are a little bit like people. And then I treat them a little like people by bringing out just one at a time, not two or three. I say if it's worth looking at at all, it's worth your whole attention. Like a person. So I don't put it on a shelf with other things, I don't compare it with other things. One at a time is the only way to treat people, especially if you have a lot of kids. So that's how I treat art."

The House has five bedrooms. (My room is not really a bedroom but a tiny corner room carved out of the third-floor attic.) Diddly and Squat share the second largest bedroom, and Mother and Eva share the largest one. (Eva sleeps in an alcove off it. Eva loves alcoves as Day and Night love boxes.) Evan and Libby each have normal bedrooms, Mister Mumm has a tiny monastic cell, and Lazarus, who is seldom home, uses the guest room/den when he is here. A tiny spiral stairway leads from the attic to the observation tower, which immediately became my favorite indoor place in the world. I call it simply "The Tower," and capitalize it in thought as well as in print. (In my world view, many things still merit capital letters.)

If The Tower is an icon of Heaven to me, the cellar is an icon of Hell. It is small, damp, windowless, low, dimly lit, and accessible only through a retractable stairway in the floor of the living room. Once you enter, you have to crouch and grope for the light pull. The strangest thing about the cellar room is a door in the wall that seems to lead nowhere except into the earth and rock itself. The door is four feet high (the ceiling itself is only four feet high at that point), held together by heavy oak planks, and locked with three padlocks. (Why?) I call it simply The Door in the Wall, because that sounds like an incantation.

Mother bakes many kinds of fresh bread every day, some of which I never heard of before. My favorite is a hot, salty poppy seed, sometimes garlicked, with a soft, airy inside and a crispy outside.

Mother gave me a lesson in baking: not *how* but *why* to bake. It's the process as much as the result. The process is fleshy, earthy, and sensual, and therefore mysterious. It's a kind of magical multisensory mysticism of touch-contact with Mother Earth and her fruits. It includes the smell of batter, the warmth of the oven, the feel of enfloured hands swimming in dough, and a sensitivity to touch and timing in this yeasty sea. (The exact point when "sticky" begins to turn to "firm" is like the point at which a wave begins to break. Baking is like surfing.) And it puts you in touch with the ageless tradition of the cycles of time, since waiting too long or too little would be fatal to the yeast—and also with place, for to care for the timing of the yeast you have to stay at home, like a plant. This restores to your life the two lost arts of simplicity and discipline. The growth of the yeasty lump is slow, like the growth of your own body and mind. You see yourself in the bread. It unites you to the earth, for the wheaten bread you eat has already eaten the earth's soil and drunk its water, and consumed hours of sunlight that caressed it and blessed it; and it now transmits these gifts to you, as a mediator, as Catholics believe their Christ transmits the very life of God to man in the bread of the Eucharist. A Muslim cannot believe this theology, of course, but he can see the beauty of the symbolism.

When I found out how cheaply nine people are so satisfyingly fed, I thought it must happen by either theft or magic. The bread is a large part of it. Its delicious varieties substitute for more expensive foods, and it seems to multiply miraculously.

Although there is always enough bread in the house, there are seldom sandwiches. Instead of processed meat on processed bread, there are chunks of real meat, especially cold chicken or sides of ham or lamb. And there are enormous salads, with many kinds of beans, cheeses, and boiled and poached eggs. Our most popular lunch is simply good bread, good cheese, and good wine or fruit juice. Evan and I do not drink alcohol, but every day we both gulp down gallons of hand-squeezed lemonade, limeade, and orangeade. Our most popular supper is fabulously fresh fish, usually from Mumbles, the old fisher-man Mother knows. Mumbles once fished from the very same shack Papa lived in years ago, before I was born. (His name really is Mumbles, and either he has no first name or he has forgotten it.) No one misses fancy food. When food is good, you want it simple. (That's true of everything else too.)

No one is afraid to eat in the living room, or afraid to spill things on the furniture. It's all well worn and well loved, like a teddy bear. You can *flop* on the furniture here. (Is that what a "flop house" meant?)

Whatever Mother doesn't have, she finds. Gifts come in and gifts go out, including clothes both rich and poor. The clothes Mother gives away look better than the clothes she keeps. She often makes house calls to deliver food or medicine or laundry to elderly or invalid neighbors. Everyone in the House, except Eva, is occasionally employed at some house repairs for neighbors, usually to the neglect of our own house.

If someone needs money, Mother begs for it. If the need is for organization or connections, she uses the phone like a weapon of war to fight others' battles for them. If the need is for food or shelter, it is never denied. Once, during a snowstorm and power failure, we had twenty people sleeping in the living room, warmed by the fireplace. I forgot to mention that we have a wide brick fireplace. We don't need much wood because we have reams and reams of paper. Everyone asks for and gets scads of junk mail, and we use it for fuel. (We clean a lot of ashes every day.) Our mailbox is a large wooden box, two feet square. Our poor mailman!—but we provide him with weight lifting exercises without gym fees.

Once I drove Mother to a nursing home to see a friend. An elderly woman complained that she didn't know what time to take her pills because she didn't have a watch. Mother immediately pulled her own watch off her wrist, put it on the woman's wrist, patted it, and said "Well, now you do," and walked away before she could hear any objections.

Three days before Christmas, kids from the elementary school flocked to the house with their report cards (this has become an annual tradition), and for every final straight-A grade, Mother gives out a gift. Most of the gifts are cheap, simple things like balls or kites. But there is a chance of receiving something extra, like a furnished doll house or a working rocket, things some anonymous wealthy benefactor gives to the House each Christmas; so hundreds of kids come, eagerly. Grades rise remarkably in the month of December in Nahant. Last year, the word spread around and kids began coming to the House from outside Nahant, so to keep the numbers handleable Mother made the simple rule that they had to come on foot. That cut the numbers and increased the exercise.

In spite of all these other things Mother always sees to it that the cooking, cleaning, and shopping is done, either by herself or by us. Almost everyone takes a turn at almost everything. Even money management, such as it is, is openly shared, and money itself is too, when it's needed. I think of Mother as an octopus, not only because of her body shape but because she seems to have eight arms and is often balancing eight things (and people) at once. I also think of her as I think of the Hill—not only because of their similar size and shape, but because both are a whole round world in themselves, a center around which everything else seems to turn.

(8) The Housebugs

I have told you of my home, my story's setting. Now I must tell you of its inhabitants. I call them the Housebugs. When I first called them this, they immediately accepted the title, conferring upon me the authority of "Resident Philosopher and Namer." Evan reminded me that "naming the animals" was a fitting task for a Ben Adam since it was also the task of the first Adam, my ancestor.

Mother

While Mister Mumm seems to be of no particular race or even age, Mother seems to be of all races at once. She also seems ageless, young and old at once, wrinkled yet vibrantly alive and strong. For each wrinkle there are two twinkles. She is primarily Jewish. (She had a Jewish mother.) If you couldn't tell that from her New York accent, you could tell it from her chicken soup and her sharp, ironic humor.

Sometimes she speaks like a sailor and sometimes like a seraph, but never like a sociologist. She ignores the whole mid-range of abstractions and seems to shuttle naturally and immediately between the two utterly concrete poles of a very earthy earth and a very heavenly heaven. She is always a million miles from psychobabble. One of her favorite responses is "Cut the baloney."

She is utterly practical, yet she can just come out with something suddenly mystical. Here are two examples.

I had asked her a question (about what? I've forgotten), and instead of answering, or cocking her head to think about it for a minute as she typically does, she became absolutely and totally still, in every cell of her body, for about two seconds, just long enough for an angel to fly past.

I asked her, "Mother, why do you do that?"

"What?"

"Stop for a second before you answer."

"OK."

"No, I'm not telling you to do it. I'm telling you you *did* it, and I want to know why."

"Why?"

"Because I think it might be a good habit for me to learn if I'm going to be a philosopher, a thinker."

"Oh." She was genuinely surprised by the compliment.

"It's because you want to take a minute to think before you speak, right? Back up and go slow, right?"

She took that two-second minute again, then said, "No, I don't think that's quite it. It's not *thinking*. It's that split second of silence just *before* you think, the one second before the words come to your mind and two seconds before they come to your mouth. That moment of silence before you speak even to yourself. That second when your spirit just *stops*. I want to stay there for a second."

"I—I think I understand, but I think I *don't* understand."

"You do understand. You just did it. The hesitation. You said 'I' twice. It's that moment—the moment between the first I and the second I. The space between your I's. The moment when you don't know who's there."

"When does that happen, that moment?"

"When you're brought up short against the question."

"What question?"

"Any question. Every question carries that moment within it."

"You mean every question is really part of the question, *Who are you?*"

"That's good, Jack, that's really good." Yak's fivefold Amen at my name then gave us five opportunities to taste the thing we were talking about. "I think none of us really knows who we are, once we stop fooling ourselves. Do you think so too?" I was silent for a moment before I answered. Mother smiled and said,

"See? That's the moment. That's where the good words come from, from that place. From the silence. The chatter comes only from other words."

I nodded. "That's the deep place. It's like the sea."

"No, I think the sea is like *it*. I think maybe that's why we love the sea so much."

*　*　*　*　*

Another time, we were talking about angels, and whether some strangers could really be angels in disguise (which we both believed). I asked, "Mother, why do you think nearly everyone in the world believed in angels, or something like angels, until—until only a little while ago? Do you think angels used to be more visible?"

"No, I think people had better angel detectors then."

"You mean they *saw* angels better?"

"Yes, but not with their eyes. You know who I mean: we call them *seers*: poets and prophets and mystics. They really *see* them, but not with these two eyes."

"Prophets and mystics, yes, but poets too? Poets are just wordsmiths."

"No. Good poets are more than that. They have to be seers. Blake, for instance. Blake saw angels."

"You mean he didn't just make that stuff up?"

"Oh, no. Poets make poems; poets don't make angels. God makes angels."

"Why can't we all see angels then? What is that other eye that seers have that we don't?"

"Oh, we all have it, I think. But we don't use it. So it atrophies, like any muscle."

"Oh." Then I took a dare. "Mother, have you ever seen an angel? I mean with your two outer eyes."

"Sure," she said immediately.

"When?"

"Every day." And she turned away to her baking. The conversation was over.

Immediately after this conversation, I climbed the Hill (unconsciously looking for angels?) and found a single grandfatherly-looking seagull standing on the summit. As I approached, he looked at me, then silently flew up but not away: he circled overhead. I watched him make three turns and then release a tiny white bomb onto the rocks twenty feet away. I heard the faint, wet explosion as the bomb hit. The gull had transformed defecation into an art form. My first thought, from the adolescent in me, was the hope that I could be a gull for a day in Paradise so I could play the Flinging Feces war game. My second thought was to hope that angels had a sense of humor.

*   *   *   *   *

Mother smiles a lot, and when she laughs it comes in waves. Her whole face is shaped like a smile because her spirit has left its footprint in her flesh.

She is always busy, yet always happy to be interrupted—a habit she tries to teach us by arranging for the interruptions from Diddly and Squat. Those two are probably the two friendliest people I have ever met in my life, so it's easy not to resent their interruptions, and this trains us not to resent others'.

I thought at first that Mother was a Muslim because she prays five times a day. But she does not face Mecca or use a prayer rug. The first time I overheard her praying (her bedroom door had come loose) I felt the *frisson* that I had previously felt only at the words of the Qur'an. The words were all silver and blue and gold. The sentences were cathedrals. They were the words of angels, not of men.

> Before the glorious Seat of Thy Majesty, O Lord,
> And the exalted Throne of Thine Honor,
> And the awful Judgment Seat of Thy Burning Love,

And the absolving Altar which Thy Command hath set up,
And the place where Thy Glory dwelleth,
We Thy people and the sheep of Thy sheepfold
Do kneel with thousands of the Cherubim, singing Alleluia,
And many times ten thousand Seraphim and Archangels
Acclaiming Thy Holiness, worshipping, confessing, and praising Thee
    at all times, O Lord of all.

This, I learned, was from the Chaldean liturgy of the Eastern church. Another prayer of hers chanted these words:

Hail, height hard to climb for human minds;
Hail, depth hard to explore even for the eyes of angels!
Hail, thou great marvel and wonder of angels;
Hail, thou great cause of wailing in demons!
Hail, fiery throne of the Almighty!
Hail, mother of the star that never sets!
Hail, dawn of the mystic day!
Hail, death-knell of Hades and bridal chamber full of light!
Hail, fiery chariot of the Word, living Paradise!
Hail, bush burning but unconsumed!
Hail, cloud full of lights!
Hail, all-holy chariot of Him who rideth upon the Cherubim!
Hail, all-glorious chair of Him who sitteth upon the Seraphim!

This, I learned, was from the Akathist Hymn to the Blessed Virgin Mary used in the Orthodox liturgy.

Mother loves both the high and the low, but she does not love what is neither high nor low, neither heavenly nor earthly. She will lovingly talk about bugs and boots and boats and bread, or about the Beatific Vision in Heaven, but not about economics, psychology, sociology, politics, or "communications." I think she is the solution to most of the problems of this world.

She seems somehow both feminine and sexless, both motherly and virginal. No one doubts her purity, yet she laughs heartily at mildly "bawdy" jokes, though not at insulting ones. She is married, but mysteriously silent about her husband. I know his name ("Josh") but little more. He seems to have been abroad for a long time on an urgent but undefined mission. Clues and speculations from the Housebugs have led us to three theories: (1) that he is a large sheep farmer in New Zealand, (2) that he is an interior decorator for a large group of mansions somewhere very far away, or (3) that he is the commanding officer of an international spy ring.

I have gathered these clues largely from Evan and Libby. Mister Mumm and Lazarus both seem to know more than they will tell. I have seen these two huddling with Mother on more than one occasion, and so has Libby: she calls them "the huddlers." Once, I was almost certain they were "huddling" about me:

> Mother was saying, "Why else would he have shown up here?"
> And Mister Mumm objected, "But we've received no orders yet."
> And Mother replied, "In time, in time. Patience, patience."
> It all sounded very conspiratorial.

When I confronted Mother about the "huddling," she admitted, "Yes, those two *are* something like secret agents, but not the way you think. I'm sorry, but I'm just not free to tell you any more just now. And neither are they."

*   *   *   *   *

Once, when I found Mother weeping, I gently asked her why, and she told me a little about a great tragedy in her life. She has a sister, much older than she, who is estranged from her and sometimes also from their father (who is still alive). The cause of the estrangement is Mother's husband. Mother would not say any more about it than that. It is evidently very painful for her.

*   *   *   *   *

Of all the House rules (and there are really only a few), the one Mother says is the most important of all is the Rule of Perpetual Hospitality: that someone has to be in the House at all times to receive and help whoever may come. And they do come, unpredictably and inconveniently. (That's the reason for training us in "the Discipline of the Interruption.") Just *being there*, Mother says, is the most important thing you can do for anyone, living or dying. She likes to quote Woody Allen's best line: "Ninety per cent of life is just showing up."

I know Mother is a holy woman. Her life proves that. But so do her words. Once, I was defending philosophy as the love of wisdom and the search for truth, and she said, "That's very good, Jack, but you also know a much more powerful way to that goal than philosophy, don't you?"

"What do you mean, Mother?"

She seemed surprised at my surprise. "Praying. You must know that. You are a Muslim, and therefore you pray. You pray, and therefore you know Allah. You know Allah, and therefore you know truth."

"Yes," I said, simply. Mother's argument was flawless, both in logical form and in content. Why was I surprised? I asked myself. I was surprised by such a mystical syllogism from such a practical realist as Mother. As if she read my mind, she continued, musingly,

"Most people don't know that, I think. They know that prayer is *good* and *beautiful* but they don't know that it's *true,* that it's the quickest road to truth, that it's pure realism—living in reality. But *you* know that, don't you?"

"Yes," I said.

"Why?" (She was not going to let me go.)

"Because it teaches me who I am and who He is."

"So tell me, then, what have you found out on this road? About who He is and who you are?"

"That He is everything and I am nothing," I said, immediately. Then, seeing Mother's face break out into a smile as broad as the dawn, I was encouraged to explain further: "Prayer is a mosque. I learn things there that I could never learn anywhere else. I learn that I am less than a subatomic particle, and He is more than the universe. The universe doesn't even *exist* in the same way He exists. It is His song. The song doesn't exist in the same way the singer exists."

"Oh, that's good," Mother muttered. "Your philosophy and your prayer say the same thing. I'm glad you're a philosopher, 'Isa. The world is dying because its philosophers don't pray any more."

Lazarus

Here is a typical conversation with Lazarus:

'Isa: Lazarus, do you love the sea too?

Laz: Yes.

'Isa: I mean, *really* love her?

Laz: Yes.

'Isa: Are there any things you love more than the sea?

Laz: Sure.

'Isa: Tell me one.

Laz: Mother.

'Isa: I mean anything except human beings?

Laz: God.

'Isa: Anything else?

Laz: Angels.

'Isa: I mean anything else here on earth.

Laz: Some of *them* are here on earth.

'Isa: Anything else, then?

Laz: Music.

'Isa: You're pretty brief today.

Laz: Yep.

'Isa: What's your favorite music?

Laz: Silence.

'Isa: Silence?

Laz: That's what I said.

'Isa: Why do you love silence?

Laz. Try it.

*   *   *   *   *

The longest conversation I ever heard Lazarus have was with Ned, a young man who evidently had known Lazarus all his life, and called him "Uncle." I don't know whether Lazarus was his biological uncle or not. Lazarus is especially close-mouthed about his family and his past. All he says about his family is that "it's big," and all he says about his past is that "it's long," and all he says about himself is that "I'm old."

Ned was a music teacher, and had just gotten his first big recording contract as the lead singer and guitarist in a new rock band. It was called "Twisted Tonsils."

Ned's new album was "burning up the charts," and he said to Lazarus, "I'm on Cloud Nine" as he broke the news. Lazarus brought him down to earth with a single syllable: "Why?"

"What do you mean, 'Why?' It's success. This is my big opportunity."

"For what?"

"For what I've always dreamed of."

"What's that?"

"What's my dream, you mean?"

"Yeah."

"The Great American Dream, of course."

"Bet you can guess my next question."

"OK, OK, what's *that*, right? Watch out, Uncle, you're turning into a philosopher."

Lazarus didn't smile, as Ned and I did. After a silence, he said, "I'm still waiting."

"You really want an answer?"

"Yep. And so do you."

"OK, so I wanna be rich and famous. Is that bad?"

"Let's see. Why?"

"You mean why do I want that?"

"Yep."

"That's a silly question. Everybody wants that."

"You're not everybody. You're you. Why do you want it?"

"What are you getting at, Uncle?"

"What are *you* getting at, Ned? That's my question. What will you be when you get rich and famous?"

"I'll be rich and famous, of course! No, I see your point. I guess I just haven't thought that far ahead."

"Do."

"What?"

"Do. Do think that far ahead."

"Oh. OK. Good advice. Some long-range planning. I should do some of that some day."

"No, not some day. This day. Now. Right here, in front of me, now."

"Hmmm. 'No time like the present,' right? I guess you're right."

"I'm still waiting."

Ned was now getting uncomfortable, but couldn't back away. "Uncle, I honestly have no idea what the future holds, and you don't either."

"You're wrong."

"What? Can you see the future?"

"Of course. You can too if you only look."

"Look at what?"

"At the others ahead of you on that road."

"You mean rich and famous rock stars?"

"Yeah. That's why I don't wish you success. I wish you failure."

"You wish me *failure*?"

"Yeah. 'Cuz I love you, kid. I don't want to see you become one of them."

"What do you mean, 'them'?"

Then Lazarus uttered the longest sentence I have ever heard him speak, which shocked Ned and me by its length as well as its language (which, I think, was exactly what he hoped it would do):

"I mean one of those smug, shallow, self-centered little pricks with shrunken souls and swollen egos who swagger around like pimps, step on their friends like bugs, forget their families, hate everything middle class, screw everything in sight, fry their brains with drugs, kill themselves at thirty, and strut into Hell singing, 'I Did It My Way.'"

Ned looked as if he had not moved for centuries. Lazarus seized the moment of silence. In a warmer voice, close to tears, he said, "I love you, kid. Don't go down that road."

Ned hesitated, then literally ran out the door. I never saw him again. But there was a long letter from him to Lazarus a few months later in the mail. I watched Lazarus's face as he read it. After the first line he let fall the quickest and smallest of smiles. "Kid's OK," he said.

Everyone needs an uncle like that.

* * * * *

Lazarus is an encyclopedia of information about ancient things. Once, someone at BC called me a name I had never heard before: "Shiloh." I thought it was an insult. I asked Lazarus whether it was familiar to him. "As familiar as my own face," he said, and immediately gave me the following eight references from memory, rattling them off as if he had just written a term paper about them. I jotted them down and looked them up in the Bible, and they were all real. But I have no idea what holds all eight together, or why someone who hardly knew me called me that arcane old name.

(1) It's a name for the Messiah: Genesis 49:10; Joshua 18:1.

(2) It's the name of a pool in Jerusalem: Nehemiah 3:15.

(3) It's a place where Jesus healed a man: John 9:7–11.

(4) It's a great river, or "great waters," in some Eastern land: Isaiah 8:7.

(5) God somehow associates the name with Himself: Isaiah 8:6.

(6) It's etymologically cognate with *shelah*, or *selah*, which is a liturgical direction appearing often in the Psalms, but no one today knows what it means!

(7) The Ark of the Covenant was there (I Samuel 1:9 and 4:3–4). The Ark was captured because "God forsook Shiloh" (Psalm 78:60). When the Ark returned, it was *not* to Shiloh: II Samuel 6:2–17.

(8) It is cursed and in ruins in Jeremiah 7:12–14.

What real thing held together these eight references? Why did Lazarus call *me* Shiloh? And why did he call it "my own face"?

*   *   *   *   *

Here is the strangest thing I ever heard Lazarus say. It was late one night when I woke at 2 or 3 A.M. to hear voices from downstairs. They sounded unfamiliar, so I went down to investigate. By the time I reached the second floor, I realized it was just the three "huddlers." I didn't want to eavesdrop, and turned back up, but I couldn't help hearing the following words. Lazarus was arguing:

"*I'm* the Jew. We need only one."

Mister Mumm retorted, "No, you don't count."

Lazarus replied, "Why not?"

"You're a Jew but you're not human." (It was the first time I had ever heard Mister Mumm make a joking remark like that.)

"What nonsense is that?" Lazarus now sounded angry.

"You're twice as old as Adam."

"So what?" Lazarus replied. Then Mother said something softly, and I heard no more. I think Mister Mumm must have said "*Ben* Adam" and meant me.

When I first came to the House, I had this short conversation with Laz. (There are no other kinds of conversation with Laz.) Knowing his laconic and cynical humor, I said to him, "I'll bet I can guess your favorite play."

"No way."

I smiled knowingly.

"So guess, already."

"*Waiting for Godot.*"

"Right!" He was genuinely surprised. "How'd you know?"

"Simple math."

"*Math?*"

"Sure. Count the average number of words in each sentence."

"Oh."

"The only long one is Lucky's three-page meaningless babble."

"Oh."

"Am I right?"

"Yes . . ."

"Why the hesitation?"

"There's another reason too. Deeper."

"Like Vladimir and Estragon, you're waiting for the Messiah?"

Lazarus looked as if I had caught him in a guilty secret. All I meant was his Judaism: most religious Jews are waiting for the Messiah. But I didn't think any of them took that so literally that they traveled all over the world to check out the candidates.

*   *   *   *   *

I once said to Mother, "I think I will become as cynical as Lazarus when I get that old."

"You may get that cynical but you'll never get that old," was her reply.

"How old is he, really?" I asked.

"Oh, about two thousand, I think."

"Symbolically, you mean."

"Laz is very symbolical."

"Well, I'm not symbolical. I'm literal. So tell me, literally, how old is he?"

Mother again avoided my question. "You like to be literal because you like to be clear, right? Like Socrates? Your favorite philosopher?"

"Yes," I answered.

"Well, Laz is like Socrates in a deeper way, I think."

"What do you mean?"

"He's waiting for the Messiah—unlike Socrates—but that's why he questions everything and everyone everywhere—that's how he's like Socrates—and he gives every one the benefit of the doubt—like Socrates—and then questions them—like Socrates—because he's got this job, this commission, from God—like Socrates— and he has so much faith in his God that he spends his whole life at this job—like Socrates. That's why he's always on the lookout—like Socrates—and why he's so cynical, because he hasn't found the really wise man yet—like Socrates."

"Wow! It's almost as if he *is* Socrates."

"Symbolically, maybe. But no, he's Israel, not Greece."

"You mean he's a Jew."

"No, I mean he is Israel. Symbolically, of course."

"He's Jewish by blood but Christian by choice, you mean?"

"He doesn't see it that way. He says he's a Jew 100%, in religion as well as blood—like Jesus! He calls himself a 'complete Jew,' like Jesus. He *is* Israel—fulfilled Israel."

"But if he believes Jesus is the Messiah, why is he still looking for the Messiah?"

Mother took in a big breath and thought (or prayed) for a minute before answering me. Then she looked directly at me and said, "Because he didn't believe in Him when He came 2,000 years ago. So his punishment is to stay alive until the end of the world, when the Messiah will come again. Meanwhile, he has to finger all the false Messiahs. That's why he's so cynical: he's seen the real one, so he can finger all the fake ones. That's what Israel is doing now, until the end."

"Israel the people, you mean."

"Yes."

"But how old is Lazarus?"

"As old as Israel. He *is* Israel."

"Symbolically, you mean."

"You could say that."

"But *he* wouldn't say that."

"No, he wouldn't."

"This is very confusing. He's an individual, but he's also a whole people. He's a Jew but he's also a Christian. He believes Jesus was the Messiah, but he's still looking for the Messiah."

"He's looking for the Second Coming. That's even in your Qur'an, you know: Jesus's second coming, at the Last Judgment."

"I understand how he can finger false Messiahs if he's literally 2,000 years old and met the real one. Is that what you say he is?"

"That's what *Israel* is."

"And he *is* Israel?"

"He identifies with Israel."

"Just because he's Jewish? You've got Jewish blood too. Your mother was Jewish, right?"

"Yes, but Lazarus is different."

"How?"

"I go back to Christ, he goes back even farther."

"What do you mean, you *go back* to Christ?"

"I was baptized."

"Why do you call it 'going *back*'? Is it like a time machine?"

"Yes. It's like a time machine. You could say it put me back into Him or you could say that it put Him forward into me. But Lazarus was circumcised. He goes back to Abraham."

"I'm getting more and more confused. Is Lazarus looking for the Messiah because he's Jewish or because he's Christian? Please be more logical."

"It's both. Christians have a Messiah detector in them because they've been baptized, and baptism puts Christ into you, and Christ is the real Messiah, and the real Messiah is the standard to judge anybody who claims to be the Messiah. The Messiah is the Messiah detector. Is that logical, or what?"

I was not convinced. "We Muslims don't look for a Messiah, or have a 'Messiah detector,' and we don't have baptism, and we don't believe God lives in our souls, so it's hard for me to understand all this."

"I think maybe you do have a kind of Messiah detector. A prophet detector, at least."

"What do you mean?"

"Your book, the Qur'an."

"Oh. Yes. The Qur'an is our detector."

"Well, our Qur'an is Jesus."

Suddenly, those four words made everything fall into place. I've read a lot of things about Islam and Christianity by scholars and theologians, but I've never found an eye as simple and clear as Mother's.

Mister Mumm

I wonder whether his name is a nickname; he is the most tight-lipped man I have ever met. But he is not at all unfriendly. All I have been able to find out about his various goings and comings is that he has to report periodically to his boss, whom he calls "Mister Mike," and that he is unusually busy this year. "Not as bad as '68, though," he muttered.

He is so self-possessed that I have never once seen him show fear or even surprise. He never looks weary. (Lazarus, in contrast, *always* looks weary.) But he is not robotic, he is very human. He smiles a lot, honestly and genuinely, and helps me at all the household tasks cheerfully, often with a little hum or whistle.

He is also capable of swift and decisive action, despite his quiet demeanor. I discovered this one November afternoon when Evan and I rowed out to Egg Rock, half a mile offshore, in the old rowboat stored in the cellar. On the way back, as the light was beginning to fade under a lowering sky, a swell suddenly capsized our little boat. I am a pretty good swimmer, but when the boat turned over I hit my head on it and was a bit stunned, barely able to hold on. Evan, who was the weaker swimmer, was floundering in the suddenly strong swells, unable to reach the capsized boat, and was drifting away. I think we both may have actually drowned if it had not been for Mister Mumm, who appeared after a few minutes of real panic. He was rowing another, faster boat, and he said he had come to get us when he saw the rising sea and lowering skies. I asked him how he knew we were going to be in trouble. He replied, "I just knew. Something just told me. I guess it must have been your guardian angel."

Libby

Though Evan is my closest friend here and a philosopher like me, I have my most interesting and numerous arguments with Libby. She is a relative of one of my favorite singers, Lou Rawls. (Libby's last name is also Rawls. "Libby" is short for "Liberty.") She was delighted when I told her that my favorite song as a kid had been Lou's Dixieland version of "Hey, Diddle Diddle" on "Sesame Street."

Libby is suspicious of men. She was abandoned (and perhaps abused) by her Pentecostal preacher father, then by her husband, whom she divorced. She then bounced into and out of drugs, and got free from them only because a social worker cared enough to come to her apartment at four A.M. one morning. This one work of mercy not only saved her life but also changed it, and motivated her to become a social worker herself. After a few years in the field, she had what she calls "institutional burnout" and left her job at the Department of Social Services to help found a private volunteer group of Good Samaritans free from government bureaucracy, who did a variety of services for women who were homeless, orphaned, abandoned, abused, raped, or simply desperate.

Libby has a wonderfully good heart, but her mind is my constant friendly-enemy. She and I can hardly ever have a conversation without having an argument. But I love her dearly, because she is *good*, in her heart and in her hands if not in her head, and because she is funny, and sharp, and satirical, and because she is a dreamer, like me, despite her practical street smarts. And because her eyes twinkle mischievously and she twitches her small, parsnip-shaped nose when she argues.

Once Libby gave me an enormous teddy bear she had won at some carnival. I politely declined it, explaining that Muslims take very seriously the commandment to make no graven images. That means images of the Creator, of course—there *can't* be any images of Him—but most Muslims apply it also to things in the creation. There *can* be images of them, but there *shouldn't* be, because God made real bears, and made everything perfect, and man should not play God and try to make another world, a world of imperfect images of perfectly-made things.

When I explained this, Libby used her favorite curse word—"fundamentalism"—to describe my subtle metaphysical truths, and even Evan (who usually takes my side against Libby) agreed. At this point Mother chimed in and said,

"You know, I think 'Isa has a point there. If there's one thing that makes life in modern America different from life in all the cultures before us, that's it: we live in a land of images."

At this point Lazarus chimed in with one of his instant encyclopedic Bible references. He simply uttered the words "Jeremiah 50:38." Of course we looked it up. It read: "A drought is upon her waters, and they shall be dried up; for it is the land of graven images, and they are mad upon their idols."

Libby then showed that she really has an open mind. She said, "You know, maybe you are onto something there, Jack. I still think it's silly not to let your kids play with teddy bears, but I think you've got a point about images: they can be dangerous, because they hit you with a power nothing else has, except maybe music. They're much more powerful than *your* thing, Jack—I mean philosophy—and your thing too, Evan, theology. Images don't have to stop and present their papers to the little guard at the gate of your mind, that little censor you call Reason. You can't stop them. So whoever controls images, controls thought."

"And whoever controls thought, controls the world," Evan added.

"But I still say the teddy bear thing is just ridiculous," insisted Libby.

I tried to explain to her the philosophical principle that images are less *real* than things, and that the material things themselves are only images of their perfect models in the Mind of God. Evan said, "That's Plato, exactly." "That's the problem, exactly," retorted Libby.

*   *   *   *   *

Libby used to have a habit of interrupting me with my name in the middle of a conversation. I'd be halfway through, she would think she saw where I was going with it (she was usually right!), so she'd say "Jack?"—with an upward-tilting lilt, so I had to stop and listen. It was a simple but subtle way of controlling the conversation. I think anyone who does that must have either studied psychology or listened to talk-show hosts. After two or three times, I turned to her and said, "Libby, don't do that to me please, ever again."

"Do what?" She was sincerely puzzled.

"Manipulate me like that."

"What the devil you mean, boy? Why are you . . ."

Now I was doubly insulted. I almost called her "white trash" in response to her "boy," but instead said simply "Libby?"

She stopped and looked at me.

"See? That's what I mean. I just jerked your chain. Please don't do that to me, and I won't do it to you."

"Jerking my chain? Oh, come on now, Jack . . ."

"Libby?"

Another silence.

"See?"

"Oh." A rueful smile, and new respect. "I see. OK, man, fair enough. I'll try to remember."

"Thanks." Now it was "man," not "boy." And from that time on, our mutual respect grew.

*   *   *   *   *

Here is the most embarrassing conversation we ever had.

Mother was puttering in the kitchen, quietly, so she couldn't help over-hearing the following conversation between Libby and me. Libby was trying to persuade me to go surfing. Evan came in too late to know what we were talking about. Mother saw him enter and put her finger to her lips lest he inter-fere with Libby's sales pitch. As the conversation wore on, though, Evan thought we were arguing about sex, not surfing. So Mother decided to play a trick on Evan by not telling him that.

"It's the greatest passion in life, Jack. You just can't think about anything else when you do it. You think about it even in your sleep. And when you're doing it, nothing else matters. Not reason, not civilization, not survival, not prudence, nothing."

"You're exaggerating," I protested.

"I'm not. Just look at the facts. For the pleasure of this simple act, we will do anything, we will endure anything, we will sacrifice anything, just for that one fleeting moment of ecstasy. It overrides even the instinct of self-preserva-tion. Sometimes we try to protect ourselves by wrapping the most vulnerable part of our body in rubber, but it's best and purest when we're naked."

Evan, amazingly, held his peace and listened.

"But our culture is making it artificial," Libby went on, almost lecturing, or preaching. "Look what we've done. We've taken this private moment and made it public, even competitive. It's become an industry, a media money maker. We use it to sell stuff. We've prostituted it. It's lost its soul. The media don't care about soul, just about image. Image is everything. They use those beautiful, graphic photos . . ."

"What's wrong with that?"

"It's unrealistic. We can't all be such perfect athletes with such perfect bodies. They paint an idealized picture of perfection so that we ordinary schnooks identify with it and buy what they advertise. And yet what do they call it? 'Hard core.' That's the latest term. But those fantasy pictures—they're not hard core. They're not anywhere near the core. The core is spiritual, and personal, and intimate. So intimate that it's impossible to put it into words."

"I follow you there, Libby. I've seen some of those full-color, in-your-face, close-up, front-view pictures. It's impossible not to watch them. It seems so beautiful."

"It is. It's a dance, a dance of desire. It's all hot and all wet at once. Fire and water become one. A great romance. It never gets boring. Never."

"Not even when you're alone?"

"Not even then. But of course, the more people you do it with, the merri-er. Up to a point, of course."

At this point Evan must have received a gift of supernatural patience. But he still said nothing.

"What's the biggest thrill of all in it?"

"Well, for some it's the foreplay, the arousal, the anticipation. Especially just before you get carried away and out of this world on it. For others, it's the moment of penetration. For still others, it's the thrill of conquest, like riding a wild horse. And for still others, it's the release."

"I would think that the biggest thrill must be that moment when all that liquid rushes through your tube, or you through it. Like a foaming white locomotive."

"Oh, yes. It's literally ecstasy: you forget yourself entirely. It's a mystical experience. It's the closest you can get to a transformation of consciousness without being a mystic. You forget all your troubles. You just can't think of anything else at that moment, and you don't want to. You don't think at all, you just feel. You feel The Meaning of Everything, and you feel it with every single pore in your body."

"I never heard you wax so poetic, Libby."

"I'll bet you would be even more poetic about it, Jack. You just *have* to try it, so that you can be its poet and its philosopher."

"OK, let's do it some time, Libby. Let's do it right here in Nahant. I almost did, once, when I was younger."

At this point Evan's patience ran out; but just as he opened his mouth Libby giggled and said, "You know, Evan, if anybody overheard this conversation, they might think we were talking about sex."

"We were talking about surfing, Evan," I explained.

The three of us dissolved into a single laughter.

Evan

Einstein defined a body as existing wherever it produces an effect; Newton defined a body as existing only inside its surface boundaries. Evan's body is Newtonian rather than Einsteinian.

He is excruciatingly *square*, in body and in spirit. He has never been able to master any dance except the square dance. The shifting of weight from one foot to another is an art as mysterious to him as it must be to a moose. His face moves almost as awkwardly as his body, and so do his social graces. He not only fails to "read between the lines," he even fails to comprehend that very concept. ("There is nothing between the lines except empty paper. How can anyone read empty paper?") Libby calls him "Mister Spock," Leonard Nimoy's super-logical Vulcan on "Star Trek."

Evan and I are both very logical (we once had a medieval Scholastic Disputation together!), but I can also dance and dodge in Socratic dialog; Evan is as straightforward as the Charge of the Light Brigade. But he *knows* he is clumsy, in mind as well as body, and he can laugh at himself and even enjoy the happiness he gives to others who laugh at him innocently and not maliciously. I think this means he is a naturally humble and holy man.

Libby's and Evan's bodies both manifest their spirits. One is a curve, a wave; the other is a straight line. Significantly, Libby's favorite place in the world is in the curl of a wave while Evan's is the straight lines of a baseball diamond. As a diehard Red Sox fan, he is of course a pessimist, and this fits his Calvinism (doom, damnation, and despair). Libby, who has survived a thousand wipeouts, both in the surf and in life, is ever the optimist. She says she "feels uncomfortable with" the word "evil." I think Evan feels almost uncomfortable with the word "good." Is that the difference between a Liberal and a Conservative?

Evan's legs look like stilts: straight, skinny, and too long for his body. His hair looks like fire: orange and untamable. His ears look like two question marks. (This gives a note of puzzlement to everything he hears or says.) His nose is long and straight like a goose's beak, and his eyes are large, green, and watery behind his high-magnification glasses. His skin is pale and overpopulated with freckles. He looks like an unfinished sketch drawn by a clumsy child. But his ready smile makes you like him instantly, in a way you can only like an ugly man.

Evan is a scientist. But his interests are in science's most philosophical areas, like the "Theory of Everything," and his inventiveness extends far beyond science, into things like educational games. For instance, he invented a game he calls "Biblenections," which Libby and I often played with him to "field-test" it. Its rules are extremely simple but its possibilities are infinite. It tests the players' understanding of the Bible but it engages not merely the factual "left brain" but also the intuitive "right brain."

All that is needed for the game are two Bibles and at least three players. One of the players is the judge. The role of the judge can rotate to make the personal interactions more interesting. But it does not have to. (I stayed in the judge's position most of the time because as a Muslim I knew the Bible only half as well as the Christians did.) Each of the other two players takes a turn at shutting his eyes, opening up the Bible at random to any page (the judge can turn the Bible upside down to confuse a player who keeps turning to the same part), and putting his finger on the page, sight unseen. He then reads the verse he picked out at random. Then he does the same thing to a second verse, in a second Bible. He then has one minute to connect or relate the two verses in any way he can. The judge gives him a grade from 0 to 10 for Biblical credibility, originality, creativity, thoughtfulness, profundity—anything a teacher would look for in a good essay. Even humor counts. The second player then does the same thing, and receives a grade from the same judge. Whoever accumulates the most points wins. There can be any number of rounds.

We found that counting points and winning was the least important part of this game. Stretching minds, by finding connections between apparently unconnected verses, was much more interesting, and always unpredictable. It also produced some great arguments with the judge (whose verdict was final, but who had to give reasons for his judgment).

For example, Evan fingers these two verses: (1) "Jesus wept." And (2) "And the angel said to Lot, Do not look back to the city of Sodom." Evan knew the context of the second verse, the story of Lot and Sodom, and he knew that Lot's wife was going to do the thing the angel commanded her not to do—look back—and she would be turned to a pillar of salt. So he answered: "Tears are full of salt. Jesus weeps over every human death. He is still weeping now, in Heaven, over the loss of Lot's wife. That is why Lot is not weeping now, in Heaven: because God promised to take all the tears out of our eyes there. Here is how God does that: in taking the tears out of *our* eyes, He puts them all into Jesus's eyes. Jesus is the tears of God." That deserved 10 for creativity, even from a Muslim judge.

A less profound example: a player finds these two verses: (1) "Wine is a mocker, and strong drink is raging, and whoever is deceived thereby is not wise;" and (2) "Then the angel standing in the sea unleashed the four winds." When Libby fingered these two verses, she thought for ten seconds, then came out with: "The angel is so foolish that he's drunk with his love of the sea, and that's why he can't control his wind." That merited a 7, and was heatedly argued, Libby maintaining that I was prejudiced against holy humor and double meanings ("drunk" and "wind") because I was a "fundamentalist." This spun off into an argument about fundamentalism. The game often does that; it is a great stimulus to philosophical and religious debate!

At first I was shocked by the game, for I would never think of doing this to the Holy Qur'an—using it for a game. I am careful not even to let another book or sheet of paper ever be placed on top of it. Yet I sensed no disrespect at all on the part of these Christians for their holy book. The spirit of the game was certainly not anything like using a crucifix for a bat to play baseball with. (When I used that analogy, Evan and Libby were both genuinely shocked.) It was more like a lover exploring every inch of his beloved's body and mind. A *holy* play.

*   *   *   *   *

Evan is an excellent friend for a philosopher like me—not because he thinks like me but because he doesn't. I am a poet; he is a scientist. We educate each other. And we surprise each other. For instance:

A few days after I first came to live at the House, I went out after supper intending to spend some time on the Hill. Evan, who did not know my habits, asked me where I was going. I replied, "To listen to the symphony."

"Oh, that's great. I didn't know the Boston Symphony were playing tonight. Do you have tickets?"

"No, not the Boston Symphony, the Nahant Symphony. I mean the symphony I hear on the Hill. There were waves today; the symphony is what they play on the rocks."

"Oh. How often do you go to listen to that symphony?"

"As often as I can. At least once a week. Sometimes, every day."

"How long do you stay?"

"For hours sometimes."

"And you never get bored with it?"

"No. Once you get the ear, it's more fascinating than the Boston Symphony.."

"Don't you like the Boston Symphony?"

"I love it. But I love the sea even more."

"But it seems the sea is only a poor imitation of an orchestra. So few instruments. So little variety."

"No, it's the opposite. The orchestra is only a poor imitation of the sea."

"Prove it." (Evan, like myself, loves to ignore social graces and cut to the quick of argument.)

"OK, I will. Some great symphonies are only imitations of the sea, like 'La Mer,' or parts of 'Scheherazade.' But the sea is not only an imitation of 'La Mer,' or 'Scheherazade.'"

"You know, that's true." (Evan is wonderfully honest. A good scientist is as eager to lose an argument as to win one, if it teaches him something new.) "Why don't we all think that way most of the time?"

"Because we think only with our heads and not with our hearts."

Later, Evan told me that that single remark, common though it was, was the catalyst, or the key, to an idea he had worked on for years for his Theory of Everything. Taking "heart" to mean intuitive "right brain" and "head" to mean analytical "left brain," the point was that only an integration of the two ways of thinking, holistic and analytic, intuitive and scientific, poetic and rational, could discover the integration of nature—if nature and the human brain corresponded. And if they didn't, then we couldn't know anything real anyway.

Eva

She is even quieter, in her own way, than Mister Mumm. She seems to be always meditating. Perhaps she has unobtrusive out-of-body experiences continuously. She practices Zazen sitting meditation (she says her "handicap" makes it easy) but when I asked her whether she was a Buddhist, she answered, "I'm me."

"Are you a Buddhist mystic?"

"No, I'm just mystic me, as you are mystic you, and she is mystic she." With her head she pointed to Mother, standing in front of the big window, *and* at the sea behind her. I didn't ask which "she" she meant; I knew she would have said "Both," or "Yes."

Eva is the most constantly cheerful person in the House, in fact the most cheerful person I have ever met. I told her that once, and asked her why, and she replied,

"You're probably thinking that you wouldn't be so cheerful if you had my handicaps, so you wonder what makes me cheerful in spite of them; but my answer is that it's not in spite of them but because of them—you see, it's easier for me to meditate, and since that's the best thing, I think the rest of you are more handicapped than I am, because I can do more with my mind than you can do with your arms, and if you put my mind and my arms together and if you add what I can do with both, you still get more than what *you* can do with both your mind and your arms." (She speaks in run-on sentences, like a shower, or a fountain.)

Once, in midwinter, when the snow was sparkling in the sun, Eva asked me, "Do you see the sea in the snow, 'Isa? Do you see the stars in the snow? Do you see the same thing in the sparkles, when you see the snow, or the stars, or the sea?"

"You mean some sort of same pattern?"

"Not just the same *pattern*, the same *presence*. Not like two faces that look like each other, but like one face behind many masks, or one player playing many parts—do you see that, 'Isa?"

I think I do, but I think Eva's eyes are much larger than mine.

* * * * *

The doors in our house are knobless and have been set so that Eva can open them from either direction without handles. Even so, it is hard for her to open doors with no arms or hands. I dared to ask her once, "Why don't you ever get frustrated or angry when you have to open a door?" She replied, "You can open these doors better than I can, but I can open other doors better than you can."

"What doors?" I asked her.

"Oh, things like the sea, and the stars, and the snow."

"Why do you call them 'doors'?"

"Because they're doors in the walls of the world, and when I meditate on one of those doors, I move through that door into the Mind of God. No, no, that's not quite right," she corrected herself, "I don't do that with my mind, I can only do it with my heart, and my mind follows like a good dog."

"What happens to your heart when it goes through the door?"

"It breaks, of course." She looked at me as if I were a stupid child.

"And what happens to the rest of you when your heart breaks and comes out of your body?"

Her look changed to one of respect. "My body gets turned inside out like a snake shedding his skin. Sometimes it feels like a piñata exploding, but from the inside. And then I just—I just disappear, like a dust speck in the sun or a moth in the fire. But I'm still there—I'm still there because I'm doing something, I'm doing the disappearing. But there's no me outside the doing. All of me is in the doing, so it feels like there's no me left at all, only the doing."

Eva and I once had a mystical conversation (does she ever have any other kind?) about colors. We both remembered the intensely self-forgetful absorption we had in colors when we were children, especially bright colors. We both remembered *entering into* the colors as you might enter into a place. Colors were nouns, not adjectives. They were things-in-themselves, Platonic Ideas. Each color had its own infinite meaning, but not one you could define, certainly not by the usual device of association (green = life, red = blood, blue = sky, etc.). Red was fascinating not because it meant something else, like fire, or blood, or war, but in itself. What it was, was something too concrete and specific, not too vague, for words. It was the words that were far too vague. Red was—just red. Or, rather, *Red!* Green was—*Green!* Each of us was surprised to find in the other someone else who had also experienced this—"You too? I thought I was the only one." Each of us could still enter into that contemplative state we felt at the age of two or three, the simple fascination with nothing but the color, the pure color.

Libby once said of Eva, "She's a little piece of God. She's broken off of God and fallen to earth. That's why she's broken." Literally, of course, that's pantheism, and idolatry. But poetically, it's profound.

Like the Sufis, Eva puzzles me. She seems to be both a theist and a pantheist. On the one hand, she loves God and not herself. She is as far from a self-righteous egotist as the east is from the west. Yet she seems to think of everything as a little piece of God, including herself. People, religions, philosophies—she knows the differences between them, yet she also believes they are somehow all really one thing.

One stunningly bright spring day, I asked her to explain this paradox. I was hoping she could help me understand the Sufis. But she did more than that for me. She said, "I think I can do that, but not here, so let's walk a little." We walked to the Drum. Though she didn't go there as often as I did, it is one of her favorite places as well as one of mine. "Just do what I do, OK?" she said. We sat and watched in silence for ten minutes while the waves marched in from the open sea to the east, each wave splitting itself into two as it hit the Drum's outcropping of rock. Then both halves of the wave spiraled around this rock and reunited on the landward side, drawn back together by their own momentum or by the universal love-potion called gravity, celebrating their reunion with spectacular pyrotechnics of skyward-zooming foam that looked like delicate white fireworks. As we watched this display, I felt the same fascination Prince Andrei in *War and Peace* felt as he watched the clash of the two great armies on the plain below him at the Battle of Borodino.

Then Eva explained her paradox in one word. "See?" she said, pointing at the battle dance. Because she had no arms, she pointed with her head, and thus with her whole self. I nodded. I saw not only what her paradox meant but also how to see it and say it. Few words said more than many, one more than few, the body more than words, and silence more than all.

$$*\quad*\quad*\quad*\quad*$$

Once, when I was alone with Eva, I asked her, "Eva, do very personal questions make you uncomfortable?"

"No, Jack, never. What do you want to know?"

"Do you ever get mad at God?"

"What for?"

"Don't you ever get mad at God for being different?"

"That would be to get mad at God for being human."

"You mean everybody's different."

"Well, of course. But what you mean to ask me is whether I ever get mad at God for being *handicapped*."

"Yes. Do you?"

"No. Do *you*?"

I was taken aback by her question. "Do *I* get mad at God for *your* handicap? No, not if you don't. If you don't, why should I?"

"No, no, Jack," she laughed, "I mean do you ever get mad at God for *your* handicaps?"

"What handicaps?"

"Oh, I don't know you well enough to know them all, exactly."

"You mean . . . we're all handicapped, in different ways?"

"Well, of course!"

I suddenly felt very stupid. "Thank you for reminding me of that. How can we forget it?"

She glanced down at her armless torso. "It's easier for you to forget it than it is for me. So that's one way you're more handicapped than me, I think."

"But don't you wish you had arms like other people?"

"Of course. And doesn't Diddly wish he could hear like I can? But I also wish I could hear like he can. And both of us are foolish to envy each other, because envy never gives anybody any joy at all. It's the stupidest sin in the world."

"What do you mean, you wish you could hear like he can? He's deaf."

"Yes, but he can hear things we can't. Like that rock." She nodded to a strangely beautiful bluish stone someone had pried loose from the beach and put on a shelf with a flower behind it.

"Diddly can hear the rock?"

"Oh, yes."

"What does he hear when he hears it?"

"The rock, silly."

"What do you mean?"

"I mean he hears the greatest miracle in the universe when he hears that rock."

"What! That rock is the greatest miracle in the universe?"

"Oh, yes."

"Why?"

"Because it exists. The sound of existence is the biggest, sweetest sound there is. But we're usually deaf to it, because we hear only the little sounds that are closer to us, like crying babies or barking dogs. He doesn't have all those little foreground noises, so he can hear the big background sound."

"The sound of silence?" I said, without thinking.

"No, the sound you can hear only *in* silence. The sound of the primary miracle. That rock says: HI, WORLD! HERE I AM! I EXIST!"

"You hear that sound too, don't you?"

Eva smiled. "Yes."

"Is that why you smile a lot?"

A bigger smile. "Yes. You do understand, Jack."

"I think so."

"Tell me what you think you understand."

"For you existence isn't just an abstract fact but a real presence. Is that it?"

"That's it. And that's the presence of *God*. Existence is the fingerprint of the Giver of Existence."

"And you hear that music playing all the time, and that's why you're happy all the time."

"Well, of course. Why shouldn't I be happy?—I'm in the Throne Room. And I wouldn't give that up for the whole world, and certainly not just for a pair of arms. I don't mean to insult you, Jack, but I'd never swap my ears for your arms."

"How did you learn to use your ears like Diddly does?"

"God taught me, of course," she answered, and I felt as if I had asked her what color an orange is.

"How did He teach you?"

She glanced down at her body. "I think He usually teaches us through our bodies—maybe He *always* teaches us through our bodies, because He never takes us out of them, or almost never." She paused, turned her attention from her body to mine, and said, "I think if I had your arms, I'd probably have your ears too." Then, seeing my abashed look, she added, "Oh, I'm sorry, Jack, I didn't mean to insult you." Her words were not meant ironically, but we both immediately broke into hysterical laughter at the irony.

Diddly and Squat

These two keep to themselves more than anyone else in the House, even though they're friendlier than anyone else (except Dudley). They are the most unbelievable characters of all of us, I think. If someone had told me a story with these two in it, I would fault the story for lacking credibility. Yet they are both very reasonable men. For they do what they do simply because it makes them happy. (That is Premise One.) And that is what everyone most fundamentally wants—to be happy. (That is Premise Two.) The logical conclusion from these two premises is that Diddly and Squat have solved life's fundamental problem. And that is what reason is *for*. So if they appear to be anything other than reasonable men to us, that fact tells more about us than about them.

They remind me of the wise farmer Mama told me about once. He was someone her family knew in Mexico. He swapped his tractor for a plow horse even though it cut his efficiency in half, and his explanation was this: "I hate tractors. I love horses. Horses make me happy. I am happy now. So what is your problem?" Yet, when some reporter wrote about this wise man in the newspaper, he received some angry letters that treated him like a traitor. But he was not surprised by this. His three-word explanation was: "Prisoners envy escapees." That story helped me choose to major in philosophy, which will not make me rich, but it will make me happy. I think Diddly and Squat may be the most philosophical of us all.

I once asked Squat, "Is everything you do something to make you happy?" I wondered whether Squat was simply a hedonist.

He answered, "Nope. Some things you do because you gotta do 'em. Like our part- time consulting work so we can make enough money to eat. And some things you do because you oughta do 'em. Like admitting your mistakes. But all the other stuff we do because we wanna do 'em. Like dancing. You know of any other good reason to do stuff besides *gotta* and *oughta* and *wanna*?"

I didn't. I still don't. I find that philosophy of life simply irrefutable.

When I mastered sign language (which was much easier than I expected), I asked Diddly whether anyone had ever accused him and Squat of acting out the old racist stereotypes of American Blacks as "funny dancers." They had just finished almost bouncing through the roof bojangling to "Alley Oop" and then "Shout." I said, "When you dance like that, you look just like what a redneck racist thinks you ought to look like." And Diddly replied, "That's right. That's how we transcend the idea."

"I don't understand."

"It's like wearing a costume for Halloween. When you put on a mask, you play that part, and when you play it, you separate yourself from it, you transcend it. You say: 'See? This is not me. This is only a role.'"

"But you look like Mickey Mouse and Goofy in an old 1940 cartoon!"

"Exactly," Diddly answered. "And who are the only people who could never *play* Mickey Mouse and Goofy? Mickey Mouse and Goofy." It made perfect sense.

Diddly is six feet ten inches tall, and Squat is four foot five. In one of their dance routines, someone asks Diddly the stereotypical question, "Do you play basketball?" and Diddly answers, "We both do," and then dribbles *Squat*, and shoots him through an imaginary hoop.

Diddly lip reads infallibly. He talks with his hands more eloquently and efficiently than I can talk with my mouth. "I'm not deaf and dumb," he says, "I hear with my eyes and I speak with my hands." Squat says he's quite happy to be blind because he isn't. He "sees." He's "awake." Squat won't talk about his past, or about his future, and therefore he won't give direct answers to questions like: "Will you make dancing a career?" "Do you ever want to get married?" "Were you born blind?" "How did you come to this House?" He explained his reluctance to answer such questions with a poem, which he sang to me:

> The philosophy of Squat:
> *Now* is all we've got.
> Yesterday is dead.
> It died last night in bed.
> Tomorrow isn't born
> Until tomorrow morn.
> *Now* is all we've got:
> The philosophy of Squat.

He explained it like this: "'Sorrow' rhymes with 'tomorrow.' That's no accident. All sorrow comes from being afraid something bad's going to happen tomorrow. Or else it's because something bad happened yesterday, and you're still living there in that tomb, with the dead."

I asked him why there can't be sorrow in the present, and he answered, "There's no *room* for it here."

Diddly is more loquacious than Squat. Sign language is itself a kind of hula dance to him. He explained how he came to the House this way:

"I was rich once," he said, then added, as an afterthought: "And smart too."

"And now you're poor and stupid?" I teased him.

"No, happy and wise."

"So *wise* is the opposite of *smart* and *happy* is the opposite of *rich*?"

"You got it, Jack."

"So you made that swap."

"Yep. Best swap I ever made. I used to work like I was in Purgatory doing penance for my sins all the time. I finally did enough penance to buy this Big, Big House. When I'd fall asleep in my Big, Big Bed in my Big, Big House, I kept getting a Tiny, Tiny Dream. In the dream, there I was, like an ant, crawling down this street *pushing* this Big, Big House in front of me. I was stuck to it like glue, like it was glued to my nose, like it *was* my nose. I knew I had to get un-glued. I'm smart enough to figure that six foot ten of flesh is enough for me to push around these streets. So I unglued myself from the house. Sold it. Didn't make a penny on it, but now I can dance. You can't dance with a Big, Big House on your nose."

"Is that why you dance so wild and free?"

"Yup. Freedom from gravity: that's the secret of dancing. It doesn't start in the legs, it starts in the nose. You gotta get that Big, Big House off your nose. And then you gotta turn your nose up to the sky and smell Heaven. And then your heart dances. And then your feet follow."

"You seem so *alive* when you dance."

"I dance on all the graves. I dance on death."

"Right until you die."

"Longer. When I die I'm not gonna fall into my grave, I'm gonna dance into it, and out the other side."

I once asked Mother about them: "You saved their lives too, didn't you?"

"In a way. We all save each other in some way. It's reciprocal. They help save us too."

"How?"

"They show us God."

"How?"

"The Discipline of the Interruption, for one thing."

"How does that show us God?"

"You should understand that. Tell me: how is the one true God different from idols, or abstractions like The Platonic Idea of the Good?"

"He speaks. He acts. He creates. He judges."

"Exactly. He interrupts. Did you ever hear of the Idea of the Good interrupting you?"

I smiled at the thought. "No. I understand who God is. But I think I don't understand who you people are. Most people hate to be interrupted. Yet you all accept Diddly and Squat's interruptions. How did you train all these people so well?"

Mother looked shocked. "*Train* them? Train *them*? I think maybe you *don't* understand who we are. We're not a circus of trained animals, you know."

At that moment, Day and Night "interrupted" us at about 25 miles per hour, fighting, as if to say "See, stupid? She can't even train her animals, much less her people."

"I'm sorry, I didn't mean that. Totally wrong word."

"Apology accepted. But you still don't understand why we love the inter-ruptions, do you?"

"No."

"Well, look. If you were suddenly interrupted by an angel, a real angel—you do believe in angels, don't you?"

"Of course. They're in the Qur'an."

"So you're visited by an angel. Do you say 'Please don't interrupt me, come back later'? All those paintings of the angel Gabriel appearing to Mary—are they called 'The Interruption'?"

"No. You call them 'the Annunciation,' I think. I understand that. We Muslims revere Mary too, for her *islam,* her surrender. So maybe I would accept an interruption from an angel too, if I saw one. But Diddly and Squat aren't angels."

"How do you know that?"

"What?"

"I said how do you know that?"

"Are you serious?"

"Serious, yes. You better believe serious. You are surprised. Why? What, can't angels be black?"

"Of course."

"Or fat? Or skinny? Or dancers?"

"On the head of a pin, maybe." (I was feeling foolish by now, so I was say-ing foolish things.)

"Don't you think an angel could really dance on the head of a pin if he wanted to?"

"Yes, if Allah commanded it, he could do anything."

"So what if He commanded it on a wooden floor?"

"Are you telling me Diddly and Squat are angels?" I was almost ready to believe her if she had said Yes.

"No, I'm saying you can't ever really be sure, can you? My holy book says, 'Do not ever forget hospitality, for some have entertained angels unawares.' Your holy book is big on hospitality too, I think—am I right?"

"Yes. But about those interruptions . . ."

"What is more interrupting than a beggar at the door? Am I right?"

"Yes."

"And isn't that what we all are to each other half the time? Am I right?"

"Yes. You are right."

"So they show us who we are. I'd say that's a pretty valuable training, now, wouldn't you?"

"Yes." (Again.)

"In fact, you know what word I'd use for that lesson?"

"What?"

"Surrender. And you know the Arabic word for that, I think."

"Islam." (Click.)

"The defense rests," she concluded, with a big smile and folded arms.

So I am no longer certain that Diddly and Squat are not angels. I am even less sure about Mother. In fact, sometimes I think I'm the only human in the House.

She added, "They teach us that discipline is dancing."

"You mean that dancing takes discipline? That there's years of hard work behind their easy dancing?"

"That's true too. But that's the half we already know: that dancing is discipline. The other half is that discipline is dancing. Do you know what I mean?"

"I'm not sure," I confessed.

"I mean that all the 'interruptions' we find so irritating are really movements in the Great Dance. They're the best things in life."

"I think I understand."

"Let's see if you do. Do you understand *why* interruptions are the best things in life?"

"Because they are God's will."

"Yes, but why is that not just *good* but *beautiful*?"

"Because it's *His*"

"Yes, but what is it like? Give me an analogy."

"There are no analogies for Allah. He is unique. He is like nothing else."

"Yes, but what is His will for us like?"

"Like a dance."

"Exactly! Like a dance. Not a whip but a baton. When we follow that baton, we dance. We make music. We all know we need discipline, unless we're fools. But we don't *like* it, we don't see it as *beautiful*. If we did, if we saw the dance, we'd love it. Because we all love to dance."

"You are indeed a wise woman, Mother."

"No I am not. But I have a wise Master."

* * * * *

What did we *do* at the House? We talked and talked and talked. Not chatted, or gossiped, but really talked, about really important things. We argued, endlessly and passionately, and with respect and even love for our antagonists, even when we had no respect or love for their ideas. I learned far more about how to do philosophy from the Housebugs than from all my classroom teachers.

Eva, Diddly, and Squat only occasionally took active parts in our arguments. Their primary languages were music and silence rather than words. Mother was almost always there, patiently hovering in the wings. Lazarus and

Mister Mumm were gone as often as they were home. That left Evan, Libby, and myself to develop a little core community of arguers. "There go the word-warriors again!" Mother would say when she saw us doing our thing.

*   *   *   *   *

The fall of 1977 was probably the happiest time of my life. New friends, new courses at BC, a new home. I have written very little in this autobiograph-ical notebook about those days; for we think and write the most not when we are the most content but when we are the most discontent. The only thing that made me discontented at that time was the dreams.

The main events of my life for the next four months were the daily changes in the exhibits in the world's most perfect museum, in which I was now living. That museum is the world itself. What a privileged life when the most remarkable events are *weather*!

There was a day in October that was so beautiful it was almost physically painful. I woke up, looked outside my window, and thought the whole of Bailey's Hill was on fire. But it was only a painting. God had dipped His brush in fire, and painted the whole slope of the Hill with it. Not only were the leaves exactly the same *colors* as fire—piercingly bright reds, yellows, and oranges—but each leaf was also *shaped* like a flame, and the wind was fan-ning the leaves into the same quivering *motion* as flames.

My first instinct was to run to a fire alarm. My second was to take off my shoes, like Moses, for the place was clearly holy ground, a burning bush. I almost expected to hear the words "I AM WHO AM" from the waves of flame.

Another preternaturally bright day, we watched from the deck as a tiny red lobster boat floated tranquilly a quarter mile offshore, surrounded by about fifty white beggar gulls on the bright blue water, waiting for their welfare dole. Libby took a photo of the scene, sent it to a contest, and won second prize of $500.

There was an evening in November when the cold fog was literally palpa-ble. The mist from the sea crept through the streets like a spy, and into the houses like a ghost, and even into souls, like an evil spirit. We could not get warm that night, even though the temperature was above freezing, no matter how much wood we put on the fire. We felt *haunted*.

The day after, every tree on the Hill was totally bare. The whole of Nahant had succumbed to winter death—except for a single leaf on a single tall tree on Trimountain Hill. As I watched, the last leaf of summer spun in the wind, gave up the ghost, and fell, fighting gravity for a full minute, surfing on the wind, until its final burial. If it had a mind, it must have felt like the last man on earth.

The first winter storm, in December, took us off the surface of the planet earth and deposited us in Heaven in the middle of angels. Every single surface in the world was coated with white ice. I thought of the prophet Ezekiel's vision of the "terrible crystal." It had rained, sleeted, snowed, and frozen during the night, a fourfold combination with a perfect temperature window that happens only a few times in a lifetime. The sunlight darted around with the speed of light, playing all day with the ice, sparkling and melting it just enough so that when the wind blew on this crystal instrument it shattered and fell all morning with sounds like an endlessly long South American rain stick.

In the afternoon the sun melted the ice more, so that thousands of tiny pins of light flashed from every surface like ignited candles. Clearly we were amid angels, and the candles were their eyes. Or the campfires of Allah's angel army. The images were from my imagination, but their presence was not. This was no fantasy; the drab, dull world of everyday, empty of angels—*that* was the fantasy. This day was the most *normal* day, the most realistic day, we had ever seen. When the sun disappeared behind a cloud, late in the afternoon, the thousand eyes closed and the curtain was lowered again.

The window to Heaven had opened for one magic day.

At the end of that day I found it hard to believe that some people actually spend a lot of time, money, and thought traveling to far countries and museums to see beautiful sights.

(9) Throwing Poems at Each Other

There are many strange sorts of unpredictable wisdom in Mother's rules for the House. One of them is The Discipline of the Interruption. Another is the absoluteness of the rule of hospitality: we may never leave the House empty. A third is Poets' Night. One designated evening each year, each of the Housebugs, without exception, must write a rhyming poem, in any regular meter (Mother insists on discipline!) about any topic close to our hearts, and put it on the table some time before the next morning. They are not to be published, or used, just collected, read, and enjoyed. We set the date months ahead of time, and we all arrange our busy schedules around this day as an assignment more sacred than any mandatory one from school or work. Mother calls it "a Sabbath from prose and the prosaic."

I asked Mother's permission to include this year's poems in my autobiography, and at first she refused, but when I explained that they were parts of myself since they were parts of the Housebugs who were part of my new family, she relented. Here are the poems, in the order in which they were finished.

ANGELS AND ANIMALS
by Mister Mumm

I dreamt that once, as I did lie
'neath single sun and single sky,
there woke in me a single eye.

I saw, with eye now newly one,
all things that swim or fly or run
as does the Angel in the Sun.

Each angel, from the first to least,
seemed one specific kind of beast
that filled the world from west to east.

I saw an angel: it was Cat,
yet it was neither this nor that,
nor white nor black, nor thin nor fat.

I saw another: it was Frog.
A third was Whale. A fourth was Hog.
A fifth was every breed of Dog.

They were not beasts, but beastly kinds.
They were not signified, but signs,
that moved only from minds to minds.

The vision gone, I closed my eye
and woke to that familiar lie:
the world in which the living die.

But now, each time I hear a lark,
or see a firefly in the dark,
I recognize the heavenly spark.

ELEMENTARY ARITHMATIC
by Eva

NONE is black, like outer space.
ONE is white, like God and grace.
TWO is blue, like heavens' span.
THREE is red, like heart of man.
FOUR is green, like grass in spring.
FIVE is gold, like lion king.
SIX is purple, like wizard wise.
SEVEN is orange, like sun at rise.
EIGHT is silver, like metal foil.
NINE is brown, like sandy soil.
TEN is grey, like foggy sea.
ALL is right, it seems to me.

THE LOVE OF GOD
by Squat

Harder than iron,
Sweeter than honey,
Prouder than lion,
Humbler than bunny,

Wiser than age,
Fresher than youth,
Darker than rage,
Brighter than truth,

Higher than sky,
Closer than skin,
Deeper than sigh,
Dearer than kin,

Longer than years,
Shorter than breath,
Weaker than tears,
Stronger than death.

DIVINE INSPIRATION
by Diddly

I find the music of the ocean
the most conducive to devotion.

The secret silence of the sea
makes a contemplative of me.

The explanation is not far:
for silence and great music are

the only languages of Heaven
still heard on earth when skies are riven.

The Ones who blow upon the sea
must be the Ones who blow on me.

IN YOUR HANDS
by Libby

This is the law of life on earth:
for every thing that comes to birth,
man and woman, child and mother,
the life of each is in the other.

This is the law of life in Heaven:
we must forgive to be forgiven.
Hands that close, and will not give,
cannot receive, and will not live.

Thus by Thy divine decree,
to each other, as to Thee,
we must say, with trepidation,
"In your hands is my salvation."

THE MEANING OF LIFE
by Lazarus

Life's a mystery, life's a race,
Life's as plain as nose on face,
Life is motherhood and pie,
Life is toys before you die,

Life is scrubbing dirty pots,
Life's a box of chocolates,
Life's a battle, life's a ball,
Life is nothing, life is all,

Life's an accident of chance,
Life's a plan, life's a dance,
Life is good, life is evil,
Life is cotton, life's a weevil,

Life's a bowl of cherries red,
Life's a bitch and then you're dead,
Life's a glorious work of art,
Life's a belch, life's a fart,

Life is anything you want,
Life is Alice's restaurant,
Life is peace, and life is strife,
Life is anything but life.

THEREFORE ALL SINS ARE SINS AGAINST THE SEA
by 'Isa

Because there is no God but God; because
there's no more second God than second sky;
because His light shines through all things like gauze;
because He is creator, and not I;
because each being is from Him alone;
therefore all waters, tides, and rivers run
according to their natures and His own,
so No to Him and No to His are one.

Therefore all sins are sins against the sea
for being wet and wonderful and wild;

against the very bee-ing of the bee;
against the very childhood of the child.

Sin seeks some little door in truth's strong keep,
where doors can never be. It gnaws on Naught.
Its sleep is waking and its waking sleep.
It does not see the Is inside the Ought.

It hurls itself against an iron wall:
the essences of things. It would be free
from That-Which-Is, but finds itself in thrall
to What-Is-Not and What-Can-Never-Be.

Therefore all sins are sins against the sea.

SURFER'S ESCHATOLOGY
by Evan

When come new heavens and new earth,
this world will be but afterbirth.
For every living thing is leaven
to fertilize our bread of heaven.
Yet every glorious thing created
shall shine in that world unabated.
And each beloved bird and beast
will be there at the wedding feast.
And all the art that men have made
will at His holy feet be laid.
His feet of fire will melt them down
into a single golden crown.
We'll go to put it on His head
And, smiling, He'll crown us instead.

Yet in those perfect heavenly places
there seem to be three empty places.
For Revelation Twenty-One
mentions three things whose life is done:
In heaven three things will not be:
no sun, no temple, and no sea.

Now we are told the deeper cause
for two of these apparent flaws:

There's no sun in the new creation

but that is not a real negation.
The Son of God will be our sun,
and moon, and stars, when day is done.

And temple mount, in all its parts,
imaged the One who dwells in hearts.
With Bridegroom here, His wineglass token
is now fulfilled by being broken.

The reason for no heavenly sea
must be the same, it seems to me.
As He's our temple and our sun,
He'll be our sea when time is done.
When this old body lies in sod,
my soul will body-surf in God.

ENOUGH
by Mother

It was not enough
being only One.
Thus His timeless act:
Fathering the Son.

It was not enough
timeless Two to be.
Overflow of love
makes them timeless Three.

It was not enough
being God alone.
Angel minds He made
to know and be known.

It was not enough
making only spirit.
He made matter's music
and the ears to hear it.

It was not enough
making minds and atoms.
Fusing them together,
He made sirs and madams.

It was not enough
giving them a Garden.
They invented sin,
He invented pardon.

It was not enough
pardoning the sinning.
God acquired a mother,
God got a beginning.

It was not enough
in their flesh to dwell.
To save their place in heaven,
He took their place in hell.

It was not enough
powers of Heaven were shaken
See upon the cross:
God by God forsaken.

It was not enough
Life becoming dead.
For our starving souls
He became our bread.

It was not enough
that He share His house.
He would share His bed,
make each soul His spouse.

When is it enough?
Ask the mighty River
flowing on forever
with Love's holy water.
Hear the answer: "Never!"

(10) The Dreams

I have a recurring nightmare.

I never used to dream much at all until I lived in the House of Bread. Then, dreams began to come like storm waves, one after the other. The first one is about a Door, and it seems to have let the others in through itself.

It's about *something* leaking out of another world—a world behind a locked Door—and into this world. I know what triggered it: it was that oak door in the cellar of the House that leads nowhere but into the earth and is locked with three very large padlocks. It looks a thousand years old.

Dream #1

The first time I dreamed of the Door, I dreamed I was utterly alone at night standing in the cellar right in front of that Door to Nowhere. I felt something wrong in the air. It was hot and stuffy, yet a cold wind seemed to be blowing in the middle of it. I looked around to find the crack in a wall or the floor through which the cold wind was coming, but there was none. I began to sweat and feel cold, even in the oppressive heat. I was afraid. I was very, very afraid.

Next, I noticed that the air had a color I had never seen before, a sickly, sticky yellowish-blue, a yellowish-blue that was *not* a green. In the waking world, yellow and blue make green, but not in this dream.

As I watched, the Door opened by itself. My legs stuck to the cement floor with fear. Through the Door crawled a Thing that I can only describe as a moving, man-sized hole of blackness. The line from *The Lord of the Rings* echoed in my head: "Far, far below the deepest delvings of the Dwarves, the world is gnawed by nameless things."

I woke up shivering and sweating and trying unsuccessfully to scream with a dry mouth. I felt I had just been shocked with an electric current.

I kept the nightmare to myself the next day, hoping there were tides of the mind, like the tides of the sea, that would clean the garbage out. But the very next night, I dreamed again.

Again I was alone at night in the cellar, and again the Door opened. The Thing came out again, but this time it enveloped me like a cloud and started dragging me through the Door, through tunnels, down into the earth. I thought: "I am going to Hell. Hell is not fire but earth. For fire needs air to fuel it, and air is heavenly." (Occasionally, I dream in syllogisms!) I was surrounded by something that felt like heavy, wet mud or cement, full of rivers of flowing urine, diarrhea, vomit, pus, and mucous. I woke up with dry heaves.

In the morning I asked Mother what was behind the Door. She said, "Nothing but the earth." When I pressed her about why the Door was there and why the three locks were on it, she said, "I don't know. I only inherited this house, I didn't design it." I wanted to ask her whether she had the keys to those three locks, but I didn't dare. I didn't really want to see them. Mother had dozens of old keys around—to what doors, I can't imagine.

When I told her about my dream, she got very serious. She took my hand, and called me "'Isa" instead of "Jack." "'Isa, even if there *were* something in the earth, the Door would keep it out. Nothing can break those locks." (This did *not* reassure me!)

Seeing my reaction, Mother then did something surprising: she simply promised me, with quiet authority, that my dream would never bother me again. And then I did something equally surprising: I simply accepted that without question. She gave no reason for her reassurance and I had no reason to accept it. Yet I did. And sure enough, that particular dream has never recurred. What powers are at work here, I wonder? Certainly many that I do not understand.

Dream #2

The nightmare stopped, but the dreams did not. The next night, I had an even stranger dream. This one was also about a man from the underground, but this one was not a monster, he did not come through the Door, and the dream did not terrify me. The man was buried in the ground, but under the stony beach outside the House instead of under it. I have always been a bit claustrophobic and afraid of cellars, but never afraid of beaches or the sea, even in storms.

The dream came to me when I was half awake and half asleep, dozing out on the back deck in the middle of the day. That was one peculiarity; another was that it included a *smell*: the smell of mingled blood and salt water.

The dream came in little bits at first: faint sounds of horns and bells, far off and muffled, yet cold and clear. Then drums. Their "Boom!" made me think: Doom. This went on for quite a few minutes. Once, during that time, I thought I heard the sound of the crash of waves against the side of a boat. When I looked (or dreamed I looked) at the sea it was totally calm. But when I closed my eyes (or dreamed I closed my eyes), I saw in my mind a different sea: a black, foaming sea gnawing at a stony beach surrounded by a harsh, primitive landscape.

(Two weeks later, I saw an Icelandic movie entitled *In the Path of the*

Black Raven, which included the exact beach scene I had seen in my dream! The scene was repeated three times in the movie. It was a beach in Iceland.)

In the dream, the Icelandic surf vision faded and was replaced by the deck of the House again, and the calm sea. Suddenly, a Frost Giant, straight out of an old Victorian illustration, arose from the sea right under the deck. I did not feel fear, perhaps because the image was familiar to me. The giant opened his mouth and sent a spray of ice, snow, water, and sand onto the beach next to the House, which opened a bus-sized cut across the beach like a sharp butcher knife into meat. From the cut emerged a Viking. The Frost Giant faded as the Viking stood up.

Its eyes were searching for something, like a searchlight. Its mouth was moving, repeating the same phrase over and over. The searchlight eyes roamed until they found me, then stopped and peered straight at me. His words then became clear, just once. They were: "WARE MY GRAVE."

At first I thought he meant "Where (is) my grave?" But then I remembered reading Shakespeare, and realized that "ware" was old English for "beware," and that he had said "BEWARE MY GRAVE."

Then I saw a beautiful girl with black hair, holding the Viking's hand. She looked more like an angel than a girl, but I think there aren't any female angels, so it must have been a girl. I tried to call out to her, and she turned to me as if she had heard me, so I saw her face for a second. It was innocent and childlike, with large wide eyes. I thought: "She is vulnerable to pain; she has probably experienced great pain." And then I was afraid for her.

But she sensed my fear, her face took on a sudden look of fear herself, and she ran away, pulling the Viking with her.

They both walked into the sea.

Dream #3

I saw a very old, very wise-looking man with a scraggly beard whose face was heavy with grief and suffering rise from the sea and walk toward me. (I don't know where I was.) The old man looked as if he had walked across the sea bottom from the other side of the world. His hair was matted with crabs.

He trooped across a lawn surrounded by red brick buildings that felt familiar, stepped onto a small stepladder, and opened his mouth. Out leaped flames. They surrounded a large, well-dressed crowd of people. The flames did not burn the people, yet they acted as if they were being burnt.

Then the flames began to *melt* the people, making them smaller and smaller. When they shrank to the size of mice, they rose in unison and ran together at the bearded man, covering his face and mouth. I felt pity for the man, but no fear.

Fulfillment: June 7th?

(Editor's Note: this last line, and other "fulfillment" lines after subsequent dreams, are written in a different ink. They were evidently added later. For an interpretation of this event, see my two-part article on Solzhenitsyn's Harvard Commencement Address in the *St. Austin Review* (StAR), July–August 2007.)

Dream #4

I saw a large squarish thing with green metal girders on the inside and red brick on the outside. It reminded me of a ferryboat, but it was much larger. It was open on top, hollow inside, and full of bright green grass. On the grass were white and grey bugs running around. Thousands of other bugs were stuck onto the inside walls of the thing. The thing was plunging up and down in the sea, sinking and then rising again. It rose one last time and then sank to the bottom, making a whimpering sound.

Fulfillment: Oct. 2?

(Editor's Note: see chapter 26)

Dream #5

I saw a frail, thin man with a pained face wearing what looked like a white, pointed dunce cap. He was riding in a boat buffeted by waves. After much toil, he sank beneath the waves, seeming to fall through the bottom of the boat. His white cap floated on the surface of the sea, and was picked up by another man, a little younger and stronger, with a sweet smile on his face. This man also sank beneath the waves, as soon as he put the cap on his head.

Then there rose from the sea a third man, very strong and muscular, almost a giant. He had a Viking-like glint of determination in his eye. He put on the cap, entered the boat, turned it around to face east instead of west, and sailed away.

Fulfillment: Rome, October?

Dream #6 (Feb. 22, 1978)

Unlike the others, this dream seems pretty transparent. I saw a ladder let down from the sky, like Jacob's Ladder. Its top went not just *to* the sky but *through* it, as if the sky were paper and had a hole in it. Its feet touched the earth at Bailey's Hill, exactly where the rocks meet the water in the Cauldron. Bright little multicolored rectangular clouds of light were climbing up and down the ladder on wheels, like trucks on a busy highway. The rectangles were all face, and each one was looking simultaneously upward and downward. Either the rectangles, or the ladder itself, or both, were singing, with a high and holy and inhuman voice that sounded inorganic yet soft and beautiful, like the "Neptune" part of Holst's "The Planets" suite.

Then I noticed a mirror image of the ladder reflected in the water, the same size and shape and angle, but all the colors were different. The first ladder was gold, the figures on it were multicolored, and the sky around it was blue. The second ladder and the figures on it were red. They seemed to be made of sparks. The space surrounding it was black. Then I realized that it was not a reflected image but another ladder, reaching down into the sea and into the earth.

Though I was repelled by the second ladder, I was so enthralled by the beauty of the first one that I wanted to climb it and leave the earth. The light at the top was intense, and the thought came to me that if I climbed up far enough I might just fade and disappear and *become* the light.

But I knew this climb was not permitted, and that I had to perform an important task before I would be permitted to disappear.

As soon as this thought came to me, I saw a tiny baby at the very top rung of the heavenly ladder. He floated down on clouds of light, singing in a baby voice, singing just one sound, which he could barely articulate with his baby mouth. It was "Ah . . . ah . . ." Then a bubble formed on his lips and it broke the "A" into two: "Ah . . . B . . . Ah . . ." "Abba." And when that word came out, all the angels on the ladder hid their faces, and the whole round universe shook. (I know they were angels. I don't know why they were shaped like rectangles.)

When I told Mother this dream, the "Jacob's ladder" meaning seemed obvious to both of us. "Jack's ladder," she called it. The angelic and demonic spirits both seem to have done their work at the Cauldron. I remembered the two contrary forces I felt there myself on that terrible night. I do not think the dream was a vision from God, because it was accompanied by doubts. I think it was simply my unconscious mind sorting out and interpreting some of the things my conscious mind remembered.

But who was the baby? And why did I get the feeling he was addressing me when he spoke? And why did that fill me with fear?

Dream #7

This last "dream" was not a nighttime dream but a waking vision, though it came to me around midnight. I was going upstairs to go to bed, having just passed Night and Day in the same second. As I passed the door to Mother's bedroom, I noticed that the door was open an inch, and I could not help seeing her through the crack as I passed. She was on her knees, praying. Nothing surprising about that. But then the house suddenly seemed to spin around her like a whirlpool. The boards of the house looked like waves, then all the other houses on the street became bigger waves, then all of Nahant became one enormous wave, whirling round in a whirlpool that kept expanding until it included the whole planet. The whole universe was turning around this place and this event, like the whorls on the soapstone spindles in the Norse myth of the Norns. Everything turned around that center, as if everything depended on it. I thought that the world would abruptly end if I had been so foolish as to have interrupted Mother's prayers. It seemed to me that events thousands of miles away were dangling at the ends of the threads she twirled in her hands, so that if she said one prayer too few, a nuclear war might break out.

If these dreams come not just from my own consciousness but from another world, I hope it is the world of the angels rather than the world of the djinni.

If they come from the minds of angels, then they are not photographs of events in our world but models for these events. For angels know events before they happen. We know them only afterwards. Angels are allowed to read some of the thoughts of the Eternal Mind; that's why they know the outworkings of these thoughts in time before they happen. Can djinni do the same? I hope not.

(11) Saint Michael's Bloody Sword

Boston is nicknamed "The Hub." The name comes from the local intelligentsia of the nineteenth century—elegant, snobbish, and breathtakingly provincial—who called their town not only "the Athens of America" but "the hub of the universe"—and meant it. To them, all land west of the Charles River was "Indian country," and the route from Boston to Florida was "through South Boston."

Boston is also called "Beantown," "the town of the bean and the cod / where the Lodges speak only to Cabots / and the Cabots speak only to God." It is also Braintown. (One of its suburbs is even called, most improbably, "Braintree.") There are more colleges per square mile here than anywhere else on earth.

Of these colleges, the most beautiful campus is Boston College. Ralph Adams Cram, greatest of post-medieval Gothic architects, called it "one of the three most beautiful campuses in America." Perched on "the Heights" at the western edge of the Boston city limits, it is a Jesuit university with a distinguished past and present, graduate schools of arts & sciences, law, nursing, and business, 15,000 students, fierce competition for admission, financial solvency, continued growth, and an ongoing identity crisis. (Students say "BC" stands for "Barely Catholic.") Each of these facts proves it is alive. It has never ceased to seek the definition of its "Catholic and Jesuit identity," and has never quite succeeded in definitively finding it. Like the Red Sox, it is both dearly loved and dearly complained about. It feels more like a family than a business.

In hidden places like the kitchens, many of the simple jobs are held by learning disabled and mentally retarded young adults who "fall through the cracks." If the prophet Jesus (blessed be his name!) returned to earth, I think he would see his own reflection there more than in the theology department. After all, according to his own parable of the last judgment, his question will be not how we thought but how we lived: "I say to you, what you did to these, the least of my brethren, you did to me." He did not tell any parables about theology exams at the golden gates. I think he would smile at the story about the theologian who died and was give the choice to go to a lecture on Heaven or to go to Heaven, and chose the lecture.

In the theology department, BC's most famous professor today is Mary Monthly (the name has been changed because of lexophobia, fear of lawyers).

Mary is a "feminist" theologian who declared in print that she was the Antichrist and that the purpose of her life and work was "to castrate God the Father." Nearly every sentence of her public speeches is laced with a blasphemy or an obscenity, not only against the Catholic religion but also against language. She consistently lives out Nietzsche's profound comment that "we atheists have not killed God until we have killed grammar."

Mary got tenure because of the expansion of the Vietnam War into Cambodia in 1969. The students went on strike and refused to attend classes. Their demands included the following, which they saw as connected in some deep, underground way: that BC's President (1) condemn President Lyndon Johnson as a warmonger, (2) condemn those who claimed Pol Pot was a tyrant rather than a liberator, and (3) give Mary Monthly tenure. They got their third demand. (Pol Pot singlehandedly instituted "the killing fields" of Cambodia, murdering one-third of the entire population of his nation, including everyone who wore glasses and therefore might have been an intellectual.)

Mary is a bit of a recluse, does not speak publicly to the Enemy (i.e. men), and teaches only one course, by many different names, namely "The Whole History of Western Civilization = Patriarchy." The very rules of Aristotelian logic are for her a form a rape: a patriarchal plot to force the minds of men upon "Womynspirit." She calls her classes covens, and will not allow any men into them.

(Editor's Note: This policy eventually got Mary fired from BC after a Harvard graduate student brought suit against her for sexual discrimination under federal laws. The fear of God never moved BC to fire the Antichrist, but the fear of lawyers did.)

The oldest and most impressive of the Gothic buildings on BC's campus is Gasson Hall, which occupies the highest point on the hilly campus called "the Heights." It is a cathedral to learning built with the faith, passion, and sacrifice of poor Irish immigrants who used their money to make magic: to make heavy building stones leap high into the sky like rockets—or angels. The cathedral-like buildings were built by people who had cathedrals in their souls. A century later, people with Bauhaus souls built Bauhaus buildings: schools that look like prisons, apartments that look like factories, and houses that are "machines to live in" (Le Corbusier).

Gasson's central clock tower can be seen for many miles. It looks like a stone cat with erect ears, listening for the signs of the times. At its center is an indoor rotunda three stories high and 150 feet in circumference. Over four stone doors are inscribed, in Gothic letters, four Latin mottoes:

(1) *"Quis ut Deus?"* ("Who Is like God?"), which is what "Michael" means in Hebrew;

(2) *"Ad Majorem Dei Gloriam"* ("To the greater glory of God"), the motto St. Ignatius gave to the Jesuits, the "Society of Jesus," which he founded;

(3) *"Quid Hoc ad Aeternitatem?* ("How does this lead to eternity?"), the question St. Ignatius told us to ask about any choice we make in this life;

(4) *"Mater Dei Est Mater Mea"* ("The Mother of God is My Mother"), a formula for stating the Christian doctrine that Mary's son Jesus is God (an idea Muslims find idolatrous), and expressing the personal devotion of Catholics to Mary as their spiritual mother.

In the open center of the rotunda stands a larger-than-life marble statue of St. Michael the Archangel in full battle gear, sword in uplifted hand, trampling on the Prince of Darkness who has taken the form of a hateful, horny, scaly dragon with hellish wings and human face. The statue rises 11 feet. Every eye is drawn to it. Gardner Brewer, a wealthy Boston merchant of the mid-nineteenth century, commissioned the statue from the distinguished Italian sculptor Scipione Tadolini. The Pope saw it and wanted it but did not get it.

Each of the four walls of the rotunda shelters an original stone statue of a great Jesuit of the past. Above them are four striking oil paintings, fifteen feet high. These were painted by Francis Schroen as a thank-offering for what he believed was Mary's miraculous deliverance from demonic forces. Rev. Charles F. Donovan, Boston College's official historian, sums up the story this way:

> Coming from a family of strong Catholic faith, Schroen attended parochial school, but some time after his marriage at age 21 . . . he ceased the practice of his religion. His wife died when he was 35, and things went worse for him. He became obsessed with spiritism and the Ouija board and had ever deeper contact with the spirits beyond until the messages he received became so obscene and blasphemous that Schroen demanded in God's name to know the identity of the being moving his hand. With violent trembling his hand wrote the word B-e-e-l-z-e-b-u-b. . . .
>
> Schroen was convinced that he was cured through Our Lady's intercession. . . . Therefore one can imagine the feelings of awe Brother Schroen must have felt in 1913 as he was creating his great paintings on the upper walls of the rotunda and looked down from his scaffolding to see the statue of St. Michael crushing Lucifer. For Schroen the vanquished was Beelzebub and the massive statuary must have represented the outcome of a battle that had taken place in his own life.
>
> (Gasson's Rotunda: Gallery of Art, History, and Religion: Occasional Papers on the History of Boston College, April 1992)

If BC had been a Protestant school, Luther's verse would have been inscribed on the statue:

For still our ancient foe
Doth seek to work us woe;

His craft and power are great,
And armed with cruel hate,
On earth is not his equal.
Did we in our own strength confide,
Our striving would be losing.

The archangel, dressed in Roman helmet and breastplate, holds a raised sword, ready to swing it down upon the neck of Satan, who grovels under his feet. The tip of St. Michael's sword, pointed to the heavens, is the focus that draws all eyes. It is at the exact center and top of the sculpture, which in turn is at the exact center of the rotunda, which is at the exact center of Gasson Hall, which is at the center of the BC campus. If you add the premises that BC is the spiritual center of Boston and that Boston is "the Hub of the Universe," you arrive at the conclusion that the event I am about to narrate happened at the very center of the universe.

*   *   *   *   *

It was six or seven A.M. on February 1, 1978. Outside, Boston struggled to awaken from the black of night to the dirty grey of dawn. A major winter storm system, perhaps a blizzard, was moving through in the next 48 hours.

The earliest classes were scheduled for 8 A.M. (There were only a very few of these. Most students' alarm clocks refused to be set that early.) The housekeeping crew was cleaning the building at about 7 A.M. Old Mrs. McGonagle, tough and gnarled as an oak, was mopping the marble floor of the rotunda, her face turned to the floor to guide her mop.

As she approached the base of the St. Michael statue, she noticed a small pool of red liquid on the floor. The thought "blood!" paralyzed her for a second. Then she heard a dripping sound. She saw a drop of the red liquid splashing down into the puddle. Curiosity conquering fear, she turned her face upward. From the tip of the archangel's sword blood was dripping, as from a leaky faucet, down his bare arm and his armor, onto the face of the terrified Satan under his feet, then splashing to the floor. One drop actually bounced Onto Mrs. McGonagle's face.

It was all far too much for her simple soul to hold. She fainted, right onto the pool of blood. When the rest of the four-man cleaning crew found her, they thought she had hit her head on the statue. But then they too saw the blood dripping from the sword eleven feet in the air.

When the cleaning crew brought university officials to the rotunda some thirty minutes later, a few students, arriving early for their 8:00 class, stood stunned and staring at the sight of the still-dripping blood. As soon as the school officials arrived, the blood stopped dripping. They closed Gasson Hall for the morning and canceled the morning classes. A police detective arrived at 8:30 to investigate the scene, and classified it as a student prank. A reporter from the *Boston Globe* interviewed Mrs. McGonagle in Saint Elizabeth's Hospital later that day, as well as a few students who claimed to have seen the blood, but the newspaper refused to print the story. One student called the paper about this and was told, "We don't do miracle stories. It's a matter of policy." I suppose when the skies roll back like a scroll, the angels blow their trumpets, the Four Horsemen of the Apocalypse ride across the sky, and the saints go marching in, the *Boston Globe* will refuse to run the story, "as a matter of policy."

One student who said he had gotten close enough to the blood to smell it said that it smelled like sea water.

The story circulated around campus that day. I do not know whether to believe it or not. I did not see any of these events with my own eyes. I have talked to one student who did. He seems sane and serious. As a student of philosophy rather than of science or history, I am even more fascinated with the *meaning* of this event than with whether it was fact or fiction. If it was a sign, what did it signify?

(12) The Great Blizzard of '78

The Great Blizzard of '78 was the most destructive storm in all of New England's history. The *Boston Globe* of 2/6/78 called its effects "the most ocean damage ever to hit New England." It was a hurricane as well as a blizzard, with winds up to 125 miles per hour in some places. At one point there was concern that an entire town (Revere Beach) would be swept out to sea. Yet there were few written descriptions of the blizzard-hurricane itself, though many descriptions of its aftereffects. This is largely because you couldn't write about it without seeing it, and you couldn't see it without risking your life.

Two weeks before the Great Blizzard, there was another one, which was striking at the time, and in fact set an all-time record of 21.4 inches of snow in 24 hours, but was almost wholly forgotten two weeks later, in the shadow of its monster brother.

For the first blizzard, the *Boston Globe* headline for January 20, 1978, read: "Worst Storm in Years Immobilizes Boston." The article read:

> With snowdrifts topping 12 feet on some roadways and . . . streets blocked by stalled and abandoned autos, the city of Boston was virtually paralyzed yesterday by what officials described as the city's worst snow storm in nine years.
>
> The North Shore's two peninsular communities, Plum Island in Newbury and Nahant, were isolated from the mainland . . . as their causeways, buffeted by high winds, became buried in snowdrifts and clogged with stuck automobiles. . . . in Nahant, local officials called in tow trucks from the National Guard to remove cars on the Nahant causeway so that plows could get through. Civil Defense officials said they considered the Nahant situation critical since, in the event of a medical emergency, it would be impossible to drive inland.

Then, two weeks later, came the real blizzard, which the *Globe* described in these words:

> It began days before, with an extraordinary interaction of the air, the sea, the earth, the sun, and the moon. These all seemed to conspire to make the Great Blizzard of '78 as bad as it could possibly be.

The storm lasted a day and a half: half of Monday and all of Tuesday. The headlines Wednesday morning read:

WORST STORM OF CENTURY . . . RECORD HIGH TIDES . . .
UP TO 4 FEET OF SNOW . . . WINDS GUST UP TO 125 MPH

Gov. Michael S. Dukakis declared a state of emergency yesterday. . . . said: "The weather situation that now exists in the state of Massachusetts is the worst in its history."

The storm imposed . . . the highest recorded tides in this century . . . more than 16 feet above normal levels. Evacuees: more than 10,000 people living on the coast. Deaths: 54 in New England, including 29 in Massachusetts. Vehicles stranded: some 3000 cars and 500 trucks just on one eight-mile stretch of Rte. 128. A governor-declared state of emergency. A president-declared state of emergency. 5000 Massachusetts National Guardsmen mobilized. 350 federal troops with heavy equipment airlifted to the Bay State. Cost: an exact figure will never be known.

For the first time in 106 years the Globe was unable to distribute its morning edition.

One cab driver, who asked not to be named, got his taxi stuck in snow while delivering a fare during the Great Blizzard Monday night. The grateful woman offered the cabbie her apartment as shelter from the raging storm outside.

By Thursday, said the cabbie, they were living together. Cross-country skier Terrance Maitland of Somerville was just gliding along the picturesque, ice-covered Charles River when he saw a fellow cross country enthusiast disappear under the ice.

"I was the closest one to him, so I took off my skis and laid on my stomach on the ice. Then I extended the skis out to him and we were able to get him out," Maitland recalls. He said the young man thanked him and skied off . . .

STORM CAN'T DELAY THE STORK

If there had been no storm, Mary Ward Christopher would have had an easy ride the block or so from her house on Tuttle Street in Dorchester to St. Margaret's Hospital, where she expected to give birth to her first child.

However, when she went into labor about mid-day yesterday, the hill to the hospital had become impassable due to snow and her husband's car was stuck fast in deep drifts.

A deputy stork in the form of a snow plow rushed to Mrs.

Christopher's aid. Wrapped in blankets, the woman climbed into the front scoop of the plow.

Reactions to the storm were not all negative by any means. There was, as the Lynn *Item* put it, definitely a BRIGHTER SIDE TO THE STORM:

> For those on the dark side of the greatest storm in history, there was nothing but devastation, desperation and even death.
>
> But, through the heartbreak of it all, there is a bright side to the whole thing. People are . . . walking neighborhoods.
>
> It's quiet, the clang of modern living muffled in the paralyzing snow. And, it seems to shatter the times and turn back the clock.
>
> Families have been sitting together by the glow of logs, and talking to each other, something they usually don't have time to do.
>
> They are all there together because the hockey game was cancelled, as was the Girl Scout meeting and the Women's Club meeting and lodge night.
>
> And there are the little things, like calling a friend just to make sure he's not in trouble; talking to a passer-by about the wonder of it all. There are things like steaming chowder and hot chocolate, which taste so much better when there is only one serving apiece.
>
> It turns time around, slowing things down to a pace where people can be people—at least for a few days.

The *Globe* noted that "PEDESTRIANS FIND JOY ON CAR-EMPTY STREETS":

> Walking along the streets has brought out the sense of neighborliness . . . cross-country skiers have glided past, some even with toddlers riding in backpacks. Jokes are called from shoveler to shoveler. Neighbors help each other with their walks and driveways.
>
> The occasional car is conspicuous in more ways than one. It commands attention as a rare sight. It also commands attention because, on these days of rare clean air, its fumes are a pungent reminder of what pollution is all about.
>
> On one street in Wellesley yesterday about 20 residents set up a table in the snow, chilled some wine in nearby drifts, and laid out a spread of cheese. "Best blizzard we've ever had," said one woman. Elsewhere, at a supermarket on Linden Street, shoppers brought along sleds to carry groceries home. And the parking lot, normally filled with cars, was crowded with sleds. Two young girls even tethered their horse in the lot. Throughout the town, observers said, there was a carnival atmosphere as people filled the streets.

Even people without power or heat for most of the storm expressed a cozy spirit. George Blackman, rector of the Church of Our Savior in Brookline, said: "Thank God for a rectory built in 1885, because we had fireplaces. And the snow had insulated things." . . . They could get light from the lanterns he and his son took Tuesday night from the cupboard where they usually sit from one Christmas carolservice to another. They used them to find leaks in the church and put buckets under them—"wandering around as if it were the Middle Ages," he said. . . . Three people walked in who had skied to his church, so he held an Ash Wednesday service for them.

ACTS OF COURAGE, COMPASSION SHINE IN STORM

Sometimes Mother Nature has to remind us that she's still running the show.

Boston never looked better on a winter afternoon because the cars, trucks and taxis were temporarily gone and there was a Sunday afternoon atmosphere. . . .

And sometimes we have to be reminded in this Age of Cynicism about the basic goodness of most people. . . .

There was a line outside DeLuca's Market on Charles Street because food was running low after the two-day storm. The people stood patiently and some were smiling.

Globe columnist Diane White wrote:

You probably know someone who chose this past week to head south, who, snug and sunburned, weathered the storm in Puerto Rico or Barbados.

On the other hand, those who weren't here really missed something. Don't laugh. . . . It was, for most of us, almost worth the trouble because it was one of those shared public events which will shape our memories forever . . . we'll be telling our grand- children, or somebody's grandchildren, about this in years to come.

There are usually only a few such events in a person's lifetime. Natural disasters. The outbreak of war. Massive technological failure. Assassination. We live through the danger or discomfort or sadness. We remember and we share a common experience that enriches our lives.

Where were you in The Blackout? When Kennedy was shot? On Pearl Harbor Day?

Where were you in the Blizzard of '78?

In years to come, when she recalls the Blizzard of '78, she will remember . . . the look on the face of the man who floated out his second story window to be interviewed by a reporter. The man stood there confused and incredulous, near his half-submerged home, while the reporter intoned, "Hull has been through this before and Hull will go through this again. . . ." She wonders if the man had the strength to slug the reporter.

She will remember a heroine of the storm, a Rockport woman whose house floated out to sea. "What now?" she was asked by a persistent reporter. She shot him a look of exquisite nastiness. "You tell me!" she snapped. Good for her.

This makes the Blizzard sound like fun. However, on the coast, the situation was far from fun:

"Tuesday morning was the worst," remembers Agnes Sheehan. "As high tide came in, houses across the street just smashed apart. They just ripped apart and floated away. Cars were floating by our window. . . ."

The tide was so high that the breakers, some 20 to 40 feet high, roared over seawalls and struck their full force against the oceanfront settlements. Houses were bowled over.

The worst destruction came to Nahant's immediate neighbors, Revere and Winthrop, where, the *Globe* reported, "houses as far away as a quarter mile from the shore were inundated."

One man was swept two blocks inland by the waves. If he had been a surfer, the sheer wonder and amazement of surfing city streets would have made him forget the danger. The streets looked like whitewater rivers. The surf delivered lobsters three and four blocks inland. After the storm, people collected them and ate them.

In Winthrop the wind screamed with such violence that a man hiding in his basement said he did not hear his house fall down above his head. The wind was so strong that salt spray was felt *fourteen miles inland*.

The Lynn *Item* described the situation in Nahant as follows:

STORM SEALS OFF NAHANT

NAHANT—Still isolated . . . Little Nahant is separated from the rest of the town . . .

The recently-built Bass Point Apartments in Nahant were evacuated last night when waves smashed in windows and bore huge rocks into the apartments and the street outside.

The entire Bass Point Road area was reported flooded by seawater and laden with huge rocks which make accessibility difficult and in many cases impossible.

The storm left Nahant a battled, reeling, isolated wreck. . . .

Huge waves and wind which reached 72 miles an hour smashed a large futuristically designed home of an architect on Bass Point Road, destroying the house.

This was the house right next door to ours.

Water three feet deep covered the Nahant Causeway, isolating the community. Persons requiring hospital emergency treatment could not be removed from the island and had to be placed under care of doctors living in Nahant.

Nahant fire fighters were inhibited in fighting the blazes by the flood waters as well as the fact that dangerous electrical currents were running through the flood waters from the burning homes. . . .

Nearly all residences in the Fox Hill Road and Castle Road areas of Nahant remained under water today.

One of the town's landmarks, the town wharf . . . caved in at 10:30 P.M. Monday. Boats crashed against one another. . . . Tudor Beach was torn up with large granite blocks of the sea wall being tossed onto Willow Road. . . . Homes on lower Willow Road were flooded and many of those directly on the ocean had front walls torn down after waves crashed through windows. Water running down Willow Road was so strong it swept several cars along with it. . . .

At 10:30, the water was a few inches deep in basements, a few feet deep on roads. . . .

At 10:31, the water was eight feet deep, roaring into basements, smashing through windows and doors.

Jiggs Donahue and his wife were 71 years old. For much of the morning, he'd stood in waist-deep water in his basement, trying to wake his boarder, Mel Demit, in his basement apartment.

When the wave crashed through, Donahue climbed the stairs to safety. The basement filled to its ceiling with water.

It was too late. If Demit was still in there, he was already dead. They hollered. They yelled. There wasn't an answer . . .

Three days later, scuba divers found Mel Demit's body in the ice and water still flooding his basement apartment.

One moment, said a spectator, a road might have only six inches of water on it and the next instant it was six to eight feet deep in boiling surf. It was like a tidal wave. It was not long until Nahant was turned into three islands. The causeway to Lynn was covered with three feet of water. Nahant was marooned and then the lights went out as the power failed. . . .

After six days of isolation the travel ban was lifted on midnight of February 12. Nahant once more joined the world after Father Neptune's greatest performance.

The day after the storm, the *Globe* told of ruins, rescues, and refugees:

All along Nantasket Avenue [in Hull] rescue crews, neighbors and firefighters were launching small boats to paddle down streets with water 8 to 10 feet deep. . . . Furniture floated on top of the ice-coated water while people, stranded in their homes for more than three days, waved anxiously from second and third story windows at rescuers. . . .

[One resident said:] "Tuesday night, we slept in shifts. We really didn't sleep. The waves kept rocking the house as they pounded against it. I tried to lie on my bed but the pounding surf just kept shaking the bed."

[Another said:] "We looked out the front windows and couldn't believe what we were seeing—huge chunks of the cement sea wall that were floating down Beach Avenue like pieces of cardboard. The waves kept crashing over the house . . . one wave right after another. . . . There was no way we could get out."

In Scituate, sand was nearly six feet deep in the street. For nearly three miles houses were tipped upside down while others were ripped off their foundations. Some had been swallowed by the sea, and several had been destroyed by fire.

Police Chief Gilbert Patterson said: "It is unbelievable and beyond expression." Patterson said that during the height of the storm waves were hurling spray 80 feet high.

In Revere, one third of the city's land area, containing about 2000 of its 17,000 homes, is under as much as six feet of water. The seawalls are completely washed away, or are just piles of rubble that leave the ocean free to reclaim some parts.

"There's no more Beachmont," said one resident.

Rescue workers spoke of the eerie feeling they had as they paddled along streets and looked down and saw the tops of cars under the water.

The most dramatic storm story of all was the following.

He named his pilot boat Can Do, and when no one else dared challenge a wild sea, Frank Quirk would say, "I've got to give it my best shot."

Gloucester had awarded him two Mariner's Medals for heroism

during rescues, defying the sea with his courage, his seamanship and his custom-made boat. On the night of Feb. 6, he set out from Gloucester in the middle of what was to become New England's worst storm of this century, hoping to reach an oil tanker aground in Salem Sound . . .

For the seamen of Gloucester, stormy weather means listening to marine radios. After lunch at the Cape Ann Marina Lounge, Quirk headed for the High Performance Marina where the Can Do was docked to listen to the radios and put the finishing touches on a boat that was always shipshape and spotless.

Late in the afternoon, his friends Dave Warner, Kenny Fuller, Dave Curley, Charlie Bucko, and young Mark Galinas came aboard.

Shortly after 6 P.M. the six heard the Greek-registered tanker Global Hope radio the Coast Guard station at Gloucester. The message was difficult to hear, but the ship apparently was taking on water in the engine room and its captain believed the hull was split. . . .

Quirk decided to help. He called the Coast Guard and told him his plan. The Coast Guard called back and told him not to, that the seas were too rough.

But as Quirk told his friend Keith Trefry, the Gloucester harbormaster, "I've got to give it my best shot."

The Can Do was under way at 7:36 P.M. by Mark Galinas' watch. The 16–year old Gloucester High School student was ashore. The last time he had gone out with Capt. Quirk he had missed a couple days of school, and he couldn't do it again. . . .

The wind was blowing between 40 and 70 knots, the seas were running 15 to 20 feet, and visibility was 50 yards at best in blinding snow.

The sea smashed Quirk's boat, taking first the Can Do's radar, compass and fathometer. Then it took the power and some of Quirk's blood when an enormous wave shattered the pilot house window where he stood.

Then, the implacable sea took Quirk and the four men who had accompanied him on his last mission.

The next day two bodies from the *Can Do* washed ashore on Nahant's Short Beach, right by the Coast Guard Station. The sea gave up her dead.

(13) Hurricano

The storm of January 20th (the one two weeks before the Great Blizzard) sent up satisfyingly sizeable waves to stare at, as they smashed smartly against the pointed prow of the deck. They deposited freezing spray all night, and in the morning the House was transformed into a fairy palace of crystal. The snow covered everything in sight with a coat of impossibly white paint from Heaven.

That evening the Housebugs talked of storms. I confessed that I longed to see a really great storm, even a hurricane. Mother retorted, "I think if you ever saw one from the inside you would not long to see another." (All mothers are practical.) Libby agreed, and told us about the San Ciriaco Hurricane of 1899, which her grandmother had seen on Puerto Rico as a child. It had raised storm waves so high that they passed over the entire length of the island, and killed thousands of people. Then Lazarus told his tale of a hurricane in the Florida keys (back in the 1930s, I think):

"Winds impaled this guy. On a two-by-four. Ran right through him. Under his ribs, over his kidneys. Doctor found him, after the storm. Offered him morphine before taking the two-by-four out. He refused the morphine. Drank two beers instead. Then said, 'When the timber's out, I'll die.'" Lazarus paused.

"Well?" asked Mother.

"Did," concluded Lazarus.

Then it was Evan's turn. His uncle had been a cook for the U.S. Army and had been in the August hurricane of 1945 in Guam. He had survived only by walking into a massive refrigerator. The building was swept away around him, but he and the refrigerator survived.

"Now that's the kind of storm I want to see," I said, impulsively—and immediately felt foolish, as every eye turned and gave me the look you give a very small and foolish child.

"Hey, Jack," Libby laughed, "you know what psychiatrists say about that Thing of yours? That fascination with disasters?"

I guessed "death wish," but Libby had a subtler answer: "It's a way of warding off depression. Really. I'll bet you never feel happier than when you're watching some disaster, right?"

I hadn't really seen any great disaster, so I couldn't say. But I tried to explain that it's not disaster I love, just storms; I have no desire to see a war, or an earthquake. "I have no need to ward off depression, thank you, but I could use something to ward off amateur psychoanalysts."

But Evan pressed Libby's point like the scientist he is: "What is it in you that loves storms so much, Jack?"

I said it was the *height*—not just the literal height of the waves, though that's a big part of it, but what that physical height seems to be a symbol of: spiritual height, or hierarchy, or the heroic. "When you see the sea rising higher and higher, don't you feel a wonderful kind of fear? Not like the fear of death or pain, but more like the fear of God. When the sea rises in power and glory, doesn't it feel like God arising? Barging into your life, interrupting, rearranging everything, killing and bringing to life? Do you know what I mean? The thrill is in the contrast, isn't it? The contrast between the horizontal and the vertical. The sea is ordinarily the flattest, the most horizontal thing we ever see, flatter than a piece of paper, a piece of paper a thousand miles wide—and then, one stormy day, it suddenly rises, it starts to *go vertical*. And our flattened spirits rise with it. They rise from the dead with each wave. *You* rise with each rising wave. Like a surfer. Watching a storm is letting your spirit go surfing when your body can't."

Evan suddenly interjected another angle into the conversation. (He has never managed the art of smooth conversation.) He said "To me, a wave is like a home run. It is an arch of triumph high in the air. The geometry of the arc is the same for a wave and for a home run, I think. Isn't it?"

Before anyone could answer, Day dashed through the room pretending to be chased by Night. "*That's* what a wave is like," chimed in Eva, joining in the tumble of metaphors. "Like a cat."

"Like a lion," I added. "Like the King of Beasts."

Lazarus had been giving Dudley a bath. Hearing my voice, Dudley escaped the bathroom and ran to my feet. Lazarus observed, "There's your wave. Better not get too close."

The warning was too late. Dudley stood directly in front of me to give me a gift of spray, right up into my face. A matching spray of laughter fell down.

"But what do *you* say, Mother?" Libby asked. "Everybody takes a turn in this metaphor-go-round. What are waves to you?"

"Angels," answered Mother. "Ascending and descending on Jacob's ladder."

We could not know that we would be plunged into those angels in a very few days.

* * * * *

The next Monday, Nature seemed to be holding her breath. There was an ominous feeling in the air. The sky was a color borrowed from one of my nightmares: grey but with a tinge of sickly yellow, almost green, like rotten mustard. Dudley whined all day and refused to come out of his bed. Night and Day no longer played. Everyone seemed on edge. Another storm was coming, and some forecasters were now predicting it would be even bigger than the last one.

I had three classes that day at Boston College. I went to my 11 and 12 o'clock classes nervously, feeling I might miss something significant in Nahant, and returned as quickly as I could in the afternoon, after my 2 o'clock class, as it began to snow and blow heavily. The second blizzard was beginning, and signs pointed to something that would break the all-time records set by the first one.

As I drove back to Nahant the heavens were falling and the sea was rising. At Long Beach the sea was all white agitation, like a bathtub filled with soap and hyperactive infants. As I began to cross the causeway I noticed, with a start, that there was no more beach. The sea had invaded and occupied all of it, and was now attacking the low little dunes that were all that stood between the causeway and the sea. Soon the causeway would be conquered by the sea from both sides, like the pincers of an army, and it would be closed. In fact, I looked into my rear-view mirror and saw the police setting up a barricade at the landward end already. I was the last car they had let through.

As my attention had drifted to the rear, I had failed to notice the alarmingly quick change in the sea at my side. It seemed now that the police had closed the causeway a moment too late. For as I passed a low dune midway across the causeway, a wave simply carved away the dune, then the whole sea seemed to rush through the newly opened breach at once. A second wave leaped onto the causeway right behind me, at an angle. I saw it approaching at an unnatural speed, driven by a sixty mile-per-hour wind. I had been deliberately dawdling on the causeway, like a tourist, watching the waves. Now, one was chasing me! I floored the accelerator. The car coughed and stalled. The wave petered out under the car. But another, bigger one moved in behind it. Since my car was a small one, I prayed the Normandy Sailor's Prayer: "Lord, Your sea is very big and my boat is very small," simply substituting "car" for "boat." I floored the accelerator and turned the ignition key. The car hesitated, then started. It began to move forward again, but with agonizing slowness. The second wave thumped the trunk and shook the car, then splattered flat underneath it. But now the third wave was coming, and it was even bigger and faster than the other two. It was coming right down the street like an animal, and gaining on me. The speedometer crept up to 20 mph. The wave was fifteen feet behind me and five feet high, higher than the car. I reached 30 mph. The wave was only five feet behind me now, but only four feet high. I reached 40. The wave took the left rear fender in its jaws and shook the car like a cat shaking a mouse. But it was only two feet high now. I skidded to the right, almost into the bay, and suddenly leaped straight ahead at 50 mph. out of the grip of the exhausted wave.

As I escaped the wave, I had the scary feeling of being watched by the water, fingered for destruction, *pursued* by some alien force in the wave. "It's out to get me!" I thought. It had risen out of its bed and come alive. It was not a lifeless mineral, or a slow-moving vegetable, but an animated animal, a hungry hound out to bite me, a cannibal determined to eat me. Of course I knew this was only fantasy. But with the flood of water came a flood of childhood memories and fears. I think the most rational philosopher in the world would have believed the sea was an animal or an evil angel if he had been with me in my car during that moment on the causeway.

The sea was doing the same thing all along the shoreline north and south of Boston: waking and rising and stalking its prey. Having conquered the beaches, it began to occupy the seaside towns. It stayed in the streets, like an uninvited guest. It lapped and panted at doors like a hungry dog. It crawled into cellars like a homeless cat. It climbed through windows like a robber. It insinuated itself into living rooms and invaded the privacy of bedrooms and bathrooms, in violation of elementary good manners. It *lived.* It was no longer sodium chloride suspended in two parts hydrogen and one part oxygen; it was Poseidon's wrath.

As I negotiated the rest of the exposed causeway, I repeatedly felt the car jump under me when the wind gusted. It felt like riding a horse. I thought the screaming wind would inevitably tear the canvas top off the convertible. Water came in even through the tightly closed windows. Outside, wind and snow and sea and spray were becoming increasingly one and increasingly omnipresent.

At the end of the causeway there is a beachfront restaurant that marks the beginning of Little Nahant. Waves were already surrounding it, sloshing at its sides. When I came to the second causeway, between Little Nahant and Nahant, the gloom cleared for a moment so I could see, out across Short Beach and the breaking waves, Egg Rock, the 55-foot-high rock a quarter mile offshore. Swells were breaking *over* it! Sixty foot swells! Not sixty foot *spray* (which I have seen before, when twenty foot waves crash) or even sixty foot *waves* (which I have never seen), but sixty foot *swells*. Breaking waves are usually bigger than the swells that cause them. If these swells crashed against a 60-foot-high sea wall they should send the spray two hundred feet up!

I could see in front of me that Short Beach was gone too, and the sea was beginning to slosh over its causeway, but I accelerated through the slosh. When I reached the higher ground by the police station at the end of the causeway, I stopped and watched, heart pounding. Many people said of this storm that they "got seasick just watching it" from land; but I was in Heaven. I don't know whether I was there for three minutes or three hours. But it was dark when I left.

After being hypnotized by the sight for so long, I suddenly remembered my friends: they might be in danger. I skidded the car through the snowy streets as fast as I dared. When I passed the row of beachfront houses on pilings on Castle Road, spray from the waves was shooting over their roofs and spilling onto my car as I drove past. The engine sputtered as I climbed the high ground at Bass Point, and I wisely parked the car halfway up Trimountain Road, high enough to be safe from the sea even if it flooded the street below.

I ran down the road and into the house. There was spray in the street but not seawater, at least not yet. Inside, I found only Mother, Lazarus, and Mister Mumm. They were tending the fire in the fireplace and listening to storm reports on the battery-operated radio. (The electricity had gone out.) The other Housebugs had evacuated to the mainland before the causeway closed. A few minutes after I arrived, police came by to evacuate the remaining residents of our street. Some went willingly, some went unwillingly, and some stayed, willfully. Mother insisted that there be someone in the house at all times—that's what a home *means*, she said—so she and Lazarus and Mister Mumm refused to evacuate. I insisted on staying too and riding out the storm with them. Mother agreed, seeing the gleam in my eye and the strength of the house. Through a crack between the boards on the boarded-up seaside picture window, I stared at the great storm, terrible and wonderful.

Swells out at sea beyond Bailey's Hill were rising thirty feet, and twenty-foot waves were pounding the foot of the Hill. They were not as enormous as the waves I had seen at the two causeways, but they were more terrifying because they were in my own back yard! They were also terrifying because I had been told that they were impossible. I once asked the scientists out at Northeastern University's Oceanographic Center on East Point how high the waves could possibly get at Bailey's Hill, and I had been assured that there was not enough fetch for a wave ever to be more than eight or ten feet high in this shallow estuary. "Highly impossible!" was what the scientist had called such waves. Well, the highly impossible waves were now impossibly high.

At first they simply spilled foam forward horizontally, but after a while they began to turn into vertically plunging breakers with "barrels" big enough for trucks to surf inside. They fell like blind giants suddenly tripping over invisible obstacles. Sometimes, after the fall of one of these giant waves, a fire-hose-like spray of white foam would rise from the place of its fall and shoot fifty feet into the sky, as the air compressed by the enclosing barrel found an outlet. Once, I saw a plunging wave simultaneously shoot *two* streams of icy spray out of its tube, horizontally rather than vertically, one on each end of the tube, like a giant violently blowing his nose without a handkerchief.

None of us slept at all that night. When the sea rises out of her bed, none of us can fall into ours.

I felt like a captain staying with his ship as it was in danger of sinking. None of us knew for sure that we would survive. Our souls were as restless as the sea. We stared, and we talked, and we prayed—and we sang. The four of us were a perfect quartet. Lazarus' gravelly Russian bass sounded as if it was coming out of the earth and out of a depth of time as ancient as Abraham. I sang mellow baritone, Mister Mumm tenor, like a bird from Paradise, and Mother a strong contralto that reminded me of Mary's voice from Peter, Paul and Mary. When we sang William Whiting's "Sailor's Hymn" a capella, we sounded like a full Russian chorus, at least to ourselves, for we were inside the music, not outside, like an audience. The waves added a fifth bass. Deep called unto deep at the noise of God's waterspouts. All His waves and billows were going over us. It was the most memorable music I have ever heard in my life—and we were *making* it.

We sang the Sailor's Hymn over and over. It is a prayer for salvation from the sea, and I felt, as sharply as a wind in my face, that we were in fact literally saving lives by our prayer-music:

> **Eternal Father, strong to save,**
> **Whose arm doth bind the restless wave,**
> **Who bidd'st the mighty ocean deep**
> **Its own appointed limits keep:**
> **O hear us when we cry to Thee**
> **For those in peril on the sea.**

We also prayed together the "Prayer to Be Used in Storms at Sea" from the Anglican Book of Common Prayer:

> **O most powerful and glorious Lord God, at whose command the winds blow and lift up the waves of the sea, and Who stillest the rage thereof; we Thy creatures, but miserable sinners, do in this our great distress cry unto Thee for help. Save, Lord, or else we perish! We confess, when we have been safe and seen all things quiet about us, we have forgotten Thee our God, and refused to hearken to the still voice of Thy word, and to obey Thy commandments. But now we see how terrible Thou art in all Thy works of wonder: the great God to be feared above all; and therefore we adore Thy divine Majesty, acknowledging Thy power and imploring Thy goodness. Help, Lord, and save us for Thy mercy's sake.**

We prayed some Psalms in Lazarus's old King James English version of the Bible, whose language is as high and stately as the waves themselves. (Flattened, modernized translations would never meet the height of these waves.)

> **We will not fear**
> **Though the earth be shaken,**

> **Though the midst of the sea become mountains,**
> **Though the waters thereof roar and be troubled.**
>   **(Psalm 46:2–3)**
>
> **Thou didst divide the sea by Thy strength;**
> **Thou breakest the heads of the dragons in the waters.**
>   **(Psalm 74:13)**
>
> **They that go down to the sea in ships,**
> **That do business in great waters,**
> **These see the works of the Lord**
> **And His wonders in the deep.**
> **For He commandeth, and raiseth the stormy wind,**
> **Which lifteth up the waves thereof.**
> **They mount up to the heaven,**
> **They go down again to the depths.**
> **Their soul is melted because of trouble.**
> **They reel to and fro,**
> **And stagger like a drunken man,**
> **And they are at their wits' end.**
> **Then they cry unto the Lord in their trouble,**
> **And He bringeth them out of their distresses.**
> **He maketh the storm a calm,**
> **So that the waves thereof are still.**
> **Then are they glad because they be quiet,**
> **So He bringeth them unto their desired haven.**
> **Oh that men would praise the Lord for His goodness,**
> **And for His wonderful works to the children of men!**
>   **(Psalm 107:23–31)**

Lazarus was the only one who dared to go out of the House that evening. I marveled at his recklessness: this old man would stand on the porch as giant waves crashed over his head. Each wave I thought would be his last, as it rose up and crashed down like a giant fist; but the shattered water just fell onto him like pieces of a broken silver Christmas tree ornament.

Then he got his high boots on and stalked up and down Bass Point Road through eighteen inches of fast-moving water. Mother did not berate him for his recklessness, but acted as if he was indestructible—which he indeed seemed to be.

I asked him, when he returned, "Weren't you afraid?"

"Of what?"

"Those rocks tumbling down the street, for one thing."

"Why should I be?"

"They can kill you!"

In reply, he looked at me strangely and muttered something that I thought sounded like "Been there, done that." But he would not explain.

But even Lazarus joined us inside when the second high tide came. And when the water rose to the level of the first floor and began pouring in through the cracks in the walls, we all moved up to the second floor with the animals. We began to hear other sounds in the water: a moaning, groaning sound like a chained giant; then a grinding sound, as big blocks of ice and boulders churned together in the giant's mixer; and then a booming sound, as if the giant's hammer struck the earth. But the most dangerous sound was the crashing of debris against the foundations of the House, and even, occasionally, against the walls.

The sea continued to slosh through cracks in the walls, and everything on the first floor was now flooded. But the angled porch deck broke the force of the waves, the house stood, and the second floor remained fairly dry. The tide was due to ebb that night. The most dangerous tide would be the third one, the next morning at 11 o'clock.

Toward dawn, I drifted in and out of sleep as the seawater drifted in and out of the House. The others slept not at all, I think. Dudley climbed up to the third floor, crawled into bed with me, and whined.

I woke early to winter's late, grey first-light dawn. The sea was still raging but the tide was low. The waves were still monstrous, but they were breaking much farther out, and only their wind-whipped spray was reaching the house. The first floor had drained, and Mother had lit the stove and was baking bread as if everything was back to normal.

Of course I absolutely had to go outside to see the storm close up, now that the tide had ebbed and the immediate danger from the waves had subsided. But the waves themselves had not. In fact, while yesterday's winds had blown the tops clear off the waves, the wind, it seemed, had now died down a little, so that the waves were able to rise even higher. Mother understood my obsession. She had to remind me to eat breakfast first. I had simply forgotten to eat, the storm was so beautiful. I gulped down some bread and tea, threw on my parka, mittens, and boots, and stepped out the front door. Evan came with me. He had a scientist's fascination with the storm; I had a poet's.

We were fortunate in timing the opening of the door. The wind had died down for a moment. But that window of opportunity soon closed as the wind began to blow at hurricane force again. I had to cup my mittened hands around my face to see anything at all; otherwise, the wind instantly whipped my eyes shut with arrows of icy spray shot from a thousand invisible bows.

I tried to say something to Evan. He was three feet in front of my face. He heard nothing. I shouted at the top of my voice. He heard nothing. We had to put our heads together and yell, and then we heard each other more through our bones than through our ears. Now I knew how the deaf hear.

What I heard very clearly was the incessant pounding of the earth by the waves. All the bones in my body heard them. The waves sounded like cracks of thunder. In fact, at first I thought it *was* thunder, and looked up at the sky. I had never heard waves that sounded like that before. Then I turned to the sea and *saw* the thunder, and was wonderfully terrified. The only thing in this world that Saint Thomas Aquinas was afraid of was thunder; imagine him *seeing* it! Today I felt as if I could actually see and hear a Viking god: these waves were the iron hammer of Thor.

The wind quickly deposited freezing water on every hair on my head despite my double parka hood. It got into my feet despite my boots, shoes and two pairs of socks. The sleet and snow were blowing through the air in everything *but* straight lines, getting into every crevice.

As soon as we took a few steps away from the protection of the House, we simply could not exhale when facing the wind. When we turned our backs to the wind, it was almost as difficult to inhale. I was drowning in an ocean of air.

We both went back inside. Evan did not go out again. "You're crazy to go out there, you know," he said to me. The first thing I did was to make a blizzard-watcher for myself, a sort of lensless binoculars, out of two metal tubes that I covered with duck tape and then taped together. This protected my eyes from watering up, icing up, or snowing up.

When I went out again, I tried taking little breaths, like a panting dog. That worked well enough to avoid suffocation, at least—for a while. But after two minutes, a sudden great gulf of air half sucked my lungs empty, and I gasped for breath. Having exhaled for me, the wind then turned and inhaled for me when I turned around, roaring back into my lungs like a wave onto a beach. I tried to keep my lips tightly shut, but my lips were forced back against my face in a contorted smile. Even through closed lips I could taste the wind. It tasted like Italian ice flavored with salt shot into my face with a gun. I thought I now understood for the first time the very first sentence in the history of philosophy, for today it had come true: Thales of Miletus' saying "Everything is water."

It took a while for me to focus in the confusion of snow, rain, sleet, salt, spray, and debris zooming together in raging confusion through the air. When I did, I noticed that the wind was not just blowing *down* bushes and small trees, it was picking them *up* and tossing them into the air. It seemed to be blowing from all directions at once, including the ground: gusts seemed to rip *upwards*, taking sheets of mud and debris with them like baby tornadoes.

Below the chaos in the air was chaos on the ground. All kinds of shapeless jetsam was lying on the snowy mud, all kinds of flotsam was lurching through the street (which was now a sloshing river), and all kinds of projectiles were being launched through the air. I was on a battlefield! An aluminum storm door with broken glass in it zoomed by on the wind. I ducked. It could have decapitated me. So much was moving so quickly that (paradoxically) it seemed to be happening in slow motion, as it does at the brink of a fall or an automobile crash. I was under a spell. I could not move.

But I could move my mind, and the next thing I turned my attention to was the sound. It was surprising that I had not noticed it immediately. Only the pain of the wind's touch could have distracted me from it. (Touch is the primal sense, after all.) Yesterday, the wind had sounded like a steam engine roaring down the tracks; today, it sounded like the screech of its braking wheels, or the incessant screaming of a mad animal, or the howls of the damned.

One continuous sound dominated everything: the screaming of the wind. Nothing else could be heard above it. But if you were close enough to the ocean, you could also hear (or rather feel) the deep bass notes of the waves accompanying the shrieking wind. And if you were near trees, you could also hear the wind *whistling* through the flailing limbs, and frequent POPs as it pulled the tortured limbs out of their sockets.

The whole world seemed to be screaming. It was the Primal Scream of a monster from pre-creation chaos. Or it was a djinn, a demon from Hell, or a demon-possessed lunatic with wild, bulging eyes howling "EEEE—EEEE—EEEE" directly into your face from a foot away without pausing for breath, until you went mad.

I deliberately attended to this horror, straining my spirit to hear the Voice of the Storm. Some primitive secret in my heart opened to the primitive secret hidden in this howling wind; something sleeping beneath the cellar of civilized consciousness. I wondered whether it was the Thing behind the Door in my nightmare.

The wind was coming mainly out of the north now, so I took refuge in the relative shelter of the south side of the house, looked left (east) to see my beloved familiar sea—and found Another in her place! It felt like suddenly hearing your mother speak with the voice of a wolf.

I knew the hundreds of different sounds the waves made on other days as well as a mother knows her baby's hundred different gurgles. Occasionally Baby will utter a new sound. But today's sea voice was *wholly* different. Its other voices had been words; this was war. They had been languages; this was the destruction of language. The birth-giving Mother had turned into a devouring giantess. Roused from her long, ancient sleep, she was in a fey and foul mood, thumping her mile-wide fists in a raging fit.

My musings were interrupted by the snapping of a tortured tree limb. It missed my head by about two feet and crashed against the wall of the House behind me. I felt as if the wind had spotted me as its target, seized a weapon, and lunged at my head with it. I blinked and shook myself free from the spell.

I next directed my spirit to leave the vehicle of my ears and enter the vehi-cle of my eyes. My spirit obeyed, got off the train and into the plane, exchanging Sound's track for Light's airspace. I turned my attention to the appalling and glorious sight of the tortured sea.

Large bits of civilization heaved in its waves. One large object—some part of a house, a closet or a shed—was being tossed twenty or thirty feet up into the air above the foam by two waves crashing against each other, like two giants playing with a dwarf. Then the sight of the waves was obliterated by driving snow as the wind shifted to the east and came off the water, at hurricane velocity. Wind and water were joined without a joint. Heaven and earth met, married, mingled, became one flesh. The horizon simply disappeared, and I was lost and disoriented in an infinite sea of whiteness. Now I understood Melville's musings on "The Whiteness of the Whale" in *Moby Dick*. The demonic here was white, all white.

There was no longer any clear separation between land and sea, between air and sea, or between air and land. The land and air had both become a sea of snow and sleet. The land seemed as mobile as the sea, the sea as whirly as the air, and the air as solid as the land. The pantheist nightmare had come true: the dissolution of all order in an all-encompassing white oneness, a churning mixture of undifferentiated ooze from the time before water, air and land were assigned their separate identities and places. The storm was a time machine, a trip back into the primal energies of the universe.

I had to see those monster waves more clearly. So I went back into the house and climbed to the third floor tower to see whether perhaps the slit in the tiny boarded-up windows (we had to board up all the windows, of course) was wide enough to see through. To my great delight, it was. And though I could not look into the wind because it blew my eyes shut, I could look *along* the wind when its gyrating spirals turned to blow out to sea, which happened every few seconds. My sight was like a kite that went where the wind carried it.

I put my eyes to the slit; the wind turned round; and time, breath, and heartbeat all stopped while my mind rushed forward at preternatural speed. As I stared at the huge waves I felt the hairs on the back of my neck stand up. Something—either my angel or my adrenaline—kept pumping images into my mind as incessantly as the waves themselves. Never had I felt such a sensory overload.

The definitive image was that of mountains. The adjective "mountainous" has become a cliché in writing about great storm waves; but it is inevitable, and remains the most accurate adjective. The sea was a range of moving mountains made of water instead of earth. Waves *shouldn't be that high*. Nothing that high should move that fast. Nothing that fast should be that high.

Imagine you are driving along a pretty country road and you come to a tall, wide, green mountain. Now imagine you see the whole mountain come to life, undulate, and rush straight at you. Now imagine not just one mountain but a whole mountain range coming at you like hungry giants who mean to eat you. This is what it felt like to watch those waves.

After the mountains came the military images. The sea was an immense, roaring battlefield "where ignorant armies clashed by night." Swell upon swell, surge upon surge they came, an endless army of waves. As each line of troops broke rank and died, it was replenished by another. I thought of Robert Frost's lines:

> **The shattered water made a misty din.**
> **Great waves looked over others coming in**
> **And thought of doing something to the shore**
> **That water never did to land before.**

The greatest power of the waves was hidden beneath the sea's surface like torpedoes, and when they hit the concrete sea wall protecting the houses on our street, the wall exploded like the hull of a torpedoed ship. Then, having been an army and a navy, the waves sent up spray that became an air force of kamikaze pilots diving down and exploding in suicide missions.

The waves were also giant earthmovers and excavators. As they receded with a hoarse, rattling roar, they scooped out great masses of sand and stone from the beach.

And then the whole sea was one gigantic witch's cauldron, bubbling and boiling, hissing like serpents, concocting all the wars in the world.

And then it was the hammer of Thor. The waves were plunging, not spilling, and making a sound that waves make at Waimea Bay in Hawaii but never in Nahant: the beating of a gigantic drum. Even from the third floor of the House my whole body could feel the pounding of the ground under the booming breakers. I thought the ground would split and shatter.

Thor's spiky gray hair streamed out like sparks from struck steel. He was in full battle gear, scornfully laughing, smashing and smiting friend and foe alike with his giant hammer in a demonic joy of formless, indiscriminate rage.

Of course I am no polytheist or idolater, but today the sea was no longer merely the sea, but something more like Thor or Earthshaker Poseidon. Clearly the shaker must transcend what he shakes; and the force now shaking the earth was obviously something more like a god than a scientific principle. Today even a good Jew, Christian, or Muslim would be tempted to polytheism. Perhaps it is good to be tempted, as long as the temptation is conquered. Never to be even tempted to see Poseidon in the sea, or Apollo in the sun, or Zeus in the thunderbolt—is that not a great loss to the human imagination?

Today Poseidon was a hamfisted colossus, wakened from drunken sleep and pounding his fists in a blind rage. The dirty water was his slobbering saliva squirting between his rotting teeth, the gasping white wind was his hysterical breath, the invisible sun his blindness, and the flying snow his hair. King Lear went mad in such a storm.

Then the waves became a berserk ballet of dancing dervishes running up on each other's backs, slapping at each other's sides, and smashing each other full in the face. Huge lumps of water rose and collided belly to belly like sumo wrestlers.

Then came the animals: thundering elephants, raging bulls, mastodons with convulsions, dinosaurs flailing and thrashing in death spasms. Then a pack of rabid wolves foaming at the mouth and swallowing their own foam, biting at the backs of the preceding waves but never catching them, and frothing in frustration. And then the horses.

Whenever the waves were big enough to ride, I have always thought of them as white-maned horses, those glorious beasts that, amazingly, let us tame them and ride them. But today they were untameable wild horses, gnashing their teeth at the land as at their food. As each wave rose, it formed a dark tube, a mouth rimmed with white foam at the top and bottom like teeth. If they had their way they would devour all the land.

The profusion of images intensified: caverns, canyons, castles, towers, rockets, dragons: a cornucopia of vertical images. For the waves were moving *vertically*. Deep aquatic caves opened between them, caverns that would suck you down into their bottomless depths forever, into the center of the earth, into hell. At the same time peaks of white leaped *up* heavenward like birds or rockets. I half expected them to fly away and never return to earth. The sea was a frantic fairyland of castles, throwing up impossibly thin towers of froth that made mad King Ludwig's Bavarian castle look heavy and earthbound—and then destroying them a second after creating them, in a fit of artistic frenzy. Then the castles became modern skyscrapers as the waves rose still higher. The wind whipping the tops off these skyscrapers was Rodin smashing Tokyo. Then the waves became Egyptian pyramids and the ocean was a dancing desert.

Finally, the explosion of each breaking wave was another Big Bang, creating new worlds, each water droplet a universe. At this point my supersaturated mind itself seemed to explode like an over-inflated balloon. I left my mind and entered into an ecstasy of adoration. Of this I will say only two things: that those waves nearly killed me, just seeing them; and that I was half way to Heaven.

*   *   *   *   *

The sea kept rising higher all morning. Mother, Lazarus, and Mister Mumm had taken refuge on the second floor after having rescued as many items as possible from the kitchen and the living room, which was now taking on water through the floor and walls.

I awakened from my ecstasy utterly unaware how long I had been in it. One part of me was aware that hunger and thirst were happening in another part of me. Seeking some cheese and bread, if any was still dry, I left my room to go down to the kitchen. (I didn't know that Mother had already taken most of the food onto the second floor.) Just as I reached the top of the stairs that led down into the living room, the Great Grey Inexorable Wave exploded, as suddenly as a bomb, right out of my dream.

It crashed through the wall that kept my dreams from entering the real world, the wall that kept the sea from entering the house. Three sounds mingled in terrible trinity: breaking glass, breaking wood, and breaking wave. The wave, having risen over the deck outside like a cobra, then opened its mouth and bit down upon the house to devour it. It crashed directly onto the boarded-up picture window between the deck and the living room. Although this window and this wall, like the deck, were turned at an angle to the sea, it was directly in the wave's impact zone. The glass and boards did not so much shatter as explode.

The wave rolled not just *into* the living room but *through* it. I was more terrified by the breaking of the boundaries than by the breaking of the glass. The ocean was now in my living room! It was Doing Things there. It was not just a wave breaking *into* the house; it was a wave breaking *in* the house. I could have surfed from the stove to the front door. The thought was as shocking as the sight.

I knew that waves come in sets of threes. All surfers know this, and all scientists deny it. So my first thought was to look through the shattered window for the next wave; and when I saw it, the rhythm of my heart and breath stopped, in deference to the rhythm of the wave. Air ceased to move through my lungs, and air also seemed to cease to move through the room as the wave displaced even the air. When It was here, there was no room for any other.

There was a moment just before it broke when it stopped, motionless, like a fist raised up in threat, or a projectile at the top of its parabola, suspended between its rise and its fall. The spell of this timeless second was broken by bouncing brine from the wave's crash. It leaped up the stairs and cut into my face with a hundred icy needles. I grabbed the banister like a life preserver. It receded, and then the third wave struck.

It hit what was left of the deck, and bounced like a giant beach ball. Twenty feet of water sent up seventy feet of foam, covering the whole house and making it disappear for a moment from the universe of light as if it had fallen into a Black Hole. When the water struck the house I felt a jolt like a speeding car slamming on its brakes. The bottom half of the wave surged through the cellar, cracked the floorboards on the landward half of the living room, and rose up through the break in the floor that it had made. It climbed up the stairs and grabbed at my legs. I fled as from a wild animal. Its tongues

lapped at me. I fancied I heard its throat panting. Then the backwash from the
wave surrounded the house. I thought it would surely rip it from its foundations and take it out to sea. I was amazed that the house still stood.

Mother caught me as I fell, whether from the physical shock of the wave
against the house or the shock of fear, I don't know. The dizzy spell passed, and
so, it seemed, did the worst danger. The house stood, and no worse wave came,
though smaller ones kept sloshing through the first floor. The sea slowly subsided, growling like a beast grudgingly giving up its lost prey. After ten minutes it was clear that the house had won. It stood in a tide of debris like a shak-
en warrior standing amid fallen comrades on a bloody battlefield. Water ran
out of it as out of a sieve. House and inhabitants alike were shaken but unbroken, except for the deck, the big window, and half the living room floor. When
the waves stopped coming in the window we all went downstairs to survey the
damage. The first thing Mother did was to open the front door and look for
refugees. There were none. Within an hour we had cleaned up the glass and
shattered wood and were able to light a fire in the fireplace to begin the dry-
ing-out process.

Day and Night would still not come down from the attic, where they had
taken refuge in each other's fur. Dudley was not to be seen or heard.

Even when the tide ebbed, the house was still surrounded by moving seawater. It was an island. That was the thing I found most fascinating of all: that
where once there was a street, now there was a sea. Ocean waves in city
streets!—an inversion of the fundamental cosmic order. It was like "Jaws"
coming right up onto Captain Quint's boat to devour him. I think that, rather
than merely drowning, is the terror of Noah's flood: the overturning of the
foundations of cosmic order, the apocalyptic trespass over God-appointed
boundaries. God's magnificent speech to Job, his answer to all Job's questions,
uses this image:

> **Then the Lord answered Job out of the whirlwind, and said,**
> **Who is this that darkeneth counsel by words without knowledge?**
> **Gird up now thy loins like a man,**
> **For I will demand of thee, and answer thou me.**
> **Where wast thou when I laid the foundations of the earth?**
> **Declare, if thou hast understanding . . .**
> **When the morning stars sang together,**
> **And all the sons of God shouted for joy?**
> **Or who shut up the sea with doors, when it brake forth,**
> **As if it had issued from the womb?**
> **When I said. . . . Hitherto shalt thou come, but no further,**
> **And here shall thy proud waves be stayed?**

The deepest terror last night was not the fear of death, or of its pain or violence—not even the fear of being smashed to pieces by a giant wave, or by a house that the wave held in its fist. That is part of the natural order. Man is *supposed to be* mortal. But the sea is not supposed to be here. Waves are not supposed to be that high. When neighbors said, "It's never come this high!" they meant "It *can't* come this high!" The sea, the biggest thing in the world, had escaped its cage, trespassed its divinely ordained natural limit ("hitherto shalt thou come, but no further"). It was an icon of apocalypse. Was it a prophetic warning of things to come? Was it a sign? If so, we do well to fear, for the sign is not greater than the thing it signifies.

*   *   *   *   *

The storm was like a drug to me. I had to have more.

The waves had waned enough and the wind had died down enough to think of the possibility of climbing the Hill without being blown into the sea. I had to try it. I had to see the beautiful and terrible sight of the raging sea from a more Godlike vantage point: from the Hill that was the navel of my world.

I layered as many dry clothes on as I could, went downstairs, stepped over the broken living room floorboards, closed the door between the living room and the tiny front entrance hallway—and promptly bumped into Mister Mumm, who was standing there keeping his eye on the street. "Going out again?" he asked blandly, as I put on the hip boots that were shared by all of us. (No one knew whose they originally were.)

"Yes," I said, "The wind seems to be dying down a little."

"It will pick up again, you know."

"Maybe. But it doesn't seem to be doing that."

"How do you know this calm isn't the eye of the hurricane?"

"It's February. This can't be a hurricane."

"Didn't you hear the radio? Its winds reached 125 miles per hour. That's a major hurricane."

"But it's a Nor'easter. It's stuck offshore. It's not moving like a hurricane. Therefore it's not a hurricane. Therefore it doesn't have an eye. Therefore this is not the eye of a hurricane. Q.E.D."

"How dogmatic you sound!" That was all he said, but it was enough to make me feel annoyed. I pushed past him and out the door without reply except an embarrassed smile.

I sloshed across the street, which was now a brook full of stepping stones, to the higher ground on the other side, and strode with determination to the Hill. The ascent was difficult but negotiable from the landward side, by the little park with the gazebo. And the reward at the summit was magnificent: the vista of a whole sea of monster waves. The gift was repeatedly given and then taken back by shifting curtains of snow. It was much colder and windier at the top than below, colder than I had counted on. But the glory of standing here, on this bald little Everest atop the whirling world, was well worth the pain of ice needles being inserted into my face. I was on the holy mountain. All was transfigured before my eyes. It was good for me to be here with the Storm Master. I would not have been surprised to see Moses and Elijah appear. If they were not here, their *dimension* was.

Then the non-eye of the non-hurricane passed, and the wind whipped round to return with impossible intensity, lashing me with lariats. The whole world began to white out in blindness and whirl in vertigo, and my spirit followed. I was now utterly unprotected on the most exposed spot on the coast in the most serious storm in recorded history. Mister Mumm was right. I was a fool. I was in real danger.

My spirit had nearly died of exultation a few minutes ago; now my body nearly died of exhaustion. You simply cannot breathe with a 90-mile-per hour wind blowing straight into your face. And you simply cannot see when the wind pierces your eyeballs. And you simply cannot hear anything except the insane, incessant screaming of the demon wind. And soon you cannot feel anything either, not even the cold and pain. That is when you know you are dying. All your senses go numb. When your spirit follows them, you are dead.

Suddenly the wind lashed out and whipped my feet out from under me. I fell onto icy snow and could not rise against both the wind and the slippery ground. I knew my only hope was to wait for the wind to abate. I was wholly at its mercy. But it had none. It was blowing straight out of Hell, and screaming "Abandon all hope, ye who enter here!" I could no more move into that wind than into an elephant. I tried to slide at an angle to it, like a tacking sailboat, but it simply spun me around. Turning my back on it would be as foolish as a surfer turning his back on a forty foot wave. The wind would simply have lifted me up off my feet and blown me off the Hill and into the sea. I did the only rational thing: I fell flat to the ground, face down, in obeisance.

Then I noticed that there was a little less wind down there, so that I could crawl on my belly through it. So I crawled fifty feet south, toward the side of the Hill nearest the House. The south side has always been more protected during nor'easters. I could stand again, once I left the summit.

But first I had to steal a glimpse down the *east* side of the Hill, the side facing the open sea. I could maintain my balance in the wind only by kneeling and crawling like a bug—which I did. It took about twenty minutes to crawl fifty feet to the east side of the summit. But the sight was well worth it. The waves were ascending the Giant's Stairway of rocks, which was now completely covered by water. This is a thirty-degree incline, with vertical obstacles every few feet, but the ocean was treating it like a sand castle. The top of the Giant's Stairway, the slabs of rock that reach halfway up the Hill, is about fifty feet above sea level vertically, and a tape stretched straight from the Drum to the top of this stairway along the thirty degree incline would measure some 150 feet long. These waves were rushing 150 feet up the Stairway right to its top, defying gravity, and spraying spume over the summit of the Hill. Impossible! Terrifying! Sublime!

But I could not stay here. I was already totally soaked, cold, and beginning to freeze. I had to turn around and go home.

By good luck or good grace I reached the bottom of the Hill without slipping. But Bass Point Road had now turned from a brook into a river. The house was an island. I was a castaway. I had to half swim, half run, to the House. Unfortunately, the "river" was flowing in the wrong direction. There was no way I could swim against its current.

Suddenly, I tripped on an icy rock and fell underwater. My lungs started filling with icy water. I expected to wake up in Paradise.

Then I felt myself being dragged through the water by strong arms. It was skinny old Lazarus, dressed only in a bathrobe! How could this frail old man endure the biting wind and icy water, undressed, and have the strength to drag me to safety? I seemed to remember (or fantasize) other times when he acted as if he were indestructible. Cars seemed to stop just before hitting him.

I was conscious enough to hear his gravelly voice above the wind shouting directly into my ear: "Stay with us, Jack! Stay awake! Keep breathing! Cough out the water!" I commanded my body to obey. It refused. It was stiff.

The front door seemed to open by itself. The two of us fell in a pile. I heard the crack of icicles breaking. My clothes came off, with no time for modesty or shame. Then a warm blanket surrounded me and I was in the kitchen before the open door of the big stove, being rubbed down.

"You make a habit of dangerous swimming, Jack!" said the voice behind the rubdown. It was Mister Mumm. "That's twice now."

*   *   *   *   *

When my body and my spirit were both dried out and re-clothed, I confronted Lazarus, my rescuer, and Mother and Mister Mumm, who stood behind him

"*What . . . are . . . you . . . doing . . . here?*" I asked, in measured tones. My close escape from death had given me the courage to be impolitely candid.

"Me? I was out looking for you, Jack."

"No, I mean all of you. What are we doing in this house?" They looked at each other as if they were hiding a guilty secret. "*You* gathered us," I said, turning to Mother, accusingly. "Why?"

"I didn't gather you. You all came to me."

"So it's just chance then?" I demanded. "Nobody planned this thing, the nine of us being here?"

"I didn't say that."

"Who did, then?"

I turned to Lazarus. "Who planned this group? You, Lazarus?"

Lazarus's response was a quiet fit of hysterical, sardonic laughter.

I turned to Mother, who was also laughing, quietly. "It was God, you mean? Divine providence? Is that all?"

"Disappointed in God, are you?"

"No, I mean—curse it all, you know what I mean. Is there some special plan here that you know about?"

Mother looked at Lazarus and Mister Mumm. All three nodded together. "Yes, Jack, there *is* a special plan for all nine of us being here. And I will tell you as much as I know and as much as I'm allowed to about it."

"How do I fit in?"

"You are a necessary part of it."

"That's why you had to be rescued," said Lazarus.

"Oh, thanks! If you weren't using me as part of your secret plan, you would have let me drown, is that it? That makes me feel really welcome!"

"No, no, Jack," Mother quickly corrected. "He didn't mean it that way. We would have rescued you anyway. We rescued you for you, but also for us. We need you."

"For what? The least you can do is tell me what you're up to."

"I'll tell you as much as I can. I don't understand it all myself, and I'm not allowed to tell you all of . . . of even the little bit I do understand. At least not yet."

"You keep saying '*allowed to.*' You have to report to some higher authority?"

"Yes."

"I think you know what my next question's going to be."

"Are we playing Twenty Questions now? Look, Jack, let me just tell you all I can, OK? We *are* here for a purpose, but I don't know exactly what we are going to be called on to do, or when."

"Is it a spy operation? A military operation?"

"Yes it is. But it's not physical warfare."

"Is it the CIA?"

"No, no, nothing like that."

"Something less than that?"

"No, something much greater than that."

"I guess we *are* playing Twenty Questions, eh? Can you please tell me how nine eccentrics can do something great just waiting around eating great bread and watching great waves and having great arguments?"

"Those are three pretty great things, I think. Don't you?"

"Don't play with me, Mother. I didn't mean great *fun,* I meant great *significance.*"

"So did I. And I think you understand something of the great significance of all three of those things too, am I right?"

"Come on, Mother, you're being evasive. What are we here for? If you saved me for some job I have to help you do, the least you can do is tell me what it is. How can I do a job if I don't know what it is?"

"Sometimes that's the *only* way you can do it," said Mister Mumm.

"We're really all in that position," said Mother.

"Once we stop fooling ourselves," added Lazarus.

"Will you all stop being evasive?" I exploded. "Just tell me what you want from me. Why *me*? Is it because I'm a Muslim?"

I don't know why I said that, but when I did, all three looked like children caught with their hands in the cookie jar.

"What, do you want to convert me?"

"No," said Mother. "We need you to be true to your faith."

"Why? I'm a Muslim, and you're a Christian, and you're a Jew," I said to Lazarus, "and you're. . . ." I turned to Mister Mumm and realized for the first time that I didn't know what this pious man was or believed.

"I'm all three," he said.

"How can that be?"

"There's only one Conductor to this music, and even though we play different notes, we'll play in harmony if we all follow His baton."

"But what's the music we're supposed to be playing here? What's the score?"

"He wants to know the score!" Lazarus echoed sarcastically.

"I don't know," replied Mister Mumm. "We don't see the score. We only see the baton."

Mother then explained: "We're all serving the same Commander, in different armies. And He seems to be changing His battle plans. He's bringing those armies closer together. That much we know: that we have to learn to work together. And to do that, we all have to practice 'islam,' submission. It's the first law of success on any battlefield: obey your commanding officer. You know that, Jack. If there's anything you know for sure, it's that."

"Yes, but we're only nine. You talk as if it's some worldwide battle plan."

"It is. We're something like a firing range."

"Firing range?"

"When you try out a new weapon, you try it out first on a little firing range, at home."

"What new weapon?"

"Us. Our cooperation."

For some unknown reason, this satisfied me. It was all so unconvincing that it was convincing. If they were lying to me, if they were making it up, they certainly would not have made up such a far-fetched thing. Besides, if I didn't trust them, I couldn't trust anyone. But I still don't know what's going on.

*   *   *   *   *

We woke Wednesday morning to a world of bright sunshine and crisp, calm air, full of the clean, empty smell of snow. Snow has a definite smell, just as water has a definite taste and white is a definite color. I think it smells like the soul of a saint.

The sea was still agitated but back in its prison cell, muttering in its beard like a senile curmudgeon. When I walked to the store across the street from Short Beach half a mile away, I saw a surfer in a black wetsuit standing on the beach holding his longboard and looking wistfully at the unrideable waves. I half expected to see the words *Can Do* on the board.

This was one of the days we brought the TV out. The electricity was still out but we had a battery-operated hookup. There was also no newspaper delivery.

I learned from the TV that two drowned bodies had washed ashore in Nahant, from the boat *Can Do*. How eerily similar to the name of Papa's boat, "Yes We Can." Am I paranoid for wondering whether there is a link? Am I supernaturally paranoid for wondering whether both proud names were inspired by the same evil spirit?

The roof upstairs leaked at all four corners, but unlike some other roofs in the neighborhood, it had not been blown off. The first floor was still cold and soggy but it warmed up and dried out quickly. We nailed up a heavy plastic tarp over the broken window and covered over the holes in the floor with wood Mother had stored in the attic for just such an emergency. The cellar was clogged nearly to its ceiling with sand, stones, shells, crabs, and dead fish, many with broken bodies. A Christmas tree ornament—a large, metallic-gold treetop star—stuck out of the top of a little heap of mud like a flying saucer that had just landed on earth.

A check outside revealed that the wind had totally sandblasted two sides of the House. Almost all the paint was gone. A professional sander could hardly have done a more complete job. The gutters had come off, or were hanging loose, but no main timbers were broken. Even the deck was intact except for its shattered floorboards, and its angled sides still pointed at the sea triumphantly.

There was a low, gnarled tree next to the house whose broken branches held some small household items stolen by the wind. A set of rosary beads dangled from a broken limb, its crucifix shaking in the wind like a metal midget with the palsy.

Our neighbor across the street, whose car had been guillotined by a falling tree, was asking the policeman, "Who can I sue for this?" The policeman replied, "You can try suing God, but I don't think you'll win."

Another neighbor, an old man a few houses down the street, who had also stayed to ride out the storm when nearly everyone else had evacuated, had a different point of view. He had had a narrow escape, and said, "I think I just got a preview of the end of the world. So quick, so quick it came. So unprepared we were. So easy it would be—it could happen any day. It almost *was* the end of the world for me."

Libby asked him, "Do you mean you almost died?" (She had come back to the house this morning on cross-country skis, since all roads were still closed to cars.)

He replied, "I mean I died inside. I was totally helpless. I didn't control my body anymore and my body didn't control my world anymore."

She said, "That must have been a horrible experience for you."

He replied, "It was the most precious experience of my life. I tasted death, and I tasted the sweet tang of life, and now I can see."

"What can you see?"

"That it's all so simple. There's death, and there's life, and there's only those two things, and life is infinitely precious."

If I am to be a true philosopher, I think I should listen to this old man a little more and to the smart young scholars a little less.

The storm had turned us all into philosophers. Everyone felt older, wiser, and humbler after the storm. The shockingly quick destruction of a small beachfront civilization that had taken lifetimes to build revealed the fragility of that civilization, and of all civilization. The mask had been stripped off with amazing ease.

The perpetrator of the crime, the sea, was now sitting quietly in her appointed place, fully clothed and in her right mind, with an innocent smile on her face. Amid the chaos of destruction the sight of the calm sea was the strangest sight of all. The timid people crept out again like sandpipers, beachcombing, playing with the fringes of the giant's dress as she heaved heavily but harmlessly in her post-orgy exhaustion.

I checked out the Hill. I expected to see broken branches everywhere, but though the trees were indeed broken, there were not many branches on the snowy ground. The wind had blown most of them off the Hill into the sea.

The Giant's Stairway, the rocky incline leading from the summit of the Hill down to the sea at the exposed eastern end, was littered with great boulders. But higher up, some seventy feet above sea level, at the summit of the Hill, looking lost and out of place, was one loose boulder, shaped in a rough square, some eight feet in diameter. It must have weighed at least twenty tons. There was no place above it from which it could have been dislodged, but there was an eight foot square depression at the *bottom* of the Hill the same size and shape as this rock. The sea had tossed it like a toy seventy feet into the air! I didn't know whether to be grateful or regretful that I was not there to see that event.

*   *   *   *   *

As I was helping repair the House a few days later, I reflected that a storm, like the sea itself, has a very definite personality, even though it is not (of course) a person. And this personality is large, wild, short-tempered, single-minded, and stupid, like the giants in the old tales. Giants ran through my memory now. Of course giants are not real; yet there is something real about them. C.S. Lewis explained it best: "Nature has in her that which compels us to invent giants, and only giants will do."

Squat told me that the word "hurricane" came from Hurricano, or Hunrahan, a Caribbean god (or demon) of Big Winds. They say you can see his evil face leering down from the clouds. They say that when the clouds get a certain dark green-yellow color, that's Hunrahan. It is a myth, of course, but what is the staying power of the myth? I find in myself, as Lewis does, something that insists on giants, and spirits like Hunrahan. I would sooner believe that Libby is an archangel than believe there are other gods, so why does it feel more right to me to ascribe a hurricane to a nonexistent god than to a real low pressure system? And why does the something in me that feels that way not feel like foolishness?

Because reducing the hurricane to the low pressure system is even greater foolishness.

What *is* a storm? Something more than wind, water, and snow. Not a person, of course, not even a spirit. But something more *like* a person than dead molecules. For a storm is not just an *event* but an *act*. An act comes from an actor. We want to know *who* it is, not just *what* it is or *how* it is. What is the first question we ask about it, the question the child in us asks? It is *not* the weatherman's question, "What physical forces caused this, and what will they cause next?" It is not the scientist's question, "What patterns of matter and energy is it made of?" It is the more "primitive" question, the question all men have naturally asked for nearly all the time they have lived on this earth, before our modern science taught us to ask the new questions and our modern philosophers taught us to forget the old ones. It is the question: "*Who's there?*"

Maybe it *is* a spirit. After all, there are many spirits, good and bad, angels and demons. And we know almost nothing about them. They're not gods, of course. "There is no God but God." But God created spirits as well as matter. Perhaps the old myths were onto something. Perhaps their cosmology erred not by excess but by defect. Was I not in the grip of giants there on the Hill? Of primeval forces more ancient, more substantial, more formidable than anything I can imagine? I opened my mind to the possibility. After all, "There are more things in heaven and earth, Horatio, than are dreamed of in your philosophies."

If life is a play, there must be more in the play than even the brightest of the players can see. For a play has an Author as well as layers, and the gap between the brightest and the dullest of the players is far less than the gap between the Author and the brightest of the players. And the Author may have written many other plays as well as this one, other creations than this universe. Perhaps he put into this play also some of the spirit-characters whose home lies in other plays. Isn't that what angels are?

It would be arrogant for us to set any limits to reality. What do we know, anyway? We do know that we humans have felt, from the earliest times, the presence of Something More, a larger world, a world of spirit, constantly pawing at the door of this one as the waves paw at the land, eager to eat their prey but held in check by a higher authority. Might not this larger world occasionally spill over into our world as a great storm spills the sea onto the land? These two things *feel* the same. The terror of seeing your yard turn into the ocean is more than the mere shock of loss and destruction of property or even life. It is a reminder of the power of the other world.

Why does the sea so naturally symbolize the sea of spirit? Because the fear of the sea of water and the fear of the sea of spirit is the same kind of fear: the fear of the Great Other breaking through.

Why shouldn't there be spirits behind hurricanes? Why shouldn't visible events have an invisible side? *We* certainly do! Every spiritual event we know has a physical side: thought uses brain chemistry, a poem's meaning uses its syllables, a picture's beauty requires paint molecules, and romance arises only when hormones flow. But thought is not only chemistry, or meaning only syllables, or beauty only molecules, or romance only hormones. In this world where spiritual things have a physical side, it seems perfectly logical that physical things also have a spiritual side.

Doesn't *all imagery* presuppose precisely that ancient world-view of a real connection between the literal-physical-visible and the symbolic-spiritual invisible? Symbolism is not *invented* by poets. It is *discovered*, it is in the nature of things.

We know that everything in the universe is physically connected to everything else, through time and space and gravity and energy and causality. If the old world-view is true, then these connections are not just physical. There are also spiritual connections. Wouldn't these connections be stronger and clearer at certain times and places, just as the physical connections are? And might not a great storm be such a time and place? A big hole in the curtain?

I do not believe an evil spirit moves the sea. It would make more sense to think of the *land* as the haunt of evil spirits and the sea as righteous, and taking its just vengeance on the polluting land by cleansing its defilement, like the inexorable justice of Allah. In that way the storm could be prophetic. Perhaps even apocalyptic.

*   *   *   *   *

Saturday evening, after we had all been working on house repairs all day, we sat around the fireplace with big mugs of hot cider, still talking about the storm. The echoes of a sound that large would reverberate in our minds and mouths for many days.

I asked each how the storm made them feel, deep down inside. Libby answered, "It feels like you had a gentle mother and she just exploded in a fit. To a kid, that's absolutely terrifying. It changes their feelings about her forever, even after she goes back to normal. And if they're young enough, it changes their feeling about everything, because for a little kid everything is just an appendage of Mommy. So afterwards, no matter how long the calm lasts, they know who this calm and gentle creature really is: she's the Mommy who went crazy once."

I said, "I understand that, but I can't feel that way. I still love the sea, even though she nearly killed me."

"Why?" Evan asked.

"I don't know," I answered.

"What kind of a 'she' is she to you, Jack?" Libby asked.

"A mystery."

"Like God?"

"No, nothing is like God. Besides, God is not a 'she.'"

Libby opened her mouth to start a feminist argument, but Evan interrupted: "I have a question," he announced, in his formal, clumsy way. (Evan always had "ay" question, not "uh" question.) "I would like to know: What words spring up into your lips first when you remember this storm? Isn't that what Freud did, Libby? I mean, to listen to what we speak when we speak before we think?"

"That's a neat way of putting it, Evan. All right, so what words come up into *your* lips?"

"Words like 'awesome' and 'majestic' and 'magnificent,' and even 'transcendent.' Unlike Jack, I see the sea as something that is a little bit like God."

"Yeah, your mind flies up to God like a balloon as soon as you let it go, Evan," kidded Libby. "You're an escapist."

"No, Libby, I am not an escapist. I am a realist. Unless God is not real. An atheist would call thinking about God 'escapism.' Are you an atheist, Libby?"

"No."

"Then God is real."

"Yes."

"Therefore thinking about God is thinking about reality. And thinking about reality is realism. And that's what I am doing. And therefore I am a realist."

Evan's watertight logic caught Libby off her guard and closed her lips. Encouraged by this triumph, Evan explained further: "Once you see one mighty act of God like that storm, you understand who it is that acts in all the quiet, little acts of nature that happen every day."

Libby persisted, "OK, you got a point there, Evan, but what does the storm teach you about yourself?"

"That I am very little."

"And does that make you happy, to know that you are very little?"

"Yes, it does."

"Why does that make you happy?"

"That is a very good question. It seems that we feel the *need* to feel little, and even the need to feel terrified, sometimes. I think it is part of realism. If we did not feel these feelings, we would not be in harmony with reality, with our real place in the universe."

At this point a question occurred to me. "But if this need comes from human nature, then why are we so different from our ancestors? They only *feared* storms, they didn't *love* them. Nobody felt that storms were beautiful until—I don't know just when, but probably around the rise of Romanticism."

Lazarus, surprisingly, interjected a scholarly note here: "No, earlier. Longinus wrote about 'the sublime' as delightful terror. And Petrarch was the first poet to see mountains as beautiful. Before, they were just obstacles to travel. For instance, in Isaiah: 'The mountains and hills will be laid low'— Isaiah meant that prophecy as a promise, not a threat." Lazarus was revealing a surprising knowledge of world literature. It was also one of the longest speeches I had ever heard him make.

Eva reinforced the point: "And the colonists who first came here to Nahant—they didn't notice the natural beauty either, because they just cut all the trees down for fuel and then started to strip the rocks to mine them—they were only interested in profit and money and survival, not beauty."

Mother added: "And in the next century they built ugly amusement parks here. You've all seen the pictures in my big old historical book—the one there on the side table. I still remember the big roller coaster they used to have in Revere. You could see it from here. Those people weren't interested in beauty either. The sellers were interested in money and the buyers were interested in pleasure."

"So you see how society changes your mind-set," concluded Libby.

"But human nature does not change," objected Evan.

Libby shot back, "It certainly does. We've just seen an example of it. What kind of scientist are you, Evan, ignoring your data?" (Evan had a degree in physics and was working for another in theology.)

Evan turned to Mother for help. "What do you think about that, Mother?"

"I think you're both right. The human spirit is always the human spirit, right Evan?"

"Right."

"And our society keeps changing because we keep changing, right, Libby?"

"Right."

"What is there in us that makes us keep changing?"

"Desire," said Libby.

"Reason," said Evan.

"Folly!" growled Lazarus.

"Love," said Eva.

"I think you're all right," said Mother. "Let's follow Libby's lead and look at desire. What do you think is our deepest desire, our deepest need?"

"God," I answered, firmly.

"Why? What is there in God that we so deeply desire?"

"Truth and goodness," said Evan.

"And beauty," added Eva. "Divine beauty, the beauty that awes us."

"Yes," I said, "Our modern society murders our awe. No absolutes, no transcendence, nothing to be fanatical about."

"Oh, sure, let's hear it for fanaticism." Libby put in.

"You know what I mean, Libby. Infinite passion. The passion it's right to have only for God and His attributes. Other fanaticisms are wrong, but that one is right. Other fanaticisms are idolatry but that one is worship. And that's what we don't find in this society. And *that's* why we love the wildness of nature, and even storms, so much more than our ancestors did. That's the answer to the puzzle."

"I don't follow your leap of logic there, Jack," Libby protested.

I explained: "They still had heroes. They still felt awe in the presence of the high and the holy. They had hierarchy. They looked up and said 'Your majesty' to somebody. We don't. But our hearts still do. That's why we have to say 'Your majesty' to nature. We say it to the great sea instead of to the great king."

Mother nodded in approval. "I think you're right, Jack. Even if hierarchy isn't good for our society, it's good for our souls. We're designed to love something awesome, because we're designed to love God, and God is awesome. I think nature is designed to feed our souls as well as our bodies. It's a museum, full of His holy pictures."

"Those waves *were* kind of like holy rollers," Libby joked. "I wish I could have surfed those monsters. Now *that* would be awesome."

"Surfing on God would be even more awesome," Eva said. "And I think that is what we are training for, whether we know it or not."

We were silent at that. The wisest answer, alas, usually has a way of ending a good conversation.

(Editor's Note: The next narrative chapter in 'Isa's autobiography is in fact a separate book, physically: a red, leather-bound, carefully-handwritten book entitled "The Book of Love." When I first read it, I thought it may have been included in 'Isa's writings by mistake, its style is so different. I found it quite surprising for a tough-minded philosopher like 'Isa. Fashionable literary critics would call it overwritten, florid, and full of "purple passages." Lovers, however, would not. I publish it because I believe there are still more lovers in the world than critics.)

(14) The Book of Love

I have never kept a diary. I always thought of that as a colossal waste of time. Worse, as something silly, self-indulgent, self-centered, shallow, and stupid. I think ingrown eyeballs are as unnatural as ingrown toenails. Allah designed our eyes to look outward. A diary is a temptation: it encourages the false perspective of judging all things from the diarist's point of view, as if the sun and moon rose and set in my back yard.

But Mara changed that. I begin this very personal diary because it is *not* primarily about me but about her. Seen through my eyes, of course; I am its writer. But she is its object. In fact nothing has ever pulled me so powerfully *out* of myself as Mara.

The Day the World Began

On May 15th, 1978, the world began, at 11 o'clock in the morning, on the summit of Bailey's Hill.

Spring had mailed itself to me in a bright yellow wrapper. The sun's sparkling image on the surface of the water was impossible to look at and impossible not to look at—like the Face of God. ("Tyger, Tyger, burning bright!") No, nothing on earth is like the Face of God. Rather, the sea stood like the soul of a strong saint, still and vast and open, enacting its islam to the sun.

All my exams and late papers were finished, as well as my job in the BC kitchen. I slept late, said my prayers with gratitude, and ate a leisurely breakfast of Mother's bread, honey and fruits, pretended to agree with Lazarus just to hear his wonderful "harrumph," kissed Eva hello and goodbye on the forehead, waited outside the door of Diddly and Squat until they finished "Mister Blue" (my favorite), wished Dudley were still at the end of that ugly orange leash which Mother will not throw away (he died suddenly of unknown causes the day after the Great Blizzard), and giant-stepped up the Hill like Tom Bombadil.

The air felt heavy with angels. The sky felt very close. It reflected a blue so brilliant it was almost painful. The air tasted both sweet and salty. The seagulls filled the sky with the sound of K's as they swooped down after fish and each other. Their swoops were the same shape as waves. (Isn't everything?) The sun made the sea shine like a second sun.

I lay down in the newborn grass, "lizarding." I smiled at the sun, which came down and played in the house of my skin. I gave myself up to the delightful deception that this world was my home. On a day like this you could not help believing the grand illusion that this earth was where you belonged forever, that even Paradise couldn't get any better than this. I thought: If I died tomorrow, it wouldn't matter, because today was eternity. Earth was Heaven, and the gulls were angels. I was happy that the world was round because that meant its circumference was closed and complete, so that nothing could break its perfection, nothing could come in from outside. You don't want additions to Paradise.

I was wrong. The planet may have been round and complete, but not the world. For something did come in from Outside.

That something stood on a low, flat rock some forty feet away. She had clearly come from Outside. The earth was not safe. Its circumference had been interrupted.

She was not from this world. Nothing in this world could have assembled her. She was not a thing but a sign, a message from Heaven. She was not a girl but an angel.

Imagine a man in a familiar landscape, shortly after sunset, looking at a familiar horizon, expecting the familiar stars to rise, or the moon. Suddenly, the arc of an enormous disc looms up, fifty times bigger than the moon, and quickly dominates the horizon: an immense new world, a new planet, unexplainable yet undeniable. He thinks: What planet am I on?

I've climbed Bailey's Hill a thousand times; how could I have suspected that this most familiar place in my world would turn into a magic door, the wardrobe into Narnia? I came here many times with Papa when I was too young to remember. I came here with my school friends to play pirates and sailors. I came here to think and pray my way through both my parents' deaths. I almost died here myself once. Here I saw the demon Hurricano, the most awesome sight I've ever seen. I've come here nearly every day since moving to the House of Bread. It is my back yard. And an angel descended from heaven right here, through some door in the sky.

Next to her was a Jacuzzi-sized puddle of water, left from last night's storm. As the sun impaled both her eyes and mine with a single arrow of light, I suddenly saw her not just *reflected* in the pool but *shining* in it, as if from her own inner light. The surface of the water was unruffled because the wind was hushed (in awe of her, no doubt). The sun was behaving like Midas, turning the water to gold at its touch.

It was not just a painting but a vision; not opaque but transparent. Her material self, real as it was, was a mere reflection of the shining Heavenly form in the water, which was her Platonic Idea. The water was the Mind of God, and I was graced with a moment of heavenly telepathy.

Everything in my life has changed from that moment on. It is now a totally unfamiliar arrangement of totally familiar things.

Then a momentous, historical event happened: she stepped down from her
rock.

It was a simple move, but I will preserve its photograph in perfect detail
in the gallery of my mind for the rest of my life. As she moved that one step
toward me, I trembled like a very small child facing a giant wave, at the brink
of a death that was both blissful and terrible.

She did not yet see me, and she stretched her body, as only a cat or a
young, willowy woman can, into that tubular position, hugging herself with
both arms. It made her look totally feminine and vulnerable; it said: "I am hug-
gable. I am lonely."

The movements of her arms were the movements of a wave. Both bodies
were obviously moved by the same spirit. If the sea was making music, her
arms were conducting it.

The gold had now turned into silver, and silver was everywhere. Silver
was not just a color but a shape, the shape of the waves of the sea and the shape
of her arms, the shape of an S. Silver was also the sound she made when she
spoke. Her voice was "the music of the spheres," the voice of the universe. It
was the soft whisper of "S," of a wave on sand. Her hair was also an S, a breaking wave, the neck of a swan, the shape of a Viking ship.

The universe looked at me with two very dark eyes. I could not meet those
eyes. And I could not help but meet those eyes. I could not look away, yet I had
to look away—or die.

I looked away. I was not shy; I was beyond shy: I was terrified.

And then, after a silence just long enough for an angel to squeeze through,
she spoke. The universe acquired a voice. It was the voice of the She, which
was the voice of the Sea: clear and bright and sparkling, like the strains of "Für
Elise" or a Chopin polonaise. It was the voice of the Elves, high yet deep and
melodious.

"Why do you look away? Are you afraid?"

"Yes." I stammered like a caught child.

"Of me?" The tone of surprise added to her beauty. It meant that this
queen was humble. O bounty too great to be true! Once in a lifetime, perhaps,
one might hope to see such a face (no, not even that, for "such a face" implies
that there might be another to match it, and that is clearly impossible), but such
beauty is usually a curse: as soon as it becomes self-conscious, it moves its
possessor to possession, to pride, and thus to an ugliness of soul to pollute the
beauty of face. To be beautiful is no curse, but to know you are beautiful is.
The Devil's secret weapon was not an apple but a mirror.

So while it was a miracle to see such beauty in a face, it was a double miracle to find such beauty in the soul that wore it. Such a double miracle would

be like lightning striking twice. She was such a miracle, and I was being struck by lightning.

"Yes," I stammered.

"Why? Why are you afraid of me?" The words bespoke innocence. Only innocence could answer them.

"I'm afraid that if you smile at me I will dissolve into ashes."

This was not clever flattery but simple honesty. I was afraid to look at her because I was afraid I would just vanish like a shadow in her sun if she did not temper its light. But I was afraid even more to look away, because I was afraid she was only a vision, not a reality, and that the vision would disappear if I looked away. She had to be made of spirit, not matter. Matter was too gross and immobile. If she was matter, it must be water, dancing and taking on new shapes and swells.

What a terrible dilemma: I would disappear if I did not look away, and she would disappear if I did. Both were intolerable.

She threatened to smile. Almost, the world collapsed. Then, a last-minute rescue. Instead of smiling, she frowned, puzzled. She looked dubiously down at me. (She was not as tall as I am, but she stood on what the world would call a rock. I would call it a throne.)

I blinked, and marveled that the vision did not fade. I still did not dare to look away. My stare must have frightened her, and she turned away.

"What is your name?" I blurted out. I suddenly understood why ancient cultures thought of names as sacred, as momentous, as power. I could not, and would not, keep her here by any physical force, but if I had her name, that would be like a magic spell. I could conjure her up by speaking her name. For the name of such a magical creature must be a magical name.

She turned her face back to me and said, simply, "Mara"—and then ran down the Hill and onto the road. I did not follow her except with my eyes. She slowed to a walk, stopped, then turned and waved at me when she reached the bottom of the Hill in front of the House. I was thrilled at her attention, like a puppy, and waved back. I think she could not see the smile on my face at such a distance; could she feel it, I wondered?

She drove off in a little yellow car, a Volkswagen bug. I thought of the union of our cars: Yellow plus Blue make Green. Green equals Life, and Hope.

When her car puttered up Trimountain Road and disappeared over its summit, I turned into a tree for five minutes. I was rooted. I could not leave the sacred spot. I stared at the puddle where she had first appeared, and at those few cubic feet of air space on her rocky throne into which a door from another world had opened. I thought it might open again at any moment.

On the way back to the House I noticed that the whole world had changed. Everything was perfect. Through the transparent water of a large tidal pool I saw a single red lobster slowly crawling across the underwater rocks. I followed it with my eyes into a tiny cave, and found that I had no temptation to extract it and eat it, as I had done a few times before. I suddenly realized that it was very ungrateful to eat an actor who has just entertained you.

I noticed that the wind had risen just enough for the sea to begin speaking to itself in the softest of whispers, each wavelet cautioning the next: "Sh-h-h!" If silence has a sound, that is it.

I had noticed when I came up the Hill that the sky was startlingly blue this morning, almost as blue as a medieval stained glass window, and that was my favorite color. Now, on the way down, the world was reversed, and medieval stained glass was almost as blue as the sky. I remembered that blue was God's favorite color. I noticed a single yellow daffodil, with the end of one tiny petal crumpled like the ear of a yellow dog who had been in a fight. It was perfect, not despite the crumple but because of it.

When I entered the House my chores awaited me, but they turned into liturgies. The vision of Mara spilled onto the old wooden floor as I swept and mopped. Each crack and splinter was like the daffodil's petal. My perfect destiny was to sweep up each perfect particle of this perfect dust into this perfect dustpan and perfectly put it into this perfect trash can. All was part of the plan, the plot, the play, and all was absolutely perfect. For

> **There is a lady, sweet and kind.**
> **No other form so pleased my mind.**
> **I did but see her passing by**
> **And I shall love her till I die.**

What has she done to my soul? What a hurricane does to the sea: a sudden, violent upheaval, a glorious revolution. When I saw her face I realized that the universe was not what I had thought it to be. She stood all things on their heads. All bets were off, all securities and predictions dashed to pieces. She is not the fulfillment of my desires; she is the instigator of a new desire in me.

All men spontaneously and unconsciously judge the beauty of every woman they see. Some of these women turn men's heads and some do not. "Man is the head of woman, but woman is the neck that turns the head." Mara has turned my head around 180 degrees. I find that I cannot help spontaneously judging all other women by Mara. I now see all "perfect" women, with "perfect" blonde hair and "perfect" curved eyebrows and "perfect" upturned noses, as being far from perfect because they are not what Mara is. And I see all other women who have dark brown hair and straight eyebrows and straight noses as being close to perfect because they are close to what Mara is.

She has instantly transformed all the silly, sentimental clichés into high and holy wisdom. Love is a many-splendored thing. Once, on a high and windy hill, in the morning mist two lovers kissed and the world stood still. Some enchanted evening you may meet a stranger, and then you will know.

You're just too good to be true, can't take my eyes off of you. I feel the earth move under my feet, I see the sky come tumbling down, tumbling down, tumbling down.

What happened today on the Hill was the thing that has happened millions of times in human history yet has never been explained, even though it is the most important thing that ever happens. (*The* most important thing? Says who? Says every single person it ever happens to.) No psychologist has ever explained it. Love is a "je ne sais quoi," an "I know not what." Yet it moves the world: "love makes the world go round." Its causes are invisible, like the wind, yet its effects are catastrophic, like the wind. Perhaps it *is* the wind.

We cannot explain it, but we can explain why we cannot explain it. How could anything less than love comprehend love?

When I see her face in my mind I am swept out of my skin and out of my time. Time dies. I cannot imagine what she looked like ten years ago, or what she will look like in ten years, or in forty. In her face there is only Today. Nothing could exist outside this moment because her face defines this moment, this moment does not define her face.

I have not yet seen her smile, but I know what it will do. If she smiles during the day, it will make the stars come out in broad daylight; and if she smiles at night, it will make the sun rise at midnight.

The Second Meeting

The next day I came to the Hill two hours earlier, my heart beating hard with hope. My longing to see her again almost paralyzed me so much that I could not climb the Hill.   At exactly eleven o'clock, the meaning of life arrived in a bright yellow Volkswagen bug. She parked at the top of Trimountain hill and walked down (through the woods, not the road) and up Bailey's Hill (by the little dirt path, not the big paved one), slowly and deliberately.

I was waiting at the summit, desperately trying not to look desperate. I was sitting up: a compromise between standing (too imperial) and lying down (too casual). As her head appeared over the edge of the Hill like foam on a breaking wave, my eyes plunged into the wave, forgetting my fear in the splash of her glory. When she was a safe twenty feet away, I spoke.

"Mara!" The invocation. The sacred name. The magic word. The golden key. "You—you're here."

"That's a safe assumption. Wherever you are, you're always there."

"I mean—you're real."

"Another safe assumption, I think."

Surprised by her sarcasm and stunned by her logic, I retreated to a safe cliché: "Do you come here often?"

"Yes." (Wonderful!—this girl does not chatter. She wastes no words. There is a concentrated power in her spirit like the power in a wave.)

Two embarrassingly obvious butterflies, splotched sun-yellow and death-ly-black, suddenly zigzagged up in front of our faces. I ignored them: our relationship was not deep enough to talk about such profound trivia yet.

"I come here too. Why haven't I seen you here before?"

"I haven't let myself be seen." (Why didn't I notice her? Why did she hide from me? How could she hide so well? Is she an Elf?)

"What do you come here for?"

"For the same reason you do. To listen."

"Yes, that *is* why I come here. What do you listen to?"

"The silence."

"I listen to the sea."

"I think it's the same thing."

"Yes, it is."

The first hint of a smile appeared on her face, and a relaxation. She said, "I come to listen to the real music, and to get away from the other music."

"The other music?"

"That horrible 'background music' that they play at you everywhere else. The Muzak. It's like Chinese water torture. Why do they have to play it all the time? You can't *think*."

"I think that's the whole point: they play it so they don't have to think. Thinking is scary."

"So is silence. I think they're afraid of the silence."

"I understand that."

"Do you, really? Or are you just trying to be polite?"

"Both. I do want to be polite to you. But I don't know how. I want to be totally honest too. Like you."

She stood still in thought for a few seconds. Then: "I can't speak with you for long. I have to go away from words, to think about them. What's your name?"

Those last three words were the most wonderful words I had ever heard. She cares about me! "My friends call me Jack."

"So what's your real name?"

"'Isa. 'Isa Ben Adam . . .'"

Her eyes and face muscles suddenly stopped moving. (Why?) "You're a Muslim." (How did she know that? Not many people know the name 'Isa. But I did not ask her. I did not want her to feel under scrutiny, as I did.)

"Yes."

"I'm a Jew." Suddenly, with these two words, we had become dogs sniffing each other out: friend or foe?

"Good," I said. "We worship the same God you do. We just call Him by His Arabic name."

"I know," she said. "But Jews and Muslims always fight."

"We shouldn't. Not if we believe in the same God. We should be dancing to the same music."

"Well, why do our people always fight then if they're both dancing to the same music?"

"I don't know," I said, rather miserably. "But I know it has to stop somewhere."

"Where?"

"Here! Let's stop it right here. Let's be friends. Let's start turning the world around."

"You want to turn the world around now?"

"Yes, I do."

"Oh, I think that's been tried before, Jack. And if you're planning to turn the world around, I think you'll find it's just a little too heavy for you."

"Heavy?"

"Heavy with too many centuries of history, and too many millions of people who think otherwise."

"No! That's the wrong way for us to think about it!" My anger overcame my shyness now. "Those centuries of history, and those millions of other people—that's why peace hasn't happened yet, because everybody thinks about those millions of others and those centuries of history. But we're not those others. And we're not history, not yet. We're the present. We can turn any way we want. We can change. Maybe we can't change a million people but we can change two. No matter how many people play war, we can play peace."

"That's a good speech, Jack, but there is a great big wall between us, because there is one between our people, and we are part of our people. You know that."

"Yes, I know that. But tell me, Mara: Do you think God made that wall, or did man make it?"

"Man."

"Then man can unmake it. What man has put together, man can take asunder."

"I hope you are right, Jack." (She hopes I'm right! She wants the wall to fall. The wall between *us* as well as the wall between our people.)

We spoke for an hour and agreed to meet again the next day on the Hill.

How wonderfully direct and un-devious she is! No gossip, no chatter, no polite, meaningless conversational gambits! Her mind is as fresh as her face! As I floated through the air back to the House my feet barely touched the earth. On the sloping, stony beach between the Hill and the House, I flew like an angel over two tiny saltwater streams returning into a tidepool from their high-tide journeys inland, even though it was an hour past the turning of the tide, like tourists scrambling to catch the last bus home.

Another angel had clearly arranged our meeting. I glanced at the teeming life in the tiny tidepool, as if to find that angel. I found instead a thought: that angels are Heaven's high tides. They come periodically, in waves of invisible predestination, to nourish the organic life on the little tidepool of Heaven that we call earth.

*   *   *   *   *

I will now attempt the impossible. I will try to tell in words who Mara is. I shall endeavor to eff the ineffable.

O my reader, I fear you may find this section of my story boring, but that is because you have not met Mara. You may skip it if you like. But you should know that nothing I have ever written is *less* boring to me.

Who is Mara? It is impossible to define her soul, so I shall describe her body, since the human body is the only image of the human soul, as the words in a book are the only physical image of the meaning of the book.

Her Perfection

Mara is not "beautiful." She is *stunningly* beautiful. But she is not "perfect," i.e., she does not conform to some abstract archetype of perfect beauty, such as symmetry. If "the perfect female form" were ever incarnated without blemish, it would not be Mara. If a computer were to discover and generate the maximally beautiful female form and face, by taking account of all perfections and imperfections and all preferences, the result—"the perfect woman"—would be infinitely less beautiful, and incomparably less *interesting*, than Mara. She would win the "Miss Universe" contest but she would not win my heart.

Perhaps no one else in the world sees Mara this way, as more-than-perfect. Let it be so; my vision is no more subjective than theirs. It is less subjective, in fact! My perception of her beauty is as objectively accurate as mathematics. Beauty is NOT in the eye of the beholder. Whether anyone else sees what I see or not, it is there.

You will smile indulgently and say to yourself that "love is blind." No. True love is not blind, it is the healing of blindness. Scales fell from my eyes when I saw her. I saw her with the mind of an angel, with the mind of "the necessary angel," with *necessity*. Henceforth, for all time, I must judge all women by this new standard. A woman is more beautiful insofar as she approximates Mara. All noses are beautiful as they approach Mara's nose. All eyes lack beauty to the exact extent that they differ from Mara's eyes. It is not an option, a choice, or an accident; it is a necessity, like 2+2=4.

Reality has strange and unpredictable shapes and edges, like a jigsaw puzzle. I did not design these pieces or this puzzle. But I discovered the piece that fits in the center of the puzzle. It (she) is as unpredictably and uniquely shaped as a key, but it is *perfectly* shaped, like a key, for it alone opens the lock at the center of my heart.

Each feature of her face shows her spirit. I could write a whole book merely on her nose. (I mean that literally. The nose, after all, is the center of the face, and makes more of a difference to the whole face than any other feature.) Mara's nose is not a tiny, delicate, turned-up nose, either short (a "button nose," "cute as a button") or long (an aquiline nose, a "ski nose"). Nor is it a large, pugnacious, intrusive nose. It is not bulbous, squashed or squamous, nor is it hooked. It is two opposite things at once: on the one hand it is like a secret, enclosed garden, something delicate, shy, reticent, withdrawn, vulnerable, and easily hurt; but at the same time it is passionate, demanding, jutting forth into the world, sharp and straight like a sail. And these two opposite things are exactly what her spirit is.

My philosophy of beauty has been revolutionized by Mara. I used to be a Platonist. No more. Mara is not beautiful because she is an image of the abstract Platonic Form of feminine beauty; that abstract Form is beautiful because it is an image of her. The universal and the particular have exchanged places, like the prince and the pauper.

Her Name

Her middle name is "Angelique"—"Angel-like." Allah, Master of Names, must have inspired her parents in naming her. An angel is a messenger of God, a piece of Paradise sent to earth. An angel is not from this world. An angel is like Mara.

Angels are not only messengers *from* God but also point *to* God. Angels are pointing fingers: we are meant to look *along* them, not *at* them, as Dante looked along Beatrice at God. He saw a ray of divine beauty reflecting off the face of Beatrice, like sunlight in a mirror. Beatrice was not simply a beautiful *thing* in this world but a *hole* in this world through which divine light entered. "Angelique" sounds like "angel leak." She is the angel leak, the hole in the wall between heaven and earth through which an angel leaked into this world. An angel fell into the sea, into *mare,* into Mara.

Her Body Language

Look at her from behind; she is an utterly feminine water sprite. Her shoulders are thin and straight and narrow, not thick and round and broad like a wrestler's. They are thin from back to front (so is her stomach) rather than from side to side. This accentuates the curvature of her breasts, hips, and buttocks. She looks fragile yet strong. Next to her grace my clumsiness is shamed. I am a beast, a barbarian, a wild boar. Libby tells me I "fell for her like a palsied mastodon."

She stands (and sits) straight up, at attention. Her body is the extension of her eyes, which are the bright, unsleeping eyes of the archangel. Yet when she walks, she walks the way a wave would walk if it took human flesh. She does not walk with her legs. She walks with her whole body. "She walks in beauty, like the night."

What is more devastating than a tornado? Mara fondling a strand of her black hair and rolling it between her fingers. (I think she does this when she is just a tiny bit nervous.) What is even more devastating than an atom bomb? Mara running both her hands through her whole hair from the neck up in an artlessly elegant upsweep, as the north wind does to the sea, making a rising wave no surfer can resist.

Her feet are the foam of the wave, the fringe. She loves to go barefoot. She also loves to wear dresses and skirts instead of jeans or slacks like a man. This makes the bottom twelve inches of her almost as beautiful as the top. When she listens intently, she stands tiptoe, like a small Victorian girl. The spiraling curves of her calves, ankles and feet when she walks are little waves. The waves of Mara are the waves of *mare.*

Her Voice

It is the voice of water: of brooks, of little rivers, of rain, of little waves. It is so utterly natural that it seems to come from the earth itself. Yet it is so supernatural that it seems to be coming from Heaven.

Her thoughts are like stars, and her words like shooting stars, meteorites gracing earth's atmosphere with their burning presence. I cannot imagine her singing because she seems to be always singing. Her words are already music.

Her Face

Her face is astonishingly active. Much of its beauty comes from its activity, like a dancer, or a violin in the hands of a virtuoso. It is a beauty of a different *kind* from mere beauty of passive geometrical form, though it has that too. I contrast it in my mind with the beauty of Kimba, a girl in my class at BC. Kimba comes from Polynesia. She is the most *perfectly* beautiful girl I have ever seen. She will be an actress or a model. Her brown skin gleams with a soft inner light. She wears a perpetual smile on her face. Her whole face and body are at peace. Her soft, round, large eyes, above her high cheekbones, are half closed, like Buddha's, or like a purring cat. She comes from Nirvana, and will take you there if that is where you want to go.

Kimba's death-mask would look more perfect than Mara's, but it would not shock you to see it. "Oh, that's Kimba," you would say, if you had known her before she died. But Mara's death-mask would be a shock: You'd say "That's not Mara!" You'd ask, "How could something so alive be so dead?" Kimba is the perfect body, but Mara is *all soul*, and when her soul departs, her body will be unrecognizable. It might just vanish. Even her body seems to be soul.

Kimba is a beautiful object; Mara is a beautiful subject. Kimba is most beautiful when you look at her. Mara is most beautiful—unendurably beautiful—when she looks at you. Kimba is a great work of art, Mara is a great artist. Kimba is a painting, Mara is a painter. Kimba is a toy, a doll, an object of play. Men call her "adorable" and "cute." It would be high treason to call Mara "cute." It would be like calling a panther "cute." Kimba's body is sexually exciting, but Mara's very *conversation* is thrilling. It would be exciting to see Kimba's bare body, but it is more exciting to see Mara's bare spirit, to be allowed into the inner sanctum of her soul.

While Kimba comes from earth, Mara comes from Heaven; and therefore her eyes are wide open like the sleepless eye of the seraphim, "the burning ones." Her spirit flutters intensely, like a hummingbird. Not *nervously*, like a drummer or a druggie, but as if she knew she had only a short time to live and learn and savor everything. Each cell in her body seems to be moving even when her body as a whole is still. She is a sea full of life. Even when she stands still in one place, she seems to be whirling in an orbit around herself like a spiral galaxy, or like the rotating lens of a lighthouse. Sometimes her eyes suddenly shine even more brightly, and her body becomes totally still, like a pointer dog or a cat stalking a mouse. She always looks like she is scanning for something. Her innermost fire seems to be seeking its opposite, the outermost sea.

Mara brings me to ecstasy. "Ecstasy" means, literally, "standing outside yourself." Kimba would bring not ecstasy but "in-stasy," self-gratification. Already Mara's face has become more familiar to me than my own, yet each time I see her anew I am taken outside of myself, startled. I feel as if I am about to levitate out of my body. Sometimes I have to look down at the ground to be sure my feet are still attached, since my head is not. My eyes tell me my feet are on the grass but my heart tells me my feet are in the sky, six feet above my head, upside down. I feel disoriented like a wiped-out surfer under a wave: up is down and down is up.

Her Eyes

There is an old Irish love song that I used to think silly and sentimental. Now, it perfectly expresses why I love Mara: "It was not her beauty alone that won me. Oh no, 'twas the truth in her eyes ever shining that made me love Mary, the Rose of Tralee." That's it exactly: "the *truth* in her eyes ever shining." Seeing her is seeing truth, seeing light.

To see her face is beatitude, "Beatific Vision." But to see her face turned to mine, to see her seeing me, is exponential beatitude, infinite bliss multiplied by itself. Surely the primary sex organ is the eye. It can actualize the intercourse of two souls.

Her eyes are large and round and bright and swift and tireless. Sometimes they sparkle suddenly like firecrackers; other times, they gleam steadily like stars; but they always seem to be generating light rather than merely reflecting it. I cannot imagine them asleep. They must remain open all night beneath her closed eyelids, like a little girl who doesn't want to go to bed and only pretends to be asleep under the covers.

Her eyes are two deep seas, trembling with living water. They remind me of Ruskin's saying: "To paint water in all its perfection is as impossible as to paint the soul." Sometimes they are stormily dark and sometimes dazzlingly bright and sometimes both at once. Like her hair, her eyes are very dark brown, almost black: a black that is the presence, not the absence, of all colors. What was only a cliché of words—that "the eyes are the windows of the soul"—has suddenly become a miracle of fact. And behind those windows lies my shrine, my Mecca. As the Prophet rode his horse to Heaven from the holy hill, my spirit rides to Paradise on the holy horses of her eyes. All the cynicism in my spirit is left behind, shattered into pieces like a fallen chandelier.

Her Pain

Mara is not *literally* Paradise, of course; that is not only idolatry but stupidity. But even speaking the language of Sufi poetry, as I do, Mara is not Paradise, because there is no pain in Paradise but there is pain in Mara. Her pain is part of her beauty. Look at Kimba and you know that she has never suffered great pain. Look at Mara and you know she has.

In her eyes I see pain but I do not see hate or resentment. I understand this. I too have been hurt, by Papa's death and by Mama's, but my spirit did not turn into a wrinkled prune or a crawly crab. Better for Papa to die in his strength in his beloved sea, than in decrepitude in some hated hospital. I still love the sea, though it was Papa's grave. I love it *because* it is Papa's grave. That makes it more sacred. Mara too has been deeply hurt, I know not how, but her soul is not prematurely aged, like the souls of most people in our culture, whose souls seem older than their bodies. (If you look at souls instead of bodies, you will not call America a "youth culture" but a prematurely aged one.) But Mara has not aborted her spiritual childhood. Her eyes tell me that. They are pure and free from the flip and jaded cynicism of her peers.

Some day I shall know her pain, and share it with her, and take exactly half of it away from her soul and into mine. I will be her road to Paradise as she has been mine. I will do it because I *will* do it, though I do not know how. Like Frodo, I will bear the Ring though I do not know the way.

Her Willfulness

Mara is willful, spirited, strong. Most men fear that. When she turns her eyes on them they blink, for the light in their eyes is dimmer than hers. The flea cannot endure the fire.

But she is not to be feared. Her willfulness is not shallow, silly, or selfish; it is simply strong. Is that a fault? Is weakness more beautiful than strength?

I want a strong-spirited woman. For I know that the joy of meeting an equal is far greater than the joy of controlling an inferior. A great king wants a queen, not a slave girl. He wants to rule-with her, not rule-over her. It takes two strong pieces of flint and steel to make a great spark. My spirit seeks a flaming seraph, not a purring pussycat.

Why fear her strength of will if her will is my will? Will we ever fight? Of course. The more ardently we love, the more ardently we will fight. But the more ardently we fight, the more ardently we will love.

Her Posture

I could pick her out in a crowd from a block away even if she was facing away from me in a fog. For her posture is as distinctive as her face, even when standing still—because, like the sea, she is never standing still. She is a bird poised to fly. For her, "standing" is an active verb. And it is a she-verb. She is thoroughly feminine.

Her Clothes

Mara dresses modestly. She does not need to increase her "sex appeal" by immodesty, as less beautiful women do. She also has no desire to imitate men's clothes, as American women increasingly do (I cannot fathom why).

She loves to wear loosely flowing clothes: dresses; robes; long, pleated A-line skirts; loose-fitting blazers of soft, thin material—anything the wind can play in and make into waves. I am jealous of the wind.

She is a mermaid on land, a wave out of the water. She is herself a little roving sea. Her surface undulates, both her clothing and her body, like the surface of the sea under the wind. I love her because she resembles the sea, but much more I love the sea because it resembles her.

Colors get new meaning on her clothes. I never liked green until I saw it on her dress. On her all colors change from dead facts into living acts. They become events. They become songs.

When she wears that sky-blue and snow-white striped jumper, she becomes so light that I'm afraid she will fly away into the sky and return to Heaven. The blue shoulder straps are ribbons of the sky and I fear they will work like magnets, lift her up, and take her Home.

Her Hair

Her hair transforms the meaning of "dark." Dark is no longer the opposite of light; dark is a certain kind of light: the opposite kind from Barbie-doll light. *Weighty* light.

She wears her hair long (proud to be a woman!) and flowing gracefully like plunging wave, swan's neck, or Viking longboat. I love her hair because it is like waves, but much more I love waves because they are like her hair. When I see a storm, I see the angel in the sea shaking her hair as Mara does.

Her Naturalness

Mara uses little or no makeup. Putting makeup on Mara would be like coloring the Mona Lisa with crayons. The only reason why any woman uses makeup is because she thinks she is ugly without it. Ugli*er*, at least. Why else would she ever alter her face?

But Mara is not proud of her beauty. She is usually unaware of it, sometimes embarrassed by it, and even embarrassed at her embarrassment. And that is so genuine that it multiplies her beauty. When she is unselfconscious, she is unselfconscious about her unselfconsciousness. When she is self-conscious, she is self-conscious about her self-consciousness. I must try to inveigle her into the waves. They wash away self-consciousness better than anything I know.

Mara as Archetype

I think too much, talk too much, and even write too much. Perhaps it is an obsession. But it is Mara, not me, that I am obsessed with. So I will chance it: I will show how Mara and I are destined for each other as Yin and Yang, two parts of one whole. In the words of the song, I am the sun, she is the moon, I am the words, she is the tune.

She is the sea, I am the land.

She is the wave, I am the rock.

She is the womb, the amniotic fluid murmuring softly and moving subtly within. I am the soldier, standing stiff like a spear at the outer walls of the world.

Her very eyes open inward, like a waterfall, or a window onto a secret garden. Mine open outward, like a sailor's stare standing at the ship's rail.

Her eyes are large and round like the world. Mine are straight and narrow, like its axis.

Her lips, like her eyes, are thick and soft and curving. My lips, like my eyes, are thin and hard and straight.

Her straight nose turns slightly up, concave like a swan. Mine turns slightly down, convex, like a hawk.

Her hair is brown, mine is black. It is not just brown, it is darkest-gold. It seems to shine from within, like the sun. My hair absorbs light, like the night. I am outer space and she is a star.

Her face is oval, mine is square. Hers is short, mine is long. Hers is smooth, mine is craggy.

Her skin is light brown, a little lighter than tea. Mine is dark brown, a little lighter than coffee.

Her flesh is soft, mine is hard.

The lines of her body are curved, mine are straight.

Her shoulders are round, mine are angular.

Her whole body is a sheath, mine is a sword.

Her legs are curved and fleshy. Mine are hard and straight and bony.

Her ankles are thin, mine are thick.

Her fingers and toes are long, mine are short.

Her chest is rounded, mine is straight.

Every detail fits. I am arid rock longing for the wash of the sea, the She, and longing even more that the sea should have an equal longing for the rock.

Her Uniqueness

Even if she is of the human species rather than Elf or angel, a new word is needed for her. And if the new word is not forthcoming, then I must use the old word "beauty" for her but deny that old word to everything else in this world. Her beauty cannot fall under judgment by any common standards; all standards henceforth fall under judgment by her beauty.

Yet she does not rival other beauties, or depress their value. They are like colors but she is like light. As light brightens all colors instead of suppressing them (*that* is the work of darkness!), she brightens all other beauties in the universe. For instance, I had never truly seen the moon before I saw her. I was surprised to find it much brighter than I had ever noticed. Everything was! Every thing looked as if had been put there a second before I looked at it. It had no past when she was not in it. Every color became dramatic, like a painter's choice. The sky said, "Look! I'm *blue*. I could have been green." Cats could have been red, or rectangular, but weren't. The first seagull that screamed at me after I met Mara was the first seagull that had ever screamed. Everything suddenly came to life. Every entity in the world became a little lightning bolt. And I was one of them. I too had just been created. The finger of Allah had just touched the finger of this Adam.

Blinders?

Some of my friends think I have lost my faith, or my reason, or both. They say love is blind, but it is they who are blind. There *is* a love that is blind. Its name is lust, which is selfish, blind desire. But the love I sing of is not desire, and therefore not blind desire. It is a vision. It opens the eyes; lust closes them. The angel of love is not a deceptive rationalization for the beast of lust. Just the opposite: lust is a deceptive substitute for love.

Their sophists say they can explain love's vision as a trick of brain chemistry and hormones, a trick to fuel the machine of biological reproduction. What pitiful souls they have! They explain everything and understand nothing because they believe nothing. They put their head in the dirt and sneer at those who have theirs in the sky, where it was designed to be. They also kick up at the heavens in rebellion, like wild horses. They are upside down.

Clearly it is the vision that fuels the desire, not vice versa. Beauty is "that which, being seen, pleases" (*id quod videtur placet* was the medieval formula). It pleases because it is seen, not vice versa.

Some of my friends call me "arrogant" for not doubting the vision. "You forget that you can be deceived," they say. "You think you see with the eyes of an angel, but you do not have the eyes of an angel. You are at best a lustful sinner like the rest of us and closer to a beast than an angel." Even Evan thinks something like this, though he tries to say it politely.

My answer is simple. I am indeed a lustful sinner. I know the power of lust by experience, alas, as well as they do. That is precisely why I know this is not lust. The claim I make is not for my purity but for my vision. This is a grace, a gift. It did not come from me but to me. Nothing that pure could come from a soul like mine. Does that argument sound like arrogance?

Idolatry?

Some friends warn me against idolatry. But the critic of love, who is so suspicious of love and reduces love to lust, is really the one who is the idolater, and also the blasphemer, for he confuses the work of love with the work of lust, the work of light with the work of darkness, the work of God with the work of Satan.

If they are right, then I have two souls, not one. If they are right, then there lies, cunningly asleep beneath the worshipping visionary, a salivating predator, a shark. But this is not so. Mara has killed the shark.

Loving her makes me humble, not arrogant; self-denying, not selfish; self-doubting, not self-confident. How could the works of darkness use such a cover? How could Satan invent such a love to be the bait concealing his hook of lust?

Lust?

The very passion of my love protects me from lust. It is a demand for perfection. Nothing less will do, and nothing that would mar the perfection is even remotely tolerable. When a man is in love with one perfect rose, he can pass through jungles without plucking a single flower.

And that perfect rose—how could one possibly pluck the perfect? How could I tear one petal from its wholeness and purity and perfection? If we ever marry, the perfect gift will be given, and taken; but the gift must be whole, not partial; free, not driven; with no fears or regrets and with absolutely nothing held back. Divine life may not be contracepted.

Lust mentally undresses its object. But I do not want to imagine her naked. I have seen something more beautiful than any body I could ever possess: her soul, her essence, which she held out to me through her eyes and her words. *That* was naked and unclothed. And her modest physical clothes express that; her nakedness would conceal it.

What I love is an angel. How could anyone lust for an angel? Do we want to copulate with the sea, or the stars? Loving her keeps me *safe* from lust. She is "tenderness vanquishing desire" (the words of the Orthodox liturgy's Akathist hymn to Mary).

We have agreed to meet only at the Hill and at the House for now, not to "date." Americans do that, not Muslims. We will not step onto the first step of the down escalator of the "Sexual Revolution." If and when our love is consummated in marriage, it will be perfectly and paradisically sexual. But to preserve that paradise we have agreed to respect it. It is Allah's paradise, and His boundaries and rules are always right.

We must not use our souls to know each other's bodies, but use our bodies to know each other's souls.

She cannot be an object of lust because she is not an object at all. She is the better half of my self.

I know this is not lust but love because I can feel both within me and they move in opposite directions. The lust to physically consummate our love would be far stronger than I have ever had for any woman if I allowed it to rage in my soul, yet it is powerless and tamed in the face of a greater force, which is not fear or duty but love. I have discovered the only thing that is stronger than evil passion: good passion.

Romanticism?

Friends call us "romantics" in the same tone as they would say "alcoholics." We *are* "romantics," but it is nothing like being alcoholics. It clarifies everything. Alcohol dulls everything.

We come from the two least romantic cultures on earth: a Jew and a Muslim. Why are Jews and Muslims unromantic? Some would answer in terms of sex: they would say that Jews and Muslims are "un-sexy," or "puritan," or afraid of sex. I know the answer goes deeper and is more positive than that. But I don't know what the answer is.

I do know that our cultures do not love each other, but we do; that our parents and our childhoods were enemies to each other, but we are not. We have conquered our enemy. When we fell in love, our childhood fell dead at each other's feet.

Chauvinism?

One cynical friend at BC calls me a "collector" who has found a gem and wants to possess it and keep it. "You Muslims don't believe in equal rights for women, do you?" My answer was: "We do not want women to be little men, if that's what you mean."

The typical Western idea is that Muslims have a low view of women, as possessions, or even as slaves. One writer even said we treat our goats better than our women. Are we supposed to bear such insults to our honor in silence? The charge stems from the idiotic Western assumption that social equality, freedom, competition, and the demand for "rights" exalts women and their happiness more than virtue, order, honor, chastity, and respect do. But Muslim women are happy and American women are not! That is *data*. And here is the explanation: Muslim women are women, American women are weird-looking men with an identity crisis.

Here is my theory about American women.

Men are not attracted to either a masculine woman or to a generic unisex woman, but to a feminine one. But three things have destroyed femininity in America: the Sexual Revolution, Americans' obsession about freedom and rights, and the death of romance. All three of these are part of what is now called "feminism." Calling that "feminism" is like calling Mao's China "The

People's Republic," or calling a cannibal a chef. The so-called feminists are the murderers of femininity. And the death of femininity is the reason why American men want to artificially stimulate their sexual appetites with images in movies and advertising and pornography. The Sexual Revolution has not freed romance; it has suppressed it. But in their hearts men still want feminine women, and women want masculine men, even when their ideology have confused their minds. Hearts are harder to fool than heads.

"Feminists" always seem to be angry. "Angry" is not sexy.

But "holy" is sexy. The same thing that makes a woman sexually attractive to a man makes her naturally holy: her submission, her surrender, her islam. Surrender is an erotic necessity; that is why American women are sexually frustrated. That is also why they are not holy.

Look at the faces of almost all young American women. They imitate their models: they are brash, blasé, bored, and jaded. And they think that is "sexy"! Where is the Victorian innocence and restraint and modesty and shyness? *That* is sexy in a woman, but to see one you have to invent a time machine, or meet Mara.

Most American women repel me. I find brazen women not only crooked but ugly. For those who stray from the Straight Path also stray from beauty. But who understands this connection? When I try to explain it to my friends at BC they call me a "snob." I do not understand this. Is it snobbery to seek the kind of woman the Qur'an directs a man to marry: modest, wise, and virtuous?

My high school friends called me "stuck up" because my standards were higher, "opinionated" because my opinions were clearer, and "hot tempered" because my spirit was stronger than theirs. Perhaps they are right; after all, only Allah sees us truly. But isn't it true that a temperature of 98.6 will seem like an abnormally high fever to the cold-blooded? And isn't it the typically American form of bigotry to judge anyone with strong convictions as a bigot?

My philosophy professor told me that if people were elements, I would be fire. Is that why I love water so much?

I cannot and do not believe that I am the last gentleman in America. Yet most of the men I know are either wimps or wolves. Like Chad, one of my most articulate friends, who calls himself a "shopper." I asked him what he is "shopping" for and he replied, "Women with big breasts and small noses."

Once, in senior year of high school, I was in a locker room debate with twelve of my friends on our baseball team. The question was: Would you rather have ordinary sex with the world's most beautiful woman, or the world's greatest sex with an ordinary woman? (I think half of them were virgins, but no one dared admit it—as if the only shame was to have a sense of shame.) The question was crude (of course), but so are boys in locker rooms (of course). I was amazed to find that I was one of the only two of the twelve who would choose the perfect woman over "perfect sex."

(The other one was a surfer who said, "No surfer in his right mind would ever give up the chance to have even an imperfect ride on a perfect wave, not even for a perfect ride on an imperfect wave. We surf ordinary waves all the time, and once in a while we do it as well as the pros. But every surfer's dream is to surf the wave of a lifetime. That's another dimension. That's unforgettable.")

The only interpretation I can put on the choice made by the other ten is that they don't really love women but only sex, the experience, the thrill, like a drug. When I told them this, they were insulted and called me "snob" and "queer." I retreated from that battlefield, but I continue to puzzle over the fact that the two boys I know who *are* "queer" seem to respect women more than most of my "straight" friends do.

A friend who knows my love for Nahant once teased me that I love Nahant as I ought to love a woman. I blushed at this, for it is almost true. I have more aesthetic passion for Nahant than for any woman I have ever met, until Mara. And throughout my high school years in Lynn I have treated Nahant like a mistress, running off like an adulterer to a rendezvous whenever I can. I hug her waves and wildness close to my heart. When I arrive, I sit by the side of the sea and listen to her sorrowful voice chiding me for being so long away, yet also welcoming me with joy once I have come.

Bringing Mara Home to Mother

I will not go into detail about this social interaction because I am not good at it. I am not Jane Austen. But anyone could see that Mara instantly took to everyone in the House, and they to her. However, after she left, Mother seemed uncertain whether to worry or rejoice over Mara's presence in my life. And Lazarus's reaction to Mara was even stranger: when she left, he sank back into his chair with a sigh and a deep smile, and muttered, "Now maybe I can rest a little."

Mara's First Smile

Next to our first meeting, the most momentous event in the history of the world so far has been Mara's first smile.

For the first few times we met, I never saw her smile, except with the corners of her mouth—sometimes with only *one* of them: a wry or sad smile. The beauty of her face was the beauty of a shadow. She was a heavenly bird with a broken wing.

Yet I have always felt unsmiling women to be unbeautiful. I classify four reasons for unsmiling women. (It is a philosopher's obsession to classify everything!) They are:

(1) dullness, passionlessness, soullessness, small-mindedness, unwillingness to think about anything but immediate and practical matters like money and tampons;

(2) the *pout* of the modern model, a mixture of pettiness, petulance, and egotism, the spoiled-brat-badly-in-need-of-a-spanking look (How can American males be attracted to this? Or how can advertisers think they are?);

(3) anger; or

(4) worry.

But I have forgotten a fifth cause: deep pain, true hurt and sorrow. And that presupposes vulnerability, and that is part of beauty.

Mara is sad and beautiful. Is she beautiful *because* she is sad? Would a smile dispel her beauty? I asked my soul this question, worriedly. For I know that the most beautiful plays are tragedies, and that the most beautiful music is in a minor key.

But my heart answered my mind's worry. It told me clearly that Mara's beauty did not depend on her sadness; that when the sun dispelled her shadows it would not dispel her enchantment; she would *not* look like all other women. She would be more Mara, not less.

So I vowed to make her smile, to bring forth her full glory. I determined to find the golden key to unlock the palace of the sun.

Although she did not smile, she sang. This made her seem happier than she really was. I had never heard anyone sing so sadly. I asked her,

"Why do you sing, Mara?"

"Sometimes I sing to remember, sometimes I sing to forget."

"To remember when you were happy, and to forget when you were sad?"

"No. Sometimes to remember the sadness."

"Why do you want to remember the sadness?"

Instead of answering that question, she said a rare and wonderful thing: "Thank you, 'Isa, for not saying 'Why *would* you want to remember the sadness?'—as if I were slightly insane. You said, 'Why *do* you?' You accepted what I do, and then you explored it with a 'why.' I appreciate that very much."

"That's very perceptive, Mara. I never noticed that I did that."

"And I appreciate *that* very much, too."

"So why *do* you want to remember sadness?"

She was silent for a short eternity. Then she answered, "I think it's like the photo of a dead friend that you keep even though it makes you cry. It's *because* it makes you cry. When you cry, that's almost like he's still there. It's the closest you can come to him now. It's even comforting. Your tears make him more alive. They almost raise the dead. They're magic water. They take the shape of your friend. They're not just *your* tears, they're him-shaped tears."

"That is unutterably profound and beautiful."

"If it's unutterable, then I didn't utter it."

"That's good logic. But is there such a 'him' that you mourn for?"

"It's not what you think."

"You mean it's not a boy friend?"

"It's not a boy friend."

"Your father?"

A sharp, defensive look, and a colder tone of voice: "No, *not* my father." The way she emphasized "not" made me suspect it *was* her father

"Then who. . . ?"

"Don't ask, 'Isa, please. Not now. Maybe some day."

"I want to know your pain. Not just know *about* it, I want to know it with you."

"You wouldn't say that if you knew how bitter it is."

"Yes I would. I'm not afraid of your pain, because it's yours."

"What are you afraid of, 'Isa?"

"*Not* knowing your pain. Not knowing you."

She was silent. I don't know why I next said what I next said.

"It's got something to do with God, doesn't it?"

"I can't say any more now." The words were like mathematical symbols, emotionless. The lid was safely, carefully, calmly replaced.

When I returned home I prayed that Allah would let me say the words she needed to hear and to prevent me from saying the words she needed not to hear. The next time we met, we just sat still watching the sun, in silence, for a long time before either of us said a word. She looked sadder and more beautiful than ever. I did not ask her anything, but I broke the silence:

"Listen to the sea."

"I always listen to the sea."

"Listen now."

She nodded. "What am I listening for?"

"God."

"The *sea* is *God*?"

"No, no, the sea teaches us to listen to Him."

"So why don't we hear Him now?"

"Because we're not listening now. We haven't learned to listen—not well enough, anyway. Not yet."

"How do we learn to listen?"

"We have to quiet everything in us."

"How do we do that?"

"We have to learn how to do nothing. I don't mean not doing something, I mean doing nothing. It's very hard."

She nodded, seriously. I'm glad I didn't ask her any questions.

After we did-nothing together for ten minutes or so, there on the rock by the breaking waves, she gave me a half-smile. "Yes," she said, simply, and was gone.

Exorcising the Shadow

I will not tell the conversations by which I discovered the causes of her shadow, but I will tell what the shadow is, because this shadow creeps over me too. What hurts her, hurts me. But there is also a more terrible reason: I am saddened to be part of the people that is responsible for this shadow.

Mara's mother, like mine, married a Muslim. She was a Jewess and he was a Palestinian Arab. She was a gentle woman; he was a rude and stupid man. She let herself be abused and beaten because this was all she knew: the pattern on the fabric of her destiny went back to *her* mother and, Mara suspects, to her mother's mother as well.

So I discovered Mara's prison. Then, one day, I found the key to unlock it. It was not words, either mine or others'. It was the sea. It was *mare* that washed the shadow from Mara.

It was late in June. The air was crisp from yesterday's storm but warm from today's sun. The air was very gold, the sea was very blue, and the two-foot-high breaking waves were very white. We were walking along Nahant Beach in our bare feet, at the exact spot where I had last splashed with Papa when he told me of the angel in the waves. There were about fifty people sunbathing on the beach but no one was in the water except a few toddlers splashing in the warmer shallows. The water temperature must have been in the high fifties, sixty at best. Mara suddenly turned to me and said, "How much do you love the sea, Jack?"

"Almost as much as I love you," I answered. Up till now, we had never said "I love you" to each other except in half-kidding, "testing-the-waters" ways. When I said this, she stopped walking, stood still for a second, and then suddenly ran into the sea, fully clothed, and threw herself into the breaking little waves. She screamed and giggled like a two-year-old. Nonsense syllables rolled from her mouth like sea foam. My smile almost broke my face in two. For a minute, I was paralyzed by shock and joy. She turned to me from the sea. I saw her soul climb up into her face and give me a look that was both defiant and afraid. The look said, without words, "Jack, if you do not understand this; if you should patronize this; if you should find this 'cute' or 'quaint' or funny; if I am an *object* to you now; then all is lost. I have stripped my soul to you. What will you do with it?"

What I did was to run clumsily and fanatically into the surf in my jeans and T-shirt, shouting "Goo-goo, ga-ga! Mama! Papa! Wee-wee!"—and then fall backwards into a breaking wave, arms extended, crucified by ecstasy.

"You too?" she said, in a birdlike voice.

"Me too! Me too! Wee-wee! Goo-goo!" I was speaking in tongues, to God and to her and to the angels. It was dress rehearsal for Paradise. "Now you know my secret. The sea turns me two too. And you too! We two! Toot-toot! Toot-sweet!

Toute suite! —It was not babble; it was the *reversal* of Babel. It was understanding. Truth sprang up from the earth and rightness looked down from heaven. It was the fourth day of creation. Allah had just created the sun. Morning broke, the first morning of the world.

Her smile was wider than the world. The sun in the sky was only a pale image of her smile, lingering long after she left like the smile on the Cheshire cat.

The smile was a miracle. On land, Mara seldom smiles. But in the sea she can never stop smiling, even laughing. Like me, she becomes a child again. I don't mean that as a metaphor; it is literal. The *body* does not suddenly collapse like a balloon and become a tiny child's body, of course, but that is exactly what the soul does. The change in the soul is just as real, as radical, and as miraculous as a sudden change in body would be from a six-foot, twenty-year-old body to a three-foot, three-year-old body.

We drove back to the House wet and giggling.

Cars and Mothers

Mara lives with her mother in Salem, about ten miles away. My first impression of her mother was that she was polite but protective, fearful and somewhat suspicious of me, even though I was very respectful. But when we made eye contact, she relaxed a bit. I think that's because she can see in my eyes that I am honest and not "conning" her to "get" her daughter.

The first time I picked Mara up at her house to drive her to BC (she's a student in the School of Social Work there), we had a "car philosophy" conversation that proved we were predestined "soul mates." As she climbed into my little blue convertible she exclaimed, "What a neat little car!"

"It's the only one I've ever had. It's almost more like a pet than a machine to me."

"I love convertibles. They let *all* the air in."

"That's what I love too."

"It must be cold in winter."

"It is. The heater isn't very good. But that's OK. It lets the winter in. I like to know what I'm in, whether it's summer or winter."

"No air conditioning either, then?"

"No. I don't like to be insulated from nature."

"Even when nature is very hot and humid?"

"No, not even then."

"I understand that. I think of nature the way I think of a mother. I don't want to turn her off even when she gets a little hot. She's part of me and I'm part of her. I don't mean in any mystical way: she's not a goddess or anything. But she is herself, and I love her."

"I feel the same about my mother—about *both* my mothers." (I had already told Mara most of the things I have put into this book about both Mama and Mother.)

"No radio either, I see."

"Nope."

"Why?"

"That helps me to think, and to listen, and to talk."

"Most of my friends say listening to the radio *helps* them to think."

"Does it help you?"

"No. I need silence to think. To think the good thoughts, anyway. The thoughts that come out of the silence are always deeper than the thoughts that come out of the noise."

"Do you ever just listen to all the sounds you never notice when the radio is on? Like the wind, or the rain, or the birds?"

"Oh, yes. All the time. And to people most of all. And to conversations, like we're having now. I think conversation is one of the best things in life, and we're losing it because of the radio and the TV." I turned to look at her large, round, honest, sincere, eager eyes. The rest of her body has grown into womanhood but her eyes were still twelve years old.

"I love your philosophy, Mara." (This was all I dared to say. It felt like saying "I love your right thumb.")

"Why thank you, Mister Philosopher."

When we got out of the car at BC, she noticed the dent in my left front fender. "Are you going to fix that dent?"

"No. I *made* that dent, with an axe."

"Ooh! Were you mad at the car?" I heard some fear in her voice—fear of finding a mean streak in me.

"No, it was calculated. When the car was almost new, I was getting so attached to it that I wasn't enjoying driving it anymore because I was afraid of getting even one little scratch in my perfect little car. So I liberated myself from my hang-up with an axe. It sounds crazy to everybody else, but it worked for me. I'm happier driving it now. I think one swing of an axe is a small price to pay for a little happiness."

"You know, I'll bet that's what a real saint would have done if he had a car!" Mara exclaimed. "He'd call it detachment from worldly riches, or 'holy poverty.'" She mused for a moment. "You know, Jack, I can almost see a rabbi's beard on you, and light circling your head like a halo."

"No, no. No halo. But I do like rabbis."

Innocent Love

Last evening was so perfect that it simply will not go into the house of words.

We met on the Hill again, in the evening of the longest day of the year, the first day of summer. It began to rain, and we discovered what rain is for: for getting wet. We stood happily in the rain, said yes to it, and laughed with joy.

Then the rain suddenly stopped and the sun came out just as it was setting, a dark red sphere under purple clouds. As it set, the sun drew the wheel of light we call Day down below the shoulders of the sea, into the dark from which the stars come up. After it set, its light still lingered. I said to Mara, "Look! Look at the sky where the sun went down. Do you see that road of light it left behind?"

"Yes," Mara said. "That's the longing."

She *understands*. I am so happy that I think I am dying.

The longing does not desire to *escape* from the world. Exactly the opposite: it longs to love the world, every precious atom of it. How could I have been so blind all my life as not to notice that everything was beautiful, not only the sea and the sky but every clod of mud, every discarded scrap of dirty newspaper, every molecule of what we call garbage—how could I not have seen this before? It is as obvious as the stars.

Mara makes me notice everything. Yesterday we watched in detail how the local species of seagulls land, gliding for six feet only inches above the water before they touch down. We watched a slim, curvaceous cormorant's fish-catching liturgy. It involved totems. First it became a cat and crouched atop the water's edge, eyeing the sea with single-minded fanaticism, its neck nervously curling like a stalking cat's tail. Then it became a boat, and sailed straight for a spot some thirty feet away, its neck now held stiff like a prow. Then it became a submarine and dove down under the surface, submerging for a full fifteen seconds. Then it became a fisherman, emerging triumphantly with a wriggling eel in its beak, swallowing it in two twitching gulps. Finally, it became a bird again and flew off into the sun, where it seemed to have come from. I thought of Stephen Spender's line, "Born of the sun, they traveled a short while toward the sun / And left the vivid air singed with their honour."

We went into the House for a late supper, then back to the Hill as the sky cleared and a large family of stars came out, like children, to play in the empty fields of sky. The star-children were not merely *there*, they were *doing things:* dancing, trembling, sparkling, singing. They were clearly alive. A few miles to the south, the Boston Harbor lighthouse hurled one javelin of light at Nahant every eight seconds, not to rival the stars but to imitate them.

As we stood between the piles of house-sized rocks on the cliffside, we heard the wind whispering whooshy secrets to the sea through the spaces between the rocks, and we heard the sea whispering splashy secrets to the smaller rocks below, hoping they would deliver its messages back to the wind. But the rocks were speaking the deepest secret of all, the secret of silence.

Mara had brought a little "boom box" and tapes, and we danced (with Victorian propriety) atop the Hill to the love song in "Scheherazade," and to

Beethoven's "Moonlight Sonata," and to Wagner's "Tristan and Isolde," and to Patsy Cline's "Crazy," and to the tinny old "Beautiful Dreamer." As we danced under the stars on top of the world, the angels danced with us, wheeling round the sky, turning the whole universe around us. We were at its center, at "the still point of the turning world." The unenvious angels celebrated our love. Van Gogh's "Starry Night" came to life. The sky was full. We looked up and saw no such thing as empty "space"; we saw "the heavens," and they were brimming with burning life.

A little later, the quarter moon rose, and with its magic wand said "let it be" to the yellow brick road of moonlight that stretched out over the sea to the horizon. All evening, light kept leaping down from the moon and dancing on the dance floor of the sea. How could we do less, on the land?

After Mara left (before midnight so as not to worry her mother) I slept on the holy hill all night and woke to the birds saying "Welcome to Paradise." I heard "Morning" from Grieg's "Peer Gynt Suite" more clearly from the morning birds than I've ever heard it from a recording. I call them "morning birds" because I don't know their name and don't want to, for I am Adam and I have named the animals, and I say these are simply "the morning birds."

It is too much bliss for this world. Perhaps we have already died and gone to Paradise. Or perhaps we should die now. For how could it get any better than this? I am overwhelmed by gratitude, the wisest emotion in the world. Gratitude for life, for our lives, and for all lives, and for all forms of life that sprang from the spring of Allah's imagination, and above all for Allah Himself, Giver of all gifts, Life of all lives, fountain of all waters, the Beneficent, the Merciful.

The World's First Kiss

There are three kinds of kisses, ranked in a hierarchy of passion: polite, erotic, and worshipful. The worshipful can be even more passionate than the erotic. Our worshipful kiss came early this morning. I had been on the beach listening to the waves late last night, too happy to sleep. When I finally went to bed, at about 2 A.M., the moon was still bright and the sea was still full of fast little waves that made a smart slapping sound in the clear air when they broke, and looked like moving mirrors reflecting the moonlight. But when the moon set and the morning dawned, the morning seemed darker than the night. For clouds and heavy fog rolled in from the sea and turned every color grey. When I climbed the Hill, I watched the fog invading the land like an army. Its effect on the ear was as striking as its effect on the eye, muting all sounds as well as all colors. The whole world was silent.

Then Mara appeared out of the silence and the fog. We simply stood two feet apart for a long time in the silence. Then we simultaneously and deliberately walked (not fell) into each other's arms and kissed, very gently and tenderly, as the fog had kissed the world. No one initiated it. It was a wave and we were two surfers who caught it.

The kiss was a world-historical event. Mara's family history is almost the history of the whole world. She comes from a line of ancestors that stretches back for a thousand years in Italy and, before that, Israel. There is a family tradition that one of her great-great-grandmothers was raped by a Viking in Italy. This would put another ancestral blood line into hers. (There is something of the Viking spirit in her, surely!) Her Jewish ancestors go back to Abraham, of course, almost 4,000 years ago, and back to Adam and Eve, like all of us. She was Eve today not only because I am Ben Adam, but also because we stood in Eden. The world was created one second before our kiss. No man has ever kissed a woman before. Today Adam and Eve kissed and history began. "In the morning mist two lovers kissed and the world stood still."

It was so perfect that we said nothing—nothing with our mouths, and nothing more with our bodies, but only with our eyes. The silence was holy, and not to be desecrated. We both understood. After standing in reverence in the thickening fog for what may have been two hours or may have been two minutes, we both wordlessly and smilingly parted, knowing that this morning was already as perfect and complete as anything in this world can ever be.

As I walked across the fog-bound beach between the Hill and the House, a sudden wind parted the fog for a second to allow a single arrow of light from the Boston Harbor lighthouse to pierce the fog and strike my eye. Simultaneously, the thought pierced my heart like a spear that the dark, the grey, and the light are all holy.

(15) The Sea Serpent

On June 30th, 1978, I, 'Isa Ben Adam, being of sound mind, saw something that does not exist. Alas for my sound mind! Or—far worse–alas for reality. I would rather have blamed my mind for the awful thing I saw than blame reality.

It was neither day nor night but that in-between time, that crack, or slit, or vent between light and darkness into which things from other worlds could most likely be poured. The sea looked like a snakeskin, quivering when the wind blew on it. I was sitting on the deck thinking about nothing for a few minutes: a daily habit of mine which I highly recommend. I was watching two cormorants standing on a rock at the edge of the Cauldron, searching the sea with their hooked necks. They looked like two living question marks. Then, without warning, I saw, or thought I saw, out of the corner of my eye, a sudden silvery flash somewhere far out on the surface of the sea. I strained to see what it was, but saw nothing. As soon as I stopped straining to see it, I saw it again, this time like a streaking fish skimming along the surface. Again I tried to look at it directly, and again it disappeared. Again I turned my eyes away, deliberately, waited for a full minute, and suddenly opened them. I was rewarded with a full view of—a sea serpent.

It appeared to be no more than half a mile offshore, about 75 feet long, and undulating, as if dancing in place. I blinked, and looked again. It was still there. I passed my hand before my eyes, as if to ward off evil spirits. The thing remained.

I looked more closely. The head looked like a thin horse's head, the neck like a fat snake's neck. Head and tail were both held erect above the surface as it moved like a sidewinder snake on land. The mouth was open and moving. So were the eyes, roving like searchlights. Then came the most terrifying sight of all.

It saw me.

I am sure of this, though I am not sure how I could be sure, at such a distance. I was prey spotted by the hunter, caught by the camera. My molecules seemed to freeze at Absolute Zero. I was unable to move either my body or my mind.

Then it quickly turned its head away, like a horse, and swam away eastward, out to sea. But after five seconds it turned its head back to me, haughtily, then submerged. I thought it was laughing at me. I felt a cold terror. Then my feet and tongue were freed, and I ran inside shouting: "Mother! Evan! Anybody! Come quick! Quick!"

Evan came first, running down the stairs. "What? What?" I grabbed his arm and pulled him through the door onto the deck. "Out there! Do you see anything?" I pointed to the spot where I had last seen It swimming away.

I looked again at the spot, half in hope, half in fear—and was rewarded with my second sight of the serpent, triumphantly breaking the surface of the sea. Though it was farther away, I could clearly see that it had its head turned toward me and was laughing, or sneering, at me. I stood transfixed, forgetting Evan, until his words threw me into nearly as much consternation as the serpent did: "I don't see anything. What was it?"

I turned to Evan at my side, confused and angry. Evan was looking at exactly the right place, and his eyes were as good as mine, but he was seeing nothing. I took my eyes off Evan and looked again to sea, but now the sea was suddenly empty and calm, without even a ripple or wake from the worm. Its only wake was the memory of its sneering head in my mind festering like a sore.

"What did you see?" Evan demanded.

I was too upset for prudence. "A sea serpent!" I blurted out. Then: "A hallucination. Of course. That's what you're thinking, isn't it?" Then the anger subsided. "So am I. I wish it *was* a hallucination. But it wasn't. It was as real as you, Evan. Not a dream."

Evan was speechless. By this time Mother had come out. I blubbered, like an infant: "It—it stared at me. It saw me. I didn't just see it; it saw me!" I began to shake. Mother quickly hugged me and set me down on the bench that hugs the deck rail, taking her black shawl full of cheery yellow birds off her shoulders and putting it around mine.

"No," I said, giving her back the shawl. "I'm not cold, and I'm not crazy. I saw a sea serpent, and it was *not* a hallucination, it was *not* a dream, it was real. I know what dreams are like. Believe me, this was real."

Mother stared at me, not in disbelief but in worry. Evan asked the reasonable question, as is his wont: "Then why didn't I see it?"

"I don't know," I confessed, miserably.

"It *must* have been a hallucination, 'Isa. My eyes are good. If something is really there, anyone can see it."

Mother turned to Evan. "Are you sure of that, Evan?"

"Why not? What do you mean?"

"Can you see your guardian angel?"

"No . . ."

"But he's real."

"Yes, but *nobody* can see angels."

"Saints do, sometimes."

`'"But—but an angel doesn't take the shape of a serpent."

"One did, once. Long ago," Mother said, softly.

"Are you saying the Devil appeared to me?" I asked, with rising terror.

"No."

"Then what are you saying? What happened?"

"I don't know. I'm only opening minds, not closing them, I hope. I don't know what you saw, Jack. But I know the world is full of strange things."

"So is the mind," argued Evan.

"That's true too," Mother agreed.

The serpent had left my sight but it would not leave my mind. So I fed my mind with two kinds of truth, the first from Heaven and the second from earth. I found the first truth in the holy Qur'an (xiv, 98–99): **"Seek refuge in Allah from Satan the outcast. Lo! He hath no power over those who believe and put trust in their Lord. His power is only over those who make a friend of him."**

The second thing I did was to walk to the Nahant library to devour all the books they had about sea serpents. The library was my second home, and I had spent hundreds of happy hours in that lovely little old English stone building that was too small for scholars but perfect for browsers.

Passing the Hill, I resisted the temptation to partake of its peace today. But as I passed I noticed that curious white bird standing on the rock in the middle of the Cauldron, cocking its head to the left and looking at me.

During the ten-minute walk to the library I mentally classified the six kinds of information I expected I would find about sea serpents. (Philosophers love to classify everything.)

The first was from psychologists, explaining the mechanisms of hallucinations.

The second was from scientists, explaining the physical possibilities of unexpected things like giant eels or squid.

The third was from pseudo-mystics or *National Enquirer*-type hacks who don't explain anything but only assert.

The fourth was from over-sophisticated philosophers and theologians "explaining" how visions could be "true" without being true.

The fifth was from good theologians, explaining how both good and evil angels could materialize as signs or instruments of God or Satan.

The sixth was from real mystics and saints who saw them.

But what I found, when I got there, was a seventh category. I was surprised to find it at all, and even more surprised to find that it was by far the most numerous and common category of writings about sea serpents: sober, literal eyewitness descriptions by ordinary people!

The first that I found was a recent book by a local North Shore native, Bob Cahill, who lived only a few miles from Nahant. I discovered that

> Over 1,000 people saw "Nellie," the North Shore sea serpent off
> the Massachusetts coast back in the 1800's, and that is more than the
> number who claim to have seen "Nessie" in Loch Ness ... the one seen
> by more people than any other was the 80-foot snake-like creature
> that went frolicking off the north coast of Massachusetts in the sum-
> mers of 1815 through 1820, 1826, 1833, 1849, 1875, 1877, and 1886.
> Over 500 people testified to seeing the serpent week after week, first
> off Gloucester, then off Lynn , Swampscott, Salem, and Nahant. . . .
> Thomas Perkins, who founded the Perkins Institute for the Blind in
> Boston, also sighted the serpent . . . "I was struck with an appearance
> in the front part of the head, like a single horn, about nine inches to a
> foot in length, and of the form of a marling-spike."
>
> In 1819, at Lynn Beach, the serpent appeared again. Samuel
> Cabot, ancestor of Henry Cabot Lodge, wrote: "My attention was
> suddenly arrested by an object emerging from the water, which gave to
> my mind the idea of a horse's head. . . . At this time he must have been
> seen by two or three hundred persons on the beach . . ." An old fisher-
> man of Swampscott . . . saw the creature from Nahant Beach. . . .
>
> The most recent reported sighting of "Nellie," as the North Shore
> monster is now called, was in May of 1975, when skipper John
> Randazza and his crew, aboard the *Debbie Rose* out of Gloucester,
> spotted her while fishing 15 miles south off the coast . . . estimated as
> 70 feet long. . . . Its head was like a horse's head."

I was especially struck by the Perkins letter, which claimed that "almost
every individual in town had been gratified with a sight of him." I wondered
how many people that was, so I looked up the old census figures, and found
that figures were available only for Cape Ann as a whole and not for Perkins's
town of Gloucester. However, Cape Ann held over 6,000 people, and
Gloucester was the largest town on Cape Ann.

The librarian also showed me a painting of the serpent that belongs to the
Nahant Historical Society. It had been made by one of the 19th-century eye-
witnesses, and is available for public scrutiny, as are all these documents. I also
discovered that Colonel Perkins bought a plot of land on Nahant overlooking
Egg Rock that year, and built the stone cottage that still stands there.

The oldest recorded sighting from Nahant seems to be the one noted by
Obadiah Turner on September 5, 1641, at Nahant Beach (which was then
called part of Lynn Beach):

> Some, being on ye great beache gathering of clams and seaweed
> wch had been cast thereon by ye mightie storm, did spy a most won-
> derful serpent a shorte way off from ye shore. He was as big round in

ye thickest part as a wine pipe; and they do affirm that he was fifteen
fathoms or more in length. A most wonderful tale. But ye witnesses be
credible, and it would be of no account to them to tell an untrue tale.

Wee have likewise heard yt Cape Ann ye people have seene a
monster like unto this, whch did there come out of ye sea and coile
himself upon ye land much to ye terror of they yt did see him.

Ye Indians doe say yt they have manie times seen a wonderful big
serpent lying on ye water, and reaching from Nahauntus to ye greate
rock wch we call Birdes Egg Rocke; wch is much above belief for yt
would be nigh upon a mile. Ye Indians, as said, be given to declaring
wonderful things, and it pleaseth them to make ye white people stare.
But making all discounts, I doe believe yt a wonderful monster in
forme of a serpent doth visit these waters.

I found another illustration, in pen and ink, of the serpent between
Nahant and Egg Rock, that belongs to the Nahant Historical Society. Nahant
had become the premier summer vacation spot for Boston's most respectable
citizens by 1819, and it was during that summer that hundreds of vacationers
and Nahant residents reported seeing the serpent off Nahant Beach (Long
Beach).

I stayed in the library until it closed, reading numerous letters testifying to
sightings like the one "which, in the presence of more than two hundred
witnesses, took place near the long beach of Nahant on Saturday morning
last. . . . The first view of the animal occasioned some agitation . . . one was
so near that the coachman exclaimed, 'Oh, see his glistening eye?'" (That
one was by James Prince of Nahant, August 16, 1819.) The sightings continued, *and centered in Nahant*—for instance, in 1832 the *Boston Sentinel* reported a sighting of the monster, again off Nahant, by Captain Sturgis of the cut-
ter *Hamilton*. The *New York Commercial* noted, wryly, "We hear that it is in
contemplation to change the name of the Boston watering-place from
Nahant to *Snake-haunt*—the vicinity being so extensively patronized by
the sea-serpent."

Even the ever-careful, skeptical, and scientific Henry David Thoreau got
into the act, in a journal entry dated June 14, 1857, in which he records sightings by his trusted friend Benjamin Marston Watson:

Watson tells me that he learned from pretty good authority that
Webster once saw the sea serpent. It seems that it was first seen in the
Bay between Manomet and Plymouth Beach by a perfectly reliable
Witness. . . . Webster, having had time to reflect on what had occurred,
at length said to Peterson, "For God's sake never say a word about
this to any one, for if it should be known that I have seen the sea ser-

pent, I should never hear the last of it . . ." So it has not leaked out till now.

The "Webster" referred to by Thoreau is the famous Daniel Webster, the dictionarian.

The great naturalist Louis Aggasiz, who summered in Nahant, said this in a public lecture in Philadelphia in 1949:

> **I have asked myself in connection with this subject whether there is not such an animal as the Sea-serpent. There are many who will doubt the existence of such a creature until it can be brought under the dissecting knife; but it has been seen by so many on whom we may rely that it is wrong to doubt it any longer.**

I was amazed to find many respectable *current* scientific texts defending the reality of the Nahant sea serpent, such as Rupert T. Gould's *The Case for the Sea-Serpent*, Bernard Heuvelmans's *In the Wake of the Sea-Serpents*, and Richard Ellis's *Monsters of the Deep*.

As I kept reading, sea serpent sighting dates, places, documentation, and names abounded like a school of fish.

Suddenly, amid the profusion of dates a thought struck me like an arrow. I followed the thought and found, to my astonishment, that each year the serpent had been sighted off Nahant, a major storm had struck Nahant: 1819, 1896, 1947. There were more "storm years" than "serpent years," but all storms were (of course) reported while not all serpent sightings were. I, for instance, am not about to go to the newspaper with my sighting story today.

I wonder if this might be a real piece of evidence for the Universal Wave Theory that Evan is working on. He thinks that there is some single force or form that connects all events on earth, and that this force, like all forms of energy, takes the form of waves. I had thoughtlessly dismissed the idea as "flaky" until now.

But even if Evan should become the next Einstein, what concerns me more than any Universal Wave Theory is the particular "wave" the serpent gave me. That stare—what does it mean? Why does it feel connected with Papa and with the dream of the Viking and the angel girl, and with my own narrow escapes from death—and, God forbid, with Mara? Why do I fear for her if the serpent was seeking *me*?

I wish this was only a dream, a fib, or a story I made up, because in a story all loose ends are tied up and all mysteries solved. I have written such stories. But we are not the author of our own story. Allah is. There is a great scrim between our minds and His. But there are some little liftings of that curtain: hints, glimpses, visions of the "more" behind the curtain of appearances. And at those lifting times, perhaps some real Things might creep out under the curtain, things we do not usually see, like sea serpents.

Allah gives us partial stories as clues to the meaning of the whole story. One of them is about a man named Adam and a woman named Eve and a garden named Eden, or Paradise, and a serpent named Iblis, or Satan, who swam into their sea of innocence and brought misery and death. What is the closest surviving icon of Eden in the world? Surely it is the sea, mother of all life forms. Was the Nahant serpent a relative of the Eden serpent as I am a relative of Adam? Was its name Kraken, or Leviathan, or the Worm Ouroboros, who eternally swallows his own tail in a blasphemous ecstasy of self-annihilation? If "there are more things in heaven and earth than are dreamed of in all our philosophies," how dare we say, "How can such things be?"

*   *   *   *   *

The next morning I went early to the Drum to hear the water music, and suddenly felt Something Very Wrong. I looked around. No one, no thing, on land or at sea. No serpent. Yet Something was wrong.

Then I saw it. One of the rocks of the Drum was missing! A five-foot boulder, rounded, half submerged at low tide. It was gone. The tide was now low, and I scampered over the dangerously wet rocks to the place where I was sure it had been. Sure enough, there was a hollow in the rocks and weeds and earth beneath, where the boulder had been. The hollow was just about the same size and shape as the boulder.

There were no telltale streaks on the other rocks to mark its passage. If it had been dragged away, or swept away by a storm (but there hasn't been a major storm for months!), there would have been scratch marks; but there were absolutely none. No clues. Yet I am sure it is missing; I know every major rock around the Drum as well as a mother knows every bump on her baby's face. Why would anyone steal a boulder? And how? It would take a crane to lift it.

I confided in Evan, back at the House. Evan and Eva were the only two Housebugs at home. I've never confided much in Eva, wise as she is, not because her handicap makes me feel uncomfortable, but because it does not feel right for a Muslim man to seek solace and wisdom from a young woman who seems to be some sort of pantheist or polytheist or nature mystic or whatever she is. Perhaps deep down I fear she is holier than I am.

Evan listened carefully to me, without patronizing, then argued back with his usual Dutch common sense: "But 'Isa, it's only a rock. What shall we do? Shall we call the police? Shall we fill out a Missing Rock Report? Shall we ask the police whether anyone has reported a wandering rock?"

"Do you think I'm going crazy, Evan?"

"No, no, certainly not. You are not crazy, Jack. But I think that maybe you are troubled and angry at your own forgetfulness. You *insist* so much.

You are so certain. You *have* to be certain. You would not make a good scientist."

"Please don't psychoanalyze me. That rock was there. I know it."

"All right. But why is it so important to you?"

"You're still psychoanalyzing me!"

"And you are still avoiding the question. That is not like you, Jack." (Evan always calls me "Isa.' He calls me 'Jack' only when he is very serious. Mother does exactly the opposite.)

I had to answer his question. "I don't know why it's so important to me. It's uncanny, that's why." Evan did not reply, but waited, in silence.

"I'm afraid," I confessed. (It is harder to deceive Evan's silence than his words.)

"What are you afraid of? Of a rock coming back to haunt you?"

"Don't make fun of me!"

"I'm not."

"I'm afraid it's a message. A warning, against something terrible. I'm afraid it has something to do with the sea serpent. No one else could have stolen that rock. But why? What does it mean?"

"Why must it *mean* something?"

"Because everything means something. Everything is a thread on the tapestry."

"That's true. We Calvinists believe in Predestination just as much as you Muslims do. But we are on the wrong side of the tapestry. We see—we see only what we see. We only see this side. Only God sees the other side."

"Alas, Evan, I wish that were always true. But I fear that some of us do see a little bit of the other side sometimes. And it's uncanny. O, I am afraid, Evan, I am afraid."

"I am more afraid of the beast within us than of any beast without, 'Isa."

"So am I, so am I. But that's the worst of it. Suppose the beast without has some connection with the more terrible beast within? That makes the fear worse. Double."

"What connection could do you think there could possibly be?"

"I don't know the limits of what's possible any more. And that's the scariest thing of all." A pause, then a confession: "I don't want to be alone today."

As if in answer to this confession, there was a knock at the door. It was Mara. Allah's angels must have sent her, for she gave me the most beautiful gift from the sea that I have ever seen, immediately after the stare of the serpent gave me the worst gift from the sea that I have ever seen.

(16) Mara's Hymn to the Sea

"Can you come to the Hill with me, Jack? I have something special to show you. You can only see it there."

"You can see it from here too," I said, thinking she had just seen the serpent.

"I don't want you to see it here, Jack. I want you to see it there."

"But I think I saw it already, Mara."

Her face fell like a mountain climber into an abyss. She held up a beautiful gold and blue box, shaped like a small treasure chest, which she had brought into the House with her. Trying to hide her anger, she said, softly, "You saw *this* already?"

"No, not *that*. I meant the sea serpent."

"The *sea serpent*? Is this a riddle game, or what?" (Like Mother, she often ended sentences with "or what?" I wondered: Was that because both were Jewish, or women, or ex-New Yorkers?)

"No, I really saw one. Only a few minutes ago."

"Oh. Then you never saw this box before."

"Of course not." I was a little annoyed that Mara found her precious box more important than my seeing a sea serpent! "What is it?"

"Oh." (The single syllable contained a continent of relief.) "I didn't *think* you would . . ."

"Would steal your stuff? Would spy on your private whatever-it-is? Come on, Mara!" I was shocked.

"You don't understand. This is . . ." She looked around to see that no one was listening. "This is the most important thing I own. And I've never shown it to anyone. And I want to show it to you. It's . . . it's . . . I can't say how close it is to me. No one but me has ever seen it."

"And you want to show it to me?" I was more than flattered.

"I think so. But I'm afraid to."

I took her hand and led her outside. Her fear drove away my desire to tell her about the sea serpent. I had to drive away her fear, not add to it.

As we climbed the Hill, the sunlight was so bright that it froze everything with its Medusa eye: the twenty little grey and white saltbox cottages that climbed Trimountain Road in a straight little row, the lobster fisherman in his red wooden boat a few hundred feet offshore, and even the speckled surface of the sea. We did not speak another word until we reached our sacred spot on the Hill.

"Why are you afraid, Mara?"

"It's something I've written."

"A letter?"

"No."

"A poem?"

"Close. Yes, it really is a poem, a long poem. But it's in the form of an essay."

"For school?"

"Oh, no! I'd never turn this in to school."

"What's it for then?"

"It's not *for* anything else except itself."

"I see. It must be very important to you. And precious. And personal."

"Yes." We were now atop the Hill, atop the world. Truth was easier here.

"What is it about?"

She hesitated. "The sea." She seemed to expect me to laugh, or to ask a foolish question, but I didn't.

"The sea is very close to my heart too. You know that, Mara. Why is it so hard for you to show it to me?"

"I'm afraid."

"What are you afraid of, Mara?"

"That you won't like it. No, something worse: that you won't understand it. And even worse, that you'll pretend to. I'm afraid it will drive a wedge between us."

"How could anything do that?"

"If we find out that we're not really the same."

"We're not *supposed* to be the same. We're supposed to be ourselves."

"Oh, I know. We don't have to love all the same things, just each other. But this is different. I . . . I so want you to understand this and to love this just as I do."

"Mara, how could I not love what you love so deeply, if I love you so deeply?"

"I don't know. I just know I'm afraid."

"I understand. I love you for that fear. It's terribly flattering." I smiled. She almost smiled back. "But we have to find out, don't we? If anything divides us, we have to find out. We can't have any fear in our love."

"Not even a little?"

"Not if we want a perfect love."

"Why?"

"Because perfect love drives out fear."

"Suppose we don't *have* 'perfect love'?"

"Then we have to *make* it perfect." I was adamant and absolute.

"How?"

"We have to expose it to the test. That way, we know it won't fail."

"Thank you, 'Isa. I will trust you too." (Mara too never calls me 'Isa unless she is very serious.) She gave me that wan little smile—the smile that was the rising sun evaporating the fogs of fear. "I keep it locked up in this special box." She offered me the box—almost offered *up* the box, as if she were a priest offering the Catholic Mass.

"Your box is like your heart."

Her smile brightened. "That's sweet of you to say, Jack. Yes, I guess it is like my heart: locked and hidden away. And . . . and I think maybe I am finding one who will unlock it and enter in. I hope I am. That is why I am afraid."

"Do I have your permission to try to explore your fear with you?"

"How gracious of you, Jack, to ask permission before you enter! You are a gentleman. That's why I trust you, that's why I come here alone with you, even though we're supposed to be chaperoned."

"That is my tradition, yes. Is it your tradition too?"

"Yes."

"I didn't know you were that Orthodox."

"And how do you feel about that?"

"Safe. We are 'on the same page,' as they say."

"But if both your people and my people would not approve of us being alone together, then 'the same page' is not safety but rebellion, isn't it?"

"I certainly hope not. How strict is that rule for you? Is it a law? A commandment?"

"Not like the moral laws, the Ten Commandments, or the kosher dietary laws, or the laws of worship. They're not 'on the books,' they're what is approved in practice. Even so, I would never be alone with any other man. Do you know why I am here with you, 'Isa?"

"Because you trust me, I hope."

"Yes, that's right. Not just because I love you, but because I also trust you. That is even more important than love. Because there can be trust without love, and that is something; but there can be no love without trust. That is nothing."

"Then can we try to explore your fear now?—why you're afraid to show me your poem?"

"All right, I think it has something to do with my Jewishness."

"I don't understand. You mean Jews aren't supposed to be romantic poets? Or Jews aren't supposed to love the sea?"

"I don't know. Maybe that's it. Have you ever read a story about a Jewish surfer, or a Jewish sailor?"

"Sure. Jonah."

"No, he was only a passenger. The sailors were Gentiles."

"I guess not, then."

"We Jews are supposed to be doctors and lawyers and financiers and journalists, right? Not poets. Maybe novelists, but not poets. Right?"

"No, I don't see why that should be right. Are you testing me with those stereotypes?"

She ignored my question, and went on. "And Jews are supposed to be pragmatists and rationalists and scientists, not poets, right? And Jews are supposed to be city people, not country people or nature people or sea people, right?" I thought I detected some agitation in her voice.

"Mara, stop!" I said, suddenly but gently. "Stop with the stereotypes. I don't see you under any stereotype at all."

"Are you sure? Are you sure you don't think of me as 'a Jew but . . .'? 'A different kind of Jew'? 'A non-Jewish Jew'?

"No, I never thought that. You don't fit categories."

"What about the category of Jew?"

"Yes, you are a Jew, and I love you as a Jew."

"But you're not glad I'm a Jew. How can you be? You're a Muslim. Don't you wish I was a Muslim?"

"Not if that made you any different than you are, no. I wish everyone was a Muslim, because it's true, and how can I not wish the truth to everyone? But it's not *in spite of* my faith that I love you as a Jew. My own faith tells me to do that. The Qur'an says there is only one true religion, the worship of the one God, and Jews and Muslims and Christians all worship the same God."

"Oh, is that why you love me? Because you're commanded to in the Qur'an?"

"No, no, all I mean is that there's no conflict, no problem for me there. I love you as a Jew, and as a romantic, and as a poet, and as a sea-lover, and as everything else you are, just because it's you. I love your Jewishness because I love your Mara-ness."

Her defensiveness began to relax. "What about Jews being sailors?" she asked, now in a half-laughing voice.

"The greatest Jew was the greatest sailor."

"Moses, you mean? In the river bulrushes?"

"I was thinking of the man I was named after."

"Jesus? How was he a sailor?"

"Didn't you ever hear the song about that?"

"Oh, 'Suzanne'? I think so. Help me remember. What are the lines again?"

And as they sang it together, the Jew and the Muslim conquered their fear through the song about the sailor Jesus.

And Jesus was a sailor
When he walked upon the water
And he spent a long time watching
From his lonely wooden tower
And when he knew for certain
Only drowning men could see him
He said "All men will be sailors then
Until the sea shall free them."
And you want to travel with him
And you want to travel blind
And you think maybe you'll trust him
For he's touched your perfect body with his mind.

Mara smiled when we finished. "You may have my poem now. But you must promise not to tell anyone about it. It's been a secret between the two of us—me and God—for a long time. Now it's got to be a secret among just the three of us, OK?"

"OK."

Without a word, she placed the box in my hands, ceremoniously, and left. We both understood that this was a sacred silence for a sacred transaction. We also understood that the last thing either of us would want would be Mara peering over my shoulder as I read it. On her part it had been freely written and freely given to me; on my part it was freely received, and would be freely read and then freely responded to.

I took the box home and read Mara's essay three times that day. It was, quite simply, the most beautiful thing I have ever read about the second most beautiful thing I have ever seen, written *by* the most beautiful thing I have ever seen. As I read it I savored each word. Pulsating rods of light and fire came out of it and into my soul. It was not just a poem, certainly not an "essay." It was a *thing*, a solid entity, a jewel, a sea-stone, a gift of the sea, a pebble of thought shaped by years of caressing waves of wisdom and love from Mara, from the sea (the *mare*) of her soul, polished until it shone. My heart received and reflected its shine.

(Editor's Note: Mara's essay is not printed here. It was posthumously published, under a pen name, as *The Sea Within* by St. Augustine's Press in 2006.)

The next day, early in the morning, we met on the Hill. We had made no verbal arrangement, we both just knew we would be there. I solemnly laid the box in her lap and said, "Now these eyes, the eyes of 'Isa Ben Adam, and no other, have seen the two most beautiful things in the world: your face and your soul. And they are one. And I am one with both of them. And if I ever see a third thing as beautiful, I know I will not be able to stand on these two feet and live, but I shall instantly die and go straight to Paradise."

She had scrutinized my face carefully, looking for the slightest sign of patronizing or fakery. When she heard these words and saw my eyes, she smiled with her whole body, as if she had just ended labor and given birth.

"You are a poet too, 'Isa," she said, "like me. Even if you are a poet of flattery, and not a poet of truth, you are a poet." Here her eyes twinkled, and almost winked. It was a test.

"Flattery? I don't know how to do flattery. I am a blunt man, Mara—too blunt for my own good, most people say. Truth is even more important to me than beauty. I meant every word of what I said to you, literally. I would sooner go deaf and dumb than lie to you."

"I'm very, very good at seeing through masks, you know." Her eyes suddenly looked inward. "I *hate* them." The last three words were suddenly hard and cold. It was as shocking as if the sun itself had turned to ice. "They kill you," she added. Then: "I can't talk any more now. Will you come here tomorrow morning?"

"Will morning come tomorrow? Will the sun be here tomorrow?" I answered.

"Now that's the difference between us, I think," she replied. "You think you're certain of that, but I only hope for it." She gave a tiny, wry smile and half walked, half danced away.

The next morning I was on the Hill long before Mara returned. She found me lying down in the little patch of grass at the summit. The pale blue sky overarched the world like a rainbow with the assurance that however tangled and vexed the red thickets of the world became; Heaven would always remain calm and blue. If God had made the sky red instead of blue, I mused, the human race would certainly have gone collectively insane by now. Mara lay down too, her head a foot from mine, her body stretched south, mine north. We lay there, flat as flounder, under the infinite sky. For 360 degrees around us, nothing but sky was visible. The horizon and the sea were *below* us.

"The sky feels close here," she said. "No, more than close—*present*. Like the breath of a very large angel."

"Yes! That's exactly how it feels," I replied.

"Or two kids taking a ride on a magic carpet," she amended. "Don't your people have a lot of stories about magic carpets? Maybe they invented them because they liked to lay flat on hills like this."

"I don't think there are hills *like this* in the desert."

Mara continued her musing: "Just imagine that this little patch of grass under our backs is the fibers of the carpet, and we're not just looking at the sky but flying through it. We're in it. We're part of the sky. We're not heavy things on the earth any more, but feathers floating through the clouds."

"Oh, yes," I said again, as the kite of my imagination caught the wind of hers. "I actually feel it. How easy it is to feel it here! It actually gives you vertigo. You know, this place has real magic in it."

"I know. Did you ever want to be a bird?"

"No, but I wanted to be an astronaut. I wanted to get into the heavens. But here, you realize that you're in the heavens already."

"You know, you're right, Jack. We are, literally. In the heavens. In a spaceship. Spaceship Earth. The most well-equipped space ship ever designed. And it's a house, too, a home, with great interior decorations."

"*Allah akbar*! God is great! *We* could never have designed it. We don't have the intelligence."

She corrected me: "We don't have the *imagination*."

* * * * *

At the mosque this Friday a strange visiting Imam spoke of the sea. His words sounded rasping, like a crow's, compared to Mara's, but I could not ignore them. They seemed addressed directly to me. They were a warning. Essentially, this is what he said:

"You live near the sea. The sea is enchanting. It casts a spell. It is mysterious. It invites you to enter into it, to become one with it. It is like a beautiful woman.

"But beauty is great power, and power is open to either good or evil. Beauty attracts us like a great magnet, to great good—or to great evil. Thus in great beauty there is great danger.

"This is especially true of the beauty of the sea. There are angels and djinni in the sea, just as there are angels and djinni in the desert. To enter either of these two places of material emptiness is to enter a place of spiritual crowdedness. They are two great battlefields for the jihad, the struggle between good and evil on this earth.

"Do not take djinni lightly."

They say that those who live by the seaside sometimes learn to hear the voices in the sea. They say that those who linger too long by the edge of the sea come to hear the voices of the drowned. Or even other voices, voices of the djinni. So they say.

(17) The Summer of Love

It is familiar but amazing how familiar things become amazing when you are in love. Mara and I visited the places around Boston that all the tourists visit, and we had seen many of these places before; yet all was new: it was now a magic carpet, it was fantasyland. It was as new as the first day of creation because it was seen through the eyes of love, the eyes which make all things new. Nantucket, Martha's Vineyard, Cape Cod, Scituate Harbor, Nantastket Beach, Fenway Park, the top of the Prudential Center, the Public Garden, the Swan Boats, the Aquarium, Fanueil Hall, Beacon Hill, the State House, the Freedom Trail, the Old North Church, the North End, Harvard, Hammond Castle, Gloucester Harbor, Rockport—we left our footprints in every one. More important, we left our soul prints. We even got lost on the subway, like "Charlie on the MTA" of Kingston Trio fame ("The Man Who Never Returned").

Though we visited dozens of beautiful places, our favorite one remained Bailey's Hill. The Hill seemed to have a power of memory in it, for I remember all our conversations there much better than any of our conversations anywhere else.

One of the earliest ones was about guano and rocks.

We were walking over the top of the Hill, toward the Drum. I was kicking golf-ball-sized rocks ahead of me, unthinkingly, as I've done since I was five. Mara noticed it, smiled, and said to me, "You're still a little kid." Then, seeing my embarrassment, added, "No, I mean it as a compliment, not an insult. You're still alive. Most people die when they grow up." I smiled back and said, "No one ever said that to me before. Thank you. That was a great gift."

By this time we were walking over the rocks that led down to the Drum. "What's that?" Mara suddenly asked, pointing to the greenish-white patches on the top of all the rocks.

"You really don't know?"

"No. What is it?"

"It's guano."

"Is that a pun or something? It's a knock-knock joke, right? I'm supposed to say 'Guano who?'"

"No, no," I laughed. It's really guano. Guano is bird droppings!"

"Shit!" Mara exclaimed, jumping off the guano-covered rock she was walking on and examining her shoe.

"That's the good old Anglo-Saxon word for it, I think," I said. "It happens, you know."

"Yuk. Don't you mind it? It spoils the beautiful rocks."

"No, I don't mind it. In fact I've learned to love it."

"How?"

"I'll tell you the story behind that . . . "

"Oh, I can't wait. A shit story. 'How I Learned to Love Bird Shit' by 'Isa Ben Adam—I can see the title now gracing the pages of the great literary anthologies for all future generations." (I love it when Mara is confident enough to be sarcastic. She is both sweet and sour, and each of those two tastes brings out the other in her.)

"Seriously, Nahant taught me to accept the guano with the rocks."

"Like 'the bitter with the sweet'?"

"Yes. Guano is beautiful too if you look at the big picture."

"Nature, you mean?"

"Yes. Nothing natural is evil. Shit isn't evil. Rape and torture and murder are evil, but they're not natural."

"That makes sense. But everybody knows *that*."

"But I think I've figured out *why*. It's because in nature there's only one path, one way, one *Tao*. But for us there are two: good and evil, natural and unnatural, following *Tao* and not following *Tao*."

"Oh!" Mara's eyes lit up. "That brings Lao Tzu and Moses together."

"You mean Moses's sermon about choosing life and the blessing, not death and the curse?"

"Yes."

"The prophet Muhammad (peace be upon him!) said the same thing as Moses: there is a Straight Path and a Crooked Path, and we have to choose to walk the Straight Path. But nature doesn't have to choose."

"But then human life can't be just part of nature, can it?"

"No. We have to choose."

"And sometimes we choose evil."

"Yes. But maybe God sees even our evil as we see these bird droppings: not wasted, but good for something, a kind of fertilizer for something good, some other part of our life. *We* can't do that. Because you have to stand outside anything to see it whole. We can do that to nature, but not to ourselves."

"I wonder whether we can do it even to nature," she protested. "Nature's a mystery."

"It's hard to do, and we can't do it well, or completely, but we can do it, I think. For instance, with guano. You didn't see it as part of the beautiful whole, but I did."

"Maybe you only thought you did."

"Maybe."

"I like you when you say 'maybe,' Jack."

We were sitting on some clean rocks listening to the water music at the Drum. Both the sea and its music were very quiet today, and you had to be quiet to hear them. You had to stop even whispering if you wanted to hear their whisper.

Suddenly, after ten minutes of silence, Mara said, "I knew someone who claimed he could hear the grass growing. He was an old hermit. He was very thoughtful, and very—*different.* I asked him once whether he could teach me to hear the grass growing, and he said, 'Only if you have a lot of time.' I think he was right. You have to learn to slow down before you can learn to listen."

"He was right," I said. "I learned that too, listening to the sea. But hearing grass grow? I don't know about that."

"Oh, I think you could hear the grass. I think you could even hear rocks. I think God hears rocks, anyway."

"How can you hear rocks? They don't *do* anything."

"Yes, they do. They just act slower than the grass. But they act. Everything acts in some way, even rocks. Everything real, anyway."

"What do rocks *do*?"

"They block the grass. And they stop the waves. And they jut out there and take up space. That's something."

"You're right."

"I wonder if I could hear rocks some day. Maybe different people have different ears. You and I have ears for the sea, and my old hermit had ears for the grass. Maybe some people have ears for rocks. "

"I think Eva said that once."

"What do you think it would be like to hear rocks?"

"I don't know, but I think it would be great to hear them, not just to see them. Hearing gets you *inside.*"

We were silent for a long time looking at the rocks. The rocks on the south and east sides of the Hill are stacked like the skyscrapers of lower Manhattan. Looking beyond them, across the water, we could see the modest skyscrapers of downtown Boston. As we were gazing at these two skylines, I asked,

"See those two skylines? The rocks and the buildings?"

"Yes."

"I wonder why the rocks look like buildings but the buildings don't look like rocks."

"I don't understand. Why is that a puzzle?"

"Because it ought to be the other way round. Art imitates nature, not vice versa."

"Oh, I see. That *is* a puzzle. Those buildings are full of planning, and mind, and reason, and art—and yet they don't have much power to suggest rocks. And the rocks don't have any human design or plan, or mind behind them, yet they have a lot of power to suggest buildings."

"And the rocks have other powers too: to inspire us, and to make us peaceful, and not to bore us. We can enjoy ourselves sitting here for hours, more than we can enjoy ourselves sitting on a city street corner for hours."

"That's true. Why is that? What's your solution to that riddle?"

"There's only one possible. There must be a mind much greater than ours behind the rock."

"You're absolutely right, Jack. I think that will be my favorite argument for the existence of God. How come that's not mentioned in the great philosophers?"

"Ah, but it *is* in a great philosopher. Her name is Mara."

She kissed me then, very quickly and gently. It was mentally (not physically) very erotic.

*   *   *   *   *

A few days after this, we were again at the Drum, listening to the sea. As our souls were in the presence of the sea, we were talking about the power of the sea over the soul.

"You're not like most philosophers, 'Isa," Mara said. "You're not a rationalist, and you're not an irrationalist either, are you? You love both reason and mystery, don't you?"

"Yes."

"Tell me why you love mystery."

"I think all deep thinkers do. They know that the only things really worth thinking about, in the long run, are the things thought can't conquer."

"That's why you love the sea, isn't it?"

"That's one of a hundred reasons."

"I mean, as a philosopher. Your *thought* loves the sea."

"Yes."

"Why?"

"Did you ever read Xenophon's *Anabasis*?"

"No. What is it?"

"It's the simple story they give second-year Greek students. These Greek soldiers are somewhere far away, in Asia, as far as India, I think, fighting for Alexander the Great, and they have to get home, and they have to march thousands of miles up-country, and they're going to die of starvation unless they can reach the sea, and the high point of the story is just two words: when they finally see the sea, they all say: 'Ta thallata, ta thallata!' 'The sea, the sea!' That's it, that's the end, the goal, the point of all their marching. Well, I think of thought as those soldiers, searching for the sea, and when they find it, that's the limit of thought. You can't march an infantry onto the sea; you can't walk on water. And our minds can't march on the sea of mystery either, as they can on the land of reason. All we can do is play in the waves, at the border, the beach."

"So the greatest philosopher is just a little kid playing at the beach."

"Yes."

"And is that what all those books finally come to? Do they just sink when they come to the sea? I mean, is the sea the enemy of books?"

"No. The sea is the biggest book in the world."

"What about the Qur'an?"

"That's bigger than the world."

*   *   *   *   *

The next time we went to the Drum, the sea was calm again, yet the music was different. Just as each storm is different, each calm is also different. The last calm was full of whispers. Today's calm was full of soft blubberings and slobberings. They came from the subsurface swells, the invisible rivers of life that stir the surface of the sea as their spiritual equivalents stir the surface of our consciousness.

"It's asleep today, but alive," I remarked.

"That's an uneasy sleep," Mara replied.

"All her sleeps are uneasy. No deep sleep for the Deep."

"Does that make her scary to you? The sleeping monster?"

"No. She's not a monster, she's a Mama. When I was little, we all slept in the same room, and it felt so comforting just to hear Mama snore, just to know she was alive. Maybe I thought sleep was a kind of death. I used to wake up in the middle of the night and my first thought was to be sure Mama was still breathing. When I heard it, I had peace, and I could sleep again."

"Do you miss the peace your Mama gave you?"

"I miss Mama but I don't miss the peace, because I still get it—from the sea."

"Do you think your Mama's spirit is moving it?"

"No, no, that's paganism."

"Then how do you explain it? How does the sea give you that peace?"

"I don't know. It's a mystery. Papa used to say there's an angel in it."

"Well, whatever it is, it works. And if it works, it must be alive. And deep. And I don't think that's paganism. Of course she isn't a goddess, or a spirit, or a person. But she *is* a mystery, just as you said. She's not smarter than you, Jack, but she's deeper."

*   *   *   *   *

The next day, the sea was whispering again. There were little waves, perfectly formed. "What do those waves look like to you, Jack?" Mara asked.

"They look like themselves."

"Yes, but don't they look like mouths?"

"Yes. They do."

"Have you ever wondered what they're saying? They've got to be saying something."

"You asked that beautiful question in your—your hymn to the sea. And you gave a beautiful answer."

"Thank you for calling it a hymn instead of an essay. No, I didn't give an answer. I didn't really figure it out."

"Then how can we hope to now?" .

"We can't. But maybe we can hope to figure out why we can't hope to figure it out. No, no, that's too clever. Let me think a minute." (A rare and wonderful habit!) Mara entered the silence and exited a minute later with this: "I think we can figure out its language, at least. It's music. It's singing. And we can't make out the song it's singing because it's too long to hear. It's millions of years long, and all we hear is a few syllables."

The fire of her spirit kindled mine. I replied, "And it's also the opposite: we miss it because it's too *short*. In words, not in time. It's not too many words, but too few. It's less than a single word, less than a syllable, even. Maybe it's just a single letter: the letter S. That's the shape of the wave, after all. Maybe it's saying 'shhhhhhh,' like Mother putting Baby to sleep. The last sound of the word 'Peace' echoing for millions of years."

"Yes, yes, that's it. And it's also something else, I think." (My fire was now kindling hers.) "S is not only the first sound of 'shhhhh' and the last sound of 'Peace' but also the last sound of 'yes.' And that's the word from the heart of God. That's like 'Be!'"

We were both silent. We had to be, before we burned each other's spirits up. We both understood that, and we both understood that we understood that. The mind-meld was almost a spiritual sexual intercourse.

* * * * *

Mara and I are beginning to talk about our future, in indirect ways, like little kids instinctively practicing for adult roles by playing at soldiers, or cops and robbers, or mommies and baby dolls.

Since we both love Nahant, we formulated a Nahant Manifesto, a proof that Nahant is the best place in the universe. The proof is mathematically perfect and infallible.

It works by a process of elimination. We draw circles, or irregular shapes, enclosing the places we want to live in and excluding the places we don't. Where all the circles overlap, that's the place—like a Venn diagram, or the old Ballantine beer signs.

First, it's got to be in America. Not only because we were born here but because despite all its deep, deep problems America is still the best place in the world to live in because it gives you the most opportunities—for good *or* for evil. Here, you can make of your life pretty much whatever you want.

Second, we need four seasons. We can't really appreciate summer without winter. And we love winter too, and blizzards. Hawaii and Florida and California are nice places to visit in January, but we don't want to live there. That would be like living without night, or pain, or death—or the New York Yankees, Evan would add. So it's got to be some place north of the sunbelt.

Third, we need the sea, as we need blood, or mothers, or air. That is totally non-negotiable. Midwesterners are really nice people, but we'd just dry up and die in Kansas.

Fourth, the ocean has to be warm enough to swim in. That means nothing north of Boston. Unless you have a wet suit or a seal's flab, you get shocked by the ocean, not comforted, when you swim in Maine or even New Hampshire. (We know. We tried it.)

Fifth, we want rocks as well as sand. North of Boston there's not much sand, and south of Boston there's not much rocks.

Sixth, we want a beautiful big sophisticated city nearby, for symphonies and museums and sports and movies and universities and libraries. Charleston, South Carolina, and Savannah, Georgia, are beautiful but have no winter. There are no other big cities on the coast until you come to New York. And the coastal suburbs of New York—New Jersey or Long Island—are pretty ugly.

Besides, Boston is history, and European architecture, and colleges, and even the world's largest per capita ice cream consumption. (That has nothing to do with it, but I just wanted to throw that in.)

Also, the *smell* of the sea is right here. A little *briny.* Smell is more important than you think: it involves you completely and defenselessly. It's the most animal sense and also the most mystical sense. It's the least rational, and the longest remembered.

Seventh, the prettiest place *and* the best beach within a few miles of Boston is Nahant. It's even an *island.* And occasionally it even gets great storms and great waves.

So Nahant is the best place to live on this entire planet. The proof is infallible, though it does not claim to include other planets in other solar systems.

Therefore we will both live in Nahant. That was said. What was not said, but what we both knew, was this: how could we ever live so close to each other without living with each other? How could we see each other on the street and not feel defeat if we were not living together as man and wife? We did not use the word "marriage" yet, but we both knew that's what we were talking about.

*   *   *   *   *

It's almost as if Mara read my last entry, for today we both spoke openly about marriage. (She probably did read my mind. It happens.) It started with a conversation about values, and then children.

We are both only-children, without siblings, and we both want to have many children. Mara's father left when she was young, and her mother never married again. She says she barely remembers her father, and avoids the topic. A cloud comes over her when she does. There is something there that needs to come to light some day.

Here is how the conversation went.

"Do you want to have a lot of kids, Jack?"

"Yes."

"What do you want for your kids?"

"I want them to be good, and then wise, and then happy."

"What about rich?"

"That comes after happy."

"Sounds like you've thought it through pretty well."

"How could you not think it through? Marriage and family is the most important thing in life. How could you not want clear maps on your most important journey? It's more tragic to lose your way and drive off *that* road than any other one in this world."

"Uh-huh." Mara just nodded, and said nothing. I don't think she was skeptical, just waiting.

"What do you think of my philosophy, Mara?"

"I love your philosophy, 'Isa. If that's really you, and if you live that as well as think it, I think you'd be the best father in the world."

"And I think that any woman who would say that to me, and really believe it, would be the best mother in the world."

Mara smiled, but in a troubled kind of way. She just sat there, thoughtfully. So I added, "I couldn't help saying that, even though it sounds too much like a marriage proposal, and I'm really scared of scaring you away."

"'Isa, that was the best thing you said to me ever, because it was so totally honest. I love you when you're vulnerable." Half the trouble left her smile.

Women always say that. Why? Why do they love vulnerable men? I guess the answer came next, when I was "vulnerable" enough to ask her whether she thought I left anything out of my values map, and her answer made me feel as if I had dressed for a formal ball and forgotten to wear pants. "Where does love fit in, Jack?"

"I guess it fits in everywhere."

"At the top too?"

"Yes. The top kind of love at the top, I guess."

"I like it when you say 'I guess,' Jack."

I don't remember what I said to that. I just remember (1) that I was confused, and that (2) that made her smile, and that (3) *that* made me *more* confused, and that (4) *that* made her smile even more, and that (5) her smile meant more to me than anything else in this world, and I was not at all confused about *that*.

*   *   *   *   *

That last conversation paved the way for a deeper one, because we have been extremely honest with each other, and intellectually intimate, though not physically intimate.

"Jack, you told me a lot yesterday about yourself, and the kind of father you want to be. You've thought about that a lot, haven't you?"

"Yes."

"Well, I wonder whether you've also thought a lot about the kind of woman you want to be the mother of your children."

We still were avoiding the words 'husband' and 'wife,' but obviously that's what we both meant. So I said, "You mean what kind of woman do I want for a wife, don't you?"

"Yes, I do, Jack. I want to know that. I know you *feel* something very deep for me, and you know I feel that for you too, but I want to know what you've always *thought* about marriage, even before you met me. Because that's what's going to shape your marriage forever: your thoughts."

"How philosophical you are, Mara!"

She smiled at the compliment, and after a minute of thinking, added, "I see it this way: I think our life is like the sea, and our feelings are like the waves, and our philosophy of life is like the sea floor. Feelings are supposed to change, like waves, but thoughts should stay the same, like the ocean floor. So I want to know your thoughts."

"All of them?"

"Just one. Give me just one. Just finish this sentence for me: 'The woman I marry will be . . .'"

"Everything," I answered instantly. "She will be everything to me. Everything. All or nothing. I will be totally faithful to her and she will be totally faithful to me."

"What do you mean by 'all or nothing'? What if this woman was unfaithful, just once, and then repented and came back to you begging for your forgiveness? Would you never take her back?"

"She would never be unfaithful, and neither would I. Never. We'd have total trust in each other. Total. It's a total risk; all your eggs in that one person's basket. That's what I mean by all or nothing. Total trust. Once that total trust is breached, everything is gone forever."

"Why?"

"Because fidelity is . . . it's just different from everything else—everything else except death and God: it's unique, it's all or nothing. Because a person isn't like a car. You can fix a broken car. You can replace anything—except God or your wife or husband."

"You don't think you can fix a broken person?"

"Of course you can. That's what doctors and psychologists are for. But you can't fix a marriage as easily as you can fix one person alone. Because marriage is different from everything else. If it's not all or nothing, then it's not marriage."

"So it's a total risk."

"Exactly. I will put my heart and my life and my total trust in the hands of one person forever, and if that one person drops my heart, then my heart is broken, like an egg. And you can't ever put that back together again. Maybe that's what Humpty Dumpty means, on a symbolic level."

"But I thought Muslims could have up to four wives. How can you give 100% to more than one?"

"Muslims are *permitted* to have four wives. Most have only one, even in the East. Most want only one. We believe one is the norm. Our prophet Muhammad allowed us four for the same reason your prophet Moses allowed you divorce."

"What's that?"

"Well, according to the Christians' prophet Jesus (blessed be all three!): it was a compromise, 'because of the hardness of your hearts,' Jesus said. But he said that God did not want that from the beginning. One Adam, one Eve."

"You'd never consider divorce?"

"Never. As I said, all or nothing."

"And that formula, 'all or nothing,' does that also mean no forgiveness, then?"

"For anything else, yes, but not for infidelity."

"Why?"

"Because of total trust. Total trust is like virginity: once it's gone, you can't get it back."

"What if *you* were unfaithful, just once, and then repented, and came to your wife confessing and begging for forgiveness?"

"That would never happen. I would never be unfaithful."

"But if you were? Would it be the same for you as for her? Do you have a double standard?"

"No, I don't have a double standard. The Commandments are the same for everybody."

"Then they're the same for you and for her."

"Yes."

"So if you were unfaithful just once, that would be the end? Would you leave her, even if she forgave you?"

"No. That would be cruel and unfair."

"What would you do, then? Not tell her? Live a lie?"

"I couldn't live a lie."

"Then you'd tell her."

"Yes, but . . ."

"And if she didn't forgive you, you'd divorce?"

"No, that would never happen either. I don't believe in divorce. I believe in divorce only for infidelity, and I would never be unfaithful. So I can't really answer your question. It's like, 'What would you do if ants talked to you?' I can't imagine that."

"You can't imagine yourself being unfaithful, so you can't really answer that question."

"Right."

"But you *could* imagine your wife being unfaithful, and you *did* answer that question. So it sounds to me like you do have a double standard in there somewhere."

I was honest enough to confess my confusion—and my uncertainty. "I've got to think more about that."

"*We've* got to think more about that," she corrected me, for the second time.

"Yes, we do. Maybe I do have a double standard 'in there somewhere.' I don't know. I don't think so. I don't want to. But one thing I do know: I will never be unfaithful to the woman I love and promise myself to. That's the most important promise in your life. If you violate that, if you're not good for that promise, you're good for *nothing*." I spoke with conviction there, not with "maybes."

Mara was silent. I asked, quietly, "Do you think I'm too dogmatic about my principles?" I was terrified that she would give some typical squishy American answer that would show me I had fallen in love with a moral relativist.

"No, 'Isa. I agree with your principles. But I think you might be a little too dogmatic about yourself."

"Mara, I know the self is a great mystery, and I don't think I've got it all mapped out. I'm just making you a solemn promise: I would far sooner kill myself than betray you."

Mara smiled, and kissed me gently on the cheek. Neither of us said anything about the sudden transition from "the woman I marry" to "you."

*   *   *   *   *

The next day, Mara came with a follow-up question, asked with a very serious face: "Suppose you proposed to me some day, and I accepted, and then we had sex before we were married. Would you consider that a betrayal? I know that's a betrayal of God, and His will, but would you consider that also a betrayal of me, or of us, or of you?"

"Yes," I answered, immediately. "I would be wronging you as well as myself and God." (Even though we had no doubt that we worshipped the same God, I usually used the generic word "God" instead of "Allah" with her—

precisely because "there is no God but God.") "Do you feel the same way, Mara?"

"I think so."

A brilliant thought leaped into my mind. "Remember that day, a week after we first met, when we promised to bring our favorite poem to the Hill and read it to each other? And we both brought the same poem, Matthew Arnold's 'Dover Beach.' Do you remember that last line?"

"Yes: 'Ah, love! Let us be true to one another.'"

"Remember what we did when we came to that last line?"

"I do. What do *you* remember of that moment, Jack?"

"I remember that we looked into each other's eyes, very seriously, and we both saw something there, we *knew* something there. And then we pulled back. And then both of us opened our mouths simultaneously and spoke those same words to each other. But this time the words weren't in someone else's poem, they were in our own hearts. We both said, 'Ah, love! Let us be true to one another.'"

"So tell me, 'Isa, what is that to you? A beautiful ideal?"

"No, it's a necessity."

"So what do you want to do about it?"

"Let's *do* what we *said*. Let's make a solemn pact right now, to each other and to God, before each other and before God, to be true to one another from this moment until we die, whether we ever marry or not. If we are meant for each other, it has to be pure, it has to be true."

Mara looked at me with increasing respect as I went on, then she answered, in a tone of resolve, "I will do that with you here, now, 'Isa Ben Adam, and I will be very happy to do that. If we marry, we will start right, not wrong; we will not adulterate, we will not spoil, this beautiful thing. And if we don't marry, if we part, well, we don't want to adulterate *two* future marriages, yours and mine."

We vowed, and we sealed our vow with a kiss of the lips and (more importantly) of the eyes.

And that's how it stands.

*   *   *   *   *

I have been thinking about our pact.

I know myself well enough to know the beast within, and the need to cage it; and I defend, to my non-Muslim friends, the traditional Muslim solution to the problem of sexual temptation, which is essentially sexual segregation and chaperones. The strategy is to control the environment so that two young people are never allowed to be alone in private with each other before marriage. Muslims don't do "dating."

This solution works. It certainly works better than the American system, which produces Sodom and Gomorrah, and is already bringing down upon America the inevitable fire and brimstone. I don't mean by that a supernatural miracle, I mean the natural, inevitable destruction of the institution of the stable family, which is woman's only security and society's only stability.

Why then do I dare to see Mara alone on the Hill and take her all around the city? Because with all my heart I meant every word I said to Mara: I would no more adulterate our love than my own life. I do not *want* "sex," I want *her*, the whole her, unbroken and unpolluted, as my wife, not my mistress.

Mother would not let us stay in the House alone together, but no one is ever in the House alone. There is always someone there. Mother also warns me about even being outside in public together, like on the Hill. Though she allows it, I know she watches us. I think she also sends her guardian angel to watch us when we're out of her sight. She is an American and a Christian, but at heart she is like a strict, old-fashioned, old-world Muslim.

At the Muslim Center they constantly debate about what they call "enculturation"—how far, and in what areas of our lives, we can be Americanized without losing our Muslim identity. This is the number one topic there every week among Muslims my age, and there is a great range of opinions, from strict segregation and chaperoning to free, unsupervised American dating. I'm somewhere between the two extremes.

Mother and I had a long conversation about this at the House one morning. I called the traditional Muslim solution "radical surgery," and she replied, "Radical diseases *need* radical surgery."

"Do you think we need it too?"

"I don't know. I *hope* you don't, but I fear you do, because *you* don't think you do."

"Don't you trust me? Don't you believe me? Why are you so suspicious, Mother?"

"I am suspicious of anyone's ability to be chaste today without a lot of social helps. In the middle of a toxic atmosphere, do you think you can stay healthy without a gas mask?"

"Yes. If I really want to, I can."

"I meant that 'you' in the plural. How can you answer for Mara too?"

"She answers for herself, and she's with me 100%."

"Good. That's good. But you can't be *sure* . . ."

"Yes I can!"

"You have a lot of confidence in yourself, 'Isa."

"No, I have a lot of confidence in the help of Allah. I don't trust myself. I trust Him." I spoke those last words with gusto, and Mother, surprisingly, looked sad. "Why do you look sad? Those are some of the most precious words anyone can speak."

"Yes, they are. But you've got them in the wrong order. You put 'I' first."

I was silent.

"You seem to think it depends on you."

"No. It all depends on Allah."

"I wasn't thinking of you and Allah, I was thinking of you and Mara. And I was thinking of why you were not thinking of her. Why did you forget her? Ask yourself that. Do you think chastity is only a man's work? Isn't the woman at least half responsible? More than half, even?"

"*More* than half? Why do you say that?"

"Because for centuries, in every culture, women have been taming men. And because in our culture here in America men have not changed, but women have. And I think you know that, Jack."

Yak sent five underlinings of Mother's word into my ears.

"Not Mara. She's different. She's pure. She's wise."

"Oh, she's like Allah, then?" The sarcasm in tone mitigated the blasphemy in content.

I was silent. "You're setting yourself up for a fall, Jack."

"By relying on the grace of God to be good? I'm surprised to hear that from you, Mother."

"No, by *presuming* on it."

"He gives His grace to whom He will—I think we Muslims know that as well as you do."

"Yes, but His grace usually comes through others. Including dead others. I mean your ancestors, your people, and their traditions. And you're *not* relying on that."

"What are you afraid of, Mother?"

"I fear you will fall, of course. I *hope* not. But I *fear* it. I fear you will fall badly."

"You think I'm pretty bad, then?"

"No, I fear you will fall badly not because you are bad but because you are good. You are a bright star. A dark star falls into the darkness and hardly notices it. But a bright star falls out of the sky and suddenly it's night. I think you know what I mean: you remember one night when you almost fell into its mouth, there on the Hill, when I first saw you."

"You think I will become something like a stone sunk in the sea?"

"No, 'Isa. I think you will bounce back, because you are strong. But I fear that maybe Mara will not."

I was doubly surprised—at Mother's concern for this relative stranger, and at my forgetting her. Fear awoke from the night places in my heart. It was a dragon with terrifying yellow eyes.

Then a fearless knight with a bright sword awoke, from the same place, and struck off the dragon's head. "You don't know her, Mother. I could almost take that as an insult to my beloved, and challenge you to a duel to defend her honor."

"Oh, stop speaking adolescent nonsense, Jack!"

"Nonsense about Mara? No, that is not. . . ."

"Nonsense about yourself. It's not as easy to be totally honest with your-self as you think it is."

If I am half as honest with myself as I think I am, I must admit that Mother has a point.

*   *   *   *   *

I must record here another conversation with Mother, that I can only call "incisive." I put it here because although it started out about God, it ended up about Mara.

We were sitting alone in the kitchen, she cooking and I eating. "'Isa," she said suddenly, "will you tell me honestly if the questions I ask you are too nosy or uncomfortable?"

"Of course, Mother. What do you want to know?"

"Thanks. I'd really like to know more about your faith."

"I'd be glad to explain it."

"I don't mean the religion of Islam. I can learn that from books. I mean the religion of 'Isa."

"I hope the religion of 'Isa is nothing more or less than the religion of Islam," I replied, firmly.

"A good answer! But what I mean is, what makes you tick? What do you love? Where does your heart move you?"

"Do you want to know how I pray?"

"Yes, but first I want to know how you *think*."

"I think as a Muslim."

"Yes, but how do *you* think as a Muslim? For instance, what saints and what writers move you most?"

"Well, to be frank, Mother, I think my head and my heart move me in differ-ent directions. My heart loves the Sufis, even though I'm what you'd call a main-line Shi'ite, so my mind can't agree with them. Maybe I don't understand them."

"What don't you understand in them?"

"How they can seem so—so *close* to Allah. They seem—they seem like you Christians: impossibly cozy. So comfortable. So close. And that would make reli-gion cheap. One of your theologians—Bonhoeffer, I think—calls it 'cheap grace.'"

"Do you think it's cheap for the Sufis?"

"No, I don't think it is. But I don't understand why."

"I can't tell you why it isn't cheap for the Sufis, but I can tell you why it isn't cheap for Christians. It's because the *price* of that closeness wasn't cheap. We believe that it cost God His own Son's blood. But I don't want to argue about doctrines; I want you to tell me about 'Isa. Tell me about your love. The Sufis talk about love. Is that why they interest you?"

"Yes. Because that seems to be a love that's not cozy and cheap and comfortable, but a fire that burns up everything evil and dishonest. If that's what you mean by love when you say that 'God is love,' then maybe we're closer than our theologians think we are. I don't know. But why do you ask me to tell you what I can't tell you because I *don't* understand?"

"I'm asking about what you do understand. I think you understand the power of love. I believe you love the same God I love. And I always want to hear how others love Him. And seeing Him through your eyes—seeing Him through other pairs of eyes—I am thinking that is a good thing too. Because if you really love someone, and you meet one of his friends, you want to know everything the friend knows about your beloved. Isn't that so?"

"Yes," I said. "But I can't really tell you much about my love for God because I don't understand it myself."

"Then can you tell me what your love for Mara looks like when you put it side by side with your love for God?"

"Yes, I think I can tell you that," I said. I was happy to answer that question because I wanted to sing Mara's praises, and my love for her, to the angels, and Mother was pretty close to angel. "They're not side by side; it's more like an egg in a nest, or an egg in a bird, or a bird in an egg."

She looked at me quizzically. "This will take a while to explain," I warned.

"We *have* a while," she replied. "A lifetime, we have. So go, already." She settled back in a big overstuffed chair, and I sat down on a hard, flat, wooden one. (My mind relaxes better if my body isn't totally relaxed.)

I hesitated so she began: "You have fallen in love." It was not a question but a statement.

"I'm still falling."

"I know. Almost every day I hear you putting on that tape of 'Hello, Young Lovers' from 'Anna and the King of Siam.'"

"Love sings," I said, simply.

"It does that. Tell me what it sings to you."

"It sings all the sweet and silly and sentimental songs," I said. "Like 'You're just too good to be true / Can't take my eyes off of you.'"

"The songs become literal." (She *knows*.)

"Yes."

"And Mara—what does she become?"

"She becomes a magnet to my soul that pulls it like a twenty-foot swell of the sea. She raises a swell in my spirit."

"Can you tell me what that means without the poetry? How does it make you feel?"

"It feels like I have no fear any more—except the fear of one thing, and that's the one thing everyone else *wants*, everyone who's not in love, I mean."

"What thing?"

"Freedom. Liberty. Autonomy. That's the one thing I *don't* want: freedom from her. I want to give her all my freedom. I want her to *take* all my liberty. And that feels like the freest thing I've ever done."

"That's exactly what Saint Ignatius said to God . . ."

"The founder of the Jesuits?"

"Yes. His most famous prayer begins with exactly your four words: 'Take all my liberty.'"

"Oh."

"Wouldn't you pray that to Allah too? 'Take all my liberty'?"

"Yes, but I don't feel anything like that kind of love for Allah. To want to marry Allah? That would be blasphemous, and ridiculous—more ridiculous than a flea wanting to marry a man. That's why we Muslims really can't understand how you Christians can use the language of romantic love for your relationship with God."

"There are big differences between us, of course. But there are likenesses too. You already told me one, about love wanting to give up liberty. I'll bet I can guess another one."

"Go ahead."

"How long does it take for you to get bored with Mara?"

"Silly question. Never."

"When you look into her eyes, could you do that forever?"

"It feels like it."

"Now what do you think you're going to be doing in Paradise forever without getting bored? Parties? Harems? Songs? Story telling?"

"No. Those are only images. They all get boring."

"Does God ever get boring?"

"Not to the pure soul."

"And in Paradise you will have a pure soul."

"Yes."

"So there you will see God—with the eyes of your soul, not your body—and not be bored for all eternity."

"So?"

"Don't you see the connection? Don't you see how that explains how you feel about Mara?"

"What do you mean?"

"I mean the only thing that never gets boring is God, and the only thing that never gets boring on earth is the image of God, another person. And love is the eye that sees it rightly."

"But—look, you want total frankness, right, Mother?"

"Yes. And I'll give it out too."

"Well, then, I think it's dangerous to call a human being the image of God. God has no images. And to call the relation between God and the human soul 'love'—that's dangerous too. Look at two horses in love. Look how human they seem—and look how horsey we seem. The horses stamp and stomp and jostle and run away and chase—look at the energy, the passion, the power! Now imagine two young lovers who have that spirit. Imagine them in a crowded department store. They can't take their eyes off each other. They're stamping and stomping with their eyes, the same spirit the horses have in their hooves. The air is charged with their electricity. It feels like the whole store is going to ignite and explode any second. They see a door. Instantly, it means the same thing to them: love. *Everything* they see means love to them. Everything is colored by their passion. A spark of instant telepathy runs between them, through the air. They stroll through the door together, pretending to be blasé, and as soon as they're through, and into some private place, they're instantly in each other's arms, smothering each other with kisses, looking into each other's eyes, emitting little cries of ecstasy, a pain that's a thousand times more ecstatic than any other pleasure. It's ecstatic static electricity. Now how could anyone possibly think that anything like *that* can go on between a man and God without blasphemy and foolishness?"

"A saint could."

"Your saints, maybe."

"Your Sufis aren't saints now? They talk that way too."

"I know. And I can't understand that. And yet I'm fascinated by them. Do you think *you* understand them?"

"I don't know, I'm not inside the soul of a Sufi. But doesn't it make sense to you, 'Isa, to say that our happiness in Heaven will feel more like sex than like morality? More like joy and beauty than law and order? Something that isn't safe, and comfortable, and proper, but wild, and ecstatic? Something more like those horses?"

"Like those horses? But then lust would be closer to God than morality."

"No, lust is *below* morality. And pure, unselfish, ecstatic love is above it."

"Hmmm . . . Don't you think there's a danger of confusing the two?"

"Oh, yes. Absolutely. That's probably why lust is the world's number one religion. It's our natural substitute for the real thing, the animal substitute for the angel-thing. But the confusion only works one way: from the bottom up, not from the top down."

"What do you mean?"

" I mean nobody who's ever experienced even a little of the higher love can confuse it with lust. But lusters can fool themselves and think they're lovers. And impure lovers can fool themselves and think they're in 'pure love' when they're not."

"Do you think that's me and Mara?"

"No, I'm not saying that. I don't know. But I do know you've got to be careful. It's easy to fool ourselves. And it's easy to fool ourselves about how easy it is to fool ourselves."

"We're not fooling ourselves. We both know what sex is for. And why it's so powerful and so holy. It's for making people; it's for letting God create more of those beings that are going to live for all eternity. America may have forgotten that but we haven't."

"Congratulations, 'Isa. In our day, that's a great achievement."

"Our two people—Muslims and Catholics, I mean—are pretty much the only people left in the world who know what sex is for. Isn't it incredible? The others all think it's for fun, and babies are 'accidents.' That's like thinking that eating is for fun, for titillating your taste buds, and health is an accident."

"You see much, 'Isa. I hope you always follow what you see, not just what you feel."

*   *   *   *   *

Mara went to a wedding with her mother last night. I was alone. I walked the beach (Long Beach) under purple skies and yellow moonlight, and the sea became Mara. Mare became Mara. (Her hair, anyway.) Then I understood: the angel in the sea that Papa told me about—it is Mara's angel.

I remembered Papa's favorite song, "Beautiful Dreamer," and how happy it used to make him. It was from another, simpler, innocent and happy era. I can still hear it playing on our old 78 rpm Victrola, in the tinny, far-away tones that sound like train whistles.

I started to sing it to the sea, and realized that I was singing it to Mara *and* to Mare. The sea looks like Mara: her hair is the waves. The sea feels like Mara: her skin is the surface of the deep. The sea sounds like Mara: her voice is the same music as the waves. The sea even tastes like Mara: her kiss, I think, is slightly salty. And the soul of the sea is deep and mysterious and full of life, like Mara's soul.

*   *   *   *   *

A perfect, perfect day. Mara and I explored the rock-strong, surf-tortured coastline of the North Shore, and of each other's spirit. I drove her home in time for supper. She had aunts and uncles coming over, who met me with much more natural, earthy, genuine acceptance than I ever felt from Mara's mother. We parted with a mutual, direct, and serious "I love you with all my heart and all my soul." When I got back to the House, I skipped supper, sat outside on the deck, breathed in the salty east wind, and watched the swells breaking on the vertical cliffs of the hill only two hundred feet away, exactly where Mara and I had stood together yesterday. A smile was glued on my face.

I declined supper and just sat still and smiling on the deck for well over an hour. Mother noticed this and came out and sat silently beside me. The silence was comfortable. Everything was comfortable. After a few minutes, she asked, playfully, "So what's the newest profundity of our resident philosopher?"

"Mara is the sea," I answered, cryptically.

"What? What nonsense is that?" Mother asked, in a voice no longer playful.

"Not literally, of course. Poetically."

"So translate, then."

"Into what language?"

"Into prose. You once spoke that language, remember?"

"That was before I met a living poem."

"And what happened then?"

"I lost myself in her. I found myself in her. It's the same thing."

"Which 'her'—Mara or the sea?"

"Both."

"So you lost your ego?"

"Yes."

"Too bad it wasn't your egotism instead."

"What do you mean?"

"You *can't* lose your ego, silly. You can't become anyone else. Never. Only your thought can do that, not your being. God created that being, and it's real, and it can't be killed, and it's not an illusion."

"Oh, I believe that. But I can give her my heart."

"You can give her the love of your heart, but you can't give her your heart. You will always have your own heart. If you didn't, it wouldn't be *you* that's loving her."

"Well, of course. But why so many philosophical distinctions today, Mother?"

"Why so *few* philosophical distinctions today, Jack? Since when do philosophers not like philosophy?"

"Since they fall in love. Do you have a problem with that?"

"With falling in love, I have no problem. With 'Mara is the sea' I have a problem. I think a few philosophical distinctions would be helpful here, such as the distinction between *homo sapiens* and an inorganic compound."

"Oh, Mother, you know what I mean. I mean I feel the same way about Mara and about the sea."

"And how is that, pray tell?"

"I want to drown in her."

"You'd better not go swimming today, then, if you still want to be here tomorrow."

"But Mother, it's only a metaphor. I don't literally want to drown my lungs in water."

"It sounds to me like you want to drown in your own feelings. I thought you liked to keep your feet on the ground and your head in the light."

"I'm surprised at you, Mother. I'm finally coming to understand your own prophet's mystical words, 'He who loses his self shall find it'—and now you're suspicious."

"You think Jesus was talking about a *girl*?"

"It's just an analogy. And it's the one you Christians use. Why are you suddenly getting so technical today, Mother?"

"Not technical. Basic. Mysticism, now—that can be very good, and true, and beautiful, but it can also be extremely dangerous. Like the sea!"

"Now I have to ask *you* to translate *your* poetry into prose, Mother. What danger do you mean?"

"Give the love of your heart to Mara. Good. But if you give your *soul* to anything else but God, you won't get it back, you'll just lose it there. And that can suck you in, that bad mysticism, because it can give you the ecstasy of losing your egotism, just as good mysticism does. It apes the true one, the heavenly one. It lures you."

"Mara does not lure me. Mara is my Beatrice. Did Beatrice 'lure' Dante?"

"I don't know what Beatrice did. What I do know—and I thought you did too—is the first and greatest commandment. For both of us, Christians and Muslims alike."

"You think I'm idolizing Mara?"

"I think you're letting the philosopher in you sleep a little, and thinking dreamy thoughts and forgetting your sane, sunny 'Straight Path.'"

"Are you saying romantic love is a dreamy illusion?"

"No, I'm saying you seem to be losing your mental edge. You're feeling the same mystical way toward Mara and the sea, and you're confusing them. But I've got news for you: Mara isn't the Atlantic Ocean and neither one is God."

"Good grief, Mother, I know that."

"Yes, you do, but you have to keep remembering it. Remember your theology: it tells you that all sin starts with 'forgetting.' *Ghaflah*, isn't it?"

"Yes," I said. "I believe that. That is why we pray five times a day. To remember Allah at all times."

"Good. And remember the sea too: how tricky she is. Especially *there*, where you've been staring for an hour." She pointed at the Cauldron.

The memory of Papa's drowning, and my near-drowning, clarified my mind. "I'll be careful," I promised, first to Mother and then to myself.

But then I thought: how could I have forgotten to address my promise to Allah *first*?

Does Mother see me better than I see myself? Could the S of the waves also be the S of the serpent?

(18) The World Splits in Two

The world ended today, on July 14, 1978.

I got a letter in the mail from Uncle Abu in Jerusalem. Abu is one of the two older brothers Papa left in Palestine. Uncle Ahmed, the younger one of the two, was the only relative who still remembered me. He wrote to me at least once every year, and sent me little gifts. And now Uncle Ahmed is dead.

Worse: not just dead but murdered. Even worse: not just murdered, but murdered by the Israeli police. His two sons were in the street, throwing rocks at the police (rocks versus machine guns!), and Uncle Ahmed ran out his door to fetch them back, to save their lives. He had heard a warning on the radio that this was not just the ordinary everyday protest and confrontation, but something more serious. One of the Israeli policemen had been killed by a Palestinian Molotov cocktail, and they were searching the neighborhood for the man they thought had done it. Some boys were hiding him and throwing rocks to distract the police. The police were in the mood for revenge and reprisals. Uncle Ahmed's oldest boy Muhammad was in the street pelting the police, and Ahmed ran out to get him, calling out threatening names. The police thought Ahmed was threatening *them*, and they called out a warning. Ahmed thought they were warning Muhammad. Muhammad threw some more rocks, with about a dozen other boys, but the police fired not at Muhammad but at Ahmed when they saw him running toward them. He was unarmed, and he was running only to bring Muhammad back, but they shot him—in the stomach. He fell dead in the street in front of his son. Muhammad went berserk. The police clubbed him and handcuffed him and put him in prison. The world is full of darkness and blood and hate!

The policeman who shot Ahmed was taken off the police force for a while, while an internal investigation went on to determine whether he was at fault for responding to mere words and stones with deadly force, or whether he was provoked and attacked, and was only defending himself. The policeman will be cleared of any charges, of course—they always are—but just for show the Israelis are running a public investigation.

But this is still not the worst of it, not by far. The darkness has a tendril nine thousand miles long, and that tendril has reached out and split my heart and my life in two just as surely as that Israeli bullet spilt Uncle Ahmed's guts and split his soul from his body. Hear now, O innocent pages of this book, how cruelly and cleverly the forces of darkness have contrived to torture me.

Uncle Ahmed had a shop on a certain corner. He lived over it. When he sent me little gifts, they bore the return address of this shop. Now comes the deadly dart. Mara came to the Hill this morning with tears in her eyes, to tell me that *her* uncle was under investigation for killing a Palestinian Muslim in Jerusalem. She even gave the address, the corner where it happened. It was the corner at Uncle Ahmed's shop.

So not just our people, but our families, are killing each other. Mara's uncle has murdered mine! How can I love her with honor? How can I embrace the family and the people who are murdering my family and my people, in fact my nearest and dearest relative in this world? How can Mara and 'Isa be two pebbles of peace that roll together down the mountainside of history and start a little avalanche of peace instead of war? How can we turn the world around from war to love if the world has already turned us around from love to war? The world has branded its name on both our foreheads: "ENEMIES." My love for Mara and my family honor have become mortal enemies to each other. The two parts of my soul have declared war against each other. But both are parts of my self, my soul, my identity, and I cannot disown myself. My identity has become an enemy to itself! How can I be healed? How can I be whole? How can *we* be whole?

Mara's words were bitter—were *mara*—to me as well as to her. She did not understand my sense of honor, my split soul. She has never failed to understand my heart before. But today we were not in America; we were in Jerusalem, and we stood on opposite sides of a street in a war zone.

When I tried to explain my pain in having my honor set against my love, she got hysterically angry. She wept and screamed at the same time. "I hate your damned honor, 'Isa! You honor those stones that your cousin threw at my uncle more than you honor me. Well, to me your murderous honor is a stone. And you are the stone thrower now, not your uncle. You are stoning me to death. You are stoning our love to death. You are stoning my heart to death. And you have turned your own heart into a stone. You are made of stone, 'Isa. Your damned honor is a stone: hard and dead and loveless. I spit on the stone of your honor!" And then she spit at a large rock at my feet and ran away, weeping in a way I never heard anyone weep before: as angry as a volcano and as hurt as a dying rabbit.

I remember one other thing she said, before the bitter words about honor. We had always agreed that both sides in the *intifada* were wrong, moved by hatred and not forgiveness. We had never fought about it. We had never identified with our mutually murderous "people" in Palestine—until now. I reminded her (foolishly) that it was her uncle that killed mine, not vice versa, and she said to me, "Your whole family has vowed to destroy my whole family. 'We will throw Israel into the sea!' Those were the words of their vow. Well, why don't you just throw Israel into the sea now and have done with it? Here!"— she ran twenty feet, to the edge of a cliff—"I'm standing at the edge now, see? You can win your family's war, 'Isa, you can throw me into the sea. Come on, do it to me now."

For the first time ever, I looked into her face and it was not pretty. She had wept before, and she was still beautiful, because we wept together. She had been angry before, and she was still beautiful because we were angry together. She was afraid before, and she was still beautiful because we were afraid together. But now that we are no longer together, she no longer appears beautiful.

I remember one other thing she said: "My mother made me promise never to see you again. And you have given me no reason to disobey her." It was her mother's brother who shot my uncle.

I am not only devastated but utterly confused. I don't know what I am now. I am nothing. I am dead. I shall never see her again; I shall never again know joy or hope or love. I was allowed to taste the apple of Paradise, and then, suddenly, the worm.

Why? Because I cannot spit on my honor, as she did. I cannot. Not "I *will* not," but *can* not. A man without honor is a man I cannot be. She has gone where I cannot follow. She wants an 'Isa without honor.

It is not that I love my uncle, or my family, more than her. I do not love anyone more than her. I do not love the whole world more than her. I love her more than my uncle and my friends and my world and my self, and I love her even more than I love my honor. But I cannot stone my honor to death.

There is an astonishingly stupid saying that many people actually believe: "Better to have loved and lost than never to have loved at all." I suddenly understood that that is one of the most asinine sayings that has ever come from human lips. No true lover who has just lost the love of his life could ever have written those stunningly stupid words.

The only hopeful sign today was the return of that curious white bird, which dropped suddenly out of the sky, perched on the Cauldron rock, cocked its head to the right, and stared at me deliberately for a full five seconds before flying away.

July 15

There is still life, still hope. After a sleepless night, I got a letter from Mara this morning. She had handwritten it and put it in my mailbox some time during the night. Apparently her night was sleepless too. At least we still share that.

The night was far worse than the night of terror when I thought we would drown in the great storm. The hole in my heart was larger than the universe, and no one could fill it but Mara. I sank into darkness and despair—but not into sleep. There was an iron ball in the pit of my stomach that I could neither digest nor disgorge.

Every one at the House understands that I do not want advice or pity or condolences, but only to be left alone. Surprisingly, Mother seemed the least sympathetic, and not upset at all. "This is a test," she said, matter-of-factly. "If you pass it, if your love survives this, then you know it is stronger than anything the world can ever do to you. If not, then it *had* to break because it would have broken later, and earlier is better than later."

"Why don't most other couples get such a terrible test?" I asked.

"Because most other couples don't know such a terrible love," she said. It was the only comforting thought I had today.

Mara's letter asked me to burn it after I read it, and not keep it or copy it. I did as she wished. But she did not forbid me to tell its contents to this book.

It began by explaining something she said to me yesterday which I had attached no importance to at the time. She said, "You're exactly like my father."

Mara never talked about her father. He left when she was fairly young, and she said she had sad memories that she did not want to dredge up, so I respected that. Now it comes out. Her father was a Muslim, and apparently not a good father to her. He was proud and arrogant and bellicose. His people came first, before his family. There were violent quarrels between him and Mara's mother. There was physical violence, perhaps sexual violence. They separated. He returned to Palestine and remarried. Mara's mother never did.

After carefully explaining the facts to me, Mara added an honest confession of fear. She is terrified that she will duplicate the pattern of her mother's life. That's why she was so hesitant toward me at first.

How do I feel about all this? Extremely confused! I am standing amid whirling cross currents of emotion that I cannot name, which spin me every way at once, like the waves I saw in the Great Blizzard. But my primary feeling now is of *life,* and hope. I thought our love was dead forever, but now there is a hint of possible resurrection. The last sentence in her letter is: "Do we have a future? I don't know. Most of the answer is in your hands."

If my hands were wings, they would fly faster than any bird to lift her face up from darkness to light, and to meet her eyes with mine. If my hands were feet, they would race faster than a cheetah to carry me to her and her to me. But my hands are hands, and they can hold a pen, and the pen can hold ink, and ink can hold words, and words can hold my thoughts, and my thoughts can hold some of my heart. I will write to her immediately, and put the letter between the screen and the window of her basement bedroom, where only she can see it, as she suggested—and then wait for her one more time on our Hill. May it be the first of many more meetings, and not the last!

July 16

We were to meet at noon at the summit of the Hill (our "summit meeting"), and we did, even though it was gently raining. At fifteen minutes before noon, I ran (not walked) up the south slope of the Hill. As I reached the top, I saw Mara emerging from the north side. She too had been running. We both simultaneously (1) stopped, then (2) for a second both pretended we had not been running at all, but walking casually, then both of us simultaneously (3) laughed at the idiocy of the pretence, (4) ran, rather than walking, at each other, like gooney birds, (5) crashed into each other's arms, and (6) started the same sentence: "I'm sorry. I was . . ." (I think I said "a fool" and she said "wrong") (7) And then, we both started the second same sentence: "I love you more than anything else in the world," (8) looked amazed at our perfect coordination, as if we had rehearsed a duet, and then (9) resolutely uttered the sentence neither of us ever thought we would utter: "I love you even more than my family." It was like a shadow puppet show: each of us exactly duplicated the movements and words of the other. (10) We then simply held each other tightly, silently, blissfully, for a good five minutes, before we unclenched, with serious smiles and yeses.

So the worst thing that could possibly happen to drive us apart has driven us together more perfectly than anything else ever could. Nothing can stop us now. The Mercy of Allah is truly beyond all human imagining.

All the more reason our love must be perfect now, and not polluted in any way. When we embraced, it was pure, and peaceful, and content—for a while. Then I felt the beast awaken in me, as I felt her leg between mine and her breasts against my chest. I do not reject her leg or her breasts, for they are part of her; but I reject the beast in me. For her sake I do this. I let her go then, and said, "I will not take your body any closer—because I want to take your soul closer. My body wants your body but my soul wants your soul even more. I want to be one with you from the inside out, from soul to soul." And she said, "Jack, that is what I want too, more than anything else in this world." And then, "I love you, Jack. I love you 'Isa. I love you, Ben Adam. I love all of you, but especially your *you*. Because with your *you,* you make me feel like a *me*."

I *believe* this trial has made our love stronger. Why can't I say I am *certain* that it has? Why this lingering doubt?

July 17

Our next meeting was on a cool and windy day. The swells were running like a pack of wild dogs, foaming at the mouth. The Drum was bubbling and squeaking, then gurgling and gasping, then growling and grumbling. Every few minutes it snorted like a rhinoceros.

This meeting was a test. That seems to be the rhythm: first joy and glory and triumph, then trial and testing, then conquest and triumph again, but a different kind, and then another kind of testing.

Women are more practical than men. They cannot afford to be romantics, as men can, for a very obvious reason. In one word, the reason is *children*.

"'Isa, will you love me always no matter what?"

"Yes, Mara, no matter what."

"I will grow old, and wrinkled, and flabby, and ugly."

"So will I. I want us to grow ugly together."

That made her laugh. Then: "Suppose I get fat?"

"You will, when you have many babies. And I will love you then, in a new way. The old way always gets weaker, when you get old. Everyone knows that. But then new ways of loving show up, and the sum of loves is even bigger. Especially because of all the children we will have. They will be *ours* even more than our feelings will be ours. They will be our love forever incarnate."

"But suppose I get crippled? Suppose I get senile? Suppose I get Alzheimer's?"

"I will care for you, like a beautiful bird with a broken wing. I will always love you, no matter what happens to your wings."

"But suppose I become paranoid?"

"Paranoid? About what?"

"About anything. Suppose I become insanely jealous of something else you love: the sea, or philosophy, or your relatives, or even our children."

"Mara, why do you ask me about something that will never be, about something you will never do?"

"To find out whether you will always love me most."

"Yes, Mara, I will always love you most. More than anything. Even more than our children. But there will never be a rivalry there, Mara. You will be the queen and I will be the king. You will be the heart of our family, Mara. I will be the head and you will be the heart, and the same blood will flow through both organs."

Mara was apparently satisfied with this answer, for she seemed to turn the conversation now: "You know, 'Isa, the sea is in our heart, literally. Blood contains salt water. And it's in our head too. So the sea brings our head and our heart together, in one bloodstream—just as the sea has brought the two of us together here."

"That's incredibly beautiful, Mara. *You* are incredibly beautiful, Mara. Yes, our blood is our ocean."

"But . . . but there are three saltwater oceans, not just one. 'Blood, sweat, and tears' are all salt water."

"That's true."

"Are you ready for the sweat and tears, Jack? Are you ready for that too? Because that's what every family has, eventually."

"Yes, I am ready. I will be your knight, Mara. I am ready to fight any dragon for you."

"Oh, I think dragons would be easy for a romantic. But sweat and tears are not very romantic."

"Ah, but I would accept them *for* the romance. For love, I mean. Why else would a man embrace sweat and tears except for love?"

"That's a good answer, Jack. I hope you understand it."

July 20

Apparently I passed Mara's test. We are now talking directly and seriously about marriage. Not sharing plans yet, but sharing dreams. It turns out that we both have thought about this seriously for a long time, and "counterculturally," and along strikingly similar roads.

We both want a large family, and would put family first. We both want strong roles for each other. If you love someone, you want them to be strong, not weak. Both of us are traditional, old-fashioned, and religious in our values, and also modern and American in our desire for openness, communication, equality, freedoms, options, opportunities, and even experimentation—not when it comes to values but when it comes to applying them to social situations. We want to help invent a better kind of family and a better kind of world.

Mara is as devoted to Judaism as I am to Islam. Yet there is no religious tension between us. That is one of the "experimental" things we want to show the world can work. We worship the same God—we are very clear about that—and live by the same morality, what we call the Straight Path and Jews call the Torah, or the Law. The last thing either of us want is to weaken the other's faith or conscience. We will worship in our own houses of worship, we will also worship together both in mosque and synagogue. She will keep a kosher kitchen and I will drink no alcohol. She will keep her Sabbath and I will keep mine, and my daily prayers, and we will help each other to do this. We each have great respect and love for each other's religions.

July 22

A very strange incident happened today. Mara works on the BC campus three days a week as a teacher's aide in the "Campus School." Campus School is a small school-within-a-school that is for children who are neither big nor smart nor prestigious, as BC is. They are the multiply handicapped. Most are in wheelchairs, many unable to speak, but all vibrantly alive and human. They smile at my blue car when I drive Mara to campus, and I smile back. Juan, one

of the tiniest (though he is in his twenties), always greets me with a six-sylla-
ble word that I have never been able to decipher, and I always respond with
"Hello, Juan!" Once in a while he speaks an intelligible sentence. If we had a
son like Juan I would shower him with love.

July 29

We spent the afternoon lazing on the Hill and in the water. There were no
waves on the sea, and apparently no waves on our sea of love, now that we had
come together in one mind and will against the *intifada* our families are fighting in Palestine and also against the beast in each of us that wants to pollute
our love. We felt perfectly happy, peaceful, and secure.

The sunset was warm and glowing with orange and golden brown. "Guess
what that sunset makes me think of," Mara said.

"I don't know. What?"

"Winnie-the Pooh's honey."

"That *is* Heaven for a bear."

"And this is Heaven for me. You are my bear."

"And you are my honey."

(I know it sounds corny. Lovers aren't afraid to be corny.)

August 5

When things go swimmingly, beware. The warmer and more comfortable the
waters, the more likely they are to hide a shark.

Each day our love and our closeness has grown. Love is alive, and whatever is alive, either grows or dies. So love either grows or dies. Ours has
grown, and grown, and grown—and now, suddenly, for no apparent reason, it
seem to be turning, and dying.

It is worse than the time when we thought our families were blood enemies. That situation was our common enemy, and eventually brought us much
closer together, like a shared suffering. We encountered heavy waves for a
while that threatened to swamp our ship, but our ship survived and got through
the surf out into the deeper sea. But no visible storm hit our boat this time. I've
heard of "joy without a cause," but this is "disaster without a cause."

Mara has been moody and bitchy for three days, and won't tell me why.
She says she doesn't know. She has been treating me like dirt. I am not thin-
skinned. In fact, people tell me I am too thick-skinned, undersensitive. So if I
sense her cat claws in the flesh of my soul, they are probably tiger claws that
I have underestimated and minimized rather than kitten claws that I have over-
estimated and exaggerated. What have I said or done to provoke this? Worse,
what smoldering chemicals are in her soul, that they can explode when

catalyzed by something so tiny that I can't even see it? Or, if it's *not* a tiny thing, then am I so blind that I cannot see the elephant in my own living room?

I know lovers have quarrels, but I thought they were quarrels *about* something. This is about nothing. It's not about her mother, or her father, or her future, or her body, or her work. Perhaps it is about her self.

August 7

I have not seen Mara for two days. We are "cooling down." I hate that phrase. I am impatient to "heat up" again. No, not impatient; desperate.

I confided in Mother. "Mother, I need your help."

"And I need to be needed. So that's a good fit. What kind of help do you need, Jack?"

"There's something I just can't understand."

"Well, now, maybe I can help you to understand it, and maybe not. What don't you understand?"

"Mara."

"I thought so. Yes, that is true, I think; you do not understand her."

How did she know that? "You are not surprised," I said, with surprise.

"I am surprised that you are surprised that I am not surprised," she said.

"So tell me, please, what is it that I don't understand? Is it her or is it me?"

"Oh, I think it is both. Yes, it has to be both."

"But why? Is it because I am a Muslim and she is a Jew?"

"No, I think it is mostly because you are a man and she is a woman."

"But I can't understand her! What am I doing wrong?"

"Nothing. God didn't give Eve to Adam so that he could understand her."

"Why, then?"

"Why, so that he could love her, of course."

"But I do love her. Totally."

"Then you're not doing anything wrong."

"But I think she doesn't love me any more."

"Oh. Now, *that* is something wrong, all right. Why do you think that?"

"Because she's treating me like dirt."

"And you think that means she doesn't love you?"

"Of course."

"Why, you stupid, stupid boy!"

I was shocked. Mother had never called me either "stupid" or "boy" before.

"But Mother, if I love somebody, I don't treat her like dirt. And if I treat somebody like dirt, that means I don't love her. That's only logical."

"Right, right, it's only logical. That's exactly why you are stupid."

"You mean women are illogical?"

"I mean *you* are."

"But . . . but . . . if Mara loves me, why does she treat me like dirt?"

"That's why, silly: because she loves you."

"How can that be?"

"Because when a woman loves a man, she wants to take him into her soul, her heart, her side, her *rib*. She wants to take his rib and make it her rib—to reverse what God did to Adam. She wants to be a mother in reverse: she wants to take the man she loves into her body. And she wants to give her whole soul to his soul just as she gives her whole body to his body and to their baby. She wants to make a soul baby with him. A oneness."

Mother paused. I listened, in something like awe, not just to her but also to my heart. And my heart told me this was true. I nodded. She went on.

"So because she wants to give her soul to you, she wants you to be where she is. She wants you to feel what she feels."

Another pause, to let the connection sink in to my thick head.

"And she feels like dirt right now. That's why she wants to make you feel like dirt too. So you can be together, even in the dirt. That's what love wants: not to be clean, or even to be happy, but to be together."

Instantly, it made sense. "I understand," I said.

"Do you? Let's see. Tell me, then, what do you think you should do, now that you understand?"

"I have to make her not feel like dirt. But how? That's the next question. What's the first thing I have to do?"

"I think the first thing you have to do is to stop trying to solve her problems by *doing* something about them. Isn't it a little arrogant to assume you can solve everybody's problems?"

"But I have to do *something* for her!"

"Do you?"

I had no answer.

"Why not try just *being* there instead? Just be there with her. Don't be her plumber. Don't fix her pipes. Just come in her house and sit down."

"You mean just feel how she feels?"

"Duuuuuh! He finally gets the point."

"But I don't *understand* why she feels that way."

"So?"

Once again I had no answer. Mother continued, "Probably she doesn't either."

"Mother, you should have been a psychologist."

"I *am* a psychologist. I'm a mother."

Of course, Mother's advice worked.

(19) The Healing Power of Surf

(Editor's Note: The following is handwritten in a separate, bright blue notebook. 'Isa wrote nearly everything in 144–page brown 4x7 inch notebooks which he always carried in his pocket, and this blue notebook begins just as the third brown notebook of his autobiography ends.)

I fell in love twice in one year. My first love's name is Mara, my second love's name is Mare, the sea.

I have always loved the sea. But only this year have I married her. Becoming a surfer is like marrying the sea.

One of my millions of reasons for loving Mara is that she was not jealous that I was married already to Mare before I met Mara. She is also not jealous of the fact that Libby seduced me—into surfing.

Mara has both great love and great fear of the sea, for she nearly drowned as a girl when her father stupidly tried to teach her to swim by taking her into water over her head and then dropping her into it. This is why it took great courage for her to jump into the cold sea fully clothed that June day.

So she is a few steps behind me. Perhaps I can seduce her into surfing some time. But not yet. Libby has seduced me into it, and I will some day pass on the gift to Mara.

(Mara and I both know that there is absolutely no erotic attraction between Libby and me, so there is no personal jealousy there. But there may be a jealousy about the sea, about the fact that Libby has shown me one of its pleasures [surfing] that Mara cannot yet share. I am hoping that this jealousy will motivate Mara to try to share it too.)

If I love the sea so much, why didn't I become a surfer earlier? There were no bodyboards when I was a kid, but there were canvas surf mats, and longboards, and there was always body surfing. I will try to explain this, as I tried to explain it to some friends in high school who invited me to go surfing with them. "It's a question of priorities," I explained.

Frank, a big, tall, handsome Italian kid who got everything he wanted, challenged me: "You mean you just don't like the ocean as much as we do."

"No, I think I like it *more* than you do. I dream of waves all the time."

"Then why not live your dreams? Are you afraid?"

"No. Like I said, it's a questions of priorities."

"What's the problem? Is it medical? Does it have anything to do with your thumbs?" (My thumb joint does not work properly, which makes me clumsy and useless for most mechanical things. That probably moved me to spend time writing when most kids were playing baseball.)

"No. I did have an operation for a brain tumor when I was six, and it left me with bad balance, but . . ."

"Is that why you don't dance or skate?"

"Yes, but that's not the reason. I'd risk my health for it."

"Then why not?"

"Look, everybody has a priority list. Most people don't think about it, but they have one. Everybody has to sacrifice *something* for something else. Sacrifice—that's what tells you what your priorities are. And I'd sacrifice any amount of money or time or power or prestige or pleasure or long life for it, but it's only #3 on my list, and it has to submit to #1 and #2."

"What's #2?"

"Mama. I dream of me surfing, but she dreams of me drowning. Ever since Papa drowned, she simply gets hysterical and out of control when I go in deep water."

"You give up surfing for your *mother*? What a powerful woman!"

"No, she's not powerful."

"Then why?"

"Like I said, priorities. Number One is Allah. And Allah gave me Mama. It's my responsibility to take care of her and keep her sane. That's my job that I have to do. So I can't disobey her because I can't disobey Him."

"So that's why you don't surf?"

"Yeah."

"Gee, isn't that hard?"

"Of course it's hard."

"But . . . if you dream about it, how can you say no to surfing?"

"Because the alternative is harder: saying no to Allah."

"But surfing is like heaven on earth."

"Maybe so, but Allah wants me to wait for heaven in heaven."

"I don't believe you. It's inhuman. You gotta rebel."

"Sure I rebel. And every time I do, every time I plan to sneak away, Mama finds out and goes nuts. Or the car breaks down. Or something. Once I was on my way to the beach and I met a girl with no arms."

(Yes, it was Eva. I didn't remember the incident when I met her again at the House, but only when I wrote these memories today. I wonder why.)

"How did that stop you?"

"It was like Allah saying to me: 'I gave you your gift, two arms and a mother who needs you. I gave this girl a different gift. Everything is My gift.' I know that's true."

"So that's why you don't surf?"

"Yes."

"That's impossible. It's like not having sex. I'll bet you're a virgin too."

"It's not impossible. Millions do it."

"It's inhuman."

"Allah commanded it. To us, to humans. He doesn't make mistakes. It's not inhuman. It makes us more human to surrender. It sculpts our souls. It gives them depth. When you get everything you want, you're shallow. You're a baby."

"Nobody believes that religious crap any more."

"You don't believe it because you don't *want* to believe it."

"Oh, yeah, Doctor Freud? Well, then, if you know so much about me, tell me why I don't want to believe it."

"That's easy, Frank. You know it and I know it and Doctor Freud knows it. It's because you don't want to feel guilty about doing it to other people besides the girl you marry."

"Damn right! That's why I say religion is crap. I'm free from that crap.

"Free from religion?"

"Yeah."

"No you're not. Sex is your religion."

At this point I think he threw something at me.

*   *   *   *   *

Libby's car has a bumper sticker, in Gothic letters, that says: "Pray for surf." I thought that meant "Pray for a trip to California." But she also has in her room a newspaper photo of a surfer taking off on a wave that looked good enough to be in any surf magazine. The caption read: "Chris making the world look stupid when it says there aren't any waves in New England."

Before she moved to Nahant, Libby lived in Boston. She didn't need a car. She surfed at Winthrop Beach, just south of Revere, by taking the subway. "It's a 20minute walk from the end of the Blue Line to the water," she explained, "but watching people's faces when they see me carry my board on the subway is worth the effort."

*   *   *   *   *

Even after Mama died, I never tried to surf because of my balance problem. When I was six, I had a brain tumor. The operation was successful, except for one lingering effect: I am clumsy. I cannot ice skate, or even dance well, because my balance is "off." The only kind of surfing I had ever heard of involved standing upright, in perilous balance, on a moving surfboard: delightful to watch but almost impossible for me to attempt.

Until this magical summer, when New England discovered the boogie board, or bodyboard.

Libby says that the three greatest Americans were all Georges. George Washington was "the father of his country"; and George Freeth, who first brought the art of surfing from Hawaii to California, was the father of his country's surfing; and George Morey, inventory of the boogie board, was the father of surfing democracy. He let us into the inner sanctum because *anybody* can use a boogie board. He did for surfing what Gutenberg did for reading.

Here is how Libby seduced me to surf.

I confessed to her that I was a little afraid to try it: not afraid of the sea but of my own inability to master this new toy. "I can't see myself ever doing anything at all like the stuff I see on TV."

"Those are the pro surfers," she answered. "I call them the surf prostitutes. For every one of them there are ten thousand good amateurs who just go out to have fun and ride waves like cowboys ride horses. And for every one of *them* there are ten more who haven't learned to be cowboys yet and who keep falling off the horse. But even for them, a good wipeout is almost as good as a good ride."

"A good wipeout? How is that different from a bad wipeout?"

"The key to a good wipeout is just to lie down and enjoy it."

"I've done that, without a board. Body surfing."

"Then you know. The best surfer in the world isn't the one who wins the most contests but the one who wins the most joy. He's probably five years old."

"That sounds like me."

"And for every standup surfer there are soon gonna be a thousand kids who use these things." She pointed to the body board. "And you're gonna be one of them."

I was convinced enough to try it.

The very next day there were rideable waves at Nantasket Beach in Hull, just south of Boston. Libby and I took boogie boards (she had two) and sneaked past the angel's flaming sword into Eden.

I thought Mara might be a little jealous if she knew that I let Libby initiate me into this Eden, but I told her we were going and invited her along. She wouldn't come, but she didn't seem threatened or jealous at the idea. Libby and I got a lot of stares at the beach, but I was too concerned with getting into this Garden of Eden to take the mental detour of wondering whether the stares were because Libby cut such a striking figure in her white-rimmed black bathing suit, or because America was less liberal and enlightened about interracial couples than I thought. (We looked like a couple, after all.)

The salty air and the burning sun were as active as the dancing sea. I twirled my tongue around my lips to taste the familiar yet wild and untamed taste of salt on them, the taste of adventure. I enlarged the area of my ecstasy by extending my tongue like an anteater to taste the salt on all the reachable flesh around my lips. I felt the squoosh of warm sand beneath my bare feet, and sent my whole soul down into the soles of my feet to feel this grace. It was not just the sand but the whole world that I felt against my skin. It is very physical, but I think it is also very holy.

It is sensual but not sexual. I understood that distinction when I once blundered onto a nude beach on Cape Cod by mistake. I was shocked not so much at these people's shamelessness as at their artificiality. They were artificially natural, unnaturally natural. They were showing off, making personal or even political statements. It was not erotic to them at all. The world was their god, not the flesh.

"I love this stuff!" I said as we ran into the waves..

"Why?" Libby asked, unexpectedly. She is not usually philosophical unless she's arguing and combative.

"Because the sea air and the sea water actually cleans my soul."

"How do you think that works?"

"It's obvious, isn't it? It gets at your soul through your skin, and your lungs, and your nose."

"So where's your soul, then? In your lungs? Or in your nose somewhere?"

"Yes! And everywhere else in your body. That's why the body is holy. Whatever touches your body, touches your soul. The sound of those gulls, and the heat of that sun, and the smell of that salt—they all don't stay out there. They come into your body, literally inside, and then they come into your soul, and your mind and your heart. Your soul is your city, and your body is the wall around it, and the senses are the gates through the wall."

"For once, you make sense," Libby said. "That explains how the surf can wash away your soul-garbage."

"OK," I said, "so let's do it."

So we did. Or rather, she did it, while I tried it, and felt like an impotent lover on his honeymoon night. It looked ridiculously easy, and proved ridiculously hard.

I have been a wave-lover and a wave-player since I was two, I think. I knew the ecstasy under the scrapes and bruises, and the taste of swallowed salt water, and the churning somersaults in nature's oversized washing machine, and the suck and pounding, and I was not afraid of that. I knew that the Great Mother will play as gently or as roughly with you as you choose to let her. Even if you are afraid of her, the fear can be part of the delight, and your helplessness is part of the thrill. I was not a stranger to the sea, and I was eager to open the yellow door to Paradise that was shaped like a boogie board..

And yet for hours I just could not open that door. I watched Libby carefully. When a wave came, she jumped forward, flopped on her belly on her board, and rode the wave's foam to the beach. It looked as easy as falling asleep. Dozens of little kids were doing it successfully all around us. I did everything Libby did, yet not a single wave did I catch well enough to ride it all the way home to its end. Most of the time, the wave would break a few feet farther in and I would be passed by, like a kid not chosen for baseball or a "wallflower" at a dance. Other times, the wave would break a foot or two too soon and slap me like a giant foamy hand. I concluded that surfing, like baseball, is "a game of inches."

Most of the waves were about four feet high, a perfect height for beginners; and the strong onshore wind moved them with good force toward the shore, but that wind also crumbled their shape. (Libby told me later that offshore winds are much better because they hold up the face of the waves and give them a more regular shape.) Suddenly, a giant wave came. It seemed twice the size of the previous ones. It broke over my head. I was desperate to succeed. I caught the foam exactly right, I thought. The wave thought otherwise. "Over the falls" I went, somersaulting down into the giant's foamy mouth. My board and I flew in the opposite direction. It became a kite. I was swallowed by the whale. I tasted its salty saliva. I rolled my body into a fetal ball and let myself sink as far down as I could, as Libby had told me to do in a wipeout, seeking the calm water deep below the surface turbulence of the wave. I was surprised and scared to find no calm at all down there. Instead, I found myself in the washing machine.

How many socks have you lost in the wash? I was one of them. Nobody knows what happens to those missing socks. They just disappear out of the universe into a Black Hole. There must be a Sock Paradise where they all go. I was going there now.

I heard a roaring, and didn't know whether it came from the wave or from my own ears. I wondered if this was what it felt like to be deaf. I lost all sense of up and down. I began to flail with arms and legs, seeking the bottom. My air-starved lungs began to hurt. (I had foolishly forgotten to take a breath before wiping out.) The concept "drowning" came into my mind. I commanded it to leave. It laughed at me. Finally, after what seemed like two or three laundry cycles, the door of the washing machine opened and I spilled out into the air—just in time to see another wave, almost as big, crashing on top of me. I just had time to draw a big, quick breath before I went down again. This time I knew what to expect. I enacted my islam, spoke my *shahadah* with the lips of my mind, and relaxed. This time the machine was on short cycle, and I was rolled, like a bowling ball, into shallow water sputtering and coughing but smiling. Whatever does not kill me makes me stronger.

This was only the first of perhaps a dozen wipeouts that day. I didn't mind the wipeouts. Even when the loose board hit me in the head once; it was soft enough not to leave a bruise. What I minded was my unexplainable inability to find the key to the door to paradise. Soon it would be past supper time. But I felt no hunger for food, only for friendly water. It was a hunger of the spirit.

Again and again I tried, watching Libby carefully. Again and again I failed. At first she couldn't stop laughing at me: so desperately earnest and yet so totally inept. "What am I doing wrong? Teach me!"

"Well, I can see one thing you're doing wrong. You're just standing there waiting for the wave. Catching it isn't passive; it's active. You've got to swim into it or jump into it as it comes. That gives you momentum in the same direction as the wave. Didn't you ever jump on a merry-go-round when you were a kid?"

"Yeah, sure." I lied. But I had seen other kids do it, so it was only my legs that lied, not my eyes.

"Well, imagine that's what you're doing. You don't just jump on it from standing still. You run with it, then jump on."

"Should I actually *jump* on the wave?"

"You can, if your feet are on the ground. Or you can just paddle into it as fast as you can, on your board. Jumping is easier at first."

I could now see what I had to do, but I still could not do it. I couldn't get the timing right. The door to Paradise almost opened, but not quite. "I'm missing the timing. Teach me the timing!" I demanded.

"I can't," she said. "You learn only by doing it. You just have to sense the right moment, and catch it just as it breaks. Waves are like measles; you just catch them."

"Teach me!"

"Measles can't be taught, only caught."

"Well why can't I catch just one measly measle?"

"There's no such thing as a measle. Only measles. Once you catch one, you catch them all. It's the same with waves. Just keep trying. If you never give up, you'll get there, I promise you. And then it will be worth all the waiting."

I kept trying. The ocean kept teasing me. "Teach me! What's the trick?"

"It's like dancing," Libby said. "You can't learn logically, step by step. You just get it. You just catch on."

"I can't dance either!" I moaned.

"You'll get it eventually. You'll catch the art."

"If I can't catch a wave, how can I catch the art of catching a wave?"

"Stop with the logic, already. Just dance."

"I'm too clumsy to dance. Maybe I'm too clumsy to surf too."

"Nobody's too clumsy to boogie board. Look, think of it as music. When you dance, you do it by just falling into the music. You forget yourself. You become the music."

"I understand that," I said, remembering an out-of-body experience I had many years ago when listening to Beethoven's Ninth. But that wasn't dancing.

"Well, in surfing the wave is the music."

"Then why do the notes keep passing me by?"

"Because you're dancing out of rhythm."

Finally, an angel lifted me up onto itself. The biggest wave of the day towered over me like a cobra. I was tempted to chicken out and duck under it, but I didn't. I turned, leaped, flopped, and was gripped and lifted up like a baby tiger in its mother's jaws. I suddenly knew the wave had chosen me rather than I it. At that moment I became a woman and entered the mystery of receiving. I just let myself be there, where the gift was given. And the gift was the fact that "there" extended a hundred feet toward the shore. I was on the cowcatcher of a steaming, speeding, churning, chattering locomotive. The foamy edge of the wave, laughing all the way, shot me onto the sand like a torpedo. As we traveled together, the sea sang and the sun shone and the wind whistled and all creation danced before a delighted deity.

Only metaphors, wildly mixed, will do: tiger, locomotive, torpedo: that is what it *felt* like. But what the wave *looked* like was a *stallion,* a giant horse of the gods. He had come across the world to this point just for me. Now he had allowed me to ride him, at the last moment of his life, which was consummated as he died and I came to life in his foam.

I plunged back in, shrieking with delight, now a hopeless addict, beyond all salvation.

From that moment on, I was doomed. Lost. Hopelessly in love. Once you go to Heaven, you don't ever want to come back to earth. I will work through a thousand more wipeouts, I will wait another whole afternoon, another lifetime if necessary, for a ride like that.

The sun set. I refused to go home. I had caught not just the wave but the catching. Nine more waves came, in three sets, and I caught one in each set. Libby told me that every surfer in the world knows that waves come in threes and every scientist denies it. Surfers also believe that the ninth wave, the third of the third, is the biggest and best. They tell tall tales about the terror and wonder of the ninth wave. Someday I will ride the ninth wave, if only when I die.

Libby was smiling proudly at me like a mother. Then, immediately as the last drop of the sun's blood disappeared over the rim of the world, came the biggest set of the day. "See if you can ride one down the face now, like board surfers do," challenged Libby. "OK," I yelled. I felt like a god, capable of anything.

The wind was blowing offshore, and held up the face of the wave. It was perfectly formed, with a slanting face six feet high. It broke gradually, right to left, like a cat moving under the bed covers, instead of just "closing out" suddenly and vertically like a pounding fist. As I started sliding down the face of the wave, *everything went absolutely silent.* I knew I had not gone deaf. I thought God had shut off all the sound. Does He have a universal remote control for earth?

Then time stopped too. Did God press the freeze frame button? Most likely, my consciousness speeded up a thousandfold. That would explain the cessation of sound too, for sound takes *time* to travel. There was not enough time in that instant for any sound.

Then, after no time and motion at all, sudden supersonic speed. Like race horses out of the starting gate. A different *category* of speed than the previous waves. I sped down the face of the wave with a rush I was wholly unprepared for. It didn't look that fast on film when "real" surfers did it. I slanted down, with gravity-enhanced speed, entered into the foam, and sped to the beach at the very front of the wave, much faster than before, when I was *in* the foam. I stood up in a foot of water, stunned and smiling, holding my board like a warrior hero's shield.

Alas, pride goeth before a fall. As I stood smiling stupidly at the land, WHAM! The second wave of the set, much bigger than the first, bowled me over like a bowling pin. I came up sputtering, scandalized, betrayed by my new love.

"Never Turn Your Back on the Ocean," intoned Libby, laughing. "You forgot the surfer's first commandment."

"Now I know what the waves are saying," I replied. "They're whispering and plotting pranks like that." But I was still in love, as I conceded defeat for the day.

On the way home Libby told me that there are three landmarks in a surfer's life: catching the first wave, riding *down* the first wave, and riding *in* the first wave, or the "green room," the hollow barrel of a big curling wave. "You did two out of three the first day. That's awesome."

"So when do I try to get into the Green Room?"

"Don't worry about it. Most amateurs never make it that far."

"I will. I have to."

"You've caught the bug, all right."

*   *   *   *   *

The next time Libby and I went surfing, we took Squat along. We went to Narragansett Beach in Rhode Island and had a ball. Squat *is* a ball. He couldn't see the waves, of course, but he could hear and feel them coming. He would just sit in the white water and let it caress him like a baby. How does Squat surf? He squats!

His shape and size made it hard for the waves to dislodge him. When a little wave came, it would pass over him like a mother's hand, leaving a smile on his face that made him look like a puppy. When a big wave came, it would upend him and send him sprawling to shore like a black beach ball with four stubby limbs. And then the smile would be even bigger. He would emit little grunts of wordless ecstasy that made him seem at once angelic and animal.

The sea and the sky today were the broken halves of the mirror of the Mind of Allah. Both were so blue that the paint was still wet. I almost could imagine Allah asking me, "Look, 'Isa. What do you think of this picture I just painted for you?" I couldn't pity Squat for his blindness; I think he sensed the elements more vividly than anyone else.

It was an "oomphatic" day. I call it that because of the Squat-like "oomphs" that the waves squeezed out of my happily battered body. I imagined my guardian angel riding each wave with me like a father riding a big roller coaster with his scared little boy.

When, back at the House, I mentioned this image, Mother looked up at me as if I had quoted the *National Enquirer*. "Oh, you surf with angels now?"

Lazarus, from his favorite chair, looked at Mother as if she were a little girl and said, matter-of-factly, "You all swim in a sea of angels every day."

"Can you map that out for me?" I asked.

"Water below you, spirit above you, you in between, bridge between worlds," he said, simply.

Nothing more to be said.

(20) Islam in the Art of Body-Surfing

When two great things enter your life, you have to relate them somehow, especially if they are two great loves. So it's inevitable that I think about the relation between surfing and Islam. (When it's three loves, it gets even more complicated. How Mara fits into all this has to become clearer soon.)

I have resolved to build a two-way bridge: to show Muslims that surfing is a great analogy to Islam, and to show surfers that Islam explains the "high" they seek, the unique experience they call "stoke." Surfers and religious people usually hang around in different crowds; I want to see them talking to each other. I want to drill some holes through the watertight wall between the two, and let the holy water rush through.

The third time Libby and I surfed, we talked about that. All our conversations in the House have been argumentative, and many have ended with her stomping out and slamming doors; but all our conversations at the beach have been forward-moving like spilling waves. The water is a great healer.

We were taking a brief rest on the sand as the tide was slack and changing. She blurted out, "Heaven must be like this!"

I answered, "Do you think Heaven has waves?"

"Sure. What's more Heavenly than waves?"

"What do you mean by 'Heavenly'? Just 'pleasant'?"

"You gotta spoil everything by philosophizing about it, don't you? Why don't you just forget yourself for a few minutes?"

"Thanks, Libby. I think that's a pretty good answer to my question, 'What do you mean by "Heavenly"?' 'You just forget about yourself.'"

"Wow! You're not going to argue with me today, you're going to compliment me! See? Surfing does miracles. You know, 'Isa, if you lived like you surfed, and if you thought like you surfed, you'd be a lot happier. You can't surf on syllogisms."

"You mean just take the wave as it comes, just accept it, submit to it, and ride it."

"You got it, man."

"As if it's a wave of God's hand."

"Hey, you do understand."

"I sure do, Libby. Because you know what you just defined?"

"Sure. Surfing."

"You just defined Islam."

She turned to me in surprise. Her first wipeout of the day was there in her eyes. "Islam? Prove it. Gimme a 'for instance.'"

"OK, I will. Just this morning, I was daydreaming about going surfing as I was washing the dishes, and I noticed that I had chipped a dish, so I felt a little guilty about daydreaming, and I wished I could be as 'stoked' by my duty and my surrender to it—doing the dishes—as I was by surfing. That's when I realized that I *could,* because everything, even doing dishes, *is* a kind of surfing. I could surf right now and every minute of every day on the most perfect waves, His will."

"Preachy, preachy! I knew it. I ask for a 'for instance' and he gives me a principle."

"No, Libby, you don't understand. Don't turn up your nose like that. Don't you see? It's concrete, not abstract. The waves of the sea are images of something even more real, something heavier than water: the waves of His will. They are just as real and just as heavy and just as perfect as the waves of water. Sea surfing is the image, islam-surfing is the solid thing."

"It doesn't feel like that."

"It can. When you surf in the sea, it's only your body that does the deed, and your soul comes along for the ride. But when you surf on God's will, it's your soul that does the deed and brings your body along."

"So?"

"Well, the soul is more solid than the body. It lasts forever. It's not an image of the body. The body is an image of the soul."

"Hmm. You're really into this philosophizing about surfing, aren't you?"

"Yes! It's tremendously exciting, like loving two women and feeling torn and guilty about it, and then one day discovering that they were only one woman in two disguises."

"OK, so surfing makes you holier when you wash dishes. Does religion make you a better surfer too?"

"Absolutely! The connection works both ways."

"How?"

"Well, for one thing, I say *Allah akbar!* after every wave I catch. 'God is great!' Because gratitude is the essence of religion, and surfing teaches me gratitude."

"You feel gratitude after every single wave?"

"I may not *feel* it, but I *will* it, because I *believe* it."

"So you say your *Allah akbar* even if you don't feel it?"

"Yes. It's not self-expression. It's more like an incantation. The words aren't just the *effect* of gratitude, they *cause* it, they enact it."

"Sounds suspiciously easy: become a saint just by having fun in the surf."

"No, no, you need the hard stuff too to become a saint. All I'm saying is that you can use the fun stuff too."

"But the fun stuff is only the icing on the cake, it's not the cake. And it doesn't make the cake different, it just adds something sweet on top."

"No, the icing gets down into the cake and makes the whole cake sweet. The fun stuff helps you to do the hard stuff too."

"How?"

"Because they're just two forms of the same thing, don't you see? Islam, surrender to the waves. Riding the water waves can train you for riding the will waves, and the easy rides can train you for the hard ones. It's like Mother's 'Discipline of the Interruption.' Diddly and Squat don't interrupt us with slaps in the face but with great music and great dancing. So when we do get slapped in the face, we're at least open to being interrupted."

Reconciling My Two Loves: Mara and Surfing

Mara and I often played in the little waves at Nahant beach after that crazy day in spring when we both ran into the cold water fully clothed. (After that, she always wore a modest bathing suit.) But when I told her of my conquest of the boogie board, and the joy it gave me, and invited her to share it, I could see something was troubling her. I asked her what she was afraid of.

"What if I don't like it as much as you do? Will I be a surf widow?"

"If you never try it, you *will* be a surf widow."

"But suppose it's worse than just not liking it. Suppose I become like your Mama. Suppose I freak out when you surf. Suppose you're torn in two between your two loves?"

"Nothing can rival you, Mara, not even Mare."

"So you say."

"I will never lie to you, Mara. Never."

"I don't fear that you are lying to me, 'Isa."

"Then what? What do you fear?"

"Maybe I fear that you are lying to yourself."

"Mara, there is one way we can resolve all these doubts. Come surf with me. Overcome your fear and mine at the same time." She was silent. I said, gently, "I know you are strong and courageous. There is something about your fear that you have not told me, Mara. Will you be totally open with me as I am with you?"

She sighed deeply. "I will. 'Isa, it's not just about the sea, or surfing, and it's not even about you, it's about . . . about my father."

"Your father? What does he have to do with surfing?"

"Nothing. But he has something to do with you." I waited (wisely), and she sighed again before going on. "My mother wants to like you, 'Isa, she really does, but she is afraid, and I am picking up some of her fear. She likes you but she does not trust you, and she tells me not to trust you either. She

can't help it. My father was so much like you. Mother noticed it before I did.
You look like him, and you even move like him. He was 'a real charmer,'
Mother says. He was also a Muslim. And he—oh, 'Isa, it's so hard for me to
say this, but I must, I must, for my sake as much as for yours—he turned into
a tyrant and he made life miserable for Mother and he began to look at her
in a new way, with such anger in his eyes, and then with such angry words
and such angry music in his voice, and then when she talked back to him he
would threaten her, and then one day he actually hit her, and I saw blood
come from her face, and I couldn't look and I couldn't hear, and I just ran
into my bedroom and screamed and put my head under the pillow, and he
came into my bedroom and said he was sorry, and I said I hated him, and
Mother said *she* hated him, and he cursed us both and stormed out and
slammed the door and . . . and he left us both alone, forever. We never saw
him again. 'Isa, *we never saw him again*. He didn't phone or write or anything. He just left."

"Is he still alive?"

"*No.*" She said it as if the words would make it happen, like an incantation.

"What happened to him?"

"I think he went back to Palestine and fought and died in the wars."

"Do you know this for sure? How do you know. . . ?"

"Stop! Stop being a policeman and questioning me! Oh, 'Isa, I'm sorry.
But you just don't understand. You can't understand." She was shaking but she
refused to come to my arms for comfort, and I didn't impose my will on her
fear.

"I think I do understand, Mara. After my parents both died, my adopted
Papa acted like that too . . . "

"No, you *don't* understand."

"What is it that I don't understand?"

"*Papa looked exactly like you.*" She spat the words out.

"Mara, Mara, do you really think I could ever become like that?"

"No, no. I don't know. Maybe. I don't know."

"Is it because he was a Muslim?"

"I don't know. I don't know. I don't know what little devils are running
around in my brain trying to stop me from trusting you. They can't stop me
from loving you, but they can stop me from trusting you. And if I don't trust
you, I won't marry you, even if I love you."

"Of course not. There has to be trust. Total trust. Both ways. I totally agree
with you." I saw some relief on her face, beneath the tears. "The question now
is *how* to find that trust."

"I'll try anything. Tell me how, 'Isa. Tell me how."

"Go surfing with me. The sea will heal us."

Mara nodded vigorously. "Right now," she insisted. "Not tomorrow. Right now."

We were on Bailey's Hill. "I don't want to go home," she said. So we ran down to the House. Libby lent Mara a bathing suit (they're the same size), and we borrowed her two bodyboards and drove to Short Beach.

"Do you think I need a psychiatrist, 'Isa?" she asked.

"Look at the thousands of free psychiatrists!" I said, pointing to the totally trustable, perfectly formed, two- to three-foot waves, one after another. There were about a dozen longboard surfers and half a dozen bodyboarders surrounded by churning white foam. The slope of the beach was very gradual, and the waves were breaking in three- or four-foot deep water about 150 feet out, so even non-swimmers could get good long rides to the beach. The faces of the waves were not big enough to surf down, but after each wave broke there was rideable white-water that did not peter out until it reached the sand. A good day for beginners.

I expected that Mara would be silent, with her fears bottling up inside her. Instead, she could not stop asking questions about surfing—which I thought was a very good sign.

"Tell me honestly, 'Isa, is it dangerous?"

"No, Mara, it's not. Not those waves."

"What about the boards? Are they dangerous?"

"Not these. They're soft. Surfers call them 'sponges.'"

"Hard surfboards can be dangerous, can't they?"

"They can."

"What happens if you get hit with one?"

"It can give you a cut, or a concussion. But nobody's ever been concussed by a bodyboard."

"What if you—what do you call it? Wipe out?"

"You will. Everybody does. But it's only water. Water's even softer than your sponge."

"But don't the waves grab you and dash you down and crash you around and—and bash your crown?" I knew she was OK when I heard the playful rhyme.

"Big waves, sure. So you start by learning to catch little ones first, like these. They can't hurt you even if you turn your back on them."

"But what happens when you wipe out in one of these?"

"Look. That kid just wiped out. See? He just comes up again laughing. All you get is a mouthful of salt water and maybe a scrape on the sand. And the salt water is good for little cuts and scrapes."

"I'm not afraid of getting cut. I'm afraid of getting drowned."

"You won't drown here unless you can't swim and you go out over your head, or if you get caught in a strong rip current. But there aren't any rip currents at this beach. At least not today, not until a big, big storm comes."

"Did you ever do anything dangerous in the ocean? I mean, besides that night when Mother found you on the Hill?" (I told Mara all about that. I think I've told her *everything* important about me.)

"Yes," I admitted. "I body-surfed in waves churned up by a hurricane once."

"Good God, Isa!"

"We must remember not to use His name in vain, Mara. We are both under the same Commandments."

"I didn't mean . . ."

"I know. We forget. Do you want to hear about my hurricane?"

"Oh, yes. You don't mean the one this year, do you?"

"No, another one, a couple years ago."

"Why did you do it? Were you . . ."

"Suicidal? No, not at all, never (except for that one night on the Hill, when I felt something pulling on me). No, it was the most mystical experience I ever had. And *that* was the danger, not the waves."

"I don't understand."

"I loved it so much that I almost lost consciousness. I lost all sense of self and self-preservation. I just sank into the sea, and became wonderfully one with it, and it was sheer bliss."

"That *does* sound mystical. And dangerous. But your reason clicked in in time. You're still here."

"Actually, my reason was part of the mystical experience—my reason was like the sand that the sea gouges out big chunks of them and eats it, and then it becomes part of the sea. In fact, it was my reason that convinced me I couldn't drown. It was a syllogism, and it came to me like a slap in the face."

"A syllogism!"

"Yes. Major premise: What is the one and only thing that can never drown in the sea, and therefore never needs to fear drowning?"

"I don't know. What?"

"The sea itself, of course."

"OK, that's reasonable. The sea *is* the sea. What's the minor premise?"

"That I had become the sea, that I *am* the sea. That was the mystical experience. So you see what conclusion logically followed. I could never drown."

"But 'Isa, you got it backwards. You said your mystical experience ate up your reason, like the sea swallowing sand. But it was your reason that ate up your mysticism. Your mystical experience was only one premise for your syllogism. It was your syllogism, it was your reason, that almost made you drown. *That's* what you have to be afraid of: your reason."

I was stopped and impressed by her insight.

We had been standing with our bodyboards, talking instead of surfing. I wondered whether Mara was shooting all these questions at me out of procrastination, as a defense against the sea she feared. So I didn't push her, but went along with her, "painting with the grain." She had more questions.

"Look! Those surfers are wearing wet suits. Why aren't you?"

"I don't need one. It's July. It's warm today."

"Is it only for warmth?"

"Of course. What did you think it was for?"

"I thought it was a kind of uniform, or a fashion statement: 'Look at me, I'm a surfer!'"

"Maybe it is for them, but not for me."

"Doesn't it insulate you from the slaps the waves give you too?"

"A little. That's why I don't like it. I like to feel every slap. I like to feel the water pouring in to every pore of my body."

"Just like the sun pours in."

"Exactly."

"So why don't you just bodysurf instead of using a board?"

"That's good too, but it's much harder. The board gives you an easier ride and a longer ride and a faster ride."

"As good a ride as a real surfboard?"

"These *are* real, Mara!"

"I mean a hard board. Can you get the rides *they* give you on a body-board?" She pointed to two standup surfers getting a beautiful, long ride.

"Yes. And it's a lot easier. Anyone can learn it right away, even little kids or old people."

"I lifted a surfboard once. It was heavy. Why are our boards so light?"

"To make it easier. For both us and the wave to catch each other."

"Why are they so much shorter than real surfboards?"

"They *are* real surfboards, Mara. Bodyboards are boards for riding the surf. That makes them surfboards."

"But if they're bodyboards, why are they shorter than our bodies?"

"They're just long enough to reach from your neck to your knees."

"Why are they soft on top and hard on the bottom?"

"Soft is for us and hard is for the water, to skim over it faster, without drag."

"And why don't we have swim fins, like those surfers do?"

"Because I forgot to bring them."

"Will it work without them?"

"Sure. We'll just jump off the bottom to catch the waves instead of swimming into them."

"They do make it better, though?"

"Yes, especially in deeper water. They help you swim faster into the wave."

"How come you never see bodyboarders or bodysurfers in the movies? All the surf movies, and all the surf advertising, always has standup surfers. Why is that?"

"I don't know and I don't care."

"Suppose *I* care, suppose I want to know. Tell me. Guess."

"I guess because bodyboarding isn't a sub-culture yet, an in-group, an 'in' thing. We just do it for pure fun."

"So bodyboarders are surfers too?"

"Bodyboarders think so."

"And board surfers don't?"

"Some don't. They call bodyboarders 'spongers.'"

"If you used an ironing board as a surfboard, would you be a surfer?"

"If you rode the surf, sure."

"Then why won't they call a bodyboarder a surfer?"

"I think they're jealous of how easy it is to learn to surf on a bodyboard. I guess they want to keep their subculture pure. Fine. Let them. We don't need their stupid subculture. We just need waves."

"Aren't surfers supposed to be airheads, or meatheads, or potheads?"

"I don't know and I don't care. I just know this one isn't."

"But don't they treat their women as toys?"

"I don't know, and I don't care. I just know this one doesn't. And I hope you know that too."

"I do know that, 'Isa. I have to trust you out of the water, so I guess I have to trust you in the water too. I'm hoping the sea can teach me to trust you more. And I'm hoping you can teach me to trust the sea. Let's try it."

I smiled, nodded, and said, "Just follow me and do what I do. OK?"

"Yes!" she said, with passion.

We strode out to where the waves were breaking I tried to give her the exact same instruction Libby had given me. I remembered all the principles, but forgot the frustration I had felt until I saw it in Mara, who missed the first ten waves, and was almost crying in frustration. "I missed my first fifty," I replied. "You'll get it. Everybody does. It's like sleeping through the night, or toilet training: every baby learns to do it eventually."

"But why can't I just do it like you do? You said it's easy, but it isn't." I could see her getting passionately frustrated. She wanted to do this more than Edmund Hillary wanted to climb Everest. I loved that in her. That's why I wasn't upset, but almost pleased, when she added, in anger, "You lied to me!"

"Never, Mara, never. It *is* easy! Only getting to your first wave is hard. Once you start, you can't stop. Here, let me put you on a wave." I took her board, with her on it, poised it atop a breaking wave, and gave her a good shove. The wave smiled and slapped her board like a tennis champ making a service ace.

The wave took her all the way to the hard sand at the edge of the beach.

Her body quivered quietly, savoring every inch. She lay there on the sand for a second, rolled off her board onto her back, picked up her board, kissed it, and ran back to me like a tornado, totally crazy, out of control with joy. Her smile was wider than the world.

"I did it! I did it! That's it! I'm hooked! Thank you, thank you 'Isa. And thank you, God, thank you, God. *Shema Yisrael, Adonai Elohim! Allah akbar!*"

We stayed at the beach for five hours, until dark. The smile never left her face.

The next day she insisted we return. The wave magic did not return with us, however; we found only the one- to two-foot waves that Nahant produces nine days out of ten, much too little to be rideable.

I looked at Mara's face and saw the face of a four-year-old running out of the house with ice cream money only to see the ice cream truck disappearing down the road. "The day is not lost," I promised. "We can still make a little magic. Watch me."

"You'd have to be a mouse to get any magic out of those waves."

"Right. And here's how to make yourself into a mouse. Do what I do." We waded out to the exact place where the little waves were breaking. Then we lay prone in the surf, right in the impact zone, maximizing its force.

"See? If we can't make the waves bigger, we make ourselves smaller. When they break on your face, you can almost imagine 12-inch waves are 12-foot ones."

"I remember how big the waves looked when I was little," Mara said. "So if you can be a child again . . ."

"Yes! If you can find that time machine, you find a little Paradise. If we can make ourselves small, we make everything else big. Small is beautiful."

We tried sitting in the low sand chairs that Mara had brought, about three inches off the ground, at the exact place where the waves broke onto our chairs. Then, we just lay on our backs prone, in the breaking waves. The sea and the onshore wind responded to our subservience by inserting salt into every pore of our skin. Grateful for this free medical service, we smiled face-wide smiles of contentment at each other. In fact I half closed my eyes and took a holiday from thinking. Something in me made a low purring sound.

"Are you *purring*?" she laughed.

A little embarrassed, I explained, "It's the sea breeze: it makes me feel like a cat."

"Why a cat?"

"The way a cat feels when you run your fingers through its fur. It purrs because it feels loved."

"You are loved, 'Isa."

"I know, Mara. By you, and by the sea too, and perhaps I may dare to hope even by Allah, not directly but *through* these two supremely lovable creatures of His, Mara and Mare. I think both of you must be stirred by His angels."

"Do you really believe it is His angels, 'Isa?"

"That's what my Papa said. He told me about the angel in the waves, the angel that troubles the water to heal us."

"Do you think maybe there is an angel in the wind too?"

"Maybe. In Greek, the same word means three things, *spirit* and *breath* and *wind*."

"What's the word?"

"*Pneuma.*"

"That's amazing. Because there's also a word in Hebrew that means exactly those three things, *spirit* and *breath* and *wind*."

"What word is that?"

"*Rua'h.*" Then, after a moment of thought, she added: "I know what happens. The angel whispers love to the sea, and the sea shivers with delight, and that's why she has all those wrinkles. See?" She pointed to the rippled surface.

"You think that too?" I exclaimed. "I thought I was the only one who thought that." (By Allah's grace I had found the only other alien on earth.)

"I will be a sea to you, 'Isa," Mara promised.

"And I will be an angel to you, Mara." I gently blew on her hair, and she smiled, shut her eyes, and purred. Time stopped.

The tide had gone out, and we were now high and dry. Mara lay her head on my shoulder. "Do you know what would make me the most happy, 'Isa?"

"What?"

"If I can still lay my head on your shoulder when I am old and wrinkled like the sea, and if you still love to blow on my hair like the angel when you are old and grumpy and complain about everything else in the world and you sit in a wheelchair in a nursing home and you have yellow spots on your arms and the skin on your face hangs like a bulldog. That is what would make me very, very happy."

*   *   *   *   *

During August we explored a new beach almost every day. We were exploring Allah's water park. (No one could possibly design a better one.) The coldest was at Hampton Beach, New Hampshire, but the beach break at "The Wall" produced the most cleanly formed surfable waves in New England, little tubes and barrels that broke in perfect circles. One day they were just big enough to get inside them but only if you were prone on a bodyboard. I thus discovered another very significant advantage over standup surfing: you can enter cathedrals with low ceilings. We each entered the "Green Room" once that day, and it was enough.

Once, off Nauset Beach in Cape Cod (where both wind and water are often colder than Nahant, though it is farther south) we saw dolphins body-surfing a break on a sandbar a few hundred feet out. I am not making this up.

Nahant's waves were rarely high enough to be surfable during the summer, but they are perfectly formed and a mile wide even when they are only a foot high. They rise up with calm, slow dignity in perfect order, like the Redcoats at the Charge of the Light Brigade, or the changing of the guard at Buckingham Palace. They are not guerilla waves. They are proper, British waves. If surfers were mice, this would be the best surf spot in the world.

No matter where we were, we never *walked* into the sea. We will still run like kids when we're eighty.

(21) Data for the Universal Fate Wave Theory

(Editor's Note: Many readers will probably want to skip the following pages. They are only notes, selected by 'Isa from newspaper headlines in the *Boston Globe* and the *New York Times*, as data to illustrate what Evan called "fate waves." These "fate waves" were not just *things* but something like words: they are *about* something. In fact, they were about five topics he believed were interrelated: (1) war vs. peace in the Middle East, (2) the persecution of Russian dissidents, (3) scientific breakthroughs in the life sciences, (4) abortion wars in America, and (5) sports events, especially the ups and downs of the Boston Red Sox, who were having the strangest season in the history of baseball. Evan, who was working on a "Theory of Everything," believed there was a discoverable formula for the correlation of all these things. It sounds pretty "flaky" and the formula is probably impossible, but the data may seem interesting in their own right, so I have included them here. Evan published a book about his theory many years later, with St. Augustine's Press, under a pen name, entitled *If Einstein Had Been a Surfer*, in which he, 'Isa, and Libby represent the three converging points of view of scientist, philosopher, and poet/surfer.)

What follows in 'Isa's notebook, and what I have here omitted, are many pages of news reports about these five things, with dates and Evan's mathematical formulas for correlating them, which I do not understand and which I suspect 'Isa didn't either.

('Isa's autobiography resumes.)

Lazarus is fascinated with Evan's "Theory of Everything," or "Universal Wave Theory," which would coordinate physical and spiritual events under one formula. All summer he has been fixated on news from Israel. Of course, as a Jew he identifies with his spiritual homeland. He was also born there. I think he suspects the end of the world is coming soon. Mother says that the founding of the State of Israel in 1948 "put a light in his eyes that hadn't been there for 2000 years."

"That's quite an exaggeration," I said.

"Not at all. For Lazarus this means the Age of the Gentiles is ending," she explained.

"And what is supposed to follow?" I asked.

"The last age," she replied.

The establishment of the State of Israel in 1948 was the first time in 2,553 years, since the beginning of the Babylonian captivity under Nebuchadnezzar, that the Jews possessed their own homeland in freedom. The 1967 Six Day War had been another subject of fixation with Lazarus, Mother said, since it was the first time the Jews had possessed any part of their Temple for 1,897 years, since the destruction of Jerusalem and of the Temple in year 70 A.D., which began the Diaspora. Now they had at least the Wailing Wall.

September 1: The unbearable sadness that comes every year when the light begins to die, the days shrink, the water cools, and the summer disappears like a beautiful coquette who has teased her way into your life and out again. I feel seduced and abandoned.

Mother showed me two startling quotations today. One is a letter from a friend in Rome, where the conclave to elect a new Pope is about to begin. It read: "I was here shortly before Paul VI died. He was very frail and sick. But he was celebrating Mass at St. Peter's and I was one of those giving out Communion, so I had a very good seat. The Pope was reading a recital of his most important pontifical activities, and when he came to *Humanae Vitae*, he placed his notes down, looked up, and said, 'I did not betray the Truth.' I found that to be a particularly dramatic moment."

The other is a quotation from an address given by a Polish cardinal, Karol Wojtyla, in 1976 somewhere in the U.S.—Harvard, I think: "We are now standing in the face of the greatest historical confrontation humanity has gone through. I do not think that wide circles of the American society or wide circles of the Christian community realize this fully. We are now facing the final confrontation between the Gospel and the anti-Gospel."

Now *that's* the kind of man they should elect Pope, if they dared! Alas, he's Polish, not Italian.

September 3. Mother insisted that she, Lazarus and I pray together for the Camp David accords. I have never seen her more insistent about anything. We did. Did it make a difference? Could it have cast the deciding vote in the cosmic election between light and darkness? How close was this election?

Was *that* what I was brought to this House for? Surely there were many other votes for light and many other votes for darkness, among both Jews and Muslims and Christians. I stood here with a Jew and a Christian in the global jihad and fought for the light against Muslims and Jews and Christians who were fighting for the darkness; and I did not feel like an infidel or a traitor.

I discontinued my Book of Dreams weeks ago, and the dreams themselves ceased. But now another one has come, and I must record it because of Lazarus's reaction to it. When I told him my dream, he spent a day doing research on the phone and in the Boston Public Library, and then the next day hopped on a plane to South America to check it out! When he returned, I asked him what he found and he smiled sardonically, as is his wont, and said just three words: "It's not him."

In the dream I see a large, hot, humid jungle compound with about a thousand people in it, most of them families with children. One man stands in the center, with everyone looking intently at him. He wears dark rimless sunglasses, short-sleeved shirt, and light trousers. He seems to be in his forties, dark haired and serious. His forearms are hairy and he has a small moustache. All these people are *his* people.   The next night, the dream returns, but this time I see this man raping a woman, after performing very bizarre sexual acts with her. I also see some of the young children in chains.

I am more terrified of this dream than of the monsters I dreamed of months ago because it seems more realistic. But I cannot make the dream stop. I next see a helicopter landing in the compound. It has the letters "NBC-TV" clearly visible on its side. Nine men and women get out. Suddenly all nine are shot.

The next scene is the most bizarre of all. The man gives out paper cups full of Kool-Aid to all his people. There is a terrible sense of foreboding. Everyone drinks, voluntarily, and falls down dead, without struggle or protest.

What does this mean? And why was Lazarus so riveted by it?

Editor's Note: The correspondence between 'Isa's dream and the events of November 20 at Jonestown are so detailed that I cannot expect the reader to believe that 'Isa's dream really occurred *before* these events—unless the reader happens to believe that there really is such a thing as a prophetic dream. How it fits into the global jihad, and the "Theory of Everything," is apparently something 'Isa "smelled," angels see, and we can only guess.

(22) The War in the Womb

September 3: Another terrifying dream last night. I think my mind would break under these bad dreams if I was not a philosopher. Philosophizing about what they mean diverts half my mind from their terror.

I was being chased all over Bailey's Hill by an invisible Presence which made a "whooshing" sound, like a vacuum. I felt its eye and its will upon me: it was a drain, and it wanted to suck me down into itself. Once, it passed before me like an arrow, and left a wake of hot air just before my face. The air simmered like boiling water, then blurred like smoke. The blur prowled around me like a hunting tiger, bending the grass. Then it circled high over my head like a buzzard. I flew down and began to spiral around me, closer and closer. I knew that when it touched me I would touch death—or something far worse.

September 4: Tonight's dream was more puzzling than terrifying.

My mind was a movie screen. On the screen appeared a line of letters and numbers, like the credits that appear after a movie. They wavered, then came into focus and spelled out "October 2, 1582." Then I heard these words, from a voice that sounded like a knife. It said: "I AM THE LORD OF THIS DAY. AND IF THIS DAY, THEN ANY OTHER DAY."

I woke up and immediately wrote down the date. As soon as the library opened in the morning, I did some research and found, to my astonishment, that October 2, 1582, did not exist. NOTHING happened on that day. In 1582, eleven days were removed by the new Gregorian calendar, to correct mistakes in the old Julian one. October 2 was one of those days.

The voice I heard was the voice of the kingdom of nothingness.

But why October 2? It is only a month away. It is a death threat? Will Nothingness invade on October 2?

September 6: Another vision last night.

First, a blue sea, as beautiful as Mara's face. It *was* Mara's face, but older, wiser.

I asked her, "Who are you?"

Silence.

"Are you the sea?" I asked.

She frowned, and corrected me. "I am the star of the sea," she replied.

Then the waves, like the nib of a calligraphy pen, wrote a name: M—A—R. But the last letter was blurry. It looked like an E. It was MARE, the sea. No, it was a Y. It was MARY. No, it was an A. It was MARA.

On this Mare or Mara or Mary(am) floated a baby surrounded by a transparent sac. On closer look, the baby looked like an angel: the angel of the sea. The sea was full of fish and plants of every color and shape.

Then a sword was suddenly thrust into the sea, not from above the sea but from below. Like a syringe, it began to suck all the plants and fish from the sea, and all the colors, beginning with the color red.

Then, sudden as lightning, another sword was thrust down out of the sky. It covered and enclosed the first sword as a large box encloses a smaller one. From this second sword red blood began to pour *into* the sea.

I looked more closely at this second sword, and it was shaped like a cross. There seemed to be many tiny splinters on it. Then my sight was clarified and magnified, and I saw that the cross was not made of wood but of flesh, and what I had mistaken for splinters were many tiny babies' bodies. All were covered with amniotic fluid, and some with blood. Some were mutilated: some had their skulls crushed, some had their skin scalded red like cooked lobsters, some had had their arms and legs cut off, some were decapitated.

Then I saw a large face—not a whole body, just a face—on the sword. Its eyes were closed, yet amazingly expressive. What they expressed was both infinite pain and infinite peace.

The face then reappeared, multiplied many times, on the face of what I first thought were dolphins swimming in the sea. But I realized that they were unborn babies swimming blissfully in the sea of amniotic fluid, in a womb that seemed as large to them as the sea seems to us. Suddenly, violently, they were stabbed, slaughtered, massacred. The sea became a sea of blood.

I woke up coughing, as if choking on blood. I suddenly realized, with a shock, that Christians believe that God was literally once a fetus.

I do not know why I seem to be having Christian dream-images. But I do know that there are no millstones heavy enough for such a massacre of the innocents.

September 21: This morning, my mind still branded by that dream, I was confronted by John M., at BC. John is chubby, cherubic, serious, saintly, and soft-spoken.

"Jack," he said, "I think you are probably the most pro-life person on this campus. Wouldn't you consider coming with me this afternoon? We're doing an Operation Rescue down at the killing factory in Brookline."

John had never asked me this before. Why today, I wondered. "Thank you for the compliment of asking me, John, but no."

"Why not?"

"It is not my 'thing.' I'm not a political activist."

"Neither am I. This isn't politics. It's life-saving. Literally."

"I admire what you do, John. Enormously. And I agree with you 110 per cent. It's part of a true jihad. But I don't see that particular part of the battle-field as my job . I'm a thinker, not an actor."

"Jack, what do you think happens down there at the abortion clinic?"

"We all know what happens. What do you mean?"

"Just say it. Tell me what they do."

"They kill their children. Mothers ask doctors to kill their own children."

"Do you really believe that? Be honest with me, Jack."

"Of course I believe that! Why do you ask?"

"Because I don't think you really do. Because if you believed that, you couldn't just sit there and think about it. You'd act on it. It's like the belief that your house is on fire."

I had no answer. "What do you think I believe?" I asked.

"I think you believe what the pro-choicers say *they* believe: that unborn babies aren't human beings yet."

"John, how can you say that? You know I don't believe that. You've heard me argue against people who say that."

"Then how can you just sit here when your house is on fire?"

I had no answer. John continued, "Suppose abortion clinics killed all these babies *after* birth instead of before, in exactly the same ways: they cut off their limbs with sharp knives, they crushed their skulls with metal pliers, they burned off their skin with salt poisons. Would you just sit there and think about it? I don't think so. I think you'd run out as fast as you could to fight a holy war to save those babies."

I still had no answer, with my lips or with my mind. John went on.

"Suppose it was your own baby brother that was going to be slaughtered. This afternoon, ten minutes away, right here in Boston. Would you sit back and say that's not your battle because you're not an activist? I don't think so. You'd run down there to try to rescue him from the people who were trying to kill him."

"You're right," I confessed. "I would. I do believe those babies are human beings—what else are they, apes? And they *are* our brothers. But that doesn't mean that *everybody* who believes that should be doing these rescues."

"Yes, it does!" John answered, with unanswerable simplicity. "And if they all did that, it would end abortion overnight. How could they jail two-thirds of the country?"

"That's how many are against abortion on demand?"

"That's what they say when the pollsters ask them to move their pencils. But it's not what they say when God asks them to move their legs."

"I thought the polls said one-third was pro-choice and one-third pro-life and one-third in the mushy middle."

"Then let one-third march against two-thirds. Are they going to put one-third of America in jail?"

John is a saint. You can't refute a saint. I will go on a rescue this afternoon.

*   *   *   *   *

John was very insistent that I understand one thing. "I know you understand that this is jihad, spiritual war. But I hope you also understand that our weapon is only love, never hate. I call it 'dripping.'"

"'Dripping'?"

"Dripping out our blood. Our life. Our time. Our sacrifice."

"Dripping onto whom?"

"Onto the two victims, the bodies of the babies and the souls of the mothers."

"That's a very Christian image," I noted. "Imitating your martyr, giving your blood."

"It's not imitation," John replied. "Our blood *is* His blood."

"So this is a Christian thing you're doing, then. But I'm not a Christian." I thought I saw an excuse opening up. But John closed it immediately.

"No, it's a *human* thing we do. It's human blood."

"But we don't have the same religion."

"So what? We have the same blood."

I nodded. John explained further, "It's not two jihads, one Christian and one Muslim, but the same jihad, because it's the same enemy."

"But your motive is Christian."

"Yes, it is," John confessed. "I do it because I believe it's what Jesus is doing. And a religious Jew does it because he wants to practice the law, God's law, Mosaic law—'choose life.' And an agnostic does it because it's just morally right. And you do it because it's the Will of Allah, and because it's your *jihad.*"

I nodded vigorously. "You will look far and wide in this world before you will find a pro-choice Muslim," I said, proudly. "The descendants of Isaac, the Jews and the Christians, are betraying the faith of Abraham, but the descendants of Ishmael are not."

John simply ignored my apologetics and continued his practical advice, like a sergeant addressing his troops. "If we agree that it's one jihad, and we're all in it together, then we also have to agree how to fight together. We've got to agree to use the one weapon that works."

"What's that?"

"Love."

"You know, we Muslims don't use that word much because we suspect that when you use it you really mean a sentiment. And you can't fight Satan with sentiment."

"No, you can't. Love isn't a sentiment. Love is a weapon. Love is holy water. When we drip love on them, we're exorcists. We're sprinkling holy water on the demon that's possessing them. And it really gets under their skin. It burns! Hate doesn't burn them, but love does."

I nodded again. John is a wise man. "Another thing," John added: "They're infected with hate, or at least despair, and if we're trying to be their doctors, we've got to be careful not to catch their infection ourselves."

I nodded again. John is a *very* wise man. "One last thing," he added: "We always win, even if we don't convince a single woman to change her mind today."

"Why?"

"Because we always change *something* in their minds, even when you can't see it. Love always leaves scars. And memories. We'll leave memories in their souls today, scars of love. They're signs, and even if they don't follow the signs today, the signs stay in their souls, and they might remember them and follow them some day."

John *sees*. How can I resist?

*   *   *   *   *

I picked up John at the Campus School, where he does volunteer work. (Mara works there too, as part of her psychology training, but on different days than John. They've never met.) Most of the kids there can't walk, and many can't talk. All they can do is love—love the little pieces of life they can enjoy, like wheelchair rides in the sun, and each other's laughter, and the sheer presence of the caregivers, which is more powerful than anything they do or say.

John stoutly insists that his work at Campus School is not charity work. "They're like the babies we try to save on rescues," he explained to me on the way down to the abortion clinic. "They're the holy innocents, the angels. We give them a little bit of our power and cleverness—that's what we have more of than they do—but they give us love. That's what they have more of than we do."

I nodded again. When I'm with John I become a bobblehead.

"They teach us who we are, you know," John added. (The thought sounded like an echo in my head. Where had I heard it before? Why had I forgotten?) "In God's eyes I think we are more handicapped than they are." (I think John is closer to God's eyes than I am.)

At first, the "clinic" in Brookline looked like an ordinary building. In fact, it didn't look that different from Campus School. Why did this surprise me? Did I expect to see a sign over the door saying "Arbeit Macht Frei"? I did not smell burning flesh. When I said this to John, he smiled grimly, and said,

"*I* did."

"You did? Here?"

"No. Not here. They cover it up well here. I smelled it last summer when we were doing a rescue in Wichita, Kansas. I'll never forget that smell. Every weekend, when they weren't open for 'business', they burnt the ashes there— the ashes of the babies they killed the past week." John saw my eyes widen. He nodded, solemnly. "I'm not making this up. They have an incinerator . Some days you can actually see the black smoke, you can see the ashes raining down on you. The ashes of our children, the ashes of our civilization's future."

John is far too simple, gentle, and honest to lie about anything. We once had a discussion about lying. I asked him a hard question, one that divides and confuses good philosophers: "Would you tell a lie to save the world from Hell?"

"No," he said.

"Do you understand how shocking that sounds?"

"No, I don't. Don't *you* understand how *impossible* that is?"

"What do you mean? Why wouldn't you tell a lie even to save the world from Hell?"

"Because the Heaven that you got to by that lie would really be part of Hell. And the Hell that you got to by being faithful to the truth would really be part of Heaven."

We went. We stood. We prayed. We gave out literature that offered these poor women real alternatives to abortion—honest, caring, practical alternatives. (Only three out of thirty women took any literature.) We pleaded, in soft, non-threatening tones. We persuaded only one woman to cancel her abortion.

There were twenty pro-life rescuers. Some held signs. Some passed out literature. Some attempted to speak to the "clients." Some knelt and prayed— like Muslims, I thought: it was the only time I've ever seen Christians kneel and pray in public. There were about ten pro-choice demonstrators. They too held signs, but they jeered at us. No one jeered at them, though they tried to inveigle us to do it.

What amazed me the most about the rescue was the contradiction between what I saw with my own eyes and what I had heard from the media. All the secular newspaper and TV media describe this battle, in words and images, as a battle between bitter, hard, nasty, intolerant, hateful, dogmatic, inhuman, absolutistic, arrogant, narrow-minded, fundamentalist pro-lifers and tolerant, compassionate, reasonable, soft, loving, liberal, open-minded, humane pro-choicers. Go to any rescue and you will see the audacity of the lie. It is astonishingly, and dramatically, the exact reverse. The one thing impossible to miss about the pro-choicers here is their hardness and their hate. Their facial muscles were tightened around the eyes and mouth. Their eyes were slit and suspicious. Their voices were harsh and bitter. The eyes accused, the voices taunted. On the other hand, every single one of the pro-lifers there was calm and serene. Many were even radiant with love.

The third group was the victims. (The adult victims, I mean.) Most of the women's faces looked battered, broken, abused, very afraid, and self-loathing, as if their souls were dried up. They couldn't *flow* any more. They were about to murder their children, but I could not hate them, I could only pity them. One pro-choicer, more sensitive to the victims' tragic look than the others were, yelled to the pro-lifers, "You should be ashamed of yourself for trying to make these women feel ashamed of themselves."

I think every one of these mothers must have been badly hurt. Nothing in nature secretes that kind of hard shell around itself unless it's been hurt, and is afraid of being hurt again. What sort of hurt are they afraid of *now*? I think they are most afraid of their own aborted children who will look at them in their dreams with eyes that ask them: "Why? Why did you do this to me, Mommy?" I think that is the deepest terror on those terrified faces: they are trying to silence those voices.

None of the women who entered for an abortion looked up, into the light, only down, into the darkness. They seemed afraid of the sky. They didn't even dare look at one another. They say they are here for freedom, for liberation. They do not look anything like people escaping from a prison. They look exactly like people entering a prison.

They see us, but they refuse to see us. They are afraid to make eye contact. Why? What do they fear to see? Not hate: they *will* make eye contact with the hate-filled pro-choicers. But they are terrified to look into eyes of love. What do they fear more than killing? Loving. What is worse for them than being killed? Being loved.

How naïve I was to be *surprised* at the lies of the media. Why should souls that do not quail at murdering quail at lying? Especially lying about those murders? This was the place of the institutionalized lie. But these women *knew* that. That's what made them so oppressed. They knew what they were doing. Women are not stupid. They are wicked—just like men—but they are not stupid.

A good-looking young couple in jeans stood there with a big white sign that said: "We are a childless couple. We would love to adopt your baby. We will give your baby love, if you will only give your baby life. This is no gimmick, this is for real. Please?"

The couple pleaded with their eyes. One woman on her way to the "clinic" turned her head, saw the sign, read it, stopped, forced back her tears, went up to them and asked, "Are you real?" Both hugged her in answer. Tears all around, and smiles—except on the faces of the pro-choice demonstrators and hecklers. Intense, almost insane, anger showed in their pinched faces and burning eyes. How awful! A human life saved, a human family saved, a woman's happiness saved. How dare these nasty pro-lifers smile? How dare they love babies, and families, and women?

That was the only baby we saved today, but one is worth it, one is worth everything. "He who saves one life, saves the world." Twenty pro-lifers gave one afternoon to save one life. It would have been worth it if it took twenty thousand pro-lifers and twenty thousand afternoons.

One other beam of light penetrated the darkness this afternoon: Sally. Sally had come to the "clinic" last year for an abortion and had been persuaded by the pro-life sidewalk counselors to look into alternatives. She came now to show everyone her "alternative," her fat, pink, healthy baby, about 3 or 4 months old. "Thank you," she said, simply, to the fat Italian priest who was organizing the rescue. The priest held the baby aloft to the other pro-lifers. "See! This is why we are here!"

The pro-choicers went ballistic. One shouted to the priest: "That baby would have been better off dead!—and you too." Another said, "Another welfare mother! She'll raise YOUR taxes."

When I heard the timbre of the pro-choice screams, I couldn't help remembering that alien identification scream in the movie *Invasion of the Body Snatchers*. The title of the movie fit too.

An angry old lady passed the priest and kicked him in the shins, cursing. He smiled and blessed her.

A teenage boy brought "his" girl through the crowd. Both looked confused and on the verge of tears, but he also looked (or tried to look) heroic. As he passed us, the boy said to the priest, "It's her problem, not yours, Father." The priest answered, "She's not a *problem*; she's a *baby*. And she's your problem too, son." But the couple went in anyway. Words seem to have little power here.

One girl stopped to talk to the priest. She was calmer than the other women who were about to abort. I didn't hear the rest of the conversation, but I heard the priest say, "Just be honest. Say honestly what you are going to do. Say it. Say 'I have a right to kill my child.' Go home and say it over and over to yourself until you hear yourself." But he did not move her.

There was one other thing I saw that surprised me and saddened me: the gay and lesbian activists that were on the pro-choice side of the driveway. (The police kept the two groups on opposite sides of the paved driveway that led into the abortion clinic.) I know Allah hates sodomy, and so do I, but I don't hate homosexuals. All of the dozen or so men that I know or suspect are gay seem to me to be nice, civil people. I asked John about this afterwards: "Why are the pro-abortionists and the pro-gays always on the same side?"

John seemed surprised I would ask the question. "Isn't it obvious? It's the jihad: life versus death."

"Explain it to me. How do you see it?"

"How much clearer could it be? Look: gays always identify themselves with what they do. And what they do is sodomy. And sodomy kills you. It turns the penis into a gun, and semen into a bullet, and it plays Russian roulette, because AIDS is always fatal. That's how it's like abortion: instead of sex creating new life, it creates new death. How much clearer can it be? You don't have to have a Ph.D. to see that. I think you have to have a Ph.D. to miss it."

John is very simple-minded. That's why he really pisses people off. I like that.

John came to the House with me after the rescue. He and Mother are old friends. We talked over supper. "I knew John would get you into a rescue some day," Mother said.

"Who got *you* into it?" I asked John.

"Doctor Stanton." (Mother nodded, recognizing the name.) "The man is a saint. If I was the Pope, I'd canonize him tomorrow."

"I thought your Church couldn't canonize a saint until after he died," I said, looking at both John and Mother for clarification.

"That's true," said Mother. "It's just an expression. John didn't mean it literally."

"Well, almost literally," said John. "He's old and frail, and one of these days somebody's going to kill him. You know, the police broke four of his ribs last year when they threw him into the paddy wagon. And when I say 'threw,' that isn't just an expression. It's literal."

I looked at the photo John showed me. "They threw that old man around? That's outrageous! Was he making trouble?"

"Not a bit."

"Did they hurt him: Is that why he's still using a cane?"

"No, he's been crippled all his life. He had polio as a kid."

"And the police took this gentle old man and . . . I can't believe it. I thought they were supposed to be *preventing* violence, not starting it."

"They were *protecting* violence. They were protecting abortion."

"They could have killed that old man."

"They were *protecting* killing."

"Good grief, it's almost like the SS protecting the death camps!"

"It *is* protecting death camps."

"Aren't you getting a little out of hand there?" asked Libby, who until then had held her tongue.

"I don't think so," John replied. "Not if you ask Chad."

"Who's Chad?"

"A marine I know who came back from fighting in Lebanon. He said that Beirut was not as frightening as this. That was hot evil, honest evil. Bullets. This is cold evil. Cold steel. Didn't you feel the wall of ice down there today, Jack?"

I felt the chill again as I remembered it. "Yes," I whispered.

"And the journalists who lie to protect the killers who lie—that's an even colder lie," said John. "You can't help but sympathize with those poor women who come in—so sad, so oppressed. But the journalists aren't poor, and they aren't sad, and they aren't oppressed. They have no excuse. If I had any mill-stones in my house, I think I'd reserve a few for them."

At that, Libby's patience expired. "Are you trying to tell me that newspa-pers get away with outright lies? All those articles about the hate and violence from the pro-lifers are just lies?"

"Yes!" said John. "Most of them, anyway."

"You can't prove that."

"Yes I can," John said, triumphantly, reaching into his big brown carrying case. He gave Libby a laminated article. "Look at this. This columnist cites a pro-choicer's claim that she was attacked by a male pro-life rescuer. (Libby nodded, believingly.) But the police records say that the police arrested *the pro-choice woman* for kicking *the pro-life man* repeatedly in the head. So this columnist apparently wants you to believe that this male pro-lifer attacked this female pro-choicer by throwing his face at her feet. You're a social worker, Libby; wouldn't you call that a rather unusual form of assault?"

Libby read the article silently. "Who knows what really happened?" was her reply.

"I do. I recorded it. On video tape. In fact, I've got over 500 hours of videotapes of rescues. And I've counted more than 700 angry pro-choice faces on my tapes, and *two* angry pro-life ones—both fat, ugly, stupid-looking peo-ple, by the way. I gave copies of all my tapes to the TV news people. Guess how many of the 700 appeared on TV? Zero. Guess how many of the two? Both. I'd call that a form of lying, wouldn't you?"

Libby was silent. "Here's another one," John said, groping into his case. "I've got extra copies of it. Take one." Libby took it and put it into her pocket. She showed it to me later, and I copied part of it.

> **MILWAUKEE—A special prosecutor was appointed to investigate allegations that Katherine Doyle, a local attorney, kicked a seven year old girl in the face . . .**
>
> **On May 15th, at approximately 9:30 A.M., Katherine Doyle argued with seven year old Katerina Engelke, as the little girl prayed outside a Milwaukee abortion clinic. According to the other prolifers at the scene, Doyle asserted that Engelke was a puppet of her parents, and that she wasn't old enough to know what goes on inside an abortion clinic.**
>
> **Engelke informed Doyle that she knows very well what goes on inside the clinics, and the seven year old then asked Doyle what she was doing at the clinic.**
>
> **Doyle said she was helping women, to which Engelke replied, "You are not; you're killing babies."**

> Doyle then, said witnesses, cursed the seven year old and kicked her in the face with such force it could be heard several feet away.
>
> When police arrived, Doyle was not arrested, even though the young girl's face was severely swollen, and there were four witnesses to the assault ...

Another article from the same paper read:

> On May 6th, two prolife citizens were assaulted as they sat in prayer, and another was bitten in the arm. The prolifers were charged with assault and arrested by police, while their attackers remained free.
>
> Assistant District Attorney Stephanie Rothstein, even though she personally saw the bite marks and a videotape of the proabortion activists assaulting the peaceful demonstrators, did not charge the proabortion citizens.
>
> She explained that she charged the prolifers because one "looked like he wanted to jump on someone" as he sat on the ground and had his hair pulled viciously by the proabortion citizens. Rothstein did not charge Treena Hass, who bit the prolifer, because "she did not mean to hurt him." ...
>
> This case of clinic violence has not been reported by Milwaukee's daily newspapers or on radio or television news broadcasts, with the exception of WVCY, a Christian station.

I have learned that abortion is the second most common surgery in America (next to eye cataract removal), that abortionists are the only doctors in America not liable for malpractice, and that their clinics are the only ones not legally subject to basic federal safety and cleanliness regulations.

When John first told me this, I expressed surprise. John retorted, "Why are you surprised at that? Were there legal and sanitary rules in Auschwitz?"

After John went home and Libby went to bed, Mother and I talked further. She seems to see abortion not merely as a great evil, but as a special *kind* of evil, something apocalyptic. She explained, "There's this prophecy in the Jewish scriptures, in the Book of Daniel, about 'the abomination of desolation standing in the holy place.' Jesus quoted that in *his* apocalyptic prophecies. He said that would be a sign of the end, a sign that the last judgment was near. I used to wonder what it meant. Now I think maybe it means abortion."

"Why?" I asked.

She answered, "Listen to the words: 'the abomination of desolation in the Holy Place.' Abortion is 'the abomination of desolation,' because the womb is 'the holy place,' the holy of holies, the holiest place in the world, because that's where God creates new immortal souls, which is a greater deed than creating the whole universe 14 billion years ago, because souls never die but the universe does, and souls can know God but the universe can't. So the supreme blasphemy would be to worship the God of death in this temple of the God of life. It all fits. It's logical."

"The god of death—you mean. . . ?"

"Many names, he's got: Baal, Ashtoreth, Astarte, Moloch, Satan, Iblis, Dracula. Under all those names, he lusts for blood, human blood, especially babies' blood."

"You put Dracula in the same category? I thought that was only fiction."

"No, it's fact. It's history."

"Oh, Vlad the Impaler, you mean? The Russian tyrant? I learned about that from two professors at BC."

"McNally and Florescu? I read their book. *In Search of Dracula*, right? That's true, but there's more to it than that, more than the historical Vlad the Impaler *and* more than Bram Stoker's fiction. There's a real supernatural force working there, working right here in history. And he's still working."

"The Devil, you mean?" I wondered how Mother knew so much about this.

"Of course. And his legions. Dracula is just another one of his names."

Evan had come in a few minutes ago and picked up the thread of the conversation. "You see, 'Isa, we Christians see Dracula as another name for the Antichrist. Antichrist is the reverse of Christ, the perfect perversion of Christ. Christ gave His blood to take us to Heaven, Dracula takes our blood to take us to Hell."

"I see. Two opposite images."

"Not just images, historical realities," Mother corrected.

"You think Dracula is as historical as Christ?" I asked.

"If Dracula is another name for the Antichrist, yes," she replied.

Evan explained, "The Antichrist is a historical figure, like Christ, according to the New Testament, and not just a myth."

"Who is he?" I asked.

"Not a man," Evan answered. "You can't see him."

I suddenly thought, with a thrill of fear, "Maybe *you* can't see him, but I think I did. Twice." But I said nothing.

"But you can see his *effects,*" Mother added: "All that innocent blood flowing into his mouth from all those abortions. That place down there in Brookline where you went today—that's a *neck*, you know; that's where Satan sucks our babies' blood, that's where we offer our neck to Dracula to suck. Women and children, that's who he wants. He's the same spirit who did the same work back in Canaan in the Valley of Gehenna. Demons are immortal, you know. They never die."

"You don't mean to say that a million American women are demon-possessed?"

"Of course not. But their work is. How else could we have reached this point?"

"What point?"

"The point where the least safe place in the world now is not the battlefield but the womb. The point where pregnancy is now a disease to be cured. The point where the most dreaded sexually transmitted disease is a child. It's insanity! Our ancestors would simply not believe it. Pagans in darkest Africa, when they hear it, literally can't believe it. No sane primitive could believe it. How could we possibly be that—that 'primitive'? I mean it: it's insanity. Literally. It's moral insanity."

"That sounds terribly harsh." (I was playing Devil's advocate.)

"It *is* terribly harsh. You'd think so too if you were on the receiving end of the knife."

"Libby would say you're laying a horrible guilt on these women."

"No, no, don't you see? It's just the opposite. I'm saying *they* can't be the inventors of that horror. They're not that evil. They're duped by the Devil, like Eve."

Mother thought for a moment, in silence, then added, "He hates women and children most of all, you know." Another silence, then: "You know what I think, 'Isa? I think that if you *don't* say this holocaust is the work of the Devil, then you must have a very low view of women."

"Why?"

"You have to have a really low view of women to believe that they *want* to kill their children. Are they that wicked? Or maybe they are so weak and passive that they just let their boyfriends or husbands tell them what to think and what to do? 'Oh, you want me to kill our baby? OK, my love, anything for you.' Or maybe they are just stupid? So stupid that they're suckers who believe whatever the media establishment tells them? That's really stupid. Think! What force is strong enough to overcome the force of mother-love, the strongest force in human nature? It's got to be something supernatural, not something natural. It's a drug, that's what it is, a supernatural drug. The Devil knows his medicine: he knows he has to anesthetize before he operates. No woman is going to let him do heart surgery on her, and let him cut out the big Motherhood Valve in that heart, without anesthesia first."

I kept nodding at what Mother said, but she saw the surprise in my wide-open eyes. "I'm surprised you didn't see that right away, 'Isa. You of all people. It's the *jihad*. It's spiritual warfare. It's supernatural."

Again Mother thought in silence for a few seconds, then shook her head sadly. "Sometimes I wonder whether you men can ever understand what the word 'mother' means."

I ignored her last remark. "So in the last analysis abortion is literally the work of the Devil?" (I was still playing Devil's advocate, to draw her out.)

"Well, it sure as Hell isn't the work of God!"

Evan was shocked at Mother's Catholic vocabulary. I continued to play Devil's advocate:

"Maybe it's the work of ignorance, and bad philosophy, and moral relativism, and selfishness, and the sexual revolution, and lust, and fear."

"Well, of course it is! And if you were the Devil, wouldn't you use all those natural forces? How would you get these poor women to do your work if you came at them without any of those disguises?"

"So what we're doing when we refute that bad philosophy and call things by their right names is more than philosophy. It's jihad! It's stripping off the Devil's disguises."

"Exactly! That's why we love you, and why we need you, and why we're with you, 'Isa: we Christians are fighting the same enemy you Muslims are fighting: the Hungry One, who wants his meat."

She was silent for a moment, looking undecided, then set her jaw and said, thoughtfully, "He captured King Herod's soul and gorged himself on soft baby flesh back then too. But the meat he wanted most escaped him and went into Egypt. Until 33 years later. And then the Devil choked on it."

"Choked on it? But your scriptures say he got his meat, when he got Jesus crucified. That's why we Muslims say you must be wrong there: God wouldn't allow His prophet to fail. What do you mean, the Devil choked on it?"

"I mean that the one thing that sticks in his throat, the one thing Satan can't swallow, is the Cross."

"But . . . Mother, that's the one thing we Muslims can't swallow in your religion: the idea of the Son of God dying on the Cross. Are you saying we're like the Devil because he can't swallow it either?"

"No, no, 'Isa. You're not a devil. You're named after Jesus. HE swallowed it. And you can too."

My words sank before I could launch them. My thoughts flowed like two opposite tides.

I went to bed with these tides in my head. The dream that followed obviously flowed out from them. I think it may also have flowed down from Heaven.

The Aztec Nightmare

As I drifted into an uneasy sleep that night, I felt myself falling from a great height. I looked down into a smoking mirror. The nightmare rose up to me out of the mirror as I sank down into it. As I came closer, a force riveted me to the mirror as if nails were thrust through my head.

Something black was swirling and spiraling in the smoke, riding the updrafts of fiery air. It looked like the ashes of a burned page of a book that was coming apart. The ashes formed themselves into a cross, and then the four arms of the cross twisted and turned like a tortured man having all four of his limbs broken, and then the arms of the cross formed themselves into a swastika, a twisted cross, which was visible only for a second before quickly disappearing on the wind.

A picture began to emerge from the smoking mirror. First, two vast oceans, one on the east and one on the west. Between them, a continent shaped like an upside-down horse with no legs, with a vast desert stretching north to south. Then, like a zoom lens focusing, I saw a great city in middle of the desert. It was built on water—an engineering marvel. A vision of the future? The work of an advanced race on another planet? Atlantis?

In the exact center of the city rose one great stone pyramid, four-sided, rising at least a hundred feet high. On each side was a steep staircase to the top, and at the bottom four gates that looked like mouths, from which came, like four long tongues, four perfectly straight ribbons of road extending out into the desert in all four directions of the compass as far as the eye could see, to the horizon.

I noticed long lines of brown-skinned, black-haired people extending down all four roads in single file. When my "zoom lens" focused, I saw that they were young boys. Their faces were filled with terror—no, with something worse: the resignation of total despair that is beyond terror.

My eyes followed the lines of boys as they climbed up the pyramid. At the top there was a square platform, and on the platform was a man whose head and arms were stained pitch black like the smoke from the mirror. His hair was very long and very dirty, matted with dried blood. I knew he was some kind of priest. As each of the boy victims emerged from the line onto the platform from the four stairways, the priest put a hook around his neck and bent him backward over a great slab of stone. Quickly, he slashed his victim's neck and chest with an immense knife with a black stone blade. He reached in and tore out the heart as it was still beating. He held the heart high in his hand for all the watching eyes to see. (Many people were watching from below in the streets.) Then the priest kicked the heartless body over the edge of the platform. As it fell, its limbs were contorted. It bounced down the steps to the bottom a hundred feet below. That bounce was the most sickening sound I ever heard, especially when the skull cracked like a pumpkin.

The priest's efficiency was amazing: each victim took only fifteen seconds. A waterfall of blood and body parts cascaded endlessly down the steps of the pyramid.

Surrounding the pyramid were well-dressed Indian people watching the ritual like an opera. Some stood and some sat in boxes full of scented roses, which failed to cover the stench of blood. I not only *saw* this but *smelled* it, and gagged. Many of the spectators fled in horror. I could not: the nails in my head were holding me down to the mirror and forcing me to look and to smell. I was choking on smoke and blood.

The blood became a giant wave, and flooded the whole country. The country looked like Picasso's "Guernica." Body parts floated in the red wave like flotsam and jetsam. They were not the bodies of Indian boys now but the tiny parts of babies, and half were baby girls. And the blood was coming not from the pyramid but from a womb, and the knives that killed were made not of stone but of steel.

I snapped awake and sprang up in bed like a spring, shuddering with cold sweats. The terror was not just in the nightmare. The nightmare was over. The terror was outside the nightmare. The terror was the fact that the nightmare was real. I did not wake up *from* the nightmare, but *into* it. And the only way I could escape this nightmare was to change it, not in thought but in deed.

It was 1:30 A.M. I was exhausted, yet I could not go back to sleep. I rose, dressed, and went downstairs, intending to walk on the beach. Then I saw a light under Mother's door. I knocked. "Come in." I stammered out my story. Mother listened, with sympathy and (more important) fascination.

"*You* know what this dream means, don't you?" I asked.

"Yes. But it's better for you to find out by yourself. Here are two books you must read. The library will have them." She scribbled two titles: *The Bernard Diaz Chronicles* and *Our Lady of Guadalupe and the Conquest of Darkness* by Warren H. Carroll.

"Who is Diaz?" I asked.

"He was the companion of Cortez," Mother answered. At the mention of the name of Cortez, something leaped up in me, as if Cortez himself had been sleeping in my spirit and Mother's pronouncement of his name woke him up.

The next morning, I immediately went to the library and found the books. I was not surprised by the outline of the story which I already knew, and or at the match between it and my dream. But I was more than surprised, I was amazed, at the details of the match. "God is in the details."

It took me less than an hour to read both books. (No one ever taught me to "speed-read," I just do it.) Back at the House, Mother saw my face, understood, smiled knowingly, showed me an icon of Our Lady of Guadalupe, and said only two words: "That's her." I knew the story behind the icon—after all, my Mama was not only Mexican and Catholic but descended from Juan Diego. But Mother then told me something I had not known: that scholars who have studied the Nahuatl language in which the Lady spoke to Juan Diego believe that when the Bishop heard the Lady's title "The Ever-Virgin Holy Mary of Guadalupe," through a Spanish interpreter, he mistook her unfamiliar Nahuatl name for the familiar Spanish name Guadalupe, which is a Marian shrine in Spain. The name the Lady actually spoke was almost certainly *Tequetalope* (there is no G or D in Nahuatl), which means "She Who Saves Us from the Devourer," or else *Coatlaxope,* "She Who Crushes the Serpent."

Mother explained that either of these titles would identify her with the "woman clothed with the sun" in the vision in Revelation 12, the one who crushes the head of the serpent who is Satan, fulfilling the first prophecy in the Bible, Genesis 3:15.

When I realized this connection, I shuddered. For I think I have seen this serpent. I first saw this lord of death swimming in the sea of life a few weeks ago here in Nahant. Then I saw him in my nightmare swimming in the dead souls of those Mexican boys, in their hopeless, haunted faces. And I saw him riding the sea of blood that poured down the pyramid: it poured into *his* mouth.

What is far more terrifying, I think he saw me.

(23) The Ecumenical Jihad

September 18: This morning Mother did something she never did before. We were all together at breakfast. Mother looked very serious. Mister Mumm was at her side, looking as serious as he can look. Mother said to us:

"Every one of you here owes me something, isn't that right?

"Mother, each one of us owes you his life in some way. We all know that. What can we do for you?" I spoke for everyone. The others nodded at me.

"I want you to do something very simple and very important. It will take only ten minutes, but it might take an hour to persuade you to do it."

"Mother, we'll do anything for you."

"Will you all to get down on your knees together and pray together?"

"For what?"

"I don't know."

"That's . . . that's . . ." I was too polite to say "crazy" but that's what I thought.

"You know you were all brought here for a reason, don't you?"

"Yes." Eight nods.

"Well, for this moment you were called."

"But why now? What's happening now? Why this morning?" I demanded.

"I don't know," Mother confessed.

Mister Mumm, uncharacteristically, spoke up: "I know *some* of you feel the forces swirling around us." Eva nodded vigorously, Lazarus looked ready to jump, and Diddly and Squat shared a small, mysterious smile. Only Libby, Evan, and I looked puzzled.

"Remember the hurricane last winter?" asked Mister Mumm. "Well, this one is bigger. But you can't see it."

"Can *you*? Can you see the invisible? Can you see the future?" I demanded. I had always kept a tiny suspicion of charlatanry in the back of my mind about this man.

"Only God can see the future," he said, simply.

"Then why. . . ? Why do we have to do this thing right now? And why do we have to do it together? Why can't we just promise to pray twice as much today in our own way? You said ten minutes; how about if we each promise to do twenty today?"

Mother answered the question I directed to Mister Mumm. "We have to do it together. It's like one of those magic stones in the fairy tales: it works only if all the parts are assembled."

"Like a spiritual machine," suggested Evan.

"No, like a body," Mother said.

Mister Mumm added, "And each of you is an organ. All of us must do it, or it may not be enough."

I wanted to ask him why he said "each of *you*" but then "all of *us*." Instead, I asked, "But who or what are we praying for? How can we pray if we don't know who to pray for?"

"We know who we're praying for. We're praying for the world," Mister Mumm answered.

"I *thought* it would take some time to convince you," said Mother. "I know your schedules. I know you can all give me the next hour of your time. So listen up while I try to explain to 'Isa here, and whoever else doesn't quite understand what we're up to."

We all sat down in the living room. Mother went on, "You all know what *jihad* means, especially you, 'Isa. And you know a new century is coming soon—a new millennium, in fact. Did you ever hear the story of the vision of Pope Leo XIII about our century? I see some blank stares. Well, a few years before the 20th century, he had a vision of its coming horrors and genocides, and the vision showed him the reason: at the beginning of history God let the Devil choose one century to do his worst work in, and he chose the 20th. The vision was so terrifying that the pope swooned away. They thought he was dead. When he opened his eyes, he told them what he had seen, and he composed the Saint Michael the Archangel prayer to get the world through the coming century, the Devil's Century, and commanded that it be said after every Catholic Mass in the world. It was—until a few years ago."

"What was the prayer?" I asked.

"Saint Michael Archangel, defend us in battle. Be our protection against the wickedness and snares of the enemy. May God rebuke him, we humbly pray, and do thou, O prince of the Heavenly host, thrust into Hell Satan and the other evil spirits who prowl about the world seeking the ruin of souls."

The words came out like notes of a trumpet. They made my bones feel like swords. I was ready for this *jihad*.

"Do you think St. Michael is still fighting for us?" I asked Mother.

"Of course. But he can't fight unless we ask him. Angels wait for our permission. And our prayers. And our passion. They won't work without that."

How did she know so much about angels, I thought. "But why *now*? What is happening now?" I asked.

"The battle lines are getting clearer. The fog is lifting. The war on earth is looking more and more like the war in Heaven."

"You mean you think the end of the world is approaching?"

"It's always approaching. It may be a millennium away, or a century, or a day, or a heartbeat, but it's approaching, that's for sure. Like an unstoppable wave."

"The last wave," Libby put in. "The last wave is always the biggest one of the set."

"I still want to know why we have to pray this morning," I insisted.

"You were never in the army, 'Isa," said Mother. "Only one of you was." She looked at Lazarus. "So you know why: orders. And you don't always know the reason for the orders."

None of us dared question Mother about how she got her orders.

"But Mother, if the 20th century was the Devil's Century, then the next one has to be better," I argued.

"I hope so, 'Isa, I hope so. And *we* have to help this poor old world to *get* there, to *make* it to the next century. And to do that, we have to stop our civil wars and start fighting our real enemy together."

"The Devil, you mean?" asked Libby.

"The Devil, I mean," said Mother.

"That sounds so . . . so *medieval.*"

Evan, surprisingly, supported Libby: "I thought the 20th century was dead to the supernatural, Mother."

"That's what the media want you to think. They lie."

"They *lie?*" Libby asked suspiciously.

"They lie. In fact, our century is *bursting* with the supernatural. The jihad is heating up, not cooling down." Mother was always frank, but this was extraordinary.

"You don't mean *literal* war?" Libby asked, suspiciously.

"Of course I do! What, do you think souls are only *metaphors?*"

"I thought you meant real battlefields, with real casualties."

"What, dead souls aren't casualties?"

"Souls can't die."

"The Hell they can't."

"Where do they die?"

"I just told you."

"Oh. I guess I meant *physical* then instead of *literal.*"

"I mean that too. I'd call the blood from 30 million babies physical, wouldn't you? That's a pretty loud voice to be calling to God from the ground for vengeance."

"Oh. But Mother, do you really believe God wants *vengeance?*"

"No, Libby. I believe that God wants love. But that *blood* wants vengeance. And God listens to that blood, because that's the blood of His own little children. Do you think He doesn't? Do you think He can stop His ears to that cry? Could any mother do that? They're His children, Libby! Think! Imagine they were *your* children."

"I thought you said God wasn't a mother. We had that argument last week . . ."

"God *invented* mothers, didn't He?"

"All right, Mother, I'm with you. Let's pray God bless America."

"I hope I'm wrong, but sometimes I wonder how much longer God *can* bless America."

"What a terrible thing to say! Why?"

"Can a Jewish mother bless the Third Reich? I'm a Jewish mother, OK? My mother died in Auschwitz. Do you think I can bless the Third Reich?"

"So what do we pray for if we can't pray for blessing?"

"Time. It's getting short."

Libby was silent. Evan took up the questioning. "So what do you think is happening now? Satan's last gasp, near the end of his century?"

"Something like that."

"And why do we all have to pray *together*?"

"Because we've been really, really stupid for centuries. We forgot the Devil's strategy, the oldest and simplest strategy of all: divide and conquer. But now General God is calling all his troops together, all of Abraham's children, Isaac and Ishmael (she looked at me), Jacob and Esau—even Esau (she looked at Eva)—Joseph and his brothers, the lost ten tribes (she looked at Lazarus), Jews and Christians, Catholics and Protestants, liberals and fundamentalists. . . ."

"But we're just nine people."

"Yes, and nine little stones can begin an avalanche. What we do here today is the beginning of a new wave, and who knows how big that wave will become, or how far it will reach around the world?"

"I thought ecumenism was an old thing," I asked. "How new can this be?"

"It's so new that it will raise the hair on the back of your neck when you see it."

Evan shook his head, still not wholly on board. "Mother, you know my suspicions of ecumenism: watering down and compromise. What do you say to that?"

"That none of us can win this battle alone."

"I don't need heretics to help me save my soul," Evan said, bluntly.

"You may save your soul alone, Evan, but you will never save your world alone. We have to fight shoulder to shoulder and shield to shield, or we will lose this world."

"But Mother, what profit is there to gain the whole world and lose your soul?" Evan was getting preachy now, and Mother was getting impatient.

"That's what I *mean* by the world, you silly boy: souls. What did you think I meant? Politics?" The last word dripped with sarcasm.

Libby chimed in: "But how can God expect Jews, Christians, and Muslims to work together when they've been killing each other for centuries?"

"He doesn't *expect* it, He *commands* it."

Libby looked in my direction. "Then the Muslims better shape up first. They've been doing most of the killing lately."

I immediately retorted, "In Belfast, for instance?"

"That's exactly what God wants you to stop!" interrupted Mother.

I couldn't help continuing the polemic: "Mother, I don't mean to be rude, but how do you know what God wants? Do you claim to be His prophet?"

"Do you not agree with what I have said about what God wants?"

"I don't know. How can I know what God wants?"

"Listen. Listen to your heart, your conscience."

My answer died in my throat. "You are right," I said.

"Now, tell me how you *know* I am right. Are *you* a prophet?"

"No, but Muhammad was, and he told us what God wants. That is how I know."

"And Jesus is our prophet, and more than a prophet, and he has told us what God wants, and that is how I know. And Moses tells Lazarus. And the Bible tells Evan and Libby, and the Church tells me. All the prophets say the same thing about God because it's the same God. So if we all obey our prophets, we will all want the same things: the things God wants. It's really very, very simple."

"All right, Mother, let's get down to business. Let's do it. What do we pray for?"

"We pray for each other's prophets. Will you pray for mine? (We nodded.) Then pray for the Pope."

"I can't," protested Evan. "I respect you, Mother, but I have to be honest with you: I can't pray for the Antichrist."

"Do you really think the Pope is the Antichrist?"

"I really don't know. But some Protestant theologians say so."

"But you can pray 'thy will be done' always, can't you?"

"Yes."

"And you can remember that you don't really know for sure what that will is all the time, can't you?"

"Yes," Evan said with a rueful smile.

"Good," said Mother.

So we all knelt and prayed for the Pope, that kindly, sweet, wise, gentle man. But how can *he* be what Mother believes he is, God's chosen general against the Devil? Especially after his church has stopped praying the St. Michael prayer and the Devil has gotten stronger and stronger all through this century?

Some of our prayer was silent, some was voiced. Everyone said something except Eva, who was the most intense of all. Diddly and Squat half-chanted, half-hummed. I felt in the eye of the hurricane, at the center of the universe, the still point of the turning world. We were the axle of the soapstone spindle turned by the Norns.

We prayed for ten minutes, after we had argued for almost an hour, just as Mother predicted. She knows that preparation is nine tenths of the work: she paints.

As we rose, I asked Mother, "Do you think the sun will shine a little more brightly tomorrow?"

She replied with a verse from G.K. Chesterton's "Ballad of the White Horse," a battle poem we both knew and loved:

> **I tell you naught for your comfort,**
> **Yea, naught for your desire,**
> **Save that the sky grows darker yet**
> **And the sea rises higher.**

I looked outside as she recited the last line. The sea was indeed restless. I fancied I could hear the sound of millions of troops being moved around like cosmic chess pieces, angels and demons jostling for position on the chessboard. Spirit wings were opening. Battle was afoot.

(24) The Angel's Fall

September 18: Mara and I stood above the Drum and watched with fascination as a nor'easter attacked the Hill today. The wind seemed obsessed with the task of blowing our heads off our shoulders. The trillion-ton sea seethed and sighed, worried and fretted. In swell after swell it rose up like a giant cobra to engulf the Drum, then crash itself into a million particles of white madness on the rocks. Wave followed wave with slosh, boom, and swish, first inhaling as it engulfed the Drum, then exhaling in a great sneeze as it splashed up the rocky slope where we were standing.

We were as entranced with the sea's untamed passion today as with her peace yesterday; was the same spirit making both musics?

September 19: Mara and I met on the Hill surrounded by a cool September fog, which made us feel invisible to the world. Yet the fog seemed to envelop only the Hill; we could see through it to the rest of the world. Indeed, we felt literally on top of the world today: seeing all, but ourselves unseen. The Hill had become Gollum's ring for us, bestowing the two gifts of power and invisibility.

I spoke not one word, but simply took her hands in mine—gently, infinitely gently—and we looked into each other's eyes for a few centuries—really looked, looked-*into*, not looked-*at*. It was the most erotic moment of my life.

Looking-into her eyes rather than looking-at them meant that I was not just seeing her but was seeing her-*seeing-me*. She was making love to me with her eyes. They were alive. They were fire. I was kindled, like a candle, with her flame. This was not pleasure; this was ecstasy. This could go on forever without the slightest chance of boredom. This was Beatific Vision, this was Paradise.

Amazing how *clear* her dark eyes were in the fog, how *bright*. Their darkness was not the absence of all colors but their presence. In fact, it was the presence of a new universe. They were two beautiful, life-giving Black Holes (not terrible, annihilating Black Holes), pulling my spirit out of the universe, out of my body, out of my very self, down two endless corridors into a new universe. Just off those corridors were doors to places where millennia of her ancestors lived. All the children of Eve lived in her eyes, the whole family of mankind, as a whole person is in each kiss, and as the whole sea kisses the surfer in each wave.

Her eyes were transparent. Soul shone through them. What was in her soul was love.

What was in that love was human but also more than human. She was the moon, and into my eyes she reflected the light and love of the sun.

And the sun is no deceiver.

The fiery love that flamed between our eyes flew so furiously fast that I could no longer distinguish mine from hers. I disappeared into the bliss like a speck of sunlight into the sea. But this was no pantheistic oneness, for *she* did not disappear but remained, and remained gloriously other, gloriously feminine, gloriously herself.

I sent the shaft of my love up from my heart, out through my eyes, into her eyes, and down into her heart. She did the same to me. The two arrows met in mid-glance and split each other apart at their tips.

It is beyond all hope that she—*she*—should love me as much as I love her. For she is incomprehensible beauty, and I am only the lover of incomprehensible beauty. And that incomprehensible beauty was giving itself to me! It was a grace, utterly undeserved, unpredictable, uncontrollable, and free. I understood at that moment that everything in the universe is a grace, a gift. And I understood that grace was not an attitude, a spirit, or an abstract force; grace was as concrete as her eyes, her body. There was no distinction between her soul and her body. I understood for the first time what her soul looked like: it looked like her body!

I stopped thinking at this point, and did not even spoil it by thinking about my not-thinking. The fire whirling from face to face intensified, in a breathtaking synergy—how far could this go? What could ever stop it? What had become of time? How long had I been not only unwilling but unable to be aware of myself? How long had I disappeared from this universe, down this beautiful Black Hole, this birth canal, this angel-opened gate to Paradise? I was swept out to sea on the riptide of her beauty, and I became one with the sea, one with the She.

Whether it lasted for half a second or half a day I neither know nor care. If at that moment I knew that I would be tortured for 24 hours a day for the next 50 years, it would not have mattered, because this moment was the only moment. There was no future and no past; no plans and no memories. There was only this moment. We simply *were*, here, in each other; and now, in the only real time, the present. Time had stopped. Nothing ever needed to happen again. In our single act there was contained more meaning than there was in all the plots of all the stories I had ever read.

I took her right hand between both my hands. (This act took place *in* that present moment, not after it.) Gently, ever so gently, my fingers touched every corner of this promised land. Her flesh trembled with the fear that is not fear. I did not move farther than her wrist, as if this was the line between life and death. Our limits were clear and severe, and allowed us infinite joy within them. No modern American who rejected such limits, and gave in to animal lust, could ever have experienced such an erotic moment.

Never before had I realized the infinite difference between my hand and her hand, my fingers and hers, my wrist and hers. Never had a hand seemed so feminine. We were donning ceremonial robes, becoming Mars and Venus, Yang and Yin. But these robes did not conceal the wearers but revealed them. These robes made us more naked.

Mara told me afterwards that when I touched her hand she had felt a burning and freezing sensation at the same time, a kind of electricity all the way from her fingertips to her toes. "I felt as if my whole body was exploding," she said. "I felt as if I was the universe and I had just now been exploded into existence by the love of God. I felt a million little acts of creation, one in each cell of my body. I felt as if I hadn't *existed* until now."

What we both felt, I think, was something far stronger than the desire of sex. It was the desire of being. We were *inside* the Burning Bush. We were *holy*. And, at the same time, embarrassed to be there, ashamed, humble. So humble that we now realized that we had never known real humility before. Confused, yet fulfilled, we silently retreated from each other with slow, solemn, ceremonial kisses through the air. We both understood, without a word. What did we understand? That we both understood, without a word.

September 9: The next day after eternity, Mara and I deliberately didn't meet. Yesterday needed time to sink in. You say "encore!" to performances, not to graces.

I wandered out to the Drum and watched the sea thrusting her waves into the spaces between the rocks, then withdraw, then thrust and withdraw again. What does the rock feel, I wonder? Unending, perpetual orgasm? Is that what Mara and I will have in Paradise with body and soul together? And a foretaste of it in the protected paradise of marriage? If sea and rock can experience it, why not us?

*   *   *   *   *

I told some friends from the Muslim Center about Mara. To my dismay, every single person older than me, and even some young people, were suspicious. A few asked, "Why couldn't you find a Muslim instead of a Jew?" But all asked why I had "dated," American style, rather than seeing Mara only with a chaperone. One said, "Aren't you letting America drag down your faith instead of using your faith to pull America up out of its decadent Sexual Revolution?" I don't agree, but it's a good question, so I have to give a good answer. The answer is No, but I have to give a good reason. Here it is:

(Editor's Note: I present 'Isa's manifesto here without editorial comment, resisting temptations to psychoanalyze, and recommending the reader do the same. I only ask the reader to remember that 'Isa is very young and very much in love, and that "love covers a multitude of sins," even literary sins, perhaps even pontification.)

This is how I perceive the meaning of the Sexual Revolution: it has changed woman, but not man. Here is how:

In all societies, either men conquered women with power and lust (which they are experts in), or women tamed men with their superior virtue and responsibility. The first alternative was the law of the jungle: rape, pillage, and war. The second was the origin of civilization. The secret of success in creating civilization is the same as the secret of success in creating art: the marriage of passion and order, blood and brain, heart and head, red and blue, animal and angel. Women are more in touch with the angel in us. (How many men do you know who are interested in angels? How many women?)

Civilization is an art, or the sum of all human arts. And the key to civilization is morality. And the hardest part of morality is taming the strongest instinct, the sexual instinct. And the keeper of the keys to that taming has always been women. Before the Sexual Revolution, that is. Up until then, the relations were clear: men tried to get women into bed and women tried to stop them. It was crude, but it worked. Men were men and women were women, and though the arrangement was far from perfect, it was fairly stable. At least it did not produce the chaos and confusion we find in America today.

What the Revolution did was to "liberate" women to be "power brokers" on a par with men: that is, to be just as greedy, selfish, aggressive, bestial, and irresponsible as men. So the source of civilizing was itself de-civilized. Eve was persuaded to eat the forbidden fruit a second time, and Adam let her. It wasn't Eve's fault; it was the fault of her feminist teachers. They changed women's model and archetype from Saint to Slut. And men's archetype from Knight to Nerd or Nebbish.

I must do for Mara what America does not do: protect her. She does not have to protect me. But she has to tame me. She does that simply by being so perfect that it would be simply unthinkable to deflower such a Heavenly flower. Not anything outside of my love, but its very tenderness, will conquer my desire. I will pour all my passion into tenderness and protection.

The Fall of the Angel

September 11: I will remember the shock of this awful date forever. Two tall towers of idealism suddenly fell today.

I must write this while I am still in the calm of semi-shock. When the shaking and tears begin, I will not be able or willing to write.

The impossible has happened. I have broken my vow, and I have broken Mara.

I will not deface the pages of this book with the telling of the details. Why should I? But I will tell the significance.

It was a submission, a surrender, an "islam"—but not to Allah's will. Nor even to my own will, or to hers. It was to the Thing that was "bigger than both of us." Its power literally swept us away like a giant wave, and the thrill of losing all control felt like the ultimate mystical experience. I was not a free man freely choosing a free relationship with a free woman. I was in a tornado.

What was this Thing that was "bigger than both of us"? Not animal desire, for it was infinitely bigger than that. Not Allah, certainly, but not our own deliberately chosen wills either. Could it have been the Devil? But how could a demon possibly endure the ecstatic joy we felt? If this was the Devil's temptation, then the Devil must be a martyr. If this deed of ours was from the Devil, then the Devil had to endure the torment of our Heavenly bliss as the price of dragging us down to Hell in our sin. How could sin be so joyful? How could joy be so sinful? I cannot understand it.

Mara and I were dancing on the edge of the cliff; and there was an instant when I first realized this, when I suddenly knew I was going to make love to Mara here and now. It was when her eyes and mine met in unspoken dialog. Hers said, "Are you going to take me now? I put myself in your hands. I give you permission. I give you my whole self, body and soul." It was by far the most erotic sight my eyes have ever seen. Her naked body in mine in the throes of mutual orgasm was not as erotic as that look of her eyes, that permission. For her soul's "take me" was free and beautifully hers, but my body's taking her was un-free, and un-beautifully mine.

Here is something even more terrifying: at that moment when I realized I was going to commit an act of deliberate disobedience to Allah's will, I felt a totally unexpected erotic thrill instead of the sense of fear or terror or horror or guilt that I had hoped would always head me back to the Straight Path whenever I strayed. Instead of that, it was the opposite: the fact that I was risking my soul, my faith, my eternal Paradise for her—the fact that I was choosing Mara, *over Allah*—was *attracting* me! It was very definitely a sexual thrill. The risk, the total, eternal risk, the giving up of my salvation for her, made the erotic "high" a whole dimension higher. It was *total* self-giving, or a parody of it. It was idolatry. I *worshipped* Mara. She was my absolute.

There is an eroticism of the animal and a very different eroticism of the human. No animal can fall in love. And within the human, there is an eroticism of the human flesh (which is already more than just animal) and an eroticism of the spirit. No atheist could possibly experience as high a sexual thrill as I did because he does not have the Heavenly coins to give away to buy it.

But this is shocking. How could the realization that I was giving up my soul be *attractive*? How could it act as a prod rather than a deterrent? It pushed me toward the cliff edge, not back, and jumping off that cliff was an unforeseen thrill. How could Death be more exciting than Life?

I am a murderer. I murdered her innocence.

I am a liar. I betrayed my promise.

I am a thief. She was not mine to take. Only marriage makes her mine. I stole from Allah.

I can say no more now. I cannot add, "Allah will forgive me" or "Allah will never forgive me" or even "I hope Allah will forgive me." I cannot pray, "Allah, the Compassionate, the Merciful, please forgive me. I throw myself on Your mercy." I wish I could say that. I can't. I don't know why. Perhaps that is even more terrible than the deed itself; a paralysis of soul, of will.

We leaped together into the abyss. Mara's eyes had said to me, without a word, these words: "'Isa, if you choose at this moment to surrender to me, to surrender to It with me, then I too will choose this with all my heart. I know this means your refusing to surrender to God. It means that for me too. If you want to give up your faith, your innocence, your vow, your islam, and your Heaven just to have me, all of me, body and soul, then I will make exactly the same choice with you, just to be with you. 'With-you' is the whole meaning of my life. I am 'with-you' now; that is not just where I am but what I am. I am the one who has surrendered to you. If you surrender to It, so do I. If you surrender to Allah, so do I. In your hands is my identity and my destiny and my salvation."

And my response to this, to the woman who loves me so completely, to the woman I say I love so perfectly, was to lead her *away* from the Source of all good. Love wills the good of the beloved. I chose not her good but her ruin. I did not love her too much: I loved her too little. I failed to love her. We did not consummate our love; we betrayed our love. And I not only committed this sin against love, but did it with mad joy. And this was not just a joy in the flesh but also a joy in the madness. It was not just the world or the flesh making me this offer; it must have been the Devil. It felt like an offer I could not refuse. It was not; he is a great deceiver.

And here is still another terrifying thing. I did not think it possible that Mara, the most beautiful thing I have ever seen, could ever possibly become ugly. I pictured her crippled or deformed, and she was still beautiful, like a bird of paradise with a broken wing. I pictured her old and wrinkled, and she was still beautiful, like an old nun in a holy place, a saint with the love-fire still in her eyes even when the fire was old and calm, or like an old stone with the edges chipped off and rounded by years of shaping by the sea. I pictured her clothed in rags, and her beauty transformed the rags. Yet after we made love, I looked on her and was shocked to look on something no longer beautiful! I was not surprised to see *myself* as ugly, but I was utterly shocked to see *her* as ugly. I have destroyed the thing I love the most: her beauty. I plucked the rose, and found the thorns.

Before this happened, I never saw her as an object to be used. Now, I see her as an object that *has* been used, like a pack of discarded cigarettes. She was the soul of the world, and now she is only a body in *my* world. She was the whole, or the center of the whole, and now she is just a part.

Only once before have I felt a shock a little like that. It was when Mama was suddenly taken to the hospital and was in a coma for a few hours. When I first saw her I said, "That's not my Mama." She looked totally different. She was just some old lady, a stranger, perhaps dead and perhaps alive but dead to me. Yet not a molecule of her body had changed. Her nose had not twisted or fallen off. All the features were still there geometrically. But they were not there spiritually. I looked on an *it*, an object, an alien, an other. Then, hours later, when she woke and recognized me, I recognized her again.

My vision of Mara after we finished was like my vision of Mama before she woke up from her coma. I say "finished"—how impersonal! No, how blasphemous! .

Not only did I betray Mara, not only did I betray our love, and not only did I betray my vow to Allah, I also betrayed my honor. She innocently trusted me to be her protecting knight, and the knight unleashed on her the dragon, whose fire consumed her innocence. Her innocence was suddenly an aborted baby lying dead at our feet.

How right the old charts were that warned: "Here there be dragons." I laughed at the charts and said, "But we are different; we are fearless." That was exactly the danger. Those who need friends and chaperones the most are the ones who want them the least.

The moment it was over, the universe vanished and was replaced by a wholly different one, which was an exact replica of the old universe, atom for atom, but it had another soul. The old universe had been haunted by an angel; the new universe was possessed. And I know the possessor. His name was 'Isa.

> To what can I compare you, O daughter of Jerusalem?
> To what can I liken you, O virgin daughter of Zion?
> For great as the sea is your ruin; who can restore you?
> Lamentations 2:13

*   *   *   *   *

What happened next was the first new thing I saw in my new universe. I wish I could believe it was only a dream, but *Mara saw it too*. There, a mile out at sea, the sea serpent raised its head and looked straight at us, with derisive laughter in its eye. It had won. It had turned us into itself. It had gotten us to crawl on our bellies instead of flying like angels. When I looked at Mara she seemed to be a serpent too.

Was what we saw physically there or only a vision in our minds? Aren't dreams and visions private and individual?

I heard in my head the music from Handel's "Messiah," "Let Us Break Their Bonds Asunder," sung by countless voices, shrill as bats, incessant, demanding, chattering, jangling, tyrannical. What had promised to be blissfully blending union had turned into searing, tearing division: of 'Isa versus Mara, and of 'Isa versus himself, and of Mara versus herself, and of 'Isa versus Allah, and of Mara versus Allah, and—worst of all—of 'Isa-and-Mara versus Allah. Only Allah remained undivided and indivisible.   I saw fear on her face. She saw fear on mine. I embraced her, but with pity, not with love. For love casts out fear.

How false this new thing felt! She wept, wordlessly. She waited for me to speak. I waited too. But I could not speak. I could not lie and I could not tell the truth. I could not lie and say "Everything will be all right." I could not tell the truth and say "I have betrayed you." What else could I say? What did I feel? One word says it, and that word was not "guilt" or "shame" or "fear" or "regret" or "defeat" or "despair" or "anger," though these also arrived and departed. But what did not depart was *confusion.* I did not know what to do now. My future became a blank. I held her, gently, for a long time. She stayed in my arms, limp but shuddering, fluttering like a small dying bird.

We simultaneously let go, and dressed, in silence. For the first time I understood why my namesake Adam had to have clothes now. We had conceived our first child, and its name was shame. I jerked out the words, "Mara, we must talk. Tomorrow?" She jerked her head in surprise at the sound of my voice. A pause, then: "I don't know. I need time to think" And she turned and walked away, very slowly.

She walked down the north side of the Hill to her yellow car parked on Willow Road. I walked down the south side of the Hill to my blue car parked on Bass Point Road. Today yellow and blue did not make green, the color of life. Today the two sides of the Hill did not make one hill.

My joy had departed. There was no place for me to go and nothing for me to do now, so why should my body move? I felt like Adam looking at the corpse of Eve, broken, beyond repair, *and I had done this.* I wandered aimlessly around Nahant all day like a zombie, feeling no hunger, wanting to feel only oblivion.

I sat down and wrote these words. It made no difference. Only when the sun set, and only when I was too weary for another step, could I weep. I troubled the innocent grasses of the Hill with my tears. I wept both loud and soft, both short and long, both angry and hurt, both like a man and like a girl. And like a child. I never knew there were so many ways to weep. If you had heard that weeping, you would have given your life to stop the sound from reaching your ears.

No words, but only music, can express such emotional immensities. Think of all the most heartbreakingly sad pieces of music that have ever moved your soul; then imagine that a single composer was the author of all of them; then imagine that one day this composer put into a single song all the variations of sadness in all of his other works, in all those pieces that have ever moved your soul and broken your heart, all in one song. That was the song my soul sang. If Allah had granted me one prayer, I would have prayed for a perfect lyre so that I could play that one song on that one instrument one time and then break the instrument and play no other song ever again.

Something strange happened while walking down the familiar little dirt path that led from the Hill to the House. The path slopes at about a 30 degree angle, but today it seemed the angle had changed, so that it was perfectly horizontal, and I was not standing straight but leaning, at an angle to it. The new sensation was so sudden and physical that it made me lose my balance. I understood immediately what had happened: the Hill was perfectly aligned to both God and Nature, but I no longer was. The wrongness I now perceived in the angle of the Hill came from the perceiver, not the perceived.

I went home to bed, without a word to anyone, and fell instantly asleep, totally exhausted. I was surprised to find that it took far more energy out of me to succumb to the Serpent than to fight it.

September 20: I woke up at first light this morning, neither tired nor hungry. No one was up yet. I went to the Hill and found my lyre. It was the only approximation to the perfect lyre I had dreamed of yesterday, on which I could play my song of all the sadness in the world. It was the Drum. When it came to sadness, Water Music could say what no other music could.

If there is still any place in this empty world that I have any desire to visit, it is Chatsworth Estate in England, to hear the music played there on what must be the most perfect musical instrument in the world. It is 24 sets of stone steps, down which water cascades, at what seems to be about a 20degree angle, to judge from the picture I've seen. Each step is about 10 feet deep and 20 feet wide, but the size, angle, and stone of each step is slightly different, to vary the sound of the waters. It is a larger, more complete Drum.

The Drum echoed my soul this morning, as I knew it would. It was moaning softly: "Oh! Oh! Oh!" accompanied by a soft, sad little wind that sounded like a little girl trying in vain to whistle. I listened for about a half hour, until the sun rose, wan and vague behind unspectacular haze. I threw a large rock into the sea, and heard, instead of a splash, a *thud*, like a sandbag being dropped to the ground. This was a thuddy day.

I think it was the Drum that encouraged me to speak. I went into the

House. Mother was up before everyone else, as usual. I told her everything. This was wise. No one can live without a mother.

Her first reaction was to praise me for telling her everything, and then to berate herself. "You failed her, 'Isa, but I also failed you. I was not Mother enough to you. I was not pushy enough. I did not stay close enough. I did not warn you enough."

"You did warn me, but I did not listen. I acted like a stupid teenager."

"I should have warned you more."

"I would have called you 'Jewish mother,' and insulted both you and all mothers and all Jews."

"Yeah, so what? That's no excuse for not doing the job I'm put here to do. Which is to be a Jewish mother! I'm named after her, after all." She pointed to an icon of Mary on the wall. "She never let *her* 'Isa down."

For the first time in my life I wished for a moment that I was a Catholic and believed in the infallible authority of the Church when she pronounces forgiveness in the sacrament of Confession. I longed to hear and believe these words from a priest: "By the authority given to me by God Himself, I forgive you of your sins." I longed for "fundamentalist" authority in the service of "liberal" forgiveness.

Mother asked me, "*Why* do you think you fell, 'Isa?"

"I was a fool. I did not know myself. I was weak, and I thought I was strong. I was proud. I should have listened to my own people. I forgot the wisdom of Islam. I was an American and a Romanticist instead of a Muslim."

"Not knowing yourself, weakness of the flesh, pride, not listening, and *ghaflah,* forgetting—that's five pretty good answers so far, I think. Can we see any more wisdom coming to you out of this?"

"What do you mean?"

"The war was between you and your flesh, and between you and your mind, and between you and Mara, and between you and your religion, but it was also between you and the Enemy," Mother added, quietly. "Blame yourself, yes, but blame him too. *This wasn't just you, 'Isa.*"

"I failed to slay the dragon."

"Yes. Do you think you *can?* Do you think anyone can?"

"Not in our own power, not without Allah's power. But does He give that power to us? What do you think, Mother?"

"We are both named after dragonslayers, 'Isa."

"Oh. But what Mary and Jesus did, whatever it was, was long ago and far away, and we are not them, even though we are named after them. How can we do what they did?"

Mother pointed to an icon of Mary stomping on Satan. "All those pictures of her, or Michael the Archangel, or Jesus, overcoming Satan—did you think they were just about the past? The battle is still going on. The battlefield is right here. You know that. You know what *jihad* means."

"I do. And *that's* the horror of it: knowing who won the battle yesterday. The dragon speared Saint George instead of Saint George spearing the dragon."

"I think you've forgotten the worst part of it."

"What's that?"

"*You* failed, yes. So, we all fail, and we lick our wounds and we go back into the battle against the dragon. But you let the dragon spear Mara."

I became all quiet inside. Mother went on, like Purgatory: "You are 'Isa Ben Adam, and you were supposed to be her protector from the dragon, like Joseph protecting Mary. But you left her to the dragon, like Adam did to Eve. Where was Adam when Eve was being speared by that dragon, anyway? Where were the men when Jesus was being speared by the dragon on the Cross? Only one stayed. The rest were women. You see, that's why I have this rule in my House: it must never be empty. Someone may need shelter from that dragon who prowls around the world seeking souls to devour."

"Do you think it was *that* dragon? The sea serpent I saw?"

"It doesn't matter what you saw. It only matters what you did. Whether the dragon you saw was real or imagined, you let the real dragon conquer Mara as well as yourself. *That's* the bottom line, that's the biggest problem now, not just you."

I was immensely grateful for Mother's unsparing honesty. Her arrows shot straight into my heart with the truth, and I think there is no hope of any victory unless that arrow flies first.

Mother continued, "You know the bitter half: to despair of yourself. I hope you also know the sweet half: never to despair of Him, the one you truly call Allah the Compassionate, the Merciful."

Hope threatened to arise in me like a dead body bursting out of its grave. It stood face to face with my despair. They were both armed men, six feet tall, with equally unyielding stares on their faces. The two men turned into two waves and crashed against each other in the sea of my heart. I could no longer distinguish the two waves in the roil and churn and confusion. But at least I was alive. At least something was happening in me. Time had not ended.

"There's something to think about now that's not just your past," Mother continued. "A very practical thing."

"What? What have I forgotten?"

"Mara."

"Mara? I've thought about nothing else! What do you mean, I've forgotten Mara?"

"Mara *now.*" The second word was the bell of an alarm clock, wakening me from my dark dream of yesterday into the harsh light of today.

"You're right. I *have* forgotten that. How confused she must feel! And how guilty! What poor miserable thing have I turned her into?"

"You may have turned her into a *mother*. And that is *not* a poor, miserable thing!" Again Mother was unendurably practical.

"Oh! How could I have forgotten that?"

"I think *that* is a bigger part of your problem than you think."

"That Mara might be pregnant, you mean?"

"That too, of course. But also what you said: *how could you have forgotten that?*"

"You mean I should have had protection? Birth control?"

"No, no, you silly boy. I mean just what I say: How could you have forgotten? I'm talking about what's on your mind, not what's on your penis."

Mother's words are like her pies: she makes no mince. Of course, I never thought to use a condom or any other kind of birth control. That would have changed everything. But *not* for the better. It would not have made our act less adulterous or sinful, it would only have made it less honest. It would have turned it into something planned and calculated and controlled.

I could not have contracepted my love. How could I have done what I longed to do the most—to give her my *whole* self—and at the same time hold back one crucial part of me, my fatherhood? How could I say Yes to the whole of her and say No to her motherhood? Is motherhood an alien creature that fastens onto a woman like Dracula to suck her blood? I always feared I might commit adultery, but never contraception. That would change natural adultery into unnatural adultery. It would make sex into a double masturbation instead of a double giving. It would adulterate adultery itself. Good grief, man, if you're going to do wrong, at least do it right!

I look at a condom as I look at a test tube. (They even have the same shape!) Birth control and test tube babies are the two halves of the same division. Sex without babies or babies without sex—what's the difference? They're both *boring*, in the long run. They're making America not oversexed but undersexed. There's no thrill left if you don't dance on the Heavenly cliff-edge of the creation of life.

Well, look at that: I think I am getting my sanity back; I'm philosophizing again.

September 24: Alas, my sanity is farther from me than ever. Mother's fears came true. Mara is pregnant.

Worse, she is withdrawing from me. I cannot put down onto paper all the words that passed between us this morning. I have never been at a loss for words before, not even when Papa died, or when Mama died, or when I almost died.

I tried to comfort her, and was careful not to be "preachy," but I must have said *something* stupid to upset her, yet I have no idea what it was. My memory seems to be passing out of my control.

I was shocked by what I saw: I saw her body stop moving. Her body is always moving, even when it is not moving; but today her whole body seemed frozen, or dead.

We spoke only a few words. I held her in my arms, but neither of us was comforted. She was a dead rag doll. She arrived confused and left confused. She refused to talk to Mother or anyone else at the House.

I walked to the Drum for consolation and found desolation. It was making throaty, gurgling, death-rattle noises. If a giant with a stone esophagus were drowning, I think that is what he would sound like.

September 25: Mara did not come or call today, or answer my calls. I have to do something, but I don't know what. I want to speak healing words, magic words, to her, but I don't know what words they are. I must wait until they come.

*   *   *   *   *

September 27: Sometimes, beyond all our hopes, our dreams come true. sometimes, beyond all our fears, our nightmares do.

The worst thing that could possibly happen, the thing that could not possibly happen, has happened. Mara says she wants an abortion.

She saw an ad for "pregnancy services" and answered it, to "clarify her options." It was run by Planned Parenthood. She would have been treated more honestly if it had been run by the Mafia. She was told she had a "choice" but she was really given only one "choice," one "option." I curse the lie called "freedom of the press," and I curse the lie called "freedom of choice."

I will not put on paper all her words and her looks today. For my whole heart's hope is that they will pass away like a cloud of dirt on the winds of the good Spirit of Allah, and I will not aid or abet the persistence of that cloud in the sky of memory by recording her words. I will not take verbal photographs of that black smear, that Karamazov. I will not be a pornographer.

I will, however, record my words to her, for unlike hers to me, they were not to be regretted or repented of. I knew it was time to speak with authority, and not *my* authority.

I said: "Mara, imagine this. Imagine an angel of God came to you and asked you to be a vessel, an instrument, a mother—perhaps the mother of a prophet. The angel did not offer you the chance to become famous, or comfortable. The angel offered you the chance to become Miryam, to become your name."

She interrupted: "You forget, 'Isa, that 'Mara' means 'bitter.' I *have* become my name. And it is you who have made me bitter."

"I know the words, Mara. 'Call me Mara—bitter—for the Lord has dealt bitterly with me.' Listen to the words, Mara: it is the *Lord* who is dealing with you—the Creator of Adam, not 'Isa Ben Adam."

"Then tell me what this Lord wants of me, 'Isa, if you are his mouth-piece!"

"The Lord wants only one thing from you, Mara: your surrender. *She* surrendered—she after whom you were named, in the plan and providence of God—*she* said Yes—'Yes, I accept this child from You, the Lord, the One, the creator of every child, the Lord God of the universe and the God of Israel and the God of Isaac and the God of Ishmael. You have spoken, and I have heard. You have said to me, 'Hear, O Israel, the Lord, the Lord your God is one; and you shall love the Lord your God with all your heart and with all your soul and with all your strength, and also your strength of body, which is your child.'

"And your namesake Maryam heard that voice, and she surrendered to it. Not to Joseph, who was not her Lord but only her husband, but she surrendered to God, who was not her husband but her Lord. She after whom you were named said, 'I surrender, I accept, I accept this child from You, God, my Creator and the Creator of every child.' She said Yes even though she too was unmarried. She would not bring into death the child God had brought into life.

"I know you will not do that either.

"This is not between you and me, Mara, this is between you and God."

It was true, and it was honest, but it was too long and it was too preachy. Mara listened, silently and sullenly, to my words, but her face looked like the face of the Mexican boys in my dream. When I finished speaking, she turned her eyes to mine. I knew who was looking at me then. It had a tail. It was hungry.

Then out of her mouth came a black cloud of burnt pages from a book, words that were weapons, stone knives to tear out hearts. At the center of the black cloud of words was a demon. The demon repeated the words of black magic, the words of the Black Mass: "This is *my* body!" The words came out of Mara's mouth and Mara's mind. Indeed, they were the fundamental "pro-choice" formula. Mara's mouth and mind were only Its instruments. I wanted to address It, and ask It what It had done with Mara, but I didn't.

The words tore my heart out from my chest cavity. The Lord of the Smoking Mirror was waiting for it, and the dogs were waiting for the rest of me at the bottom of the pyramid.

I was desperate. "No, Mara, no! That is *not* your body. That is *another person's* body. That is our child. If you abort him, you abort me. That's me in you, Mara. Please don't kill me."

"Just who the hell do you think you are, Jesus?" The words came out like arrows.

"No, Mara, I am not Jesus. I am 'Isa. Once I was inside your heart, and then I was I was inside your body, and now I am inside your womb, and I want to stay there, in your heart and in your womb. I know I was there once, inside your heart. Tell me how I can stay there."

"You can come with me to the clinic and pay for my abortion," she said, in a flat voice.

"Pay a man to murder our child? Pay blood money? A minute ago you called me Jesus; now you want me to be Judas."

She looked steadily at me for a full five seconds. Before that moment I had no idea what the word "hate" meant. I saw the fire arrows aimed at my heart. I saw the sneering face of my enemy pulling the bowstring. Then Mara spit at my feet and walked away.

On this holy hill a few days ago Mara and I had spoken holy words to each other. We said, "This is my body" to each other. We said these words not with our mouths but with our bodies as we gave them to each other, holding nothing back, including our fertility. And when we said, "This is my body" to each other, we meant: "This, my body, is your body now."

We gave to each other. And we took from each other. But we also took from Allah, and that was theft. Although we played His holy music of love, we played it by our time, our rhythm. We seized the Conductor's baton. We did not wait for the wave, the wave of the baton.

And therefore we spoiled the music. Now she hates me, and will not marry me, so we will *not* say "this is my body" to each other with the rest of our lives, with our children, with our old age. We let the Deceiver in and he has made us enemies, so that Mara now says to me "This is MY body" and she means her child's body too—*our* child's body. She wants to steal our child's body from our child. Those holy words of life have become the unholy words of death.

Adam spoke those holy words to Eve in submission and obedience to Allah, and that is why all humans after him have life, why there are many sons of Adam, many Ben Adams, including 'Isa Ben Adam and 'Isa of Nazareth (peace be upon him!).

The Catholics believe absurd things about 'Isa of Nazareth. They believe he is Allah's son. But Allah cannot have a son. They believe his body is Allah's body. But Allah cannot have a body. They believe he died on the cross. But God cannot die. And Catholics believe that in the Mass he keeps saying, "This is my body" and changes millions of little wafers of bread into his body in a "house of bread" called a church. But Allah is one and cannot be multiplied.

But although He cannot be rightly worshipped in a Mass, He can be blasphemed in a "Black Mass," and I have helped the Enemy to do this blasphemy.

I know who the Enemy is. His name is Iblis. He is the Deceiver and the Twister, who twists all good into evil and deceives us with it. He deceived Mara and me into twisting Allah's very good "this is my body," His invention of marriage, into a parody of itself; and now he twists Mara's words and says through her mouth, "this is my body" of our child in her womb. He wants that body, and hers too. He says of all bodies, "this is my body."

I must unsay the unholy words of the Enemy. But how?

October 1: Mara had not answered my phone calls. I almost gave up all hope. But I went to the Hill—*our* Hill, it used to be—at eight in the morning, hoping against hope that she would come. And, beyond all hope, she did.

She looked and sounded different today, like a wet, shivering kitten. She ran up to me, weeping and trembling, and said, without any preliminaries, "'Isa, please be with me, even now. Please love me. Please understand me." Her eyes were red from a whole night of weeping.

"Oh, I *am* with you, Mara. And I do love you. I do. I do."

"But you don't understand me. Why don't you understand me? Why can't you understand why I have to do this?"

"Mara, you are right, I do *not* understand why you think you have to do this. I do not understand you *because* I love you! I love you because you are beautiful, in body and in soul, and I do not understand why you who are so beautiful want to do this thing that is so ugly. I want to be with you in everything, but I cannot want to be with this deed. How can I be with you in murdering our own child? That is like murdering *us*. I feel as if you just asked me to join you in a double suicide pact."

"I'm not asking for your permission." The kitten had suddenly become a tiger, and her words were cold and clenched.

"What do you want from me, then?"

"I want you to stay with me when I go to the clinic. It is a terrible thing, and it will be more terrible if I have to be alone."

"I want to be with you always, Mara, but how can I be with you *there?* How could you possibly think I could be with you *there?*"

"*There* is where I will be. If you will not be with me there, you will not be with me."

For the last few minutes I thought I would collapse and die, but now a righteous rage arose within me and gave me sudden strength. "I thought you knew me, Mara. But if you think I could help you do this, you do not know me at all. And I thought I knew you too. I was wrong. I do not know you. Who are you? *What have you done with Mara?*" I now dared to address the demon.

I expected an angry reply. But instead, she stepped up to me and touched her hand gently to my cheek. Her touch was soft, oh so very soft, softer than a cloud. I resisted the temptation to answer softness with softness. I would not yield to Iblis. I steeled myself. I stood stiffly, shaking my head.

Mara withdrew her hand. Her last words were even softer than her hand: "I forgive you, 'Isa." And then she ran away down the Hill. I did not follow or call after her. My mouth and legs were paralyzed.

I felt as if I had just beaten both my mother and my daughter and then buried them alive, and they had reached up out of the grave one last time to touch me with the tenderness that I had refused to them. I was beyond tears. Sometimes the soul has to go into a coma to survive, just like the body.

I spent most of the day on the Hill alone, praying. Not with passion. I was a stone, a machine. I felt nothing at all, not even despair. I was beyond despair.

Mara came back for a second conversation in the afternoon. She found me at the same spot she had left me. "I still feel the same, 'Isa. I still want to do it," were her first words. "Do you still feel the same?"

"What do you mean?"

"Do you still reject me?"

"No, I do *not* reject you, Mara! I love you. That's why this hurts me: because I see how it hurts you."

"No, 'Isa, it hurts *you*."

"It hurts our child."

"There will be no child."

"There *is* a child."

"No. I will not be a mother."

"You already *are* a mother."

"No! I am free to say no. I have to be free."

"You cannot be free from what you are, Mara."

"I *can* have an abortion. And the abortion will free me from what I am not, from what I do not want to be."

"No, Mara, no, it is a lie. It will not free you. It will enslave you. You will regret it later. Most women do."

"You've been reading that pro-life literature. I don't believe their propaganda."

"It's not propaganda. It's true, it's data, it's statistics, it's surveys. You don't *want* to believe it. Because you're scared. In fact, you're terrified."

For the first time, a new light came into her eyes and she looked directly into mine. "Yes, I am, 'Isa. You see that. Good. And do you know what I'm most terrified of? That you won't understand me."

"I know that, Mara, and I'm very happy you still care about me that much. But I think I know something else that you are even more terrified of, deep down."

"What?"

"God."

"NO!" she almost shouted. Then, softly but firmly, "God will forgive me."

"Mara—dear Mara—dear, dear Mara, God will *not* forgive you."

Fire came into her eyes. They narrowed. "*Your* God, maybe."

"No, yours too. There's only one. God will not be *able* to forgive you."

"God can do anything."

"No, He can't. He can't give you anything if you don't take it."

"You've got an answer for everything, don't you?"

"No, no, Mara, this isn't about me, or even about us, it's about you. You and God."

"God is not like you, 'Isa. God is pro-choice."

"Yes, God *is* pro-choice: He created us with free choice. He won't force you, against your will, to choose the right thing. It's got to be your choice. That's what your prophet Moses said: '*Choose* life!' So do it! Listen to your prophet! Be both pro-life and pro-choice."

"My prophet tells me God is full of mercy."

"Mine too! Allah is full of mercy. But mercy is a gift. And a gift has to be freely received. And freely receiving mercy means repenting. So if you don't repent, you can't receive mercy."

"I *will* repent."

"Of what?"

"The deed I am going to do."

"If you are planning to do it, you are not repenting. You can't choose sin and repentance at the same time."

"I'll repent later."

"Mara, what do you think it means to 'repent'?"

"Feeling sorry for your sins."

"No, no, that's what wimpy teachers say, the ones with their brains pickled by pop psychology. They make everything a matter of feeling. They have no spine. No, no, Mara, it's a choice of the *will*. And you can't will to kill and will to repent at the same time. You're willing to kill, and that means you're NOT willing to repent. If you repent from sin, you turn *away* from it, not *to* it. You don't *do* it! Repenting isn't about feelings, it's about choices."

"I never heard anyone talk to me like that. You are cruel."

"No, your *teachers* are cruel. They give you false peace."

"You're not my teacher, 'Isa. I don't trust you anymore. I don't care what you say."

She went away again. Did I make any inroads? Or did I harm her more? I tried to free her, but I was in a state of panic, I was desperate, I didn't know what to say, and when I don't know what to say I just blurt out the truth. Can that be bad? Can truth harm her? Did I lie to her by telling her the truth?

That night, I got a phone call from Zoe, Mara's best friend at BC. Mara had confided in Zoe because Zoe had been in the same situation last year and had had an abortion. Zoe is still pro-choice but she regrets her abortion. Mara will listen to Zoe, I hope, even though she won't listen to me. Here is what Zoe told me:

"I asked Mara, 'How do you think you will feel afterwards?'"

"She said, 'Very sad, and very tired, but free.'"

"'No,' I told her. 'You are forgetting something.'"

"'Guilt, you mean? Don't worry, I'll handle that.'"

"'Maybe you won't. Maybe your guilt will be harder to abort than your baby. But I wasn't thinking of guilt. I was thinking of the haunting.'

"That seemed to shock her. 'What haunting?' she asked me.

"I told her: 'The dreams of your baby. You can't make the dreams stop coming.'

"'It's like a *haunting*?'

"'No, it's not *like* a haunting, it *is* a haunting. It's not just my conscience that's haunting me, it's my baby.' That made Mara silent. 'When I went into that place for my abortion, I had one terrible thought on my mind: two people will go in and only one will come out, but at least the one who comes out will be free. Well, I was wrong. Two came out, but one was a ghost.'

"I think that got to her, Jack. That's all I can do for her, tell the whole truth."

"I guess that's all any of us can do for her," I replied.

"No, Jack, I think there's one thing *you* can do for her that nobody else can."

"What?"

"Love her no matter what. Love here *and* be *in*-love with her."

After that, I drove to Mara's house. Of course she wasn't there. And of course her mother wouldn't let me in.

That evening the fatal telephone call came. It was from the clinic. I took the call privately. (We have only one phone in the House, with a long cord.) I could not share this with anyone yet, not even with Mother. This was an absolute dishonor. My hands were full of dirt and blood, and I did not want them to be held by larger, older, cleaner hands.

The voice told me that Mara had insisted that the clinic inform me that she had done it. It was a woman's voice, or the voice of someone who had been a woman once. The voice was cold as death. I wonder what kind of voice informed my family in Palestine that my uncle had been murdered. I don't think *that* voice was cold. I think it was hot. I think it was a human voice, even when it was not a humane voice. I would have preferred to hear that kind of voice. I should have lived in Palestine instead of America. There is something more honest about the carnage there than about the carnage here.

I ran upstairs and fell upon my bed. Mara's deed had rammed into my soul like a bullet from an elephant gun, and my soul imploded like a burning building. My eyes closed, mirroring my soul. I don't know whether I was awake or asleep. I saw in my mind's eye an image from the dream I had a few weeks ago: I saw two tall buildings, straight and square, being hit by burning things— rockets, or missiles with wings—then falling, falling straight down, vertically, into themselves. Clouds of dust and debris rose up like the smoke from the burning mirror of the Aztec dream. The image was my soul drawing its own self-portrait, no doubt. The buildings were Mara and I.

I let out one single sigh—I think it was the longest sigh in human history—to release all the breath and life and hope that was left within me. I was surprised to see that my body could still live after my soul had died. I knew then what a zombie was.

I went to bed, without supper, at 6 P.M. I never wanted to get up again.

October 2: The next morning, a call came, from Mara herself. "'Isa, it's over. It's over. I did it. I want you to know. I need you to know. And I had to tell you myself."

She did not say "I'm all right." I did not ask whether she was all right. I did not want her to be all right.

There was a long silence. What could I say? Only one thing, if I followed my heart. "No." The single syllable expressed all that was in me.

"I'm not asking you, 'Isa, I'm telling you. It's done. 'What's done cannot be undone.'"

"No." I could say nothing but that one syllable. Nothing else meant anything. "No. No. No. No."

"You never say Yes to me anymore, 'Isa. You only say No. Once, I thought you were the one who would say Yes to me, but you turned into the one who says No. I'm glad I found that out before I married you."

"But Mara, my No is a Yes. If I said Yes to you now, that would be a No."

"Stop playing logical tricks, 'Isa. Stop playing with words, like a little boy."

"I'm not playing with words, Mara. It's true. I know the deed is done, but if I believed it was *you* who did *that*, if I believed you were the kind of person who could do that, then I would have lost faith in you. I would be saying Yes to your No."

"That's what I want you to do, you fool! That's where I am now, and you're not with me anymore."

"How can I possibly be with you *there?*"

"Because *there* means freedom. You don't really believe a woman should be free, do you?"

"I don't believe my wife should be free to kill my son, no."

I shouldn't have said that. There was a silence that was sharper than any words. Then, from a clenched jaw: "You abandoned me!" She started weeping. "It's the way you looked at me. I can tell everything from your look. First you turned me into a slut and then you *looked* at me as a slut. I see your mind in your eyes, 'Isa. You can't lie to me."

"Mara, Mara, I didn't want to abandon you then, and I don't want to abandon you now. Please tell me what can I do for you, even now. I'm all confused."

It was the first time my admission of confusion didn't move her. "I'll tell you what, 'Isa: now that you've killed my soul, why not just finish the job and kill my body too? Why don't you just push me over the _____ rock into the _____ sea?"

Mara never used language like that before. She had disappeared into her name, Bitterness. "Mara! This isn't you."

"Mara's dead. I'm answering the phone for her. Go kill yourself, 'Isa."

"Mara doesn't talk like that. Let me talk to Mara." I didn't mean this as a joke, or an insult, or an exaggeration, or a psychological trick. I meant it literally: I was talking to Another.

"Mara talks like that now."

"That is *not* Mara," I declared. I addressed my enemy in thought. "Mara is dead and you killed her," I thought, not daring to speak the words.

Then I heard exactly those seven words from her lips: "Mara is dead and you killed her." After a stunned silence, there came forth four final words: "I hate you, Jesus!" She uttered the words coldly and deliberately and put the phone down quietly. It was far more devastating and final than an angry shout and a slam of the phone.

Why did she call me Jesus? The name shocked me even more than the hate. I remembered when Mother had first called me "Jesus" on the night when she saved my life. "Jesus" was Mother's first word to me and Mara's last.

I stood as if in a trance. I looked down at my hands. They had taken Mara's hymn to the sea out of my pocket. I had taken it out of its precious little box and held onto it as a kind of talisman of the old Mara. I saw that I had been twisting it, grasping it like a drowning child grasping a rope—or was it like a murderer twisting the neck of his victim?

I replaced the phone with a blank face. Mother rushed by me on her way out. "Jack, take care of the House and Yak for me, OK? I'll be back for supper." I nodded, automatically. She had been unusually busy, and I had not told her of Mara's abortion (it's not something you quickly drop into casual conversation!), and she was in too much of a rush today to notice my face.

It was ten A.M. I went out into the back yard under the deck and cried a little sea of tears into the larger sea for two hours. I washed the wound in my soul with sea water. (Tears *are* sea water: water and salt.) But it did not heal the wound. The wound was mortal. I had died inside. Yet, amazingly, the rest of the world was still there. I went back into the world, or that part of it that we called the House, just in time to hear the front door open noisily and see Evan greeting me with the happiest face I have ever seen on him, too happy to even notice my despair.

"Jack! You'll never guess what I've got. Two tickets to Armageddon." He waved the two tickets in his hand. I shook my head in confusion. "The showdown," he explained. "The one-game playoff this afternoon. This is going to be the greatest game in history. John got the tickets yesterday at Fenway Park. They sold them after the last game. John had tickets to the game, the last game of the season, and we won and the Yankees lost, so there's a one-game playoff today, winner take all, showdown, gunfight at OK corral."

"Why isn't John going?"

"He got violently sick today, so he gave me his tickets. We can still make game time if we leave now. You've got to come, Jack. I have no one else to go with."

"I can't, Evan. I'm totally depressed. More than depressed. Mara and I just broke up. Worse than just broke up. It was terrible, terrible."

"All the more reason, Jack! You absolutely need this for diversion. The more you're hurting, the more you need an escape." I certainly did need an escape. Desperately. But my heart was no longer in my body. It was in Mara's. As if reading my mind, he added,

"Mara needs time to cool off too. She is still too hot to touch."

I almost smiled at Evan's clumsy attempt to be colloquial, and I couldn't help feeling a little better in the presence of his irresistible boyish enthusiasm, but I shook my head. I didn't feel like arguing.

But *he* did. "What else will you do? Stay home and mope all day? There's nobody home."

"I've got plenty to do, Evan. I've got to patch it up with Mara somehow."

"Of course you do. But not *now*. Reasoning with a woman when she's still mad—that is truly mad."

I smiled again at Evan's clumsy attempt at psychology.

"I'd like to go, Evan, but Mara just might show up here again, and I want to be here if she does. Everybody else seems to be gone today. Where did they go, anyway?"

This was extremely unusual. Mother made sure someone was at home every hour of every day, to receive whatever unexpected guests might be sent to us from the Higher Authorities we all served. A plaque on the wall read: "Forget not hospitality, for some have entertained angels unawares."

"Well, Mother went to some conference or other, I think. It must have been really important: she *never* goes to those things. Hates them. And Mister Mumm left an hour ago with the kind of smile on his face that I have never seen on him before. He said he had 'permission to take the day off and have some fun.' I wonder what that means."

"Where's Libby?"

"Surfing. What else is new? And Diddly and Squat both went out looking for gigs, or new jobs, or something like that. But they went *separately*. Can you believe that? They each took separate taxis. And Laz is off on another trip to South America—that place called Jonestown, I think."

"So nobody's home but us? Somebody's got to be here."

"Oh, Eva is home, of course."

"Where is she?"

"She's sleeping. She tried some stupid experiment this morning—something to do with 'sensory deprivation' that was supposed to make her relaxed—how can she get more relaxed than she is, I wonder?—but it did the opposite, it exhausted her."

"I can't come with you, Evan. Mara might come here, and it would be terrible if I wasn't here."

"Leave a note."

"We've never done that before: left the House empty. Mother wouldn't like it." I remembered her insistence on staying in the House even on the night of the hurricane, because someone might need her. I remembered how she had explained it. She said: "My namesake was always there: Mary was always home for Jesus. And everybody who comes here because they need something *is* Jesus."

"Oh, bother Mother!" Evan said, with an attempt at a British colloquialism.

"Mother is *not* a bother," I answered, defending her honor like a knight. "Mother is Mother."

Of course Evan didn't mean it. Mother was certainly not a "bother." And Mother herself was in all her rules, so her rules were not a bother either. They were the shape of her hospitality. They were the same shape as Mother was. Large.

"Look," Evan said, reasonably, "If somebody's got to be here, then wake up Eva. There's nobody better than Eva to talk to Mara if she comes here agitated. Except Mother, of course. Besides, she left Yak home. He's a watchbird. If anybody comes, he'll wake up Eva."

Half of me couldn't help agreeing with Evan. The dreadful deed was done. The worst had already happened. And I didn't *want* to meet Mara again today. Each of our last three meetings had been more disastrous than the one before. I couldn't endure the next one if we kept moving down that road, and I didn't know how to reverse our direction. My mind had failed me, and my only hope was that perhaps tomorrow it would not, that *time* was the magic that would heal this terrible wound. I needed to buy time.

Evan seemed to be reading my mind: "Come on, you need a time out. You need an escape. You need a diversion. This is therapy."

"How can a game divert me from something so serious?"

"It's not just a game. It's serious."

"Come on, Evan, baseball is great, but it's just a game."

"Maybe baseball is, but the Red Sox aren't."

"What are they? Your religion?"

"No, they're a key to my Universal Fate Wave Theory."

"You're serious about that, aren't you?"

"You know I am, Jack. All summer you've been with me following the trail of this beast. Please don't abandon me now. (Why did he have to use *that* word?) This is the crucial day—not only for the baseball season, but also for the Universal Wave Theory. It's like a solar eclipse. Like the one that proved Einstein's Theory of Relativity when they measured the swerve of the light from the distant stars when it passed by the sun's gravity field. This is a once-in-a-lifetime opportunity. Incidentally, it's also going to be the most memorable game of baseball ever played."

"How do you know that?"

"I don't know how I know it, but I know it, and I know I know it, and that's all I know."

I was captured by his philosophy. "OK, my friend," I sighed. "I'll come with you." I just didn't know what else to do. I couldn't face the emptiness at home.

"Good. Besides, there's no car here but yours—the others took all the other cars. And the game starts in an hour."

"Why didn't you tell me that in the first place?"

"Because I didn't want you to come only out of charity. I want your company, not just your car."

So for the first time ever, we left the House empty, except for a sleeping Eva, with no one to give the cup of cold water to the thirsty stranger. The little white iron gate creaked loudly as we opened it, even though I had oiled it a few days ago. For a second, I fantasized that the gate was the mouth of a bird uttering prophetic warnings. I shook my head, as if to shake out the scruples, and drove off with Evan to the navel of the universe, Fenway Park.

(25) Armageddon at Fenway Park

(Editor's Note: 'Isa evidently wrote this account many days afterwards, since the events immediately following paralyzed him for a week. Though this is a long interruption of the main thread of his story, I have put it here for the sake of chronological order. Readers who hate baseball can skip this chapter without any penalty, and pick up the narrative again on page 330.)

Early in the 1978 baseball season I had two memorable conversations with Evan about the nature of the game. The first compared it with music and the second with football. These were the two conversations that made me a baseball fan. They were Evan's "missionary work."

I had often heard classical music coming from his room, so I asked him, "Evan, why do you love classical music?"

"Don't you like it, Jack?"

"Oh, I do. That's why I want to know why you love it."

"I just do, I don't know why. I'm not a philosopher like you, so I never asked myself that question. What about you? What does it do for you?"

"I think it does the same thing the sea does for me: it frees me from slavery to time."

"How does it do that?"

"I think it's mainly the beat. Every other kind of music you hear on the radio has a hard beat. It's slavishly regular, like a slave driver on an old Roman galleon beating the drum so that the slaves all row to his beat. In classical music, the beat is the servant, not the master."

"That's true. Then you should love Gregorian chant, because that frees you from time even more, because it has even less beat."

"That's true. That's why I do love Gregorian chant."

"Then that's why you should love baseball," Evan replied. "Of all games, it frees you the most from time."

"How do you figure that?"

"Most other games—football, basketball, hockey—are slaves to the clock. The clock is the boss, more and more as the game moves on. And the clock is also the *enemy*: one team has to "*beat* the clock" at the end to win. But in baseball the clock is not the boss or the enemy, because the clock does not exist! There *is* no clock time in this game, it exists only in the world outside the game. All the time inside the game is lived time, human time, *kairos* instead of *kronos,* if you know Greek." (Evan was a seminarian and knew Greek for the same reason I knew Arabic: it was the language of his holy book.)

"I know those two words," I replied. "It's an important philosophical distinction."

"You *can* use clock time to measure baseball games, of course—you can say a game takes an average of three hours—but then you're using something outside the game to measure it. All clocks are outside the game. The game itself is clock-timeless. In that way, it's a Heavenly game, because there will be no clocks in Heaven. Yet there will be events. Things will happen."

"You know, Evan, I think you're onto something there."

My conversion to baseball fandom was just in time, for it was the beginning of the summer which future generations will surely call baseball's most dramatic summer ever, and the greatest drama took place right here in Boston's Fenway Park. Evan's missionary work succeeded: despite everything else that was crowding my life that summer, I became a Red Sox fan(atic).

*   *   *   *   *

A few days later Evan and I had another "missionary" conversation about baseball. He said, "You must love baseball if you are a Muslim because every element in baseball is based on the religious philosophy of life. It's the exact opposite of football that way. Baseball is Jesus and Muhammad; football is Machiavelli and Marx."

I challenged him to back up that claim with specifics. So he took a long page of yellow legal paper, drew a line down the middle, and wrote "baseball" on the left and "football" on the right. "Watch how these the two philosophies of life unfold," he explained, "detail by detail."

He wrote the number 1. "First, where is baseball played?"

"In a ballpark."

"A *park*! How natural! How beautiful! And where is football played?"

"In a stadium."

"See? And next (he wrote down a '2'), what is at the center of the ballpark? A baseball *diamond*. How beautiful! But the football field is called a *gridiron*."

"I'm beginning to see the two philosophies emerging," I admitted.

"Third, when does the baseball season begin?"

"In the spring."

"The season of life. And when does the football season begin?"

"In the fall."

"The season of dying."

"I see."

"Fourth, what are mistakes called in baseball?"

"Errors."

"And in football?"

"Penalties."

"Wow, everything fits. How many of these differences have you got up your sleeve, Evan?"

"Oh, at least a dozen."

"You made this up all by yourself?"

"No, actually I stole some of it from George Carlin, the comedian. I have this very funny tape of his, called 'An Evening with George Carlin'—no, actually it's called 'An Evening with Wally Londo'—here it is, listen to it some time. (He handed me a tape marked 'L.A. Little David Records Company, 1975.') But I added some things to it."

"Go on."

"Number 5: baseball is optimistic because some batter is always *up*. But football moves by *downs*."

"This is all certainly more than a series of coincidences."

"Exactly. It's philosophy. Two opposite philosophies of life, each logically consistent."

"Go on."

"Number 6: look at the words for football's penalties: *clipping, piling on, spearing, spiking, hitting, unnecessary roughness, personal foul, late hit, roughing the passer, grabbing the face mask.* How many of those does baseball have?"

"None."

"Right. But it does have—the *sacrifice*."

"I see. Does that make it the Christian game?"

"Of course. In fact, it's Trinitarian. Let that be Point Seven. Look: three strikes, three outs, three outfielders, six infielders, nine players in all, ninety feet between the bases, sixty feet, six inches from pitcher's mound to home plate, 360 feet around the bases to home. All multiples of three. So that's Point 7."

"You really love numbers, don't you?"

"That's the secret of success in science."

"Hmmm. But you could say baseball is a Hindu sport as well as a Christian one, because it's played on a mandala." I was really "getting into it" now.

"What is a mandala?" Evan asked.

"It's a famous visual meditation aid in Hinduism. It's a shape like a baseball diamond stretched out a little bit and rounded at the corners."

"What is it for?"

"To enclose a sacred space. To focus all your consciousness on the center. The pitcher's mound is the center of the action in baseball. When you watch baseball, that's where you focus your attention. In football your focus is not on any one absolute center, not even the quarterback, but on the whole field. A football field is empty space, with no center, no absolute. It's relativistic."

"That's a good point. You are really getting into this game, Jack. All right, let the mandala be point 8. Now here is Point 9: baseball has a *relief* pitcher come in. Football has the *kicker* come in."

"Everything is consistent so far. What's point 10?"

"Baseball has the 'seventh inning *stretch*.' Football has the 'two minute *warning*.'"

"I see. And I think I have Point 11 for you: time. That's the most philosophical point of all. Football is ruled by the time clock, by chronos time, external time, impersonal time. But baseball is timeless, just as you said the other day. You make your own kairos time. You never run out of time. You never have to beat the clock. It's like being in Paradise, in eternity. I never realized how philosophical this game is! What else?" I was on the hunt with him now.

"Well, here is Point 12: baseball has 'extra innings.' Football has 'sudden death.'"

I immediately added, "And here's Point 13 for you: baseball isn't played in the rain. Football is—in any kind of weather, even snow. I think there was even a famous Yale-Harvard football game that was played during the great hurricane of 1938."

"And the object of the game in baseball is—to get *home*. The object in football is to *conquer the enemy's territory*." (Evan wrote down a "14" for this point.)

He continued, "And you do that by a ground *attack*, or an aerial *attack*, and *punching holes* in the enemy line, and *riddling the defense* You *march*, and *bomb*, and *blitz*, and *spear*, and *sack*. And don't forget the *shotgun*, the *bullet pass*, and quarterback *sneaks*. All terms of war. But in baseball, you *walk*, you *stretch*, you *toe* the rubber, you *play* ball, you *tip* your cap, you *tap* your spikes—it's a gentleman's game." He wrote down Point 15.

I added, "And when the play stops in baseball the runner is *safe*. In football, play stops when the runner is *brought down*." That was Point16. We were both "on a roll."

"And in football the defense has to *tackle* the runner to bring him down. But in baseball, that's *interference*. So that's Point 17."

"And in baseball you wear a *cap*. In football you wear a *helmet*."

"That's Point 18. And here's Point19: a baseball is a *horsehide*, while a football is a *pigskin*."

"And here's Point 20: in baseball it's a *fault* for the pitcher to hit a batter. In football, defense and offence *have* to hit each other. And that's because baseball is Platonic. The pitcher's target is the strike zone, and that's an objective, impersonal thing, like a Platonic Idea. Baseball is the Platonic game. It's got absolutes, ideals. It's a saint's dream of order. Football is like a street brawl, where violence is rewarded."

"See? Two opposite philosophies of life."

"You know, Evan, I think that explains the story Art Dodge told me. You know Art—the big tall fat guy who batted .400 for the BC baseball team last year. I asked him how he got into baseball instead of football, since BC is a big football power and Art has the body for a football player. He said his high school coach took him and twenty other kids out into the forest the first day of the semester and made them all run as wild and fast as they could. The kids who crashed into the trees went on the football team. The others went on the baseball team."

We had a good, silly laugh together as we imagined this. I added, "You could see those same two philosophies of life in surfing and golfing too, point by point. Look. Point One: half the golfers in the world have broken their clubs in anger; but no surfer ever did that with his board. Two: golf is played on the hard ground, but surfing is done on the soft seawater. Three: the golfer aims at a little hole in the ground, a symbol of Hell; but the surfer aims at the sea, a symbol of Heaven. In fact, riding inside the wave is called 'the green cathedral.'"

"That's what a baseball field is called too!" Evan noted.

"See? There is a spiritual affinity here. Four: surfers smile a lot even after they wipe out, but golfers curse a lot when they make bad shots." I was keeping track of the numbers on my fingers. "Five: you can surf without a board, but you can't golf without a club. Nobody ever goes body-golfing. Six: golf goes by numbers, surfing doesn't. Seven: you often surf alone, but you hardly ever golf alone. Because surfing isn't competitive, even though professional surfers are. (Professional surfers are prostitutes.) But golf is almost always competitive. Eight: golfers 'strike' the ball, surfers 'ride' their board. Nine: golfers begin with a 'drive,' surfers begin with a 'duck dive.'"

"Enough, Jack. You've proved your point, and mine. Two philosophies of life. The saint and the barbarian."

*　　*　　*　　*　　*

I need to add a little history to explain the connection between the religious philosophy of life and the Boston Red Sox.

New York City has ten times more people than Boston, yet Boston has ten times more philosophers than New York. Why? That does not sound logical. But it is. Reality is always logical. Here is the logic:

1. Philosophers do philosophy.
2. Philosophy is the love of wisdom.
3. Wisdom comes through suffering.

5. Boston has the Red Sox.

6. Therefore Boston is full of philosophers.

Being born into a family of Red Sox fans is being born into a torture chamber; not just into a life of loss, but *crushing* loss. The Red Sox are not just losers; they are smithereens. The only possible explanation, the only logical and scientific explanation, is not "coincidence" or "chance" but Higher Forces at Work.

A knowledge of the Red Sox explains one of the most famous images in poetry: the image of the lowest circle in Hell in Dante's *Divine Comedy* as a region of ice. Everybody knows that Hell gets *hotter* the deeper you get into it. Why then did Dante make the lowest region of Hell a region of *freezing*?

The Red Sox fan's answer is this: because Dante had a vision, and in this vision, he saw a man in the lowest region of Hell. The man was Harry Frazee, the owner of the Red Sox who sold Babe Ruth to the New York Yankees for $100,000 after the 1918 season just so that he could finance a third-rate Broadway musical, *No, No, Nanette*. Babe Ruth was the greatest player in history, the man who *was* baseball even more than Pele was soccer or Bobby Orr was hockey. It was the worst deal in the history of sports, and it established the Yankee dynasty and its total, demoralizing domination of the Red Sox for many generations, perhaps for the rest of recorded history.

Frazee was sent to the lowest region of Hell, where his punishment was to have to watch every Red Sox collapse from 1920 until the end of time. The sign over his torture chamber said, "Here Is Frazee." But Dante misread the sign when he visited Hell in his vision. He thought it said, "Here Is Freezing."

An alternative explanation for Dante's choosing ice rather than fire for his image of Hell is that he was given the prophetic vision that one day the Red Sox would actually win the World Series. And that can happen, of course, only when Hell freezes over.

(Editor's Note: if you combine the snow index and the cold index, the winter of 2004–2005 was the severest in Boston's history. Meteorologists did not know why. Sox fans did. When the Red Sox won the World Series in 2004, for the first time in 86 years, Hell froze over.)

Before Frazee sold Ruth to the Damnyankees (that's one word up here), Boston won five of the first 15 World Series. The Yanks could never beat the Sox before the Sale. After it, they could never lose. As of now, 1978, the score is 20 Yankee World Series championships to none for the Sox in 60 years.

A few years ago I went to a game at Fenway Park and sat in the bleachers next to a tall Irish kid with bright red curly hair. His name was Dan O'Shaughnessey, or something like that. I told him I was interested in philosophy and he told me he was going to become famous some day by writing the most philosophical book about baseball ever written. It would be about the Red Sox, of course, and it would explain the mystery of their doomed history by proving that they were under a curse for selling Babe Ruth to the Yankees. He would call this book *The Curse of the Bambino.*

Our history has shaped our psyche in Boston. We are Calvinists even if we are atheists. We believe in doom, damnation, destiny, and despair. Yet we still hope. The unique combination of hope and despair that defines the psyche of the Red Sox fan can be defined by three signs. One is the sign a fan brings to every Opening Day. It reads: "Wait Till Next Year." A second sign reads: "Any Team Can Have One Bad Century." And the third sign was the one glued to the lintel over the doorway to the Red Sox Ticket Office. It was the quotation from Dante's "Inferno," the sign over the gates of Hell: "ABANDON ALL HOPE, YE WHO ENTER HERE."

Those gates of Hell have always prevailed against the cursed Sox. Yet millions enter these doors, voluntarily, year after year, to suffer anew "the slings and arrows of outrageous fortune." We Sox fans love to suffer, *have* to suffer, to preserve our identity. If we ever won it all, we simply would not know what to do. A strange sadness would settle over us. It would be a fate worse than death: it would be normalcy.

We are abnormal. We are special. We are loved. We are Charlie Brown waiting for Lucy to hold the football, waiting for our kite not to catch in a tree, waiting for the Messiah, for redemption and triumph and glory. We wait forever.

And we secretly love it. We are the Mass. Masochists, and we give thanks to the Yanks for their spanks. Our biggest fear is that our Messiah may really come some day. We are Vladimir and Estragon waiting for Godot yet terrified out of their minds when they think they hear him coming. That would destroy our job security. Our job is unique, you see: it is to wait forever for the Messiah until the end of the world, like the Wandering Jew.

And that is why we are unconquerable. Winning is conquerable; losing is not. If you expect to win, you can be disappointed; but if you expect to lose, you cannot be disappointed—unless you win. We have discovered the secret of success, the secret of invulnerability. We win even when we lose. *Especially* when we lose. And if we ever do win and not lose, why, then, if we win we will win. So we win either way. We have found the formula. Our hearts are broken, but we understand: they are meant to be broken. That is the key to wisdom. For most of life consists of losing, not winning, and that is why most folly consists of illusion and self-deception, while wisdom consists of disillusion and undeception.

This wisdom goes even deeper. The reason *why* our hearts are meant to break, the ultimate reason why wisdom comes through suffering, is because "this world is not my home, I'm just a-passing through." Our lives in this world are *supposed* to be failures. Only Paradise is our success.

That is the wisdom of our greatest literary form, tragedy; that is what we learn from our greatest plays, from Oedipus, and Antigone, and Job, and Hamlet, and Lear, and Romeo—and from the Red Sox, especially from their greatest drama, the epic tragedy of the 1978 season.

We learn the same lesson from our music. "Romantic" music is the most realistic music because only at the end does the Promised Land appear. Look at Sibelius's Seventh symphony, or Beethoven's Ninth. Renaissance and classical music *begins* with Heaven, with harmony, with its feet on home ground. Romantic music only ends there.

The Red Sox are our greatest music. The list of teams that have won the world championship in the years after 1918 is long and easily forgotten. The list of teams that have never won it is short and memorable. Chicago Cubs fans and Boston Red Sox fans remember their history in the wilderness better than other teams remember their history in the promised land. We tell our tragic tales around more campfires, and pass them down more lovingly through more generations, than anyone else. Both North and South still love and remember Robert E. Lee. Few love or remember Ulysses S. Grant. We love and remember the Jews, not the Babylonians, Assyrians, or Philistines.

Red Sox fans are not cursed. We are blessed. If and when we ever enter this promised land, in this world or the next, we will taste a joy no one else can possibly appreciate.

Between 1918, the last time the Red Sox won the World Series, and 1934, the year Ruth retired, the Red Sox played sub-.500 ball *every season* for 16 years. In 1934, on the exact anniversary of the day Ruth was sold (January 5th), a four-alarm fire nearly destroyed Fenway Park.

In 1965 the park drew 461 fans to one game. It drew 409 to another. After that season, it was scheduled for demolition in two or three years. Only the "Impossible Dream" season in 1967 saved it. The Sox had finished dead last in 1966, and in 1967 the oddsmakers gave them the longest odds in baseball history, 500–1, to win the pennant.

Which they did.

Each time they come close to winning the World Series, however, Higher Forces intervene. Or perhaps it is Lower Forces. There is only a very slight chance that it might be their own forces, an inherent death-wish. The best way to summarize the trading strategy, the managing strategy, and the batting and base-running strategy that has typified the Red Sox for the last sixty years is Abba Eban's description of the Palestinians: "They never miss an opportunity to miss an opportunity."

How long will the curse last before baseball's chosen people are allowed to enter their Promised Land? God only knows. Perhaps until the end of time. That is my belief. Someday I shall write a short story about the end of the world. It will happen at 3 P.M. on October 19th, and the clearest sign of the apocalypse will be given right here in Boston, when the Red Sox are on the verge of winning the seventh game of the World Series. They will be ahead by a comfortable margin—perhaps half a dozen runs. Their opponents are down to their last strike. There are two outs. The bases are empty. The third strike is thrown by the Sox pitcher. But the catcher never receives it, nor do the fans receive their Promised Land, because just before the umpire's right hand goes up and the fans storm the field in the greatest riot since the Boston Tea Party, the skies roll apart like a scroll and a voice that sounds suspiciously like Charlton Heston intones these words: "Now, My children, those of you who are wise know that this is the one thing I cannot allow in your world, only in Mine. History is over. Welcome Home."

My fundamentalist Christian friend adds confirmation to this prediction. He uses the Scofield Reference Bible, whose marginal notes claim that the world was created in 4004 B.C. This was the calculation of Archbishop Ussher, a 17th century British Bible scholar, on the basis of his literal calculation of the years in the Old Testament genealogies. But three things were not clear about Ussher's date. First, why was the date four years out; why not exactly 4,000 years between Creation and Christ? Second, why did Ussher pinpoint the date of creation as October 19th? Third, why did he further pinpoint the time or creation as 3:00 P.M.? The Red Sox supply these missing clues, and complete the prophecy, as follows:

In the late Middle Ages, the Christian calendar was discovered to be four years off. Jesus was not born in the year 0 but in the year 4 B.C. (That is the year there was such a remarkably close conjunction of the three brightest nighttime planets that they could have appeared as a single star, or star cluster, or constellation, leading the Wise Men from the East to Bethlehem.)

And one of the Psalms says that for God "a thousand years are as one day and one day as a thousand years." Interpreting the numbers literally, as fundamentalists do, that means that the six days of creation equal 6,000 years, and after that comes the seventh day, the eternal Sabbath, eternity. So the world that began in 4004 B.C. will end in 1996 A.D.

October 19th is the most likely date for the seventh game of the World Series. Just check the schedules.

And if it is a day game and if it is played in Boston, it will start at either noon or 1 P.M. If it starts at noon, it will end at just about 3, for the average length of a nine-inning baseball game is almost exactly three hours.

Finally, we have the key to understanding the end of the world. Finally, we know both the how and the where and the when. Finally, we know more than Jesus, who said that even he did not know when the world would end. (See Matthew 24:36.)

Yes, of course this is absurd; this is fantasy. We Red Sox fans are good at fantasy. We have been living in it since 1918.

We are the Jews of baseball, chosen to suffer. The Jews are the world's greatest comedians because they are the world's greatest experts in suffering. Only the absurdity of laughter can survive the absurdity of suffering. Laughter does not take away the suffering, but it distances you from it, like watching a tragedy in a theater. You can't objectively observe and subjectively experience the same thing at the same time. The more you observe it, the less you experience it. That's why we love to watch tragedies even though we hate to live them.

The two great centers of tragedy in the world today are Boston and Jerusalem. Boston is a theater, where a Greek tragedy may be observed every year at Fenway Park. Jerusalem is a battlefield, where real tragedy is lived every year.

When you live in a tragedy, it is difficult to see it. You have no distance. The eye needs distance to see anything. Neither the French nor the Russian soldiers saw the Battle of Borodino as well as Prince Andrei, in Tolstoy's *War and Peace*, for Andrei was observing it from a distance. But it was a close distance. Too much and too little distance both make objects invisible.

Therefore the best place to understand the conflict at the center of world history is Boston, where a great Greek theater called Fenway Park hosts a great Greek tragedy called the Boston Red Sox. But this tragedy costs no literal blood.

Boston is called "the Hub"—the hub of the universe. The phrase was meant literally by the old "Boston Brahmins." And they were right, for there is a connection between Red Sox history and world history:

Western civilization lost its innocence in April, 1912, when the *Titanic*, technology's supreme achievement, "the unsinkable ship," sank on her maiden voyage. Fenway Park opened the same week the *Titanic* sank.

World War I, the brutal fulfillment of the loss of innocence symbolized by the *Titanic*, shortened the baseball season. The World Series began on September 5, 1918. It was the last time the Red Sox won the world championship.

Man escaped his earthly womb and walked on the moon on July 20, 1969. July 20, 1978, was the date the Red Sox walked on the moon: they led their eternal rivals the Yankees by the astronomical margin of 14 games. Unfortunately, what goes up must come down.

After they sold Babe Ruth to the Yankees, the Sox finished in last place 9 out of the next 12 seasons. The Yankee team that won the World Series in 1923 had 11 former Red Sox players. Red Ruffing was one of the worst pitchers Boston ever had; when he was traded to the Yankees, he became one of the best in baseball history. (He is now in the Hall of Fame.) The same thing happened to Sparky Lyle half a century later. Last year (1977) Lyle won the Cy Young award and helped the Yanks again win the Series. The Sox deliberately passed up the opportunity to get or keep Pee Wee Reese, Jackie Robinson, and Willie Mays for almost nothing when they were rookies. All are now Hall of Famers.

When Ruth set his astounding record of 60 home runs in 1927, 11 of them were off Sox pitchers. In 1961, when Roger Maris broke Ruth's record at 61, he did it off Sox pitching on the last game of the season.

It's not just that they lose, it's how they lose. In every World Series they play, not just bad things but unbelievably bad things happen to them, almost anti-miracles. For instance:

In 1946, after the first 42 games, the Sox were 33-9, and already selling World Series tickets. They entered the Series with unheard-of odds: 20-7 favorites with the bookies to beat the St. Louis Cardinals. But Higher Forces inserted six strange events between the Sox and their prize:

1. Ted Williams, "the greatest hitter who ever lived," was hit in the elbow by a pitch in a meaningless exhibition game that the management had set up before the World Series to keep the players sharp. He played in the Series, but was ineffective.

2. Another Sox "great," second baseman Bobby Doerr, left Game 4 with a migraine and missed Game 5.

3. Sox ace "Boo" Ferris pitched the deciding seventh game. The score was tied 3–3 in the inning. With two outs, Dom DiMaggio, Joe's little brother, a light hitter but the best fielding centerfielder in baseball, doubled, but pulled a muscle hustling into second base, and had to leave the game. Had he been in centerfield during the next inning, he would have stopped one of the most remarkable plays in baseball history (below, #6).

4. With the go-ahead run on base, Ted Williams was up. The greatest hitter in baseball history, in the most important at bat of his career, popped up.

5. In the Cardinal half of the 8th, Boston manager Joe Cronin inexplicably pitched right-hander Bob Klinger instead of veteran lefty reliever Earl Johnson even though two left-handed batters were up. One of them, Cardinal outfielder Enos Slaughter, singled and eventually scored the winning run.

6. With Slaughter on first and two outs, Harry Walker singled softly just over shortstop, to left-center field. Ordinarily, a runner on first can't even make it to third on such a play. Slaughter made it to *home*, because centerfielder Dom DiMaggio's injury had brought sub Leon Culberson into centerfield. DiMaggio always played his position short, and caught many such "dying quail" singles on the fly. Before Slaughter's hit, Dom had been frantically signaling from the top step of the dugout for Culberson to move in and to the left (exactly where the ball turned out to be hit). But Culberson didn't see him, and when Walker hit the single Culberson waited for the bounce, then threw a soft "rainbow" (or "lollipop") to shortstop Johnny Pesky, the cutoff man. Pesky

held the ball for half a second, was surprised to see Slaughter 15 feet from home, then threw home half a second too late.

In 1947, on May 17, a seagull flew over Fenway Park and dropped a three-pound smelt smack on the face of St. Louis Browns pitcher Ellis Kinder. Kinder and the Browns beat the Red Sox anyway, 4-2.

In 1948 the Sox finished tied with Cleveland. They lost the one-game playoff to Cleveland, 8-4, because Danny Galehouse, probably the worst pitcher on the staff, pitched. No one knows why. Supernatural managerial brain cramps are invisible.

In 1949 the Sox went into the last two games of the season leading the Yankees by one game. All they had to do was win one of the two games at Yankee Stadium to win the pennant. I need not even write the next sentence.

In 1967, after eight consecutive losing seasons and after finishing in last place in 1966, the "Impossible Dream" team beat the impossible odds to win the American League championship on the last day of the tightest season in baseball history. (One day earlier, four teams were still in the race; on the last day, three still were.) Ace Jim Lonborg pitched and won on the last day of the season, so he could not pitch game 1 of the World Series against the Cardinals (again!). Cardinal ace Bob Gibson won all three Series games he pitched with complete games. Gibson dominated Games 1 and 4; Lonborg dominated Games 2 and 5 but could not come back on just two days' rest in Game 7 against Gibson.

They should have gotten into the Series in 1972 but didn't because in the last series of the season, Luis Aparicio, whom the Sox got for his great running ability, fell down twice while rounding third with the tying run, ending the rally that would have won the game and the pennant. They finished one game behind Detroit. The next year they finished one half-game behind Detroit.

In 1975, Vietnam had just ended, with America's first and only military defeat. We were still shaking from Watergate. In Boston, there had been riots in the streets about forced bussing. We needed escape. And the Sox needed a Series win against the Cincinnati Reds, "the Big Red Machine," for their charming long-time owner Tom Yawkey, who was dying.

Game 3 of the Series featured the worst umpiring call in history. With the score tied in the 10th inning and a runner on first, Reds batter Ed Armbrister tried to sacrifice bunt but missed the ball entirely. The runner had taken off for second and could easily have been gunned down by the great arm of Carlton Fisk, the Sox's Hall of Fame catcher. But the batter stood over the plate, blocking Fisk's throw. It was blatantly obvious interference. Fisk's throw seemed to come out of two bodies, tangled together: his and Armbrister's. The throw went into centerfield, the runner was safe and eventually scored the winning run when Joe Morgan singled. Umpire Larry Barnett stubbornly refused to call interference on the play. Barnett could never again appear in Fenway without being mercilessly reviled by the fans. Hundreds of them wore dark glasses to the next game he umpired at Fenway.

The sixth game was played after waiting out three days of cold and rain. Many writers called it the greatest baseball game ever played. (Until then, that is; October 2, 1978, trumped everything.) Ray Fitzgerald called it "a Beethoven symphony played on a patch of grass." Bernie Carbo's pinch-hit homer in the last of the ninth tied it, and Carlton Fisk's homer, which hit the left-field foul pole, won it in extra innings, at 12:34 A.M. Organist John Kiley broke into the "Hallelujah Chorus."

"Spaceman" Bill Lee started Game 7. Leading 3-0 in the sixth, the pitcher-comedian threw power hitter Tony Perez a "moon ball" or "eephus pitch," a 55-mph rainbow. Spaceman's moon ball was returned to sender. Score tied, 3-3.

After the game, Lee said, "I had been having good success with Tony throwing him my moonball, so I thought it would be a good idea to throw it to him again. Unfortunately, so did Tony. He hit the ball over the left field screen and several small buildings." Lee described the 1978 season this way: "we were about to go down in infamy with the '64 Phillies and the '67 Egyptians."

Having pitched flawlessly except for the one "moon ball" to Perez, Lee broke a blister on his pitching hand and had to be lifted in the seventh inning for ace reliever Jim Willoughby, who also pitched flawlessly. But the manager got one of those brain cramps that Heaven sends down at crucial times in Sox history: he removed Willoughby for a pinch hitter (Cecil Cooper) with the bases empty. Cooper fouled out to end the inning. Johnson replaced Willoughby not with his other ace reliever, Dick Drago, but with rookie Jim Burton, a kid as scared as his manager. Burton gave up the winning hit to Morgan, a little flare single with two outs in the ninth. Another Series lost in the seventh game.

The Sox had led in all seven games of this series, yet lost four of them.

If the history of the Red Sox was a movie, it would be a very bad movie. Everyone would complain that the plot was totally unbelievable.

Losing a won game is as difficult an art as winning a lost one. The Sox should be proud of their unique achievement.

How long can this go on? Forever? Perhaps. Will Sox fans see future World Series lost by errors of fielding, base running, or managing that a five-year-old would not have committed? Why not? Anti-miracles and supernatural brain-lock are ordinary occurrences to the Sox.

If the Red Sox ever win a World Series before the end of the world, there will have to be some cosmic catastrophe during the final game. At least an eclipse.

Editor's Note: 'Isa wrote this in 1978. I am writing this in 2008. If this book were fiction, and its characters merely my own inventions, I would at this point have Evan prophesy some of the future anti-miracles that would continue to bedevil God's Chosen Team until the End of History finally happened in 2004, such as (to take only the few most famous examples):

The most famous error in history: 1986 World Series. Shea Stadium, New York. Sox ahead of the New York Mets 3 games to 2. Sox ahead by two runs in Game 6. Last of the ninth. No one on base. Two outs. Two strikes on the batter. After just one more strike, Red Sox fans will finally hear the sound of the archangel Gabriel's trumpet announcing the triumphant end of the old era. The trumpet will sound like a thousand corks popping from champagne bottles, releasing bubbles of long-pent-up joy. A 68-year-old vintage champagne, bottled in 1918. But . . . a bloop single, then a walk, then another single, then a wild pitch, then Mookie Wilson's slow roller to first baseman Bill Buckner. I could have caught it. I'm 71. It went through Buckner's legs like a bowling ball finding its way between two pins, or like matter disappearing into a Black Hole, and the winning runs scored. Buckner had a bad leg, and he was still playing only because of another supernatural managerial brain cramp. Any Little League manager would have remembered to make defensive replacements in the last half inning.

Everyone in Boston knew the Sox were doomed to lose the seventh game the next day, even when they were ahead 3-0. You could sense the hopelessness. It was palpable, like the air before a storm. Red Sox fans are not quite human: they are like animals who can sense disasters coming much better than humans can. They *expect* terrorist attacks. They share a common border with the terrorists (Yankees). It's called Connecticut. Connecticut is outstanding for the number of mixed marriages (between Yankee fans and Red Sox fans) and for divorces.

Not only can the Sox lose when there's only one out to go, they can lose even *after* that last out is made! Impossible, you say? You forget that God is a Yankee fan and that with God all things are possible. On September 19, 1993, in Yankee Stadium, the Red Sox led the New York Yankees 3-1. Last of the ninth. Yanks up. Two outs, no one on base. Light-hitting Mike Gallego up. Suddenly, Heaven intervenes for the next five batters, i.e., the next six plate appearances. (No, that was not a misprint.) (1) First, Boston relief pitcher Greg Harris hits Gallego with a pitch. (2) The next batter is pinch-hitter Mike Stanley. Harris gets one strike on him, then throws the final pitch of the game, for Stanley flies out to Mike Greenwell in left field for the third out. What could possibly happen next? Changing the past by a time machine? Yes! An umpire time machine. The umpires ruled that they had called time out just before the last pitch was delivered, in fact between the time Harris began his windup and the time the ball left his hand, because a fan had stepped onto the field at that exact moment. (Was it a fan or was it an angel in disguise, an evil angel working for the Evil Empire?) (3) Back to the plate goes Stanley, for a second try. He singles on the next pitch, between third and short. (Another Black Hole.) (4) Wade Boggs, the next batter, grounds to second. Ordinarily, this would be the last out, either at first or at second. But second baseman Scott Fletcher knocks the ball down and can't make a play at either base. Gallego scores. The Yanks are still down by a run and down to their last out. But (5) the next batter, Dion James, walks, and (6) with the bases loaded and two outs, Don Mattingly hits a two-run single. Yanks 4, Sox 3. The Red Sox file an official protest with the earthly officials of Major League Baseball. The protest was probably referred upstairs, and God laughed at it.

The most recent supernatural brain cramp came in the seventh game of the American League championship series in 2003. It had been their most beloved and memorable season, the "We Believe," "cowboy up" season. Ace Pedro Martinez had a consistent track record of being nearly infallible for his first 100 pitches, then suddenly falling from Olympus, like a penguin stepping ashore. Pedro had thrown 100 pitches, and was coming totally unraveled. One of the best bullpens in baseball was waiting to bail him out. Every brain in the world was saying "take him out" except two. Unfortunately, those were the two conferring on the mound. Those with mystical gifts of perception saw the hole in the sky and the bolt of dark lightning that came down it and froze the grainy little brain of the Red Sox manager (he who shall not be named); but the rest of the world saw only the effect rather than the cause. The effect was that the Yanks tied the score, sending the game into extra innings. Lights-out Yankee reliever Mariano Rivera entered, and the Sox countered with Tim Wakefield. Wakefield can pitch knuckleballs almost forever, while Rivera is ordinarily a one-inning-only closer. He rarely pitches two innings. Now, he pitches *three*. But after three he is "tanked." All that Wakefield has to do is go one more inning, and the Sox are sure to score off the rest of the Yankee bullpen. But Aaron Boone, the maligned Yankee third baseman, who has been a total disappointment all season, homers to win it all.

After the Red Sox won the World Series in 2004, for the first time in 86 years, Dan Shaughnessy, author of the whole idea of the "Curse of the Bambino" (in his wonderfully funny book by that title), wrote:

"The Red Sox as we have always known them are gone forever. They never again will be the cuddly team on a near century-long quixotic quest. They are no longer cursed. . . . The ghosts are purged. . . . Now the men who play at Fenway Park are simply the World Champion Boston Red Sox. The best team in baseball.

"I guess we'll have to settle for that."

Oh—and there *was* an eclipse—a total eclipse of the moon—at the exact time the Sox won the final game of the 2004 World Series.

From this little exercise in editorial self-indulgence, I now return to 'Isa and to 1978.

* * * * *

By the season's midpoint, on July 9th, the Red Sox had an astonishing won-lost record of 57-26, and were 11½ games ahead of the second-place Damnyankees.

But great tides turn, tides of fate as well as tides of water. And so did this one.

The Yankees fired their hated manager Billy Martin on July 24 and replaced him with the beloved Bob Lemon. The Yankees' boat began to be lifted by the changing tide, and the Red Sox's boat began to sink. Fans sensed the tidal change before the team did. After a fairly good 19-10 record in August, shortstop Rick Burlson complained, in print, that "We were written off by the Boston fans in late August. And we had a 7½ game lead!" Boston fans are Calvinists: doom, despair, damnation, and predestination.

The first 16 days of September brought only 3 wins and 13 losses. The worst of these were 4 consecutive *slaughters* by the Yankees at Fenway Park, by a combined score of 42-9. These games were so traumatic that they generated their own name, "the Boston Massacre." The Sox entered them with a four-game lead and exited with none. By September 16 they had lost another five out of six. A sign held up by a Sox fan in the bleachers offered a solution: "Get Exorcist!"

But then the tide turned again. The Sox won 12 of their last 14 games and ended the season in an exact tie with the Yankees, winning on the last day of the season, while the Yankees lost. So it came down to a one-game playoff. The war between the Red Sox and the Yankees cannot end in a tie. Peace cannot have the last word in baseball.

Not even when peace can, apparently, have the last word in Israel. The same page of the *Boston Globe* that reported the Red Sox victory on October 1 and the Red Sox-Yankee Armageddon on October 2 reported that "Egypt and Israel have reached agreement to open peace negotiations in Washington on October 12. . . . Egypt is inviting the United Nations to take part in the negotiations . . . the negotiations are expected to produce a peace treaty ending 30 years of war."

Evan insists there is a connection. Although I doubt he will find its scientific formula, I believe he is right. I deduce this "flaky" conclusion from the most certain of all premises: that "there is no God but God." In a world whose story has only one Ultimate Storyteller, in a world where history is His-story, everything *is* connected.

* * * * *

Evan and I arrived at the cathedral just in time for the liturgy. Entering this green cathedral for the first time feels very much like catching your first wave:

almost everyone remembers that first time. I had been sad and silent during the hour of driving to the game, because of Mara, but when I penetrated the veil and entered the holy of holies I smiled for the first time in a week. Green cathedrals have healing powers.

The wind was blowing from the east, and the sea air was joining the olfactory alliance of hot dogs, pungent mustard, Italian sausage & peppers, cigar smoke, and the farts of the fat man directly in front of us whose bulging butt was ballooning out of his absurdly skinny seat.

We sat in the centerfield bleachers, just behind the bullpen. They are the best bleachers in baseball, with such a close view of home plate that we could judge balls and strikes with the naked eye. We were surrounded by Everyone. Baseball draws a more diverse crowd than any other game. I smiled at the twenty-something girl in a Red Sox cap sitting in front of me and wondered why baseball caps made plain girls look so pretty. I don't like other boyish clothes on girls—slacks, for instance—so why do I like baseball caps? I don't know the answer, but here is an analogy or parallel: the red clay around home plate is also ugly—it reminds me of the dry, hardscrabble soil of the South—yet it looks beautiful here. Why? Perhaps the green cathedral transforms matter as it transforms time.

"Look at those two," Evan said, pointing to two fans getting into their seats two rows below us. "I'll bet you can tell which one is the Yankee fan and which one is the Red Sox fan even though they don't have caps on."

"How?" I asked.

"One swaggers, the other stoops."

"You're right. It's obvious," I admitted.

"Red Sox fans are the South of the North," Evan explained. "It's the romance of the Confederacy, the lovable underdogs, the lost cause. Like Sisyphus with his rock."

"I wonder why we love them?" I mused.

"The heart has its reasons which the reason does not know," Evan answered.

"But *why* do we do it? Why do we let our hearts be broken year after year?"

"Because our hearts know that they're *meant* to be broken." As soon as Evan said this, he regretted it. I remembered my own broken heart, and suddenly my smile disappeared.

Most of the adults in the park had "anticipated tragedy" written on their faces. Even after yesterday's Sox victory and Yankee loss, and even with a frail, tired Ron Guidry going for the Yankees against a tough, rested Mike Torrez for the Red Sox, and even with home-field advantage, fans with memories Just Knew. They knew the laws of Greek tragedy. They smelled the Angel of Death hovering heavily in the air. The only question was not What but How. How would the unthinkable happen this time? (Sox fans alone can think the unthinkable, eff the ineffable. Their team has made them mystics.)

More than any other major league ballpark, Fenway looks like an expanded version of your back yard. It is full of nooks and crannies, like an old house. The outfield has *17* distinct angles. The right-field foul pole (the "Pesky Pole") is only 275 feet from home, but the low wall then angles away to centerfield so gradually that if you follow it out for only 115 feet more you find that the stands are now already 375 feet away from home plate. It is not rational, like other ballparks. It is crazy—like its fans. They are like your family, and it is like your home.

There is very little foul territory. The spectators are right on top of the play. Fans in the first row of box seats are so close that they could literally spit on the players. (Of course, Bostonians don't do that; New Yorkers do. That's why Yankee Stadium has much larger foul territory than Fenway Park.)

The left field wall, the "Green Monster," is Fenway's most obvious piece of weirdness. Line drives to left that would be homers in any other park bounce off the wall and become singles here. Pop flies that would be routine outs everywhere else fall into the net as homers here. (So many homers are hit over the Monster that they literally collect the balls in a net. New England Calvinists are frugal.)

The Monster looks like a photo of a 40-foot wave frozen in time. You expect it to break out of the photo and onto your head at any moment, inundating the field with green foam. You want to catch it with a surfboard. Even though it stands still, its standing there is an *act*, the act of a living creature. It is making itself present as obviously as an elephant standing in your back yard.

The park is small, dirty, crowded, old, irrational, and inconvenient—like your family. The men's rooms have soapstone *troughs* to pee in rather than private, individual china urinals. The corridors are concrete tunnels with peeling paint. The pizza is astonishingly inedible, barely distinguishable from its cardboard containers. The hot dogs are overpriced and tasteless. (Fenway Franks are exactly the same product, and made by the same company, as Yankee Franks. Only the labels differ. This is Hindu theology: Vishnu the Preserver and Shiva the Destroyer are really the same Brahman.)

(Editor's Note: Twenty-four years after Evan wrote this, the new owners of the Red Sox renovated the team's ballpark, its food concessions, and its on-the-field fortunes, all with spectacular success. From having the very worst food in baseball, it has gone to having one of the two or three best. "Monster seats" were installed over the "Green Monster," where the net used to be. And all the pee troughs are gone. Real Red Sox fans liked the old place better, of course. It said: "Suffer." It spoke their name.)

On the highest vertical surface in the park, the right field roof, hang four retired numbers: 9, 4, 1, and 8: Williams, Pesky, Cronin, and Yaz: four men that have become gods and have been taken up into the sky as their heavenly reward. Another holy icon is the glowing red triangle of the Citgo sign a block away, in Kenmore Square, that hovers over left field. It was declared a historic landmark, to be preserved forever: the only neon "historic landmark" in America.

The liturgical chants—"Hot Dogs Here!" and "Hey! Ice Cream!"—are announced by leather lungs and repeated like mantras, but no one notices the sound except the hungry. The worshippers fix their attention on the grassy altar where the sacrificial victim is offered up. However, the peanut vendors' accurate pitching of peanuts to customers sixty feet six inches away does draw your attention, especially compared to the Sox bullpen.

John Kiley, the Red Sox organist, is the only person in the world who has played for the Celtics, the Bruins, and the Red Sox at different times in his life. The organ is played only between innings. At most other ballparks the organ blares continually (like the DJ who takes over the wedding reception), reducing the game to lyrics for the organist to put to music. Why does there have to be an *organ* at a ballpark in the first place? Because it's a cathedral, I suppose. But some day I will get my revenge: I will interrupt an organ concert by playing baseball in the concert hall.

Unlike the organ music, the hawking of the vendors belongs to the Game as much as the hawking of the gulls belongs to the sea. The muttering of the fans sounds like the muttering of the surf, like "the sound of many waters" in the Apocalypse. (The writer of that book was probably hearing the fans in Heaven's bleachers.)

The most magical sound in baseball is the crack of the bat. Every hit sounds just a little different. If Squat were a baseball fan, I'll bet he could tell from the sound alone where and how far the ball was going every time it was hit. There is something in that sound that makes it one with the squawk of the seagull. The two sounds play the same keys on your spirit's organ, though they are played by different hands, one with a beak and one with a bat. You can recognize the same Composer in both musics.

Just before the game began, two biplanes circled the park like patrolling angels. They trailed banners, as angels do in medieval icons. I wished for a moment that I could not read English: the trivial content on the banners spoiled the wonderful flamboyance of form.

A single lost pigeon circled under the overhang like a caged tiger. (Evan noticed it and tried in vain to lure it close with a piece of popcorn.) Everything moves like that pigeon, I thought: in spirals, in the form of a wave. Even the galaxies spin like the spiraling waves circling round the Cauldron on Bailey's Hill. Even straight lines are really circles, according to Einstein, so that if I threw a baseball in a perfectly straight line, and if it had infinite momentum, it would eventually come back and hit me in the back of my head. What a wonderfully liquid universe! How like a wave! Everything in the universe is round except time.

When the game began, the fat man in front of us sat back with a deep, contented sigh and a wide smile, turned to his companion and said, "I love this shit!" Suddenly he was a friend, not an annoyance. Smiles are highly contagious.

Evan explained to me that Ron Guidry, the skinny Yankee pitcher, had an unbelievable 22-3 record, but was pitching on only three days' rest for the first time all year. He was tired. His arm was tired. His fast ball was tired. He was throwing 85 percent sliders. Meanwhile, we had Mike Torrez, former Yankee, on the mound. He was a horse, a Clydesdale. I foolishly asked, "What odds would you give to the Sox today? Two to one?" The fat man heard me, turned around, and said to me, "They'll find some way to blow it, no matter what the odds. I know dese bums. I bin followin' 'em fer forty years." This was the man who had just smiled contentedly and said, "I love this shit." This is a masochist.

Nothing very interesting happened in the first inning, except the passion of the fans at every pitch. Then, in the second inning, Yaz came to bat, the now-aging hero of the "Impossible Dream" team of '67. The greatest batter in baseball got a fast ball from the best pitcher in baseball and smashed a line drive home run into the right field seats fifty feet to our left. We could see the ball coming as soon as it left the bat.

At least six other Sox drives drove Yankee outfielders to the warning track during this game, but no others quite reached the stands. The Sox bats were alive, but so was the wind, which kept swirling and changing, and seemed to turn and blow *in* whenever the Sox came to bat.

Even though the Sox led 2-0 by the sixth inning, you could feel the worry in the air. Then, with two men on base, came the first crucial and crazy play of the game. Fred Lynn got the inside pitch he wanted and drove it to deep right field, right in front of us. But the Yankee right fielder Lou Piniella, surprisingly, caught up to it—only because he was playing thirty feet out of his normal position. When asked about that after the game, Piniella just shrugged. Lynn said, "I don't know what he was doing over there. Piniella was playing me as a pull hitter. I haven't put five balls in that area all season against a lefthander. I can't figure out why he was there."

I can.

In 1912, just before the deciding game of the World Series, Sox right fielder Harry Hooper ran out to right field to play his position, found a little piece of paper on the grass, picked it up, discovered that it was a Catholic prayer card, read it, and prayed its prayer for a Boston victory. Later in that game Hooper made one of the most incredible catches in history, snaring what would have been the winning home run ball with his bare hand, only because he was waiting, way out of his usual position, in just the right place at the right time. Piniella was also a pious, praying Catholic, and he was waiting in the same spot as Hooper.

We were sitting behind Piniella. The sun was shining over home plate, to the southwest, shining right into his eyes. If you drew a line from our eyes to the sun, the line would go through Piniella's eyes. The light that blinded Piniella blinded us too.

As Lynn's ball approached, I saw *something* that seemed to be moving on its trajectory, something white or silver against the backdrop of the yellow, late-afternoon sunlight. It was like an invisible bird that ruffled the curtain between the invisible and the visible skies for an instant. It didn't look like an angel. It didn't look like anything. But it looked like *something*.

Despite the sun in his eyes—or perhaps guided by it as the Wise Men were guided by the Star of Bethlehem—Piniella made a running catch on Lynn. End of inning. Piniella, by the way, is usually such a bad fielder that people laugh at him when they see him. He is the anti-gazelle: slow afoot and stocky. He looks like Fred Flintstone—or Babe Ruth. All he can do is beat you.

"Did you see that?" I said to Evan.

"No. What?"

"I don't know. Just—just light. But not *ordinary* light."

"Not many things are ordinary here."

The next half inning was the Yankee seventh. Torrez had been terrific: a two-hitter so far. He had struck out the dangerous Yankee catcher Thurmon Munson three times. But apparently he was tiring now. For with one out, Chambliss and White both singled. Pinch-hitter Jim Spencer flied out for the second out. The Yanks had no one left to pinch-hit for the light-hitting little shortstop Bucky Dent, batting ninth, so Dent had to bat for himself.

On the first pitch he swung at, the ball fouled off his foot. He jumped back, obviously hurt. But he had to stay in the game. Willie Randolph, who could play either second or short, and who was a much better hitter than Dent, had been hurt, and the Yanks had already pinch-hit for light-hitting utility infielder Brian Doyle the previous inning, so there was no one else who could have played shortstop but Dent. So the little nobody had to bat. Play stopped for a few minutes while the Yankee trainer put something (probably cortisone) on his foot. Mickey Rivers, the lead-off batter, was in the on-deck circle.

According to the "*Globe*" the next morning, Rivers said after the game that "Bucky and myself use the same type of bat . . . about noontime today, I asked our clubhouse guy if he had any of those bats in our bag. The one we had been using was a little chipped. The clubhouse guy looked in his trunk and came up with a new one, a Max 44 model. It was the last one left in the bunch. I taped it up before the game the way we liked it and I told Bucky I had a new one that felt good. He said he was going to stick with the old chipped one. I was on him to change, and he wouldn't. I was even yelling to him from the on-deck circle that I had the bat with me. Finally, when the ball hit his foot, and he was being treated, I grabbed the bat boy and told him to take the bat up and take away the one Bucky had."

Evan and I were both smiling at the Yankees' plight. Dent versus Torrez was David against Goliath, and David was both wounded and deprived of his own slingshot. Torrez's next pitch was exactly where he wanted it, a fast ball in on the hands, virtually unhittable unless you had twice as many muscles in your arms as Dent has.

Dent seemed to pop it up to the left side. We smiled. Our first thought was for Burleson, the shortstop, to go out and get it. Then the ball sailed higher in the wind. It was going out to left field for Yaz. Fine. Yaz is a great fielder.

The wind had been blowing strongly *in* from left field at the start of the game. It had blown back a couple of Sox fly balls during the last few innings that looked like sure home runs when they came off the bat. But between innings, the wind had shifted 180 degrees and was now blowing *out*. The Bucky ball looked to everyone in the park like an easy pop fly. But as it rose, the wind began to carry it. Yaz backpedaled a little, without haste or worry. But the wind had become mightier than anyone thought, and Yaz was now nearly at the warning track, for it looked as if the ball might even go over Yaz's head and scrape the Green Monster.

The flight of that ball is etched on 35,000 memories in agonizingly slow motion. Dent was running like a rabbit out of the batter's box, hoping the ball hit the wall and hoping to stretch a single into a double. To everyone's amazement, especially Dent's, an invisible divine hand that was made of wind carried the ball over the wall by about three inches and deposited it into the net, softly—ever so softly. Torrez stood on the mound like a man who had just been shot. His jaw hung open. Yaz's knees buckled, and he punched the ground.

Three-run homer. (Dent had hit only five homers all season.) Lead change. Momentum change. Tide change. No boat can sail against the Universal Fate Waves. Low murmurs of astonishment and despair, more silent than silence itself, rose like waves from the sea of fandom. The earth itself was weeping.

"Bucky Dent" is now a primal swear word in Boston. The inevitable middle name is always added.

I suddenly understood how New York is unique: it is the city that never weeps. Sensitive souls, forced to watch slow torture, will weep. But New York has no sensitivity and no weeping. New York is also "the city that never sleeps." If you never sleep, you're bound to be irritable.

Torrez worked the next batter, Rivers, to 3-2, then walked him. Manager Don Zimmer, whom Bill Lee called "the gerbil" (he looks like Socrates!), immediately yanked Torrez, even though (1) he insisted he was still strong; (2) he *was*; (3) he had thrown only one damaging pitch, the one to Dent (in fact it was a *good* pitch); (4) he had struck out Munson, the next batter, three times, (5) all four of his pitches were working, and (6) he was getting out both right- and left-handers. But that invisible hole in the sky opened up and the invisible lightning zapped Zimmer into the sudden mental paralysis that is the endemic disease of Red Sox managers. Worse yet, instead of bringing in Dick Drago, who had a much better ability to hold runners on base, Zimmer brought in Bob Stanley. So of course Rivers stole second on him (he wouldn't have stolen off Torrez or Drago), and came in to score on Munson's hit (Munson hadn't come anywhere near hitting Torrez all day). The tide had changed from 2-0 Sox to 4-2 Yanks in just ten minutes.

In the next inning, the 8th, Reggie Jackson made it 5-2 with a towering 480-foot homer off Stanley (aided by the turning wind, of course) into the cen- terfield bleachers just to our right. (Torrez had gotten Jackson out handily.)

The Yanks had already brought in their closer, Goose Gossage, in the 7th inning. Goose was strong—he and Nolan Ryan are the only two people in his- tory who were recorded to throw as fast as 103 mph—but closers rarely pitch two innings, and almost never three, and Gossage was struggling by the 8th In the bottom of the 8th Jerry Remy doubled and Yaz singled him home, making the score 5-3. Foolish faces around us began to brighten. With Yaz on first, Fisk fouled off four straight two-strike pitches, then singled. Lynn singled Yaz home for another run. 5-4. Still only one out. But Gossage was wisely left in. (Dark angels do not fly through open sky holes into the brains of *Yankee* man- agers.) He sidestepped further damage by getting Hobson to fly out and Scott to strike out.

Half an inning later, it was the last of the ninth, the hour before the end of the world (though the big clock reported the totally irrelevant time outside the park as 4:05). The Sox needed only one run to tie, against a tiring Gossage. With one out, Rick Burleson walked, then Jerry Remy hit a solid line drive to right field.

Burleson, a possible threat to steal, had a good lead off first. If he takes off as soon as the ball is hit, he makes it to third easily. Both first base coach Johnny Pesky and third base coach Eddie Yost know that Remy's ball is a base hit. In fact everybody in the park knows it's a base hit. But Burleson doesn't. He thinking, If this is a fly ball out, I don't want to get doubled off first to end the game. So he waits a split second before taking off, doesn't hear Pesky say- ing "Go! Go!" behind him, and runs with his head down, not watching Yost at third. The ball is going to bounce twenty feet to the left of Piniella and fifty feet in front of him, so Burleson can easily make it to third even if Piniella fields it cleanly. And apparently he *can't* field it cleanly, because he is trying to shade his eyes from the sun, and obviously having trouble. Everyone in the park except Burleson knew Piniella had lost the ball in the sun. It was obvious- ly going to bounce past him and roll to the wall, scoring Burleson to tie the game and sending the speedy Remy to third or even home with the winning run. Thirty-five thousand throats are shouting to Burleson "Go! Go!"

But Burleson stopped halfway between first and second to see if Piniella had caught the ball on the fly. When he saw the ball bounce and saw Piniella's confusion, he ran to second, but then he stopped *again* ten feet past second instead of going to third. He turned his head and saw the ball bounce into Piniella's glove. He still might have made it to third, even after the double hesitation, but didn't want to take that chance, especially with Rice and Yaz coming up next. This over-cautious base-running on their part was going to cost the Sox the pennant in 1978 just as the risky base-running by Enos Slaughter of the Cardinals had cost the Sox the Series in 1946.

Piniella didn't see the ball until it bounced. But he pounded his glove confidently to decoy the runner. The decoy worked. The ball then bounced 20 feet to his left. It was a hard-hit ball and was coming at him fast. After the ball bounced, Piniella *again* lost it in the sun. He lunged clumsily to the left and put up his glove like a hockey goalie trying to stop a slap shot. He had only the vaguest idea where the ball was. He couldn't see it, but suddenly he *felt* it—in his glove! The ball was hit so hard that its force (plus the surprise) moved Piniella backwards a foot, like the recoil from a gun. There was no way he could have thrown out Burleson at third after that. But Burleson wasn't going to third. A Fate Wave stopped him, like a force field. For if Burleson had been on third, he would have easily come home with the tying run when the next batter, Jim Rice, hit a long fly ball to right, a perfect sacrifice fly. In fact, the ball Rice hit would have been a home run an inning earlier, when the wind was blowing out. It was much harder hit than Dent's. But the winds of destiny had changed on schedule. IF Burleson . . . . IF the wind. . . . IF Robert E. Lee's scout had told him to occupy Little Round Top Hill at Gettysburg, the South would have won the Civil War.

The *Globe* reported Piniella saying after the game: "I never saw the ball. I never saw the ball at all. I didn't know where it was going to land. Over my head, in front of me, I didn't know if it was going to hit me on the head. . . . Somebody told me later that Burleson was watching my face instead of his coach at third. I guess I looked like I was going to catch it. But I had no chance. That ball gets by me, that's the tying run in. But it didn't."

Now I will tell you something that will make you jump out of your seat. As soon as Remy hit that ball, I literally jumped out of my seat. But not at the hit. I caught a glimpse of the same kind of light I had seen the previous inning. But it was clearer this time. It was very large, very light, and very fast, and it was not just light, it was a *something*. It looked as if the curtain of air *ripped* for just a split second to let that "something" through, and then immediately took it back.

What was that something? It did not look like an angel. It didn't look like anything. It trembled on the brink of visibility but did not quite fall over it. But it left ripples in the air, like the wake of a boat.

I ask myself, What color was it?

I answer, A color I never saw before.

I ask myself, How can that be?

I reply, Draw a triangle. Put white on top, gold on the right and silver on the left. Now put a point in the center. That's where this color was.

Our minds and bodies were both very quiet for the rest of the game. But the fans were making as much noise as they could to cheer for the next two batters, Rice and Yaz. But Rice flied out to Piniella, without the aid of the angel. This time the ball was hit high enough to escape the sun corridor.

We were down to our last out. Yaz was up. Classic showdown. Casey at the bat. Gunfight at OK corral. Baseball's greatest clutch hitter versus baseball's greatest clutch pitcher. Drama dripped from the sky like rain. It was too perfect, too contrived, to be believable. The fingerprints of the heavenly baseball writer were embarrassingly visible on the crime scene.

Gossage fed Yaz nothing but fastballs. Yaz knew they were coming. Gossage is a fastball pitcher. Yaz is a fastball hitter. Gossage was tired. It was his third inning of relief. He had lost his control. The Sox had been getting to him for the last two innings. Now a single would tie the game. A double would win it.

The first pitch was a ball. Hitter's count coming up. If the ball is on the inside half of the plate, Yaz will cream it, with that beautiful arc of an upswing, jerk it out of the park. The ball came over the inside half of the plate. Yaz gave it that beautiful arc of an upswing and jerked the ball—straight up.

Yaz took one step toward first, then stopped and looked away in shame.

Gossage said, afterwards, "Yazstrzemski's the greatest player I've ever played against. I just wound up and threw it as hard as I could. I couldn't tell you where."

Thirty five thousand screaming fans were suddenly silent. No rumble of discontent followed this silence, as it did after Dent's homer. This was final. This was the end of time, and the end of hope.

The ball froze in time. It never came down. It entered eternity. The rest of time would be too painful to endure if it were allowed to flow back into Fenway Park, if that ball ever came down.

But the unendurable was endured. No angel intervened. No bolt of lightning impaled that one little ball, but a bolt of darkness impaled 35,000 hearts like a spear. The sound the ball made on the leather of third baseman Graig Nettles's glove was clearly audible to us, 300 feet away, for it was surrounded by a roaring cataract of silence. The silence lasted for at least as long as it takes to drown. No one spoke. I have never heard a silence like that before or during a game. Then only one sound came weakly out of the silence: the voices of the few Yankee fans there. The sound soon changed from rejoicing to taunting. (Saints rejoice; demons taunt.)

Fisk said, after the game, "I was trying to will that ball to stay up and never come down." It was Fisk who had willed the ball to stay fair for his home run that hit the left field foul pole to win the 6thgame of the 1975 World Series, the most famous home run in Red Sox history. But he couldn't will this ball to defy gravity. The gravity of history and destiny was stronger than the human will. The headline in the *Globe* the next day read: "Destiny 5, Red Sox 4."

The editorial said, "Don't blame the Red Sox . . . they were just being faithful to their nature and to their destiny." Even the *Globe*, one of the most liberal papers in the country, understands the truth of conservatism when it comes to the Red Sox. Conservatives do not believe in progress. They believe in evil.

Somewhere in Connecticut, a bartender with a long memory of heartbreak shut off the bar's TV after the last out, and said, to the dumb hush that followed, "The sons of bitches killed our fathers and now they're coming after us."

After the game, hundreds of Red Sox fans were seen walking the streets like zombies.

Let me think seriously about the theology of this event. Could it have been an angel? Of course it could have. The cliché says that "baseball is a game of inches," and others say it is a game of angles; I say it is a game of angels. Nations as well as individuals have guardian angels, so Red Sox Nation probably has one too, for it is truly a nation. Why wasn't that angel saving Western civilization instead of fooling around in right field at Fenway Park? What serious task was neglected by its delinquency?

What did I see on that beam of light? What did Piniella see? The sun blinded him. It is ancient wisdom that the blind are the true seers: Homer, Tiresias, Milton, Helen Keller. We all know that that's true; that is why something in us can believe, contrary to reason, that Luke Skywalker can be a better swordfighter by closing his eyes and just "trusting The Force." Faith is stronger than sight. It's like Islam ("surrender"), and like surfing. Maybe Piniella was surfing on angels.

I had a conversation with Evan about that on the way home. When I suggested that I had really seen an angel, he disagreed: "Angels are either wholly good or wholly evil, from Heaven or from Hell," he argued. "Neither kind of angel would be somewhere in the middle and fooling around with balls in Fenway Park. Angels don't *play*. They're serious. Both kinds of angels are."

"I disagree," I said. "I think angels are whatever God is. They take their cue from God. That's Premise One. And God plays. That's Premise Two. God has a sense of humor. Look at all those strange fishes! Conclusion: therefore angels can play too. Good ones, anyway. So it has to be a good angel out there. But what's so good about putting a curse on the Red Sox? Are we the Evil Empire?"

"Just the opposite," Evan said. "We are the Jews of baseball. We are the Chosen People."

"Nonsense," I said. "God doesn't *favor* His chosen people with a *curse*. That's logically self-contradictory."

Evan then gave me some theological argument that I simply could not understand about Jesus deliberately bearing the curse of the Cross for us, and about the redemptive meaning of suffering, and about why the Qur'an is supposedly so deeply wrong when it says Jesus couldn't have been crucified because Allah would never let His chosen prophets suffer public disgrace and failure. I wanted to challenge his theology, but I was not in the mood to argue now—not so much because the game was lost but because it was over and could no longer distract me from my worry and depression about Mara.

*   *   *   *   *

But I can't stop wondering: Who was that angel? And what was he doing? I will try to think the problem through. Reflecting on this some weeks after the terrible events that were about to happen at the House (which I will narrate shortly), I have to begin with data from my own experience and confess that this day was not the first day I think I saw an angel. It was the second.

The first time was when I was about six years old. It must have been a vision, or a waking dream, but it did not feel at all like a dream; it felt exactly as real as every ordinary day's consciousness.

I saw a sea of fire. The sea of fire had waves. The waves were not made of water but of angels.

I focused on one angel, and his glance was like the shining of fire. Beams of light *bent* beneath him like a willow tree under a hurricane. He strewed light around him like a dog shaking water droplets after a bath.

Because I remember this vision, I understand what the poet meant when he wrote about "the *necessary* angel." (Of course I could not have formulated it like this at the time.) It was not a *contingent* thing. It was not an item in the world of time, which time could have made different. It was not enclosed by space or time; space and time were enclosed by it.

The angels in my vision were arranged in order, rank on rank, extending without visible limit, like the sea. There were more angels than all the people in the world. I knew this because my vision was given the gift of instant multiple magnifications, like those scientific films of the universe in which the camera keeps backing up and you see first the local scene, then the city, then the continent, then the planet, then the solar system, then the galaxy, then the supergalaxy. It made me think that the whole universe is probably only an atom in another universe, and each atom in our universe is a whole universe in itself.

Even though the number of angels I saw seemed limitless, yet the angel army had form, structure, and rank. Like the waves of the sea. The whole host was moving, but since all space and time were inside them, they were not moving *from* or *to* anywhere but simply singing or dancing or spinning in place, like the rings of Saturn.

In my vision I also saw the angels flying through the world, and they were going *through* things: not just the air but the ground and mountains, and steel skyscrapers. They were not filmy and wispy like ghosts but *solider* than steel. They were to metal what metal is to air. They could fly through the metal as metal planes could fly through the air.

They were singing and playing music. As my conversation with Evan made clear, playing music is a lot like playing baseball: time is measured by it rather than it being measured by time. So angels *do* play.

St. Thomas Aquinas says that higher animals (like otters and dolphins) play, while lower animals (like worms and sharks and TV executives) do not, because only the higher animals have leftover energy in their "forms," souls, spirits, or life-force even after that form has done its practical work of structuring the body's organic chemistry and giving life to its animal senses and instincts. So the amount of play is an index of the amount of spirit. The higher the animal, the higher the spirit and the more the play. And man plays much more than the highest animal. So angels probably play more than we do, and God plays most of all. (Do you really think that the Creator and Designer of the platypus does not play? He does everything good, and play is good.)

Some day, I hope, Allah will allow this human philosopher to climb inside the mind of an angel.

In the Qur'an, as in the Bible, angels often visit us, usually disguised under human appearances. But they do not stay. Why must they always hurry away? What business are they about? In *The Lord of the Rings,* the hobbits asked the same question about Gandalf (who, Tolkien explicitly said, is an angel). And our dogs ask the same question about us when we leave the house. Why and where do we go? How could they possibly understand our answer? How could we understand the angels'?

Angels fascinate us because they are unknown. If our science eventually comes to know everything in the universe, our sole source of fascination will be the angels.

Rilke says that "beauty is only the beginning of a terror we can just barely endure." He must be speaking of the beauty of angels here, because the beauty of Allah we cannot endure at all, and the beauty of material things we *can* endure.

Augustine says, "Every visible thing in this world is put in charge of an angel." The sea is the largest visible thing in this world, so the sea is probably put in charge of the largest angel.

Who is Mara's angel?

(26) Into the Abyss

October 16: It has been a long time since the greatest tragedy of my life. I take up the pen again today, and I wonder that I can still write at all. I suppose words are my therapy. They don't work, of course. All words are meaningless now. But I am not able to stop them. The only word that is meaningful to me now is "Mara." But the other, meaningless words keep arranging themselves on the paper.

The October 2nd disaster at Fenway Park that Evan and I went to proved to be only an elaborate joke compared to the serious slice of Hell on earth that I found when I returned to the House. I had dropped Evan off at Gordon College, on the North Shore, at the house of his favorite professor, Tom Howard. (His friends all called him Tom Chrysostom, "The Golden-Tongued," but not to his humble face.) I returned to the House just at that time when Evening had swallowed Day and was beginning to digest it. I was alone and depressed, but fully dressed and in my right mind.

As soon as I parked in the driveway, I sensed something terribly wrong. The air felt charged with electricity—literally, physically. As I got out of the car, I looked up at the Hill and saw, standing on the summit of the Hill on the south side, right above the Cauldron, what looked to me like a man made of sparks.

His body was bright red and sparking like an electrical fire. I blinked once and rubbed my eyes. He was still here. He looked like a ghost on fire. I vigorously pinched my skin until it really hurt. He was still there. I was not dreaming.

I will not call him "he" but "IT." IT could not have been a man. I do not think it was any kind of real entity in this universe. I think a tiny Black Hole whose sole activity was to drain something *out* of the universe.

I stood transfixed in the front yard, magnetized, unable to move. IT too was standing still, though the sparks in IT were not. I thought of the Burning Bush. But this was a *dark* fire.

Then I noticed an agitation in the sea some forty feet below IT. The high tide had filled the Cauldron, and the agitation came from there—from the place that had claimed the life of Papa many years ago and then had nearly claimed my own life. Then I saw the source of the agitation in the water: the Serpent was there, just outside the Cauldron's spiraling waters, making a second set of spirals in the deeper water. I knew it was waiting for prey. I blinked twice, hard, but the Serpent was still there. For the first time in my life I began to doubt my sanity.

Then a came a third sight which I know was not a hallucination—alas!—for it was infinitely more terrifying than the first two. *Mara* stood between IT and the edge of the cliff!

I had not noticed her at first because she stood as rigid as a rock. The Serpent waited below her, IT waited above her. In the growing darkness, I could not see her eyes with my eyes, but I could feel her soul's terror with my soul.

Then a third impossible figure arose, and when I saw it I was almost completely convinced I was either insane or asleep. "Three strikes and you're out," I thought. Only one, or at the most two mythological figures could be allowed into the real world, but not three. The third one was the giant Viking that I had seen months before in my dream. He was dressed in armor and held a long, straight sword that gleamed in the dying light. He came out of the earth, through the layer of stones on the beach, strode through the shallow sea to the Cauldron, and began to wrestle with the Serpent. He leaped on the Serpent's back and rode it like a cowboy at a rodeo. It could not shake him off. Then he started hacking at its twisting neck with his sword.

As soon as Mara saw the Viking, she turned away from the sea. Then she saw IT. Just as the Viking lifted up his sword to bring it down on the serpent's neck, IT began to *sizzle* like a branding iron plunged into ice. At that moment my life ended. For at that moment Mara Angelique, Mara the angel, fell, or jumped, or was pushed, into the sea.

It is more than a matter of life or death to me *which* of these three it was. It did not look like a fall, for her feet did not slip from under her. It did not look like a push, for her body did not tumble forward headfirst. And it did not look like a jump, for her legs did not coil and uncoil. It looked like a locomotive plunging through a train station whose floors collapse one by one as the great machine falls into the earth smashing through each floor.

Then came the most nauseating sound I have ever heard in my life: the thud of her head against the rocks before she hit the sea. The exact place on the rock is chiseled in my mind forever, the last place on earth that was privileged to touch her body. When her head was crushed by the unforgiving rock, my heart was crushed in exactly the same way by the unforgiving fate. For my heart was not in my chest, it was in her head.

Her motion seemed to stop, but the rest of the world did not. I had the strange sensation that her body was not moving at all but the whole rocky cliff was being *thrown* at her. She was being stoned.

Then time began again. I saw, as well as heard, her head split open. Blood spurted out, mingling with the sea. When her body hit the water I heard a hiss.

Then a second hiss, which sounded (to my mind, not my ear) like one terrible word, from an unseen mouth. The word was: "MINE!"

The only thought that kept me even slightly sane at that moment was another word, a name, a title, which came into my mind by the mercy of Allah. It was the name of the mouth that spoke that terrible word "MINE." The name was "The Father of Lies."

When Mara's body entered the sea, I no longer saw either the Serpent or the Viking. IT had also disappeared with that last hissing sound. All that was left was the empty Hill and the empty sea. There was no agitation in the water. It was as if she had slipped between the folds of a watery sheet without leaving a single wrinkle.

I stopped breathing. It was impossible to believe that my heart still beat. All life, all heat, all movement throughout the universe must now come to an end. Nothing could ever happen again. Absolute zero had been reached.

My stomach turned to mud. There was a big iron ball in the middle of the mud, and it was pulling me down, down, into the bottomless darkness through the cellar of my soul.

I did not immediately run to see or retrieve her body. I'm not sure why. Perhaps I thought she had in fact left this universe through a Black Hole, or slipped between the sheets of time and space. Perhaps I held out hope that I would wake from this nightmare. Or perhaps I simply refused to live in the heartless, indifferent world that still dared to live, unperturbed, when its finest flower had died.

After a full minute of total paralysis, I fell on the grassy turf of the front lawn, still dotted with dandelions, and *hit* the earth, again and again, targeting all the dandelions within my reach. How dare they keep smiling out the color yellow *now*? After flailing at the earth with both arms, I jumped up to *kick* it, loosening clods of grass. Then I *spit* at it. In these liturgies I spoke dark words in dark tongues, cursing the earth with curses that I had never learned, in words I did not understand.

How could I not hate the universe? The sun, the sun of that new day that had risen when I first saw her, five months ago, on the first day of creation, had just blinked out forever. Forever! How could I not curse the darkness? That curse was my only sanity. To surrender now, to be reconciled to it, to accept it, would be truly insane. It would be to give up my humanity and become a worm. I could not surrender, submit, or accept. I had lost my islam. I had lost my faith. I could no longer say the Shahadah.

I stood up with dirt on my face and in my mouth, my fists clenched and ready to defy the heavens themselves if they were allied with this accursed earth.

Then I sensed IT.

The figure of the Man Made of Sparks had disappeared, along with the

Serpent and the Viking, but IT had not. IT was not simply the Man Made of Sparks; IT was his puppeteer. Perhaps all three figures were only creatures of my imagination, but I knew that IT was real. Perhaps the Viking hero and the Serpent were only puppets in ITs puppet show. Perhaps the whole world was that! Perhaps I myself only jangled at the tip of ITs string. The thought almost made me literally lose my mind.

Then another thought came to save me: the thought of Mara. Mara was not ITs puppet. Mara was ITs victim. Mara was real. Even though Mara was dead, Mara was real, Mara was not IT, Mara refuted ITs claim to be the universal puppet master. She refuted IT more convincingly than I did, even though she was dead and I was alive. I might be seduced to believe that I was only ITs puppet, but I could never be brought to believe that Mara was. That thought of Mara was the "necessary angel" that saved my sanity and my soul. Mara saved my soul even after she may have lost her own. Mara kept me alive even after she was dead.

IT still hung there in the air, invisible but present, hovering, vulturing, waiting. Waiting for what? IT already had Mara. What more did IT want? Then I knew, and shivered: IT was waiting for me.

What was IT? IT was a mouth, a maw, but there was no personality behind the maw. The maw had already committed suicide; it had killed whatever shards of personality it once possessed. IT had eaten itself, like the Worm Orouboros, swallowing itself by its own tail. IT was certainly not human and certainly not animal and certainly not part of this world and even more certainly not part of my fantasies, however awful and consuming my fantasies may have been. IT was so evil that it was beyond good and evil. And IT wanted to eat my soul as it had eaten Mara's body. IT wanted to persuade me that there was nothing but IT. For if that was so, then death was our only good, our only hope, and birth was our supreme mistake. That was ITs dark philosophy, and that philosophy had devoured Mara, and now IT wanted to devour me.

A feeling I had never had before arose in me: pure, righteous hate. I had never had any qualms about hating evil in the abstract, but evil had always appeared in this world as some twist, some perversion in a concrete entity which was good. All entities were good, for all were creatures of Allah. I had always felt guilt in hating entities, whether evil persons like "Uncle" or even evil forces like the wave that killed Papa, or even the Sea Serpent, which had such a beautiful shape. Now I felt the thrill of a perfectly righteous hatred, a Godlike hatred. IT was no longer a creature, IT was a false creator, a false God. IT deserved to be hated and killed exactly as Allah deserved to be loved and surrendered to; and I was right to rejoice and be glad in hating it and killing it, if I could.

Something in me that was not my own mind or will cried out "Allah akbar!" Instantly, IT disappeared, totally and unmistakably. In the shadow left by ITs departure, a huge, wordless longing hung in the air over the sea like a cloud, as palpable as a *thing*. The cloud was as wide and empty as the sea itself, and as heavy.

What waited behind that cloud? I do not know. But as soon as I formulated that question in my mind, the answer came, unwilled. It was a haunting quotation from T.S. Eliot: "some infinitely gentle, infinitely suffering thing."

How can I believe that?

Then I saw the clouds part just enough to let through a tiny light, the eastern sky's last reflection of the sun that had long since set in the west. By that light I saw a flow of water down the face of the rock where Mara had fallen. It was not rainwater, for it had not rained for days. It was not seawater, for the sea was perfectly calm. It was tears from the rock. The rock itself was weeping. Or else it was Heaven weeping, a tear falling to earth from the Throne of Mercy. That tear was to me the only thing of beauty left in this world.

Out of the fading light two white herons suddenly appeared, like angels, suspended between heaven and earth, then disappeared into the unattainable sky.

I heard a sound in the little waves on our rocky beach that I had never heard before. It was the sound Vergil heard more than 2,000 years ago, the sound he called *lacrimae rerum,* "the tears of things," the sigh of the whole world weeping. The sound spoke to my heart. It said that the world was not my enemy but my sorrowing friend.

I replaced the clods of dirt I had kicked up, gently weeping, apologizing to the ruined earth. The fit of mad rebellion had passed like a tornado, leaving in its wake only unalterable death, inconsolable grief, and incalculable loss.

I went into the House. It was a dead house. (Why not? It was a dead world now.) Eva was still sleeping. So were Day and Night and Yak. No smell of bread came from the kitchen. No music came from the music room. I walked upstairs. I fell into bed, and became a stone, a coma, or a corpse—or perhaps merely a totally exhausted, totally defeated son of Adam.

The next thing I remember seeing was the next day's morning light, and the next thing I remember feeling was surprise that I was still alive. What a fool Descartes was when he pointed to his own existence as the most certain, self-evident thing!

Mother had come home late in the evening. The police had come, with searchlights and divers, and dragged Mara's body out of the sea. There were two other people who saw her fall, one from a neighboring house and one from a lobster boat at sea. Both people were almost as close as I was: about 500 feet away, but (as I found out later) neither one saw the Man of Sparks, the Serpent, or the Viking.

I do not believe I was hallucinating. I believe I saw things that were real but invisible to other eyes. How many such things are there in this world? How small-minded must we be to avoid that question all our lives?

I lay awake in bed for perhaps half an hour, thoughtless and feelingless. What could possibly be worth doing any more? Why should I ever get out of bed again? What did get me out of bed was a loud wail from the kitchen downstairs. What worse thing could possibly happen now, I thought. The parting of the sky and the end of the world would be only a triviality now, a welcome diversion. Alas, a worse thing *was* happening. I knew the meaning of the wail. The meaning was something about Mara. The meaning of *everything* was something about Mara now. Mara's absence was the empty sky; it was spread out over the whole world. I glanced at the eastern sky. My hypothesis was confirmed: the sun had risen bloated and bloody. It looked like a bleeding heart. The sea had had its heart torn out.

I ran downstairs and into the kitchen to find Mother showing Eva a wrinkled note. I grabbed it from her hand before she could stop me. I read its words in an instant. Those words, and that instant, are inscribed in my soul as deeply as the Grand Canyon is inscribed on the surface of the earth.

YOU WERE MY LANCELOT, YOU WERE MY KNIGHT.
YOU WERE MY 'ISA, YOU WERE MY SAVIOR.
YOU WERE MY MOON'S SHINING ROAD ON THE SEA.
YOU WERE MY ONLY DOOR OUT OF THE WORLD.
YOU WERE THE ONE THING THAT I HAD TO LIVE FOR
AND NOW YOU ARE GONE.

(27) Recovery

I remember very little of the next few days. Reading Mara's note felt like the last event of my life. For days—seven, I think—I was unaware of events in the outside world at all, though Evan and Libby later told me that Mother took care of all my physical needs, like a baby. I was not in a coma, but I was almost comatose. I did not want to wake up. I did not want to live. What life was left in me? Not even the life of a ghost. Not even the ghost of a ghost.

I do remember a few things, though. One of them was Mister Mumm telling Mother what happened in six words: "The angel fell into the sea." It was the exact sentence I remember Papa speaking, like an incantation. Days later, when I was capable of conversation again, I told Mister Mumm that my Papa had said that sentence when I was very young. Mister Mumm he asked me what I thought Papa meant.

"I don't know," I replied. "He was telling me a story about why the sea is so alive, and why we love it so."

"And what did you think when your Papa told you that story?"

"I think I took it literally, and I actually believed it."

"You were wiser then than you are now," said Mister Mumm.

"But," I asked, "why did you say 'The angel *fell* into the sea'? Angels don't *fall*, like us. They'd have to *leap*." We both knew we were playing with the double meaning of "angel," and that it was terribly important for me to know whether Mara had freely chosen suicide or not.

Mister Mumm's answer was merely: "What do you know about angels, anyway?"

* * * * *

I remember going to Mara's funeral in a sort of trance. Her mother refused to allow me to attend the shivah—quite naturally, she holds me responsible for Mara's death. But the funeral was public, and Mother insisted that I come with her. We inserted ourselves inconspicuously in the back pew of the temple. It was an open coffin funeral, and the undertaker had done a miraculous job. Mara's head had cracked open, but the crack was only in the back, under her hair, unseen. Her face had apparently been untouched by the rocks and now seemed untouched by pain or fear. Her limbs had been broken, but they were reset and lay naturally. She looked comfortable and at peace. When I saw her body, I shook my head and insisted, to Mother, that this was another person, a mistake, the wrong body. I do not remember anything that Mara's body wore, in the coffin, yet I remember vividly the loose threads on Mother's purple sleeves that day.

* * * * *

One other incident that I remember from those hazy days was a set of apparently meaningless nonsense words that kept coming to me, over and over, whether I was fully asleep or only half-asleep. (I think I never was fully awake during those days.) The words were: "DOMINATE KNOWN SOME THICK-NESS AT INTEREST SUBTRACT TOM TOMATO. SAID TOM-TOM DICK FUR-BALL, IT'S A NOBBY TOUR RONNIE MOM MAYO." I kept repeating these words at night in my dreams, and Mother heard them, for she was often at my bedside. She was the umbilical cord who brought me back into the world. She insisted that I write the words down, in my own handwriting. When I asked her why, she said it was so that I could know later that it was I and not she who uttered them. She said they were Latin (they certainly did not look like Latin), and she said that she understood what they meant, but she refused to tell me. "The time is not ripe for the fruit to fall," she said.

One of the first conversations I remember after I emerged into the world again was the only argument I ever won with Mother. She said to me, "Your heart is broken. But that is a good thing." I replied, "But my soul is also broken, and that is not a good thing." She did not reply. She wept.

* * * * *

Nothing educates your mind like a broken heart. It makes you doubt what you once knew, and know what you once doubted. Things that had been close and familiar are suddenly taken far away, and things that had been terrifyingly unfamiliar become more familiar and inescapable than your own skin. (Gandalf said that when he came back from death.)

The most terrifying new thing is my inescapable knowledge that the unspeakable ecstasy that all my life had hovered invisibly just beyond my grasp all of my life was now gone forever, because when it put itself into my hands, I crushed it to death like a butterfly. I think I know how the damned in Hell feel: "Abandon all hope, ye who enter here."

* * * * *

I also remember hearing all the clichés about death and grief buzzing into my ears like flies from the open mouths of otherwise wise and good people who clearly intended the best for me; and I remember wishing I dared to tell them the truth about how insipid and hypocritical they sounded.

One day Eva came to sit beside me on the Deck, where I had been spending most of my waking hours just staring at the Cauldron. After a few minutes of respectful silence, she said: "Jack, this is not the end. This is a wave. You know the law of the wave. After each trough a crest, after each crest a trough. We ride the waves, and they wash us. Remember how we used to talk about that?" She spoke more slowly, quietly, and in shorter sentences than I had ever heard her use before.

"I remember with my head but not with my heart. I cannot feel anything any more."

"You can't even feel the waves any more? The waves that are bigger than we are, the waves that wash everything in and out of our souls?"

"No, Eva, I cannot feel them any more. The waves are not big enough. The galaxy itself is not big enough to wash away the dirt out of my soul, so how could the waves be big enough?"

"Because the waves come from the galaxy-maker, and He is big enough. Nothing is too big for Him. He can wash your soul."

"I do not feel His waves, and I do not feel His wash. I feel only their undertow, and it is unstoppable."

"Yes, that is unstoppable. That is the power of the planet calling each wave home like a mother calling a child."

"I asked Allah to call me home, but He would not do it. I do not have His permission to go." I said this not out of piety but out of desperation. I knew that suicide could never reunite me with Mara, in any world.

"You had a great joy in your love, Jack, before it was taken away."

"It was not taken away. I killed it."

"*It was taken away*," Eva replied, simply.

Those simple words washed a little of the dirt out of my soul's wound. Eva is a wave.

*　*　*　*　*

Another memory stands out from those dim days: the memory of the police coroner assuring me that Mara's brain activity had stopped at the moment she shattered her head on the rock, and that she was dead *before* she hit the sea. To me this was a crucial fact, for it meant that when her body entered the Serpent's realm, her soul was no longer in it; so that whatever lured her down into itself, whether serpent or spirit or Satan, feasted only on her corpse. If the fate of her soul was severed from that of her body, that fate is not a matter of knowledge, and therefore it can be a matter of hope.

The other source of my hope was what the Viking did. He did not conquer the Serpent, but he did distract its eye from Mara long enough—a second is long enough—for her to turn away from it, and from the edge of the cliff for just a moment. At least this is what I think I saw: that one last moment of right direction in her life. If this is true, then the Man of Sparks made her fall contrary to her will. The angel *fell* into the sea; she did not jump. The Viking did not save her body, but he may have saved her soul.

Poor Evan. He seemed to think that I was oppressed more by my own guilt than by Mara's death. Perhaps his Calvinism conditioned him to think that way. Libby thought the same, from her very different conditioning, from modern psychology. But she at least had the wisdom to say nothing, and to just hold me in her arms like a baby for a long while. She looked into my eyes with deep sorrow, and kissed my face, very gently, with her tears and with her lips, especially my eyes. Her eyes understood my eyes even if her mind did not understand my mind.

Poor Evan tried to comfort me with philosophy. That is like propping up a locomotive with soda straws. He explained that my fate was not my choice. "When you are in an enormous wave that destroys everything, you are one of the things destroyed, you are not the destroyer. You are not the wave. The wave is fate. The waves of water come from the other side of the world, from Greenland, from Palestine, and so do the waves of fate. They come through many miles and many people. A wave of water comes from a thousand years ago, and so does a wave of fate. If the winds were a little different a thousand years ago, the waves of water would be a little different now. If one of your ancestors had done something just a little different, you would not be in this wave of fate now. Scientists sometimes call it "the butterfly effect": one more butterfly in Brazil beating its wings can make the difference that makes a hurricane form in Florida a week later."

"Yes, Evan, but I am that butterfly, and I beat my wings in the wrong place and time, so that Mara and all her descendants—all *our* descendants—down through a thousand generations, to the end of the world, and all the good things they would have done, have been condemned to nonexistence. Because of me."

"No, 'Isa. It happened because of your fate, because of the waves, not because of you. You are not the master. You cannot stop fate waves."

"Why not?" I asked, like a pouting child.

"Because of where you stand: you do not stand outside that ocean but in it—in the ocean of fate that flows around the whole round world."

I was not comforted by the combination of good intentions and bad philosophy. Mother knew this, and added, "Here is something you have forgotten, 'Isa. Our fates happen only together, never alone. You think you are alone, and that is why you are in guilt and despair. . . ."

"I *am* alone, and I *am* guilty, that is why I am in despair," I protested. "Those three tortures are *mine*. You can't take them away from me!" I was as ready to fight to defend my guilt and despair as a soldier is ready to fight to defend his country.

Mother did not back away. "Yes, you *are* in guilt and despair, but you are *not* alone, 'Isa. We are with you in your guilt and in your despair, and in your fate. Our fates are never alone. They are always bound together. Like pages in a book."

I was silent. Mother inserted into that silence: "And you know Who is the Author."

I then added the sins of blasphemy and apostasy to the sins of fornication, abandonment, and despair by saying: "No I don't. I no longer know Him, Mother. If He is the one who wrote the story of Mara's fate, how can I say I know Him, and how can I surrender to Him?"

I remember my question vividly but I do not remember Mother's answer. For the first time, she talked to me (gently) about Jesus, but I did not understand a single word of it.

*   *   *   *   *

Here is another remembered incident from those semi-conscious days. One day, as I was entering the kitchen, I heard the sweetly sad strains of "Traces" coming from the kitchen radio, and angrily threw a dish at the radio, breaking both. Mother looked at me seriously, but not with that "You're crazy" look, and said nothing. I think she understood that I could only feel that song as a travesty. I had made no such outburst at Diddly and Squat even when they danced a happy Irish jig, for that was simply irrelevant to me. But "Traces" was intrusive, pharisaical psychobabble.

Later that day Mother played a breath-stoppingly beautiful tape of an English boys' choir singing Joseph Barnaby's "Now the Day is Over":

> **Now the day is over;**
> **Night is drawing nigh.**
> **Shadows of the evening**
> **Steal across the sky.**
>
> **Grant to little children**
> **Visions bright of Thee;**
> **Guard the sailors tossing**
> **On the deep, blue sea.**
>
> **Through the long night watches**
> **May Thine angels spread**
> **Their white wings above me,**
> **Watching round my bed.**
>
> **When the morning wakens,**
> **Then may I arise,**

Pure and fresh and sinless
In Thy holy eyes.

The angelic innocence of the voices and the words, and the beauty of the music, moved my soul. But the beauty of the music did not make my soul beautiful.

*   *   *   *   *

The first three days after Mara's death, I sat out on the Deck unmoving all day, like Christopher Reeve at the end of the movie *Somewhere in Time.* Some time during the third morning, Mother sat her whole considerable self down in front of me on a big old unpainted wooden chair, looked me straight in the eye, and saved my soul. She destroyed my *ghaflah,* the forgetfulness that leads to damnation, by saying, simply, "She is not God, 'Isa. She is not God. Only God is God. *La illa'ha illah' Allah!"* (She chanted it as powerfully as a *muezzin.* Our neighbors must have raised their heads and wondered.) I had neither heard nor said the Shahadah for many days. It was the first drop of water in my desert.

I compared Mother's words with Eva's, running both over in my mind like two melodies in a fugue. Both spoke truth, but Mother spoke the absolute truth. Buddha was wrong about one thing: his absolute. He called it the "pure and spotless eye of the *dharma."* It was the law of *samsara,* the law of all life on earth, the law of the wave, the law of birth-and-death, the law that "whatever is an arising thing, that is also a ceasing thing." This is the law that Buddha called the "diamond" that cuts through all other truths. But it is not the diamond. There is another diamond that cuts through this one. Allah is that true diamond. For it is not true that the only alternative to *samsara* is *Nirvana,* the extinction of *samsara.* The alternative is Allah. It is true, as Buddha said, that everything in the universe is birth-and-death; that everything is a wave. Buddha came close to finding the final formula, the Universal Wave Theory. But he forgot there is also Allah, who transcends the wave.

The thought came to me that I can still sit in the waves of water, which are Allah's waves, Allah's psychiatrist couch, and that may be healing for me.

The next day I did exactly that, on Short Beach, and it was the beginning of my return to life.

Mother told me later that it was not her words that brought me back to life. It was the holy water she threw on me when I refused to hear or speak any words all through the first day after Mara's death. I was so close to coma that I did not even notice the water.

I do not believe the Catholic superstitions such as holy water, and sacraments. But I do not think it is superstitious to remember facts, and it is a fact that water is holy. Water is Allah's second invention, after light, and it reminds us of Him. It has the same paradoxical properties as His angels. On the one hand it is very heavy. Try to lift a filled fish tank, or a fully clothed man whose clothes are soaked. On the other hand, it is also incredibly light: sparkling, transparent, a mirror for sunlight. And it is as agile and active as an angel. (As *its* angel?)

*   *   *   *   *

A few days later (I do not remember how many), I had a conversation with Mother that went something like this:

I was in the middle of a late breakfast of bread and tea. Mother, Yak, and Mister Mumm were the only ones around. I suddenly blurted out: "Maybe it's all meaningless. Maybe this is the time for me to formulate a new philosophy."

Mother immediately shot back: "You're overwrought. This is the *worst* time to formulate a new philosophy."

"Maybe not. Maybe it's the best time, the time of disillusionment. I never noticed that word before—'disillusionment'—what's dissed is illusion!"

"Fine. Diss illusion. But don't diss reality."

"What reality? It's all illusion. Nothing is real, nothing is solid. Deep down, it's shallow. The ultimate is Nothingness. There's nothing really real, really true, really good, or really beautiful any more." I was not posturing; I was speaking what all my emotions and half my intellect actually believed.

Mother just listened. (Toilets wait patiently for excrement.) I went on: "Great thinkers have said so. Schopenhauer, Sartre, Nietzsche, Ecclesiastes, even Buddha. Prove to me they're wrong."

Mother suddenly sprang up. "I'll do better than that. I'll *show* you. Here!" She snatched up the loaf of bread from the table. "This, this thing here. Look at it! Here is your data! When you ask your question, don't forget your data. Start with your data. Maybe there *is* truth and goodness and beauty and maybe there isn't, but you can't find out which it is without any data. Here, smell your data. Touch your data. Eat your data. Then you can say your Shahadah."

"I can't say my Shahadah anymore."

"You *can*, but you won't."

"I want to, but I can't."

"Do you? Do you really want to? 'Isa, you have never lied to me. Is this true? Do you want to?"

"Yes."

"Then I will show you the way from *want to* to *can*. Do you want to be shown the way?"

"Yes."

"Here!"

I thought she was saying: "Hear," in the imperative, but she was pointing to her bread and saying "Here" in the declarative.

"Eat your data, 'Isa. Eat my bread."

I got suddenly suspicious. "I'll eat your bread, Mother, but I won't eat your Catholic mind. You saved my life, and you're my best friend, and I love you. But not your philosophy, or your religion. I've put a stake through its heart. It's a corpse, it's a fake, it's a lie."

"But what about *your* religion, 'Isa? Do you say the Qur'an is a lie now too?"

"Yes! No. I don't know! Maybe all faith is a lie."

"Is Allah a lie?"

I could not say that anti-Shahadah. "No. But Allah is not data. No one has ever seen him."

"But you *have* seen this loaf of bread! You can deny your unseen data, if you insist, but not this. Hold onto this bread, 'Isa. It will bring you back to God, and to hope. It's your life preserver. But you have to hold on to it. Here, smell it."

"Why should I surrender to bread any more than to Allah?"

"Because bread is here, it is data, it is not nothing."

"Maybe both are nothing, both bread and Allah, the creature and the Creator. Maybe everything is nothing!"

I spoke these words, but I cannot honestly say whether I believed what I said with a little of my soul, or with half of my soul, or with most of my soul. It felt like most.

Mother stopped me in my tracks with: "Do you also say that Mara is nothing?"

I shivered. Mother insisted on an answer: "Is she also nothing? Is that your new religion and your new philosophy?"

"Yes! I killed her," I sobbed. "I killed her, and now she is nothing."

"Will you now kill her again with your philosophy? Do you say she is nothing with your tongue, now, here, in my kitchen?"

It was cruel but effective. "No," I sobbed. "I will not say Mara is nothing. But . . . but *I* am nothing. I feel dead. Deader than Mara."

Mother then just hugged me, and I became limp as a corpse in her lap. "You will rise again, 'Isa. Now eat a piece of my data. It's raisin. Your favorite."

Mothers have mysterious powers.

"But Mother, there is one thing you do not understand. You said I *will* not surrender. But I *cannot*. It is not my will, or my mind, but my pain, that is rebelling."

"Yes, 'Isa. I know. But you *are* not your pain."

When I had digested that piece of her bread, she added another: "And Mara *is* not her death."

Only after I nodded did she add her third piece: "And neither are you."

"But I am a failure. I killed Mara."

Mother did not contradict me.

"I am no longer Allah's servant. I am a rebel. I am a failure. Religion is not for rebels and failures."

"Yes it is, 'Isa, yes it is! Religion is for failures and rebels who repent. Religion is a crutch, for cripples, and we are all cripples. Didn't Eva and Diddly and Squat teach you that?"

Mother's words gave me the ability to pray for the first time since Mara's death. It was only a confession and a cry: "O Allah, the Compassionate, the Merciful, unless You save me, I will perish! Unless You give me the power to surrender to You, I will deny You. Unless You perform a miracle in my soul, I will not have the strength there to do that first thing, that most necessary thing, that surrender. Unless You give me Your miracle, I cannot give You my surrender."

And Allah the Merciful, the Compassionate, blessed be His name forever, reached down and gave me that miracle. No psychologist could understand it. He gave me a terrible and wonderful gift, a double gift. I confessed to Him these two terrible truths: "Now I know who I am and who You are. I am the one who is nothing, and You are the One who is everything." And at that moment, for the first time, I think I understood my beloved Sufi teachers.

This brought me back to the place where I could now ask the question millions have asked: Why does the good God let us suffer so much? The question was about Mara's suffering more than mine. I deserved my suffering; she did not.

When I asked Mother that classic question, she smiled, ever so slightly, and then answered with utmost seriousness and simplicity: "We have to learn to suffer so that we can suffer God, as the beach suffers the waves."

She added, "He is like the sea, and He wants to flood us. Drown us, even."

*   *   *   *   *

My first *hopeful* prayer was the hope for Allah's just *punishment*. "Your wrath, O Lord, is better than man's love," I confessed to Him. "I need Your wrath, because it is Yours. I want to place myself into the fire of Your judgment. I fear it, but it is Yours, and therefore it is right."

I prayed this at the Drum, which seemed somehow smaller than ever before. I looked for the curious white bird who seems to live there, but did not find him, though a flock of similar but far tinier birds fluttered up and away at my approach. I caught a glimpse of a man on the rocks of Bass Point, a quarter of a mile away across the water, and he too seemed impossibly tiny, almost invisible in the surrounding immensities. I myself felt tiny. Unseen voices from the sea seemed to be saying to me: "Take comfort, Small One. You are not the meaning of the world. We and you are both threads in a greater tapestry of a high and holy weaving." I realized that my own habitual perspective, in which I loom so large, is an illusion; that my body takes up half my eye but far less than half the world; that things appear big only because they are so close.

Yet even as these voices reminded me of my unimportance, they also reminded me of my importance, saying something like this: "You also speak to us a meaning we cannot speak for ourselves, for you have the gift of thought. *You* must lift us up to Allah in praise and surrender."

Then, as soon as these voices from the sea magnified my image of myself, they humbled it again: "Yet in some ways your role is less than ours. For we can live without you, but you cannot live without us."

The sea was prophesying, and the point of its prophecy was the holy word of peace through surrender. Every one of Allah's creatures, beginning with His largest creature, the sea, spoke the same word: *islam,* peace through surrender. I knew now why the sea so drew my soul: it was a mighty prophet, a concrete Qur'an. It, and all the smaller seas in the world, in fact all of Allah's creatures, spoke the same single perfect word, and I alone was resisting it.

When I saw this, I stopped resisting it. I said my Shahadah.

*   *   *   *   *

When I returned to the Islamic Center, I had a long talk with the imam, a wise and holy man. He said I had nearly lost my faith because I am an intellectual and a loner and do not live with other Muslims. "Our faith is not just a creed for the mind of a philosopher, 'Isa. It is a whole culture, a whole way of life. You should live with Muslims, not Christians. You are vulnerable now, because you are in pain, and your soul is soft with pain. They will take advantage of this. They will try to make you a Christian. That is what they are commanded to do by their holy book, to convert the world to their religion, just as we are commanded to do."

"No, they will not do that. I know them. They have never taken advantage of me that way. They are my friends."

*   *   *   *   *

But if the imam had heard the conversation Mother and I had that very evening, he would have said, "I told you so."

I had had a fit of guilt and despair as soon as the sun went down. (I was never afraid of the dark before. But now it brings with it an inner darkness.) I blurted out, "Nothing can make this right. Nothing can heal this wound."

Mother was silent.

"Tell me what can heal this wound. You can't tell me, because there *is* nothing."

"I can tell you. There is something."

"What? Tell me. Don't hold it back. I want to hear it."

"No, you don't."

"Don't tell me what I want to hear! Tell me what you have to say. Tell me what can heal me."

"The blood of God."

"Blasphemy! Idiocy! God is perfect. God cannot bleed. God cannot suffer."

"God can do anything."

"God cannot suffer."

"Then you have no hope. For then you can do something God cannot do. You can suffer."

"Why are you so cruel today?"

"It would be more cruel to lie to you. Other people lie to you. The modern world lies to you. America lies to you. I will never lie to you, 'Isa."

"Do you believe Islam lies to me?" My eyes narrowed.

"Islam tells you truth, profound truth."

"If you believe that, why are you a Christian? Why aren't you a Muslim?"

"Maybe I can explain it this way. Science tells you truth about the world, doesn't it?"

"Yes."

"But Buddhism tells you a deeper truth about the world, or about our desire for the things of the world, a truth that science doesn't tell you: the truth that our selfish desire for the things of the world distorts everything in us and everything in the world. Is this not so?"

"Yes."

"But Buddhism doesn't tell you about Allah, does it?"

"No."

"But Islam does."

"Yes. What's your point?"

"That even profound truth isn't necessarily the whole truth. That even deep truth isn't necessarily the deepest truth. I believe Islam tells you the truth about God. I even believe it is God's truth, divine revelation, whether it came from the Jews and Christians that Muhammad met or whether it came directly from Allah through the angel Gabriel, as you believe. Truth is truth. And your God is the true God. But I also believe that Christ tells you more about God, about the one true God."

"What's the 'more'?"

"That God is love." She saw my scowl, and immediately added, "You know I don't mean sentiment. I mean a love that's so tough that it can bring good out of evil, even great good out of great evil."

"Even Mara's death?"

"Even Mara's death.

"What good could come from that?"

"Good grief, I don't know. I'm not God. But God *is.* *'There is no God but God'*—remember? And He can do *anything.*"

"I know what you're thinking, Mother. You believe He did something like that 2,000 years ago when He let Jesus be killed. Well, I don't believe that."

"I know. I'm not trying to convert you. I'm just telling you what I believe."

I believe her, though I don't believe what she believes.

*   *   *   *   *

One of the reasons I trust Mother is that she seems almost as shattered by Mara's death as I am, though she hides it better. I think her soul has many layers of fat, like her body, while mine is thin and bony. She really believes it when she says that we are all responsible for Mara's death. She doesn't minimize my role, she just adds hers and everyone else's. We all forsook the House that day, for the first time ever—every single one of us. Even Eva wasn't really *there.* One person's presence would have made the difference.

We all failed Mara. It was *our* failure, even if 99% of it was *my* failure. Mother says she blames herself the most. "What did you do?" I asked.

"I loved the House more than the work of the House."

It turns out she did *not* go to the conference, as I had thought, but went to see a lawyer to prevent the mortgage company from repossessing the House. And she got back late because she missed her bus. I told her, "That sounds like a pretty good excuse to me."

She replied, "When we start giving excuses, the time has come to do what we give excuses for not doing. I broke the Rule of Perpetual Hospitality. I stayed here even for the hurricane, but I didn't stay for Mara."

"You're being too hard on yourself," I argued. "None of us can be perfect all the time."

"Indeed! That's why we have to cover for each other. That's why Mister Mumm was there to save your life when you and Evan foolishly rowed out to Egg Rock that day. I should have made sure someone was covering for me, but I didn't. I forgot that we're at war. No soldier would do that on a battlefield."

You can't argue with Mother.

She added, "Mary was always there for Jesus. I wasn't there for you. I didn't live up to my name."

"Neither did I. I didn't save Mara. I was born to do that, and I didn't do it."

We all failed her. Evan and I were at the game. Libby went surfing. Diddly and Squat were out making money. Everyone was "doing their own thing." But that's not why we exist. We exist to do each other's things.

Where was Lazarus? He was in jail, of all things, for contempt of court. He had refused to take off what he calls his "Jewish crucifix," a golden gas chamber which he wore around his neck in public. This offended Jews,

Christians, *and* atheists! I thought that was a great achievement, and told him so, but he replied, "I thought I went to jail for love. I didn't."

Mother blames Mister Mumm especially, though for the life of me I can't see why. I don't know where he was, or why.

I keep turning over and over in my mind the three figures I saw. They sound like something out of a fairy tale. But this story didn't turn out like the fairy tales. The Viking didn't slay the dragon. That's one reason why I can believe that what I saw was not a fairy tale, but real.

When I told Mother about the Viking, I asked, "If he was real, why would God send him to slay the serpent and then *not* decree that he do it? Why send him at all? He looked like a mighty warrior, but he didn't save Mara."

"I don't know," she confessed. Then she came up with a fascinating answer: "Maybe it was for *his* salvation. Maybe he had to fight that fight to redeem himself for something evil he had done. And maybe he had to lose his fight to win it. Remember what I said to you yesterday about losing? Losing is something we all need just as much as winning, you know. Maybe that was the first battle he ever lost, the first failure he ever had to accept. Maybe that was his first surrender, his first islam. Maybe that was the only way he could become a good Muslim."

I think Mother is wiser than my imam. I know my imam is wrong about Mother: everything she has ever said or done to me has made me a better Muslim.

*   *   *   *   *

I was so fixated on the Viking that I decided to do some serious research. And this is what I found!

(28) Vikings on Nahant

After believing for centuries that Columbus discovered America, America at last discovered its discoverers: the Vikings.

They were beautiful and terrible long men in their beautiful and terrible longboats. The boats looked like giant wooden swans with proud, curved necks and high-held heads. Their boats looked like their souls. The men who made and sailed them were "proud" in both the good and bad senses of the word: they were noble and valiant and heroic, but they were also cruel and violent and arrogant. They were the "blond beasts" that haunted the dark dreams of Nietzsche and the darker dreams of Hitler; the primeval heroes whose image would give the Nazis a mythic dimension that no other modern tyrants ever had. A thousand years after the Vikings died, the bored and decadent spirit of Europe would prove to be more defenseless against their spirit than its lands and beaches had been against their boats.

Viking longboats weighed eight tons, yet drew only three feet of water. Their lines were the most graceful lines in the history of human transportation, perfectly adapted to the swells of the sea, offering the least resistance and the most cooperation with the fundamental forces of nature. "Soul surfers" would see the longboats as the world's first longboards. They did not "conquer" the waves, they became part of the waves.

Most of the Vikings' artifacts had the distinctive shape of the wave: swan's neck, gull's belly, serpent's curve, dragon's tail, lunar crescent, flying wing. No other culture has been so in love with the form of the sea's waves, even though no culture has ever lost more of its heroes to the sea's waves. The wave could not be their enemy because it was their identity.

Vikings from Norway had settled in Iceland by 870 A.D. When they arrived they found a people they called "Scotties" or "Culdees" who had already been there for 100 years. Some of them were the descendants of Irish monks who had fled the Viking invasions that had destroyed their monasteries in Ireland. Icelanders today consider themselves of mixed blood, part Norwegian, part Irish.

By 978 A.D. over 5,000 people lived in Iceland. One of them was Erik the Red, the 22-year-old red-bearded head of the Thorvaldson family. Erik's temper matched his beard. He killed two of his neighbors over some land, and the case went to court. The Vikings in Iceland, who settled disputes by a legal council called "Althing" ("the Thing"), banished Erik from Iceland for three years.

Erik took his family, three friends, and two servants in a 60foot boat 200 miles northwest to Greenland, to wait out his exile there. Greenland had been discovered in the year 900 by a merchant from Iceland named Gunbjorn. The standard view among historians is that the name "Greenland" was a "salesman's pitch," a creative lie; but Erik found grassy pasturelands and ten-foot-high willow and birch trees in protected fjords along the southern coast, with plenty of fish, seals, and edible animals. When he returned to Iceland in 986 he persuaded many Icelanders to join him in colonizing Greenland. Twenty-five ships and 750 people set out, but only 14 ships and 480 people arrived at Eriksfjord on the southwest coast. Storms sank or turned back the others. But within ten years there were 2,000 Icelanders in Greenland.

In 999 A.D., according to the *Floamanna Saga,* "**Leif, the 17 year old son of Erik the Red, in year 999 A.D., sailed to Norway with goods from Greenland to trade.**" He spent that winter in Norway, where King Olaf taught him the new religion of Christianity. Olaf had converted a few years before, and Norway was now officially Christian. Leif returned to Greenland in the spring as a missionary as well as a merchant. One of his converts was his mother Thohild (Tjodhild), who had the first Catholic church built. Another was his younger brother Thorvald (Thorwald).

While visiting all the outlying houses in Greenland as a Christian missionary, Leif met Bjarni Herjolfsson, who 12 years before had sailed south and landed somewhere in North America, discovering three lands, one rocky ("Helluland" ["Rock Land"]) and two forested ("Markland" ["Wood Land"] and "Vinland" ["Vine Land"]). Leif decided to explore these new lands himself.

According to three handwritten sagas (*Flatey Book, Hauksbok,* and *Eiriks Saga,* also called *Vinland Norse Saga,* written by Ari Thorgilson 100 years later), Leif bought Bjarni's boat and sailed with 35 men south to find this new land. It was 1000 A.D., 620 years before the Pilgrims stepped ashore at Plymouth Rock. In 1000 A.D., Christian Europe awaited the end of the world. They were right. It *was* the end of *a* world (*aion,* eon, era), though it was not the end of *the* world (*ge,* planet earth).

Leif found Helluland, and the sagas say that **Leif and his men saw no grass, but only craggy flat rocks between sea and ice. It was barren, with no good qualities.** This was not Labrador, for the Vikings already knew and named that place. Its name was "Furdustrand" (Frost Land), and they imported timber from there to Greenland, since that was the thing they most sorely missed. Birch and willow wood, which grew in a few sheltered parts of Greenland, were not strong enough for boats or roofs. Norse historian Hjalmar Holand deduces that Helluland was the northern tip of Newfoundland.

Leif then sailed even farther south from Helluland and reached Markland, which he described as **a flat, forested land.** This was perhaps Nova Scotia. A nor'easter arose, and they had to put out to sea. Nor'easters usually last for three days, and blow ships in a southerly direction. The sagas say that after this they **sighted land again after two days of sailing in a southwesterly direction.** This probably brought them to New England.

This third land they called "Vinland" because of the abundance of grape vines. Now grape vines are not found in abundance as far north as Labrador or Newfoundland, which are the locations some historians identify with Vinland.

> **The discovery of the wild grapes establishes the position of Wineland as somewhere at any rate south of Passamaquoddy Bay (Maine) in latitude 45 degrees, the northern limit of the vine in America.**
> **(T.D. Kendrick,** *A History of the Vikings*)

> **Many consider that Vinland extended as far south as New England . . . The northern limit along the east coast in North America for the growth of wild grapes is approximately 42 degrees north, in Massachusetts.**
> **(Helge Instad,** *Westward to Vinland*)

In *Eiriks Saga* Leif described Vinland as full of (1) wild grapes, (2) self-sown corn, (3) wheat, (4) sweet dew, (5) a snowless winter, (6) and frost-free ground all year. This does not match the usual limitation of Vinland to locations north of Massachusetts. Not a single one of these six items occurs north of Boston.

And it stands to reason that adventuresome, fearless and inquisitive men like these, in search of warmer southern lands, would have sailed farther south than Newfoundland, where their settlements have already been identified.

Edward F. Gray, in *Leif Eriksson, Discoverer of America*, also notes that

> **Various writers have appropriately drawn attention to the similarity of the Cape Cod region and its products with the descriptions and products of Vinland in the Sagas. . . . Not a river, cape, island, hill or bay in Vinland is assigned a different consecutive position in the Vinland voyages to those we can easily trace in the southeast portion of the Commonwealth of Massachusetts. (p. 85)**

Robert Ellis Cahill writes in *New England's Viking and Indian Wars*:

> **The Norse Sagas' descriptions of what Leif saw in this new land fits many places, but none, I think, more perfectly than Cape Cod, Massachusetts. The island of "sweet dew" could be one of many off the seaward side of the Cape, possibly Nantucket Island. One island has actually disappeared over the centuries off the Cape due to**

currents and sand erosion. The shoals at the "elbow" of the Cape near Monomoy Point continue to be a dangerous entry to the west for boats, and Bass River, which leads to an inland lake at South Yarmouth, fits the Sagas' description to a T. Also, there is no other distinctive northern facing cape or peninsula in New England but Cape Cod . . .

It almost goes without saying that anyone staying the winter north of Boston would see snow, and a lot of it, as would anyone wintering anywhere else in New England except possibly Cape Cod. At the Cape, a winter without snow has occurred a few times even during my lifetime. Because of the Gulf Stream, the seaward side of the Cape is warmer and is often without snow.

There are many other pieces of physical evidence of the Viking presence in New England, such as stones with Viking runes, possible Viking towers, Viking coins, and even what seems to be a Viking corpse:

Provincetown, where the Mayflower made first landfall in 1620, may well have been Thorwald's "Keelness." It was near here, with the Mayflower anchored off Provincetown at the tip of Cape Cod, the Pilgrims dug into an Indian mound, hoping to find dried corn that the Indians had stored for the winter. Instead, they uncovered . . . graves. . . . The body of the man had "fine yellow hair still on it, and some of the flesh unconsumed," writes Plymouth Governor Bradford. . . . Buried with him were . . . three old iron things and a knife." This obviously was not the grave of an Indian.

Leif and his 36-man crew sailed back north in the spring. Passing Helluland, they saw five "Skraelings" (Indians, literally "screamers") on an island. They landed there and the Skraelings ran away, but two women and a bearded man "sank into the ground and disappeared." The Vikings captured two boys and brought them back to Greenland as slaves. They were not Indians but white people who spoke Gaelic and were understood by two of the Vikings, Haki and Haekia, whom the Vikings called "Gaelic runners" (scouts). The two boys said,

Our houses are underground, and we are castaways from our people, who live across the water . . . we are ruled by two kings, Avaladamon and Valdidia, who dress in white robes.

The Irish "Culdee" monks whom the Vikings drove out of Ireland and who settled in Iceland wore white robes.

The narrative of our story now passes to *Eiriks Saga,* and to a third voyage. (The first was Bjarni's, the second was Leif's, and the third was Thorvald's.)

Now there was much talk about Leif's Wineland voyage, and it seemed to Thorvald, his brother, that the land had been far too little explored. Then Leif spoke with Thorvald: "Off you go, my brother, if you want to, to Wineland."

And so it was done. Now Thorvald got ready for this voyage with 30 men, under the direction of Leif his brother. Then they readied their ship and stood out to sea, and nothing is told of their voyage before they reach Wineland at Leif's Booths, and laid up their ship and did not stir over the winter and caught fish to eat.

And in the spring Thorvald said they must put their ship in order, and that the ship's boat with some men in it should go westward around the shore and explore there during the summer. The country seemed beautiful to them and well wooded, and not much land between the shore and the woods, and white beaches. It was thick with islands there, and much shallow water.

They found no men's houses. . . . But they came on a grain barn made of wood. They found no other trace of man's hand, and they came back and arrived at Leif's Booths in the fall.

And the next summer Thorvald took the ship eastward and then north around the coast.

(The coastline of America curves continually eastward and north from North Carolina to Nova Scotia. The coastlines of Newfoundland and Labrador, however, curve the other way, westward and north.)

Then a gale struck them, off a headland, and drove them ashore there, and smashed the keel under the ship, and they had a long hold-up there and repaired their ship. Then Thorvald spoke with his crew: "Now I want us to stand this keel up on the headland here and call it Keel Ness (Kjalarness, Keel Cape)." And so they did.

Coincidentally, Cape Cod is shaped like the keel of a Viking longboat.

Then they put out from there and . . . along the shore . . . and up to th headland that jutted out there. It was all wooded.

If you look at a map, the first headland that you will see jutting out into the Atlantic northwest of Cape Cod is Nahant. Henry Cabot Lodge wrote:

The men of our race who first set eyes on Nahant . . . were Norsemen, followers of Leif and Thorwald. . . . That the Norsemen came as far south as Rhode Island seems reasonably certain. The long boats of the Vikings must at that time have passed East Point (on Nahant), and it is not beyond the bounds of fair conjecture to identify Nahant with one of the most striking scenes of the old tales. Thorwald, who came

after Leif Erikson, on his return passed by the point of Cape Kjarlanes or Keel Cape, which is considered to be Cape Cod, and thence steering westward he came to a bold promontory stretching out into the sea. There he anchored and there he was attacked by the Skrellings, as the Norsemen called the natives. They beat off the red men, inflicting heavy loss upon them, but in the fight Thorwald was killed. On the rocky promontory he was buried, and the point was named Cape Krossanes (Cape Cross). This identification of the places mentioned in the Sagas is largely guesswork, but we have fair ground to suppose that Thorwald, one of the old Norse fighters, lies buried somewhere in Nahant.

(Henry Cabot Lodge, *Nahant: A Historical Address*)

William Howgaard states, in *The Voyages of the Norsemen to America*, that **"Cape Cod itself may have been Kjalarness. Krossness may have been Nahant."** (p. 226; cf. also p. 248.)

There are three rocky fingers that Nahant stretches out into the sea: East Point, Bass Point, and Bailey's Hill. The only one that has a shallow bay next to it suitable for landing a boat is Bailey's Hill. Tiny Nahant harbor sits next to it today, with its fishing fleet.

Then they bring up their ship and run gang-planks ashore and Thorvald goes up on the land with all his men. Then he spoke: "It is beautiful here, and here is where I would build my farm."

The parallel account in *The Greenlanders' Saga* has him say: **"Here I will make my home."** The wording becomes important in light of the prophetic way he interprets it in his dying speech later that same day.

Then they go to the ship, and they see across the dunes in from th headland three humps, and they went over and saw three skin boats (canoes) there and three men under each.

Eskimos (Inuit) do not make any kind of boat big enough to cover three men. Thus this incident must have taken place in Indian country, to the south, not Inuit country, in the Arctic. Yet many historians identify these Native Americans with Eskimos. But the Vikings' name for them, "Skrellings," means "screechers." How many times have you heard Eskimos war-whooping in the movies?

Then they divided their force and seized them all, only one got away with his boat. They kill the other eight and go back up on the headland and looked about and saw humps further in the firth, and reckoned that people would be living there.

Did Thorwald regret these killings? Was his next decision, to defend but not attack, an attempt to do penance for them, in obedience to the new law of his new God, and the new notion that wars must be just and holy? In any case, it came to that: to be killed rather than to kill, this time; to be sacrificed for his people, like Odin according to the Norse story, and like Jesus, according to the Christian gospels—as we shall see from what happens next:

After that such a heaviness comes on them that they could not stay awake, and they all fall asleep.

This is utterly out of character for Viking warriors in the middle of the day, who can stay awake all night on watch. The saga clearly suggests that this was a supernatural torpor, for it required a supernatural wake-up call:

Then a voice called to them and they all woke up. Here is what the voice says: "Wake up, Thorvald, and all your men, if you want to stay alive, and get to your ship, you and all your men, and pull away from land as quickly as you can."

Where did this voice come from?

Then down the firth came hundreds of skin boats and made for them. Then Thorvald spoke: "We must get wattle on board and shelter as well as we can, but hardly fight back."

Another strange thing! It is not like Vikings not to fight back. Was Thorwald making a last attempt to obey his new God? *The Greenlanders' Saga* has Thorwald say:

"We must defend ourselves, but not attack. Up the breastworks on the gunwales." Then they raised a shield-wall along the boat's gunwales. So they do, and the Skraelings shot at them for a while and then flee away as fast as they could, each a different way. Then Thorwald asked his men if they were wounded at all; they said they were not wounded.

Notice Thorwald's selflessness and his success in saving every single man alive, just as the Voice had promised—except one:

"I have got an arrow wound under my arm," says he, "for an arrow came between the gunwale and my shield and in under my arm, and here is the arrow, and this will be my death."

What are the chances of an arrow getting exactly through that narrow opening, and of striking just that fatal soft spot on Thorwald's body? There are just too many strange coincidences about this story to make sense of it without a Higher Hand at work. Next come his prophetic words:

"Now I advise you to get ready to go back as quickly as you can the way you came, and me you must take to the headland that I thought was so good for a farm. It may be that the truth was on my tongue, that I

should dwell there for a while. There you must bury me and put crosses at my head and feet, and call that headland Cross Ness from now on." Now Thorvald died and they did everything as he had told them.

The Greenlanders' Saga has him say:

"Carry me to that headland where I so much wanted to make my home, for it seems it was the truth I spoke when I said I should dwell there for a while."

Note that both sagas say not "forever" but only "for a while." Thorwald seems to be predicting some further migration or movement of his body, or his spirit, after "a while."

But his body was never found, though his brother tried the next year:

Now Thorstein Erikson is keen to go to Wineland for the body of Thorvald his brother, and he got the same ship ready and chose a crew of tall strong men and had 25 men with him and Gudrid his wife, and they sail out to sea when they are ready, and out of sight of land. They were blown about all summer and did not know which way they were going.

After Thorwald's death Leif's third son Thorstein was angry at Thorwald's crew for giving him a Christian burial. Thorstein, like his father Erik, had remained a pagan, and strongly believed that a dead Viking warrior must be placed in an afterboat, ignited, and set out to sea where the god Odin would escort his soul to Valhalla. But the storm blew him so far off course that he sighted the coast of Ireland. He gave up the quest for Vinland and Thorwald's body, returned to Greenland, and died a few years later of the Black Plague.

So say the sagas. *The Greenlanders' Saga* and *Eirik the Red's Saga* are both available as translated by M. Magnusson and H. Palsson in *The Vinland Sagas* (London, Penguin Books, 1965).

According to the *Hauksbok,* Thorfinn Karlsefni succeeded in finding Vinland in 1010 A.D. He planned to settle there permanently with 158 other Greenlanders in three boats, loaded with livestock. They found Keel Cape, with Thorwald's broken keel still standing. They also found grapes and corn. Sailing north from there, they found a large river with an island and strong currents at its mouth. Up the river there was a small lake, where they built houses along its shores. There were marsh grasses here for the cattle to eat, and bird eggs so numerous that **you could not walk without stepping on them.**

They called the place "Straumfjord" and wintered there. Straumfjord may well be the Kennebunc River just south of Bath, Maine. Norse artifacts have been found there.

*   *   *   *   *

Pope Alexander VI described Greenland as "the world's end" when he sent missionaries there. The Vikings loved this wild, untamed land. It was an icon of their own spirit. But the sundering sea, the advancing glaciers and cold after 1200 A.D., and the small numbers of the Viking population, all ensured their eventual death. In 1341 the Pope sent a priest, Ivar Bardson, from Norway to Greenland to be Greenland's bishop. It was thought that 9,000 people lived there, in two settlements. But Ivar found no one alive, only wild chickens, cows, and sheep.

Some believe the Vikings died of starvation because of their stubborn unwillingness to adapt to the land and to Eskimo ways. Others believe they were killed by the Eskimos. Others believe they died of the Black Plague. Still others believe they intermarried with the Eskimos, adopted their way of life, and disappeared into them like a cloud into the sky. A last theory is that they emigrated to Vinland, intermarried with the Indians, and assimilated to *them*. There are serious problems with each theory.

Perhaps there was another cause as well, which historians who see only this side of the tapestry are forbidden to speak of: according to the annals of the Bishop Gisli Oddsson, they abandoned their new God. When their faith died, they died. Fate replaced faith, and the dooms of Odin fell upon them.

Thorwald was the first man of the Old World to die in the New, baptizing it in his blood. If he was buried here on Nahant, his spirit seems to have been so dominant that it kept all others out, for Nahant is the only town in Massachusetts that has no ghost stories at all, despite its long, crowded, and famous history. Perhaps that work was his penance.

*   *   *   *   *

Scientists now think that humanity originated either in Africa or the Near East, and then migrated for hundreds of thousands of years. One group turned east to Asia and eventually North America by way of Alaska, when there was a land bridge across the Bering Strait. The other group turned west to Europe. Humanity completed its great circle at the first meeting of the Europeans (the Norsemen) and the native Americans. The first literal contact was the contact between Thorwald's flesh and the arrow that found its way under the gunwale and into his armpit.

The death of Thorvald **"was decisive for more than Thorvald. It made Karl Sefni realize that though the land was good, they could never live in peace there . . . so Karl decided to abandon his attempt to establish a permanent colony in Vinland."** (Patrick Huyghe, *Columbus Was Lost,* p. 149) If Thorwald had *not* been killed—if that one odd arrow had not defied all odds—history would have changed enormously, for the Vikings would have colonized America half a millennium before Columbus.

(29) Tying Up Destiny's Threads

Long before discovering that Thorwald may well be buried here on Nahant, I found myself repeatedly, irresistibly, and unaccountably drawn to Bailey's Hill whenever I came to Nahant. Only afterwards did I discover that Thorwald Erikson may well be buried on the beach that is now literally my back yard.

When I was about ten I did not dare to go down to the cellar of my house for many months because I had a recurrent nightmare about a giant buried in the earth underneath the cellar, on the other side of a round wooden door in the wall that led nowhere but into the earth. The giant looked like a Viking. This was probably the forgotten source of that first nightmare that I had after coming to live at the House, the dream of the giant coming out of the ground.

I cannot help philosophizing: What threads bind Thorwald Erikson to me?

All threads are held by the hand of Allah, and they are invisible to us (unless we are angels). But occasionally we see a few protrude from the underside of the tapestry.

Take Joseph, for instance. If the story in the Jewish scriptures is true, all Jews in history owe their existence to Joseph's cheap Egyptian tailor. For after his brothers sold him into Egyptian slavery, and after he worked his way up into the position of steward of the house of Potiphar, Pharaoh's general, if his tailor had not cheated on the threads of his mantle, that garment would not have come apart in the hands of Potiphar's wife when he fled from her seductions, and it would not have constituted the circumstantial evidence that put him in prison and in a position to prophetically interpret the dreams of his fellow prisoner, Pharaoh's ex-baker, that he would be restored to favor, then win Pharaoh's attention and trust by interpreting Pharaoh's dream when the baker remembered Joseph in prison, and save Egypt from famine by understanding the dream of seven skinny cows eating seven fat cows as predicting seven years of plenty followed by seven years of famine, and save the lives of his seventy relatives, the only Jews in the world so far, whom he inveigled down to Egypt to survive. Every Jew alive today owes his life to one cheap Egyptian tailor.

You yourself probably owe your life to a broken thread of leaf that held an acorn fast until a frisky squirrel one day accidentally swatted it down into a pile of dry leaves ten feet to the right of your twenty-year-old grandfather, who, being right-handed, habitually looked left. But this sound turned his head to the right and made him notice your great-grandmother for the first time, a pretty girl sitting on a park bench fifty feet away. One thing led to another and here you are.

If one thread of protoplasm had impeded that sperm cell that carried half your genetic code before it entered the taxi of your mother's ovum, you would not exist.

This is the way world history moves. Compared with real history, dragons and elves are not fantastic at all.

"Some say that to the gods we are like flies idly swatted by boys on a summer day. Others say that not a hair falls from our head without the will of the Heavenly Father." (Thornton Wilder, *The Bridge of San Luis Rey*) Either everything is, ultimately, chaos, or else everything is, ultimately, divine providence.

All great cultures have believed in some form of divine providence, or destiny. Either it was a fate that ruled over men and gods alike, like the Norse Norns or the Greek *Moira,* or it was the will of the one Creator-God. For without a Destiny there is no Story.

The Norse thought of Destiny as *threads,* woven on soapstone spindles by cold, old, horrid, heavenly hags called Norns. The spindle whorls shaped the threads into the form of waves. The threads went round the spindle, round the spinning world of time. Spindles are spirals, and spirals have two dimensions, a vertical as well as a horizontal; so the threads not only connected temporal events in our world, but also connected our world to eternity.

Alyosha Karamazov saw those threads. He saw them at that turning point in his life, midway through *The Brothers Karamazov,* when he had his transforming mystical vision of the earth that enabled him to love it even in all its horror and pain and injustice and kiss it, as his brother Ivan could not do, beyond reason but not beyond vision:

> **"The vault of heaven, full of soft, shining stars, stretched vast and fathomless above him. The Milky Way ran in two pale streams fro the zenith to the horizon. . . . The silence of the earth seemed to melt into the silence of the heavens. The mystery of earth was one with the mystery of the stars. Alyosha stood, gazed, and suddenly threw himself down on the earth. He did not know why he embraced it. He could not have told why he longed so irresistibly to kiss it, to kiss it all. But he kissed it, weeping, sobbing and watering it with his tears, and vowed passionately to love it, to love it for ever and ever. . . . There seemed to be threads from all those innumerable worlds of God, linking his soul to them, and it was trembling . . . something firm and unshakable as that vault of heaven had entered into his soul. . . . Never, all his life long, could Alyosha forget that minute."**

Those threads are real. They are the warp of the tapestry of Destiny. Human choices are its woof.

Destiny is real, and enlarges us. Both Fate and Chance are illusions, and both diminish us. Fate is an iron chain which reduces us to slaves, and Chance is a sandstorm which reduces us to "dust in the wind." Both Fate and Chance are idols, and God is an iconoclast.

Divine predestination and human choice are implied in every story, as Destiny's warp and woof. Every story we tell is full of predestination, from its author, and full of free choice, from its characters. This is true of the stories we live as well as the stories we tell. We fulfill our destiny *by* our free choices.

Destiny comes in waves. Sometimes the waves are too tiny to see, when nothing deep or dense with Destiny seems to be happening. But even then, the little waves are imperceptibly changing the shape of the shoreline and wearing away the rocks. And far out at sea larger waves are being prepared in Destiny's womb. Sometimes the waves of Destiny make safe little tidal pools to play in, and sometimes they make riptides that carry you out to dangerous depths.

Sometimes we are little children playing in the shallow tidal pools like the sandpipers at the edge of the wavelets that keep bubbling the shore with their sudsy baby breath. Sometimes we are like older children venturing out to where the waves break, showing off our ability to endure them. Sometimes we are mature athletes, riding the waves like horses, either bareback or with saddles (surfboards). Either way, we are at their mercy. But we can ride their mercy.

When we get old, we no longer venture out as far. It is enough then just to see the waves rather than to ride them. An old Nahanter told me that when she first moved to Nahant she had to get in the water every summer, and a cold and cloudy summer was a real loss, but "now it's enough just to watch. I don't need to *do* anything any more, just *being* here is enough."

But until we come to that point in our lives, we have to move, like sharks. We are detectives, on the hunt for clues. We are Ariadne seeking the secret thread of our destiny through the labyrinth.

We *smell* our destiny more than we see it. It has the scent of salt.

*   *   *   *   *

Tonight I heard Mother "huddling" with Lazarus and Mister Mumm again. (They thought I was asleep.)

"What a great loss!" Lazarus said.

"Greater than we know," added Mister Mumm.

"I thought she was supposed to be the missing part of the puzzle. And now sometimes I'm not even sure 'Isa is the right part." Mother's voice was sad.

"Of course he is. He was sent here," Mister Mumm declared, quietly.

"I thought he would be a Joseph and she would be a Mary and he would be her protector. And what a son they would have! He would have made peace." Mother's voice was very sad.

"Stop dreaming," said Lazarus.

"I'm not only thinking of Israel," Mother replied.

"Of what, then?"

"Of your pot that's boiling down there."

"Jonestown, you mean?"

"Yes."

"What do they have to do with that?"

"You know better than to ask that question, Laz. Everything has something to do with everything."

"That's true," Laz admitted.

Mother added, "One more prayer might have prevented Mara's death."

"One more presence certainly would have," said Mister Mumm.

"I know, I know," Lazarus answered. "Six more righteous men in Sodom would have saved the city. I know. I was there."

"And one more saint today could save the world," said Mother.

"And one more fake Messiah could destroy it," answered Lazarus.

"Well, *this* one's not *that*." Mother's voice was insistent.

"'Isa, you mean?"

"Yes. He's neither a fake nor a Messiah. So you can end your investigation now."

"Number 665," Lazarus said, thoughtfully.

"Is that all you've checked out, Laz? Only 665? After all those years?" Mother's eyes and voice twinkled.

"I was joking. To get to the next number."

"You're not a good joker, Lazarus," Mister Mumm observed.

"Down to business then! Well if Mara wasn't the Jew, who is? Me?" cackled Lazarus. "That *is* a joke!"

"It must be you," said Mother.

"No, it's you," said Lazarus.

"No."

"Why not? What are you, then?"

"I'm the Mother!" This silenced all of them.

If I had not known these people like family, I would have run from that house and never come back. I may still do just that.

Instead, I poked my head into the room and said, "I heard that. And I don't like it. I feel *used*. Tell me why I shouldn't feel used."

"You *should* feel used," replied Mother, promptly. "We're all being used. We're servants. And if our Master was only a human being, we should all resent it. But He isn't." This was said firmly; then, with sudden gentleness, "Jack, you know *that* as well as anybody in this House."

The compliment dissolved my resentment, but not my determination to know more. "If that's true, Mother, then I should be let in on your 'huddles.' I know there's a lot of things that you know about what's been happening here that I don't. Will you share them with me now? Haven't I paid the price for it these last few weeks?"

Mother's eyes widened. She nodded, and looked to Lazarus and Mister Mumm, who nodded back. "Do we know much more about it than you do? No, we don't. But do I think you deserve to know whatever we can tell you? Yes I do. So ask, already. Pitch me some pitches and I'll try to hit a few back to you."

I wanted to ask about Mara above all, but something prevented me. Perhaps it was the pain. Instead, I asked about what I had seen the day she died. "I've told you the three creatures I saw at the Cauldron. Tell me what *you* think: was I seeing things?"

"Of course you were," Mother replied. "But what you want to know is whether those things were really there as you saw them."

"Please don't play word games, Mother."

"I'm not evading, Jack. I'm clarifying. I hope I am, anyway. Hey, you're not the only one who saw the serpent. I know he's real."

"He bit her son's heel," Lazarus explained in a hoarse whisper.

"Now, Laz, don't hide behind puzzles. Not to Jack. He's one of us."

"I know the prophecy," I said. "And I know who the serpent is. I even know his name. We call him Iblis. You call him Satan."

"Well, that's settled, then," said Mother. "We know our enemy."

"Who was Sparky, then? His puppet?"

"That, I don't know. Nobody else saw him—ever, as far as I know. That doesn't mean he wasn't there. He was. He made Mara fall. *He* did it, Jack, not you." I was not convinced of this. And the third figure remained a puzzle. "Who was the Viking then?" I demanded.

"You know his name, Jack. Say it." Mother had read my essay on Thorwald.

The command to speak his name made me afraid. I knew the power of names: they could make present the one named. I summoned up my courage and said: "Thorwald."

Nothing happened. Not the slightest ripple on the waters of my soul.

"He's gone now, isn't he?" asked Mister Mumm knowingly.

"Yes," I said, surprised at his knowledge. "I wonder where?"

"Paradise," he answered, simply.

"Finally!" Lazarus added. He sounded envious.

"But why *then*? And why *me*? What does he have to do with me?"

"That's a long story," answered Mother, "and most of it is guesswork. But I think we can patch some of it together. Let's see, now. Let's take your second question first. Why you, Jack?"

"Yes, why me?"

"What's your favorite place in the world?"

"Here, of course. This House."

"Indoors or outdoors?"

"Outdoors."

"What part of outdoors?"

"Bailey's Hill, of course."

"And on the Hill?"

"The Cauldron. At least it *used* to be the Cauldron."

"You used to go there every day. You invested a lot of yourself there, a lot of your time and love, a lot of your emotional energy."

"Are you saying that my 'emotional energy' called up the ghost of a dead Viking?"

"No, but I'm saying it may have cut a channel through the rock, like centuries of waves, a channel of communication. But there had to be a deeper channel first in you: your heredity. Your paths may have crossed a thousand years ago."

"And I think I know how," I said. The puzzle pieces were fitting together. "Mama used to tell me this story that Papa told, about Muslim pirates from the Barbary Coast of Africa sailing all the way up to Iceland, capturing some of the people who lived there, and selling them as slaves in the markets of Istanbul. The Vikings had enslaved some of us Muslims, centuries earlier, and now we enslaved some of them. I remember the words Papa used for it; it was like a liturgical formula: 'raiding the raiders, looting the looters and sacking the sackers,' he called it. And one of those Viking slaves was supposed to be one of Papa's ancestors."

"You may have a second ancestor involved too," Mister Mumm added. "Thorwald was killed by an Indian arrow. What tribes were here in New England a thousand years ago, and what modern tribes are the branches that come from them? Do the research."

"If you know, please tell me what I will find."

"You will find that one of those modern tribes is the Mohawks. It may have been the Mohawk ancestor of Kateri Tekakwitha, 'the lily of the Mohawks,' who shot the arrow that killed Thorwald."

Kateri Tekakwitha was a Mohawk who converted to Christianity, the earliest-born North American Catholic saint, or soon to be canonized as a saint. Mother had a picture of her on her wall.

"What does that have to do with me?" I asked.

"Your Mama's blood is hers," answered Mister Mumm. "That's why Kateri hovers over this place."

The weight of fate was suddenly becoming too heavy to bear. But there was more. "That's only half the picture," Mother said. "Mara fits in too somehow."

I felt guilty that I had thought of myself before Mara again. "You're right, Mother. And I think I know how she fits. Mara told me. Her family had this story of how a giant Viking raped one of her ancestors, and that's why some of her family had blond hair and blue eyes."

"There you are," said Mother. "Thorwald's purgatory. He's the one."

"But . . . but he *lost*. We lost. We lost Mara. He *didn't* save his great-great-granddaughter from the serpent. We failed."

"Yes. That's why I think it was his purgatory. What do you think purgatory is for, anyway? To pay for your failures by successes? To pay for your sins by virtues? You can't do that. Purgatory is for fully seeing and admitting your failures."

"But I thought Thorwald was there to save Mara, a thousand years later, to pay for his rape of Mara's great-great-grandmother a thousand years earlier. I thought that's why Allah arranged for him to be buried on just that beach."

"The time and place *was* arranged, of course. But it wasn't to pay for his sins. We can't do that."

"Well, that's *your* theology, anyway."

"Yours too. What do you plead at the Last Judgment? Justice? Or Mercy?"

"Mercy," I admitted. "But how was Thorwald's failure Allah's mercy?"

"Maybe his purpose for being there wasn't to save Mara at all, but to save himself."

"I thought you believed you *couldn't* save yourself, that Jesus saved you."

"It's both. When God saves you, He doesn't turn you off; He turns you on. Our Bible says, 'Work out your own salvation with fear and trembling, for it is God who works in you.' It's a paradox. But let's not argue theology. Let's just *look*. What did Thorwald *see?* What did he see that he hadn't seen before?"

"Mara."

"No, I think he saw Mara long ago, afar off, from the other side of the sea of time and space. But he saw something else, something new, that day, here by this House: his own failure. And I think that's the hardest thing for a Viking to admit. Isn't that so, Jack?" She asked me as if I were a Viking.

Mister Mumm put in, "Thorwald does not delay and Thorwald does not fail."

The words sounded like another incantation. "Where did you hear that?" I asked.

"That was Thorwald's motto. I did some research," he explained.

I felt that Mister Mumm was not being totally forthcoming with everything that he knew, and for a moment I had a wild fantasy that he was really an angel in disguise, that he had been Thorwald's guardian angel a thousand years ago, had failed in his task, and had been assigned this time and place as his penance. Do angels do penances? I'll bet he knew the other names of the serpent too, like the Kraken, and the Worm Ouroboros, and the Basilisk— knew them from experience and memory, not "research."

"So you think Thorwald's failure was his purgatory?" I asked, in a tone almost sarcastic. "I don't see it. The pieces don't line up: Paradise, Purgatory, Justice, Mercy, Success—and Failure? All of those pieces are gifts of Allah, but Failure isn't. That doesn't fit into the equation."

"Yes it does," Mother retorted. "Thorwald's purgatory was God's mercy because it gave him the one thing he lacked: failure."

"Maybe that's your theology, but it's not mine. Allah does not fail. And He does not let His prophets fail."

"Of course He doesn't fail. But He does let His prophets fail. And you should understand why."

"I don't."

"You should. You can deduce it, philosopher. Look: What is Allah's intention to us? Mercy. Grace. Allah the Merciful, the Beneficent, right?"

"Of course."

"And what does He want to give us most? His Paradise, right? Heaven."

"Yes."

And what is Islam but a "Straight Path" to Heaven, right?" "*The* Straight Path," I corrected her. "Yes. That is why I am a Muslim."

Mother refused to be distracted by my correction. "And 'islam' means 'surrender,' right?"

"Right."

"And pride keeps us from surrendering, right?"

"Right."

"And humility is the opposite of pride, right?"

"Right."

"And humility is admitting our failures and sins, right?"

"Yes . . ." I was beginning to be suspicious.

"So how can we admit our failures unless we fail?"

"So you're saying we have to fail in order to succeed, in order to be saved?"

"In a world of sin, yes. Failure is to sin what pain is to disease. It's a light, it's an X-ray, it reveals, it rubs our nose in it.

"In what?"

"In our own spiritual shit."

The word was not too strong for me after what I had done, or not done, to Mara.

"So Thorwald had to wait a thousand years in his grave on that beach, by that rock," I thought aloud. "He had to learn to wait. Because he had *not* waited when he raped Mara's great-great-grandmother." (And *I* did not wait when I did the same, though more gently, to Mara.)

Mother added, "He had probably never failed at anything important in his life. So he had to learn failure after his death."

The pieces were coming together. "He failed to save Mara even though he fought the serpent with all his Viking courage and strength," Mother explained. "He had to learn that all his strength wasn't enough. He had to learn that nothing we can do is enough. He had to learn surrender. He had to learn Islam. Life's last lesson." She looked at me. I felt stripped.

"All right, so Allah did that for Thorwald's benefit. But how was it for ours? He may have won, but we lost. We lost Mara."

"Mara went out a door," Mother corrected, "and we can't see through to the other side of that door. So we don't know whether Mara is lost."

"I saw the serpent eat her!" I wailed.

"Thorwald and Kateri may have pulled her through the door to Paradise just in time."

"What are the chances of that? How much time did she have?"

"*God* is the master of times, not the serpent."

"But even if Mara is not lost, we are."

"What do you mean?"

"We lost her."

"Yes, but we may have found ourselves."

"You, maybe. Not me. I lost myself."

"And maybe that's how you're finding yourself. Your heart is broken, 'Isa, but a broken heart is the only kind of heart that can ever be whole."

I was silent, within and without. I had heard someone say those words before. I did not understand them then. I was beginning to understand them now. I confessed, "I think I am learning what cannot be put into words."

"Thorwald did that too," said Mister Mumm.

"We *all* found ourselves when we lost Mara," added Mother. "And something else we found, too: we found ourselves *together.* Look: Thorwald, a pagan who became a Christian, used a Muslim—you—as his champion, his knight, to save his great-great-granddaughter, a Jew. What does that look like? It looks to me like part of Heaven's new strategy for the ecumenical jihad."

"But we lost. The alliance didn't work. If we were God's firing range for testing His new ecumenical weapon, the test failed."

"Maybe not completely. Maybe the cooperation itself is the real victory. What do you think Abraham is thinking now if he's seeing all this? Don't you think he's excited to see his children finally fighting together against the real enemy instead of against each other?"

I had not felt so hopeful in a long time. It was not a wholly satisfying ending to the story, as in a good melodrama; but real endings never are, in this world. In this world, the last word is often simply the word "wait." The Jew's last marching order is to wait for the Messiah. The Christian's last marching order is to wait for the Messiah's second coming. The Muslim's last marching order is to wait for Allah's Last Judgment. I think perhaps we can march together if we can learn to wait together.

*   *   *   *   *

On October 18, for the second time this year, Mother insisted that we all pray together for the Pope that is to be elected. (The cardinals are meeting in Rome now.) The last time we did this, he died! Are we God's supernatural hit team?

I am getting used to this ecumenical thing—perhaps because it is the only new thing in my life now that Mara is gone. When I told the imam about our prayers together, he frowned and shook his head sadly.

"These are the people who believe all religions are equal, 'Isa," he said.

"No, they are not, " I replied. "They are the people who believe that all *people* are equal before God—as we do! All people who believe in Allah and the Last Judgment, anyway. And they believe *that* only because they believe 'there is no God but God'—as we do! And they believe that it was not God but man who created religious divisions—as we do! In other words, they are the people who believe very much of what we say we believe."

"No, no, 'Isa. It is *not* the same things that we believe. And we should not pray with them. For we are not praying to the same God. Their God is not our God," he argued. "Their God has a son. Allah has no son. They are Associators, polytheists. And their Jesus is not our Jesus. They worship him. And their Mary is not our Maryam. Their Mary is almost divine herself."

The imam came here from Cairo in 1974. I asked him, "When you were in Cairo, did you see the apparitions of Maryam in Zeitun?"

He admitted that he had. Two million people saw this miracle, more people than had ever seen any other miracle in the history of the world.

"Do you believe it was Maryam herself that appeared?"

"I do," he replied. "*Our* Maryam, the Maryam of the Holy Qur'an. When we saw her standing on the roof of the cathedral making the sign of peace, all the Muslims chanted from the Holy Qur'an, 'Maryam, Allah has chosen you, and purified you. He has chosen you above all women.'"

I replied: "And this Maryam caused Muslims and Catholics and Orthodox to pray together in public—something you tell me not to do even in private. She did not ask Muslims to become Christians."

"She also did not ask Christians to become Muslims," he replied.

We were friendly but cool when we parted.

*   *   *   *   *

We knelt together at the House tonight, and fought side by side against the same invisible enemy. I knew we were in the hot heart of the jihad. I saw in my mind a stone tower of defense: it was ourselves. Arrows of fire filled the air and arced into our tower. The arrows were mockings and tauntings and sneerings. The arrows pointed at my own sins. I began to defend myself, to justify myself, to explain my past failures. The tower weakened, leaned. I suddenly saw my folly and my weakness in praying backward instead of forward. I abandoned my past. I let it fall. The attack went on, but the tower stood. Minutes later, we all sighed, knowing (without knowing *how* we knew) that it was ended.

Each of us then heard a voice, the same voice. Yet each heard a different message.

Mister Mumm "spoke in tongues" and Mother "interpreted" the message to *her* as "When you know and love My Word better than your separated brethren do, they will come home to you. Only when you learn from all My other children, will you be able to unite them all."

Evan "heard" this: "Look not at the different roads to Me but look *along* them at Me. Only when you do that, will you see how much each one is Mine."

Lazarus heard these words: "You are my first people, still chosen, chosen forever. When you follow your own prophets and your own scriptures to the end, all your problems will be resolved."

I was skeptical but open to such "prophecies," and I too seemed to hear a voice in my spirit, which said "Follow your own scripture when it tells you to love all the People of the Book. You learned of Me from these people, and now they stand in need of learning of Me from you. Teach them the heart and soul of all true religion, teach them the total surrender to Me that makes them saints. But teach them by love, not hate; and convert them to Me, not to you."

After I spoke those words aloud, Mother said, "Something new is happening." We all sensed it.

"Make yourselves donkeys. Make yourselves rideable," said Mister Mumm, with terrible quietness.

He then whispered something in Mother's right ear. Yak had remained on her left shoulder, quietly, during all our exertions, as if he too had been praying. Mother then said to us, suddenly, as we silently rose to go our separate ways, "When you read the papers tomorrow, do not ask yourself what your role was. He does not want you to know, only to do."

The strangest thing of all tonight was how Mister Mumm had suddenly seemed to assume command and how right this felt. But because of Mother's last command, I did not dare to give voice to the question in my mind, which was whether he knew the angel in the sea. Or whether he *was* the angel in the sea.

(30) The Last Dreams

Although I can think and write again, still the echoes from the shock of Mara's death have not ceased. Nor has my sense of guilt or loneliness. But despair has been exorcised.

I am falling behind in all my courses. I have skipped most of my classes. It does not matter. Greater things are happening in the world, though I know not what they are.

My dreams have accelerated. Since I have lived in this House my dreams have gotten closer and closer to me, like a *doppelganger.* At some point I think it will be impossible for any more to come. For at some point, if they get any closer to me I will not survive. They will touch me, and I will disappear like a moth in the fire.

In one dream, I am sitting in a theater. The heavy stage curtain is down to the floor. Then, the curtain is pulled aside at the lower left corner, lifted just a few inches, allowing me to see, in a second's glimpse, what is behind the curtain. The whole stage was full of fire. The fire was not ordinary fire. It was chariots. In these chariots tiny human beings were being carried to and fro.

In another dream, I see an enormous sea, full of swells. Then I "reverse zoom" up to a great distance and see the whole sea, so that I can see its shape. It was shaped like a heart. The swells were its heartbeats.

The heart then changed into a great white bird. It looked like a dove. The waves of the sea became the waves of its wings. The thought came to me that each event in time is a beat of this bird's wings. Everything that has ever happened has happened only because this bird's wings were beating the air, and its wings were beating only because its heart was beating with blood.

Then I knew what I was seeing. I was *seeing* Evan's "theory of everything." These waves of air from the bird's wings were the universal fate waves.

I then saw a word spelled out on the feathers of the bird. The word was written in Hebrew, but in the dream I could understand it, even though I have never studied Hebrew. It said: I AM WHO I AM.

The word then took a shape: the shape of a vertical column of white fire simultaneously rising from the edge of the sea and descending from the sky. The column of fire then became an enormous harp string, and the wind played one note of music on it. The note was a single word. The word was "islam."

Then the bird flew high into the sky and hovered, looking down at everything at once, as if choreographing all the waves below. The bird then turned and looked at me, opened its mouth (it did not have a beak, it had a mouth) and spoke another word, a single word, in a whisper so soft that it could not be ignored. The word was "shalom." When this word was whispered, I heard a perfect harmony from the waves and the harp string.

I wanted to stay inside this dream forever, never to have another. But this was not granted. Instead, still another word broke the harmony. I could not hear where the word was coming from, but it assailed my ears with pain and interruption. Then I recognized what the word was.

It was my own name.

I opened my mouth and asked the unknown voice who spoke my name: "What is 'Isa? What is this the name of?"

And the voice replied, "It is the name of some infinitely gentle, infinitely suffering thing." It was the haunting quotation from the poet T.S. Eliot, but I knew that the Voice was not echoing the poet; the poet was echoing the Voice.

*   *   *   *   *

The next night I had another dream. I was standing in chest-high waves. A giant wave approached from far out at sea. When it arrived, it did not break or recede, but it *stood* motionless like an ancient Greek statue, with white foam on its head like the hair of a wise old man.

The wave seemed to be carved out of rock. Looking into it, I saw a face— a great, rugged, rocky face. It was a man's face, but ageless: both young and old at once. Its skin had wrinkles that looked unfathomably deep and scars that spoke of unfathomable suffering. The expression was infinitely gentle. It was indeed the face of "some infinitely gentle, infinitely suffering thing."

Nothing happened for what seemed like centuries, until I dared to address it: "Who are you?"

The reply was as soft as down and as heavy as thunder. It said: "I am the Mercy of Allah."

The statement stood in stone. So did I. Nothing moved. All was silent, within and without. I stood there for many more centuries, it seemed. Then I dared to ask again: "Who are you?"

And the answer came again: "I am the Mercy of Allah."

I had to test the vision. I said: "I am a faithful Muslim. Are you the Allah whom I worship?"

"I am. I am the Mercy of Allah."

"Are you Allah Himself, or are you the Mercy of Allah?":

"Allah and His mercy are one."

"Why have you come to me?"

"Because of who I am and because of who you are. I am the one to whom you have surrendered."

"What do you want with me?" (I trembled with fear.)

"I want to give you a gift." (I trembled with joy.)

"What gift, Lord?" (I trembled with hope.)

"Myself." (I trembled with confusion.)

"I surrender to Allah alone!" (I trembled with suspicion.)

"Rightly so! That is why I have come to you: because your surrender has come to me. I am the One to whom all true surrender comes."

I still felt like a knight lost in a dark forest, surprised by a strange beast, not knowing whether it was friend or foe. So I drew my word-sword. I cried: *"La illa'a illa' Allah!"* The *Shahadah* sprang out of the scabbard of my soul and into the hand of my lips. This was the supreme test. This sword would slay all false gods.

"Yea and amen! *La illa'a illa' Allah!* And I am the Mercy of Allah."

I surrendered. I threw myself upon the wave, and it received me. And there at the heart of this wave I found a peace that passes all understanding.

"What do you want of me, Lord?" I asked.

"Your surrender."

"I have surrendered."

"To whom have you surrendered?"

"To Thee, Lord."

"And what have you surrendered?"

"My all."

"Have you surrendered all your work?"

At these words, a huge pile of paper appeared before me. It was all the things I had ever written or would ever write. I reached out and placed the whole pile in the invisible hands of the Speaker. My signature disappeared from them. They were taken up to Paradise, where people read them without reading my name. I knew I too would read them there, and be blest, forgetting that I had written them. For I had not. All my best work was not mine. It was His.

"I am pleased with your surrender." My heart leaped up. "But it is not enough." My heart fell. "Will you also surrender all your virtues?"

"I will."

A golden crown then appeared on my head. It had a few beautiful jewels in it, and many empty places where many more jewels should be. I immediately took it off my head and cast it down at His feet, enacting justice, giving Him what was His own.

"I am pleased." My heart leaped up again. "But it is not enough." My heart fell again.

"What more do you want from me, Lord?"

"What I want from you most of all, 'Isa Ben Adam, is your sins."

My heart and mind both stopped. But the Voice did not:

"For I have wiped out your name from them also." My heart leaped again. "And I have written that name on my palms." (My heart turned inside out.)

Then I saw the all-holy Hands of Allah. The upturned palms were bloodied. And the blood spelled out my name.

"You are 'Isa Ben Adam," the Voice said, "and you are a mystery."

Editor's Postscript

These are 'Isa's last written words. I do not know whether he is alive or dead.

I can think of five hypotheses that explain 'Isa's disappearance.

1. He may have committed suicide, deliberately or not. He believed that he could not live without Mara, and Mara was gone forever from this world.

2. He may have run away from the world, but not by suicide. He may have become a monk, or a hermit—opportunities which are open to nearly all religions—to do penance and humiliation for his guilt, or simply because after Mara there was nothing left in this world for him to love.

3. He may have run away with Libby, who also disappeared without a trace. She may have become a Muslim, or he may have become a Christian, or they may have had a "mixed marriage" like so many of 'Isa's and Mara's ancestors.

4. 'Isa may have joined the Palestinian *intifada*. There was a man who may or may not have been the same 'Isa Ben Adam who turned up in Palestine as an underground agitator in the year 2000. He was hated by both Israel and the PLO politically, and by both Jews and Muslims religiously. He began underground worship services in which Jews and Muslims worshipped together. (His congregations were very small!)

'Isa Ben Adam was either his name or one of his pseudonyms. He died in Jerusalem, near the Temple Mount, assassinated by a conspiracy. He was wearing a bullet-proof vest, but someone threw a long knife at him, which found its way through a small opening in a balustrade of a curved wooden bridge and pierced his armpit. His companions were armed, and wanted to take revenge, but his dying command to them was to "forgive them, and escape." They swore that "from 'Isa's blood a movement will rise." So far the movement has no name.

5. The last hypothesis is probably the most fantastic of all.

I ask myself: What do I know about the truth of 'Isa's story? Not much, really. I have never met Mara. I never set foot in the House of Bread, or met its inhabitants, before it was destroyed by storms. For the first time, now that I have finished the final version of 'Isa's papers, and made them into this book, I begin to entertain a fantastic doubt: that Mara, the House, and all its inhabitants were fictions of 'Isa's imagination, either (1) an elaborate set of notes for a creative fantasy, a long mythic fiction like *The Lord of the Rings,* or (2) such an ongoing hallucination as can occur only to a great genius, as in the movie *A Beautiful Mind*.

The House is gone now, weakened by the storm of '78 and finally destroyed 13 years later by the "no-name" Halloween nor'easter that was the background for *The Perfect Storm*. I have found no photos of it. The only evidence I have that it was there is its three concrete pilings, which I photographed after it was demolished. Another house, small and ugly and modern, has since been built on those pilings. I hope we can build something better than that on 'Isa's words. That is why I give them to the world.

After-word

Dear reader, if you have given my long book so much of your precious life-time, I am grateful to you for your gift. And if in return you are grateful to me for this book-gift to you, I make bold to ask you for a second gift, far more important to me than the first gift of your reading it. Pray for me, and for all those I love, for my family. For "more things are wrought by prayer than this world dreams of." If we were allowed to see all the effects of the smallest of our prayers, down through the centuries, all the ripples of the prayer-pebbles we throw into God's ocean that is so full of angels, I think we would never be able to get up off our knees again for the rest of our lives.

If I am dead by the time you read this, then pray for the eternal happiness of my soul, as well as my family. If you do not believe in God, pray anyway. For God believes in you. He has an incredible sense of humor.